LINDA LAEL MILLER

The daughter of a town marshal, Linda Lael Miller is a *New York Times* and *USA TODAY* bestselling author of more than one hundred historical and contemporary novels, most of which reflect her love of the West. Raised in Northport, Washington, the self-confessed barn goddess now lives in Spokane, Washington. Linda recently hit #1 on the *New York Times* bestseller list for the fifth and sixth times with the first two titles in her Big Sky series, *Big Sky Country* and *Big Sky Mountain*.

Linda has come a long way since leaving Washington to experience the world. "But growing up in that time and place has served me well," she allows. "And I'm happy to be back home."

Dedicated to helping others, Linda personally finances her Linda Lael Miller Scholarships for Women, which she awards to those seeking to improve their lot in life through education. More information about Linda and her novels is available at www.lindalaelmiller.com. She also loves to hear from readers by mail at P.O. Box 19461, Spokane, WA 99219.

RAEANNE THAYNE

USA TODAY bestselling author RaeAnne Thayne finds inspiration from the rugged northern Utah mountains, where she lives with her hero of a husband and their children. Her books have won many honors, including three RITA® Award nominations from Romance Writers of America and a Career Achievement Award from *RT Book Reviews*. She loves to hear from readers—she can be reached through her website at www.raeannethayne.com.

BESTSELLING AUTHOR COLLECTION

#1 *New York Times* Bestselling Author

LINDA LAEL MILLER

Here and Then

HARLEQUIN®
entertain, enrich, inspire™

ISBN-13: 978-0-373-18058-5

Recycling programs for this product may not exist in your area.

HERE AND THEN
Copyright © 2012 by Harlequin Books S.A.

The publisher acknowledges the copyright holders of the individual works as follows:

HERE AND THEN
Copyright © 1992 by Linda Lael Miller

DALTON'S UNDOING
Copyright © 2006 by RaeAnne Thayne

www.Harlequin.com

Printed in U.S.A.

CONTENTS

Dear Reader,

Welcome to the unpredictable world of time travel, one of my personal all-time-favorite subjects to write *or* read about.

The idea for *There and Now* and *Here and Then*, the stories of Elisabeth and Jonathan and Elisabeth's cousin Rue and Farley—and their adventures in not just one world, but two— came to me in a memorable way. Long ago and far away, my good friend Debbie Macomber and I were driving through the countryside on our way to…somewhere. Truthfully, the destination eludes me, but it was probably a book signing. We were laughing and swapping stories (what we both do best) when we spotted this farmhouse, all alone in the middle of a field of some sort. It was your regulation farmhouse, ordinary in every way, except that there was a door in the second-floor wall—leading nowhere.

I turned to Debbie (I think she was driving) and said, "What if you opened that same door from the inside, and found yourself *in a room?* And not only that—what if it suddenly wasn't now anymore, but a hundred years ago?"

Well, since "what if" is the classic plotting question for writers, we were off and running. The result was *There and Now,* a story about a woman who opens a door just like that one, and finds herself in the Puget Sound area of another time. I hope you'll enjoy both Elisabeth's story and Rue's. I promise, their men are worth loving.

Also, be sure to visit my website, www.lindalaelmiller.com, for excerpts from upcoming books, contests, videos of very sexy cowboys and news of my annual Linda Lael Miller Scholarships for Women program, plus a daily blog.

Be well.

With love,

Linda Lael Miller

HERE AND THEN

Linda Lael Miller

Chapter 1

Aunt Verity's antique necklace lay in an innocent, glimmering coil of gold on the floor of the upstairs hallway. An hour before, when Rue Claridge had been carrying her suitcases upstairs, it had not been there.

Frowning, Rue got down on one knee and reached for the necklace, her troubled gaze rising to the mysterious, sealed door in the outside wall. Beyond it was nothing but empty space. The part of the house it had once led to had been burned away a century before and never rebuilt.

Aunt Verity had hinted at spooky doings in the house over the years, tales concerning both the door and the necklace. Rue had enjoyed the yarns, but being practical in nature, she had promptly put them out of her mind.

Rue's missing cousin, Elisabeth, had mentioned the necklace and the doorway in those strange letters she'd written in an effort to outline what was happening to her. She'd said a person wearing the necklace could travel through time.

In fact, Elisabeth—gentle, sensible Elisabeth—had claimed she'd clasped the chain around her neck and soon found herself in the 1890s, surrounded by living, breathing people who should have been dead a hundred years.

A chill wove a gossamer casing around Rue's spine as she recalled snatches of Elisabeth's desperate letters.

You're the one person in the world who might, just might, believe me. Those wonderful, spooky stories Aunt Verity told us on rainy nights were true. There is another world on the other side of that door in the upstairs hallway, one every bit as solid and real as the one you and I know, and I've reached it. I've been there, Rue, and I've met the man meant to share my life. His name is Jonathan Fortner, and I love him more than my next heartbeat, my next breath.

A pounding headache thumped behind Rue's right temple, and she let out a long sigh as she rose to her feet, her fingers pressing the necklace deep into her palm. With her other hand, she pushed a lock of sandy, shoulder-length hair back from her face and stared at the sealed door.

Years ago there had been rooms on the other side, but then, late in the last century, there had been a tragic fire. The damage had been repaired, but the original structure was changed forever. The door had been sealed, and now the doorknob was as old and stiff as a rusted padlock.

"Bethie," Rue whispered, touching her forehead against the cool, wooden panel of the door, "where are you?"

There was no answer. The old country house yawned around her, empty except for the ponderous nineteenth-century furniture Aunt Verity had left as a part of her estate and a miniature universe of dust particles that seemed to pervade every room, every corner and crevice.

At thirty, Rue was an accomplished photojournalist. She'd dodged bullets and bombs in Colombia, photographed and later written about the riots in Jakarta, and nearly been taken captive in Afgahnistan. And while all of those experiences had shaken her and some had left her physically ill for days afterward, none had frightened her so profoundly as Elisabeth's disappearance.

The police and Elisabeth's father believed Elisabeth had simply fled the area after her divorce, that she was lying on a beach somewhere, sipping exotic tropical drinks and letting the sun bake away her grief. But because she knew her cousin, because of

the letters and phone messages that had been waiting when she returned from an assignment in Mos-
cow, Rue took a much darker view of the situation.

Elisabeth was wandering somewhere, if she was
alive at all, perhaps not even remembering who she
was. Rue wouldn't allow herself to dwell on all the
other possibilities, because they didn't bear thinking about.

Downstairs in the big kitchen, she brewed a cup of
instant coffee in Elisabeth's microwave and sat down
at the big, oak table in the breakfast nook to go over
the tattered collection of facts one more time. Before
her were her cousin's letters, thoughtfully written,
with no indications of undue stress in the familiar,
flowing hand.

With a sigh, Rue pushed away her coffee and
rested her chin in one palm. Elisabeth had come
to the house the two cousins had inherited to get a
new perspective on her life. She'd planned to make
her home outside the little Washington town of Pine
River and teach at the local elementary school in the
fall. The two old ladies across the road, Cecily and
Roberta Buzbee, had seen Elisabeth on several occasions. It had been Miss Cecily who had called an
ambulance after finding Elisabeth unconscious in
the upstairs hallway. Rue's cousin had been rushed
to the hospital, where she'd stayed a relatively short
time, and soon after that, she'd vanished.

Twilight was falling over the orchard behind
the house, the leaves thinning on the gray-brown
branches because it was late October. Rue watched as

a single star winked into view in the purple sky. *Oh, Bethie,* she thought, as a collage of pictures formed in her mind...an image of a fourteen-year-old Elisabeth predominated—Bethie, looking down at Rue from the door of the hayloft in the rickety old barn. "Don't worry," the woman-child had called cheerfully on that long-ago day when Rue had first arrived, bewildered and angry, to take sanctuary under Aunt Verity's wing. "This is a good place and you'll be happy here." Rue saw herself and Bethie fishing and wading in the creek near the old covered bridge and reading dog-eared library books in the highest branches of the maple tree that shaded the back door. And listening to Verity's wonderful stories in front of the parlor fire, chins resting on their updrawn knees, arms wrapped around agile young legs clad in blue jeans.

The jangle of the telephone brought Rue out of her reflections, and she muttered to herself as she made her way across the room to pick up the extension on the wall next to the sink. "Hello," she snapped, resentful because she'd felt closer to Elisabeth for those few moments and the caller had scattered her memories like a flock of colorful birds.

"Hello, Claridge," a wry male voice replied. "Didn't they cover telephone technique where you went to school?"

Rue ignored the question and shoved the splayed fingers of one hand through her hair, pulling her scalp tight over her forehead.

"Hi, Wilson," she said, Jeff's boyish face form-

ing on the screen of her mind. She'd been dating the
guy for three years, on and off, but her heart never
gave that funny little thump she'd read about when
she saw his face or heard his voice. She wondered if
that meant anything significant.

"Find out anything about your cousin yet?"

Rue leaned against the counter, feeling unac-
countably weary. "No," she said. "I talked to the
police first thing, and they agree with Uncle Mar-
cus that she's probably hiding out somewhere, lick-
ing her wounds."

"You don't think so?"

Unconsciously, Rue shook her head. "No way.
Bethie would never just vanish without telling anyone where she was going…she's the most considerate person I know." Her gaze strayed to the letters
spread out on the kitchen table, unnervingly calm
accounts of journeys to another point in time. Rue
shook her head again, denying that such a thing could
be possible.

"I could fly out and help you," Jeff offered, and
Rue's practical heart softened a little.

"That won't be necessary," she said, twisting one
finger in the phone cord and frowning. Finding Elisabeth was going to take all her concentration and
strength of will, she told herself. The truth was, she
didn't want Jeff getting in the way.

Her friend sighed, somewhat dramatically. "So
be it, Claridge. If you decide I have any earthly use,
give me a call, will you?"

Rue laughed. "What?" she countered. "No violin music?" In the next instant, she remembered that Elisabeth was missing, and the smile faded from her face. "Thanks for offering, Jeff," she said seriously. "I'll call if there's anything you can do to help."

After that, there didn't seem to be much to say, and that was another element of the relationship Rue found troubling. It would have been a tremendous relief to tell someone she was worried and scared, to say Elisabeth was more like a sister to her than a cousin, maybe even to cry on a sympathetic shoulder. But Rue couldn't let down her guard that far, not with Jeff. She often got the feeling that he was just waiting for her to show weakness or to fall on her face.

The call ended, and Rue, wearing jeans and a sweatshirt, put on a jacket and went out to the shed for an armload of the aged applewood that had been cut and stacked several years before. Because Rue and Elisabeth had so rarely visited the house they'd inherited, the supply had hardly been diminished.

As she came through the back door, the necklace caught her eye, seeming to twinkle and wink from its place on the kitchen table. Rue's brow crimped thoughtfully as she made her way into the parlor and set the fragrant wood down on the hearth.

After moving aside the screen, she laid twigs in the grate over a small log of compressed sawdust and wax. When the blaze had kindled properly, she added pieces of seasoned wood. Soon, a lovely, cheerful fire was crackling away behind the screen.

Rue adjusted the damper and rose, dusting her hands off on the legs of her jeans. She was tired and distraught, and suddenly she couldn't keep her fears at bay any longer. She'd been a reporter for nine eventful years, and she knew only too well the terrible things that could have happened to Elisabeth.

She went back to the kitchen and, without knowing exactly why, reached for the necklace and put it on, even before taking off her jacket. Then, feeling chilled, she returned to the parlor to stand close to the fire.

Rue was fighting back tears of frustration and fear, her forehead touching the mantelpiece, when she heard the distant tinkling of piano keys. She was alone in the house, and she was certain no radio or TV was playing....

Her green eyes widened when she looked into the ornately framed mirror above the fireplace, and her throat tightened: The room reflected there was furnished differently, and was lit with the soft glow of lantern light. Rue caught a glimpse of a plain woman in long skirts running a cloth over the keys of a piano before the vision faded and the room was ordinary again.

Turning slowly, Rue rubbed her eyes with a thumb and forefinger. She couldn't help thinking of Elisabeth's letters describing a world like the one she'd just seen, for a fraction of a second, in the parlor mirror.

"You need a vacation," Rue said, glancing back over her shoulder at her image in the glass. "You're hallucinating."

Nonetheless, she made herself another cup of instant coffee, gathered up the letters and went to sit cross-legged on the hooked rug in front of the fireplace. Once again, she read and analyzed every word, looking for some clue, anything that would tell her where to begin the search for her cousin.

Thing was, Rue thought, Bethie sounded eminently sane in those letters, despite the fact that she talked about stepping over a threshold into another time in history. Her descriptions of the era were remarkably authentic; she probably would have had to have done days or weeks of research to know the things she did. But the words seemed fluent and easy, as though they'd flowed from her pen.

Finally, no closer to finding Elisabeth than she had been before, Rue set the sheets of writing paper aside, banked the fire and climbed the front stairway to the second floor. She would sleep in the main bedroom—many of Elisabeth's things were still there—and maybe by some subconscious, instinctive process, she would get a glimmer of guidance concerning her cousin's whereabouts.

As it was, she didn't have the first idea where to start.

She showered, brushed her teeth, put on a nightshirt and went to bed. Although she had taken the necklace off when she undressed, she put it back on again before climbing beneath the covers.

The sheets were cold, and Rue burrowed down deep, shivering. If it hadn't been for the circumstances, she would have been glad to be back in this old house, where all the memories were good ones.

Like Ribbon Creek, the Montana ranch she'd inherited from her mother's parents, Aunt Verity's house was a place to hole up when there was an important story to write or a decision to work out. She'd always loved the sweet, shivery sensation that the old Victorian monstrosity was haunted by amicable ghosts.

As her body began to warm the crisp, icy sheets, Rue hoped those benevolent apparitions were hanging around now, willing to lend a hand. "Please," she whispered, "show me how to find Elisabeth. She's my cousin and the closest thing I ever had to a sister and my very best friend, all rolled into one—and I think she's in terrible trouble."

After that, Rue tossed and turned for a while, then fell into a restless sleep marred by frightening dreams. One of them was so horrible that it sent her hurtling toward the surface of consciousness, and when she broke through into the morning light, she was breathing in gasping sobs and there were tears on her face.

And she could clearly hear a woman's voice singing, "Shall We Gather at the River?"

Her heart thundering against her chest, Rue flung back the covers and bounded out of bed, following the sound into the hallway, where she looked wildly in one direction, then the other. The voice seemed to be rising through the floorboards and yet, at the same time, it came from beyond the sealed door of the outside wall.

Rue put her hands against the wooden panel, remembering Elisabeth's letters. There was a room on the other side, Bethie had written, a solid place with floors and walls and a private stairway leading into the kitchen.

"Who's there?" Rue called, and the singing immediately stopped, replaced by a sort of stunned stillness. She ran along the hallway, peering into each of the three bedrooms, then hurried down the back stairs and searched the kitchen, the utility room, the dining room, the bathroom and both parlors. There was no one else in the house, and none of the locks on the windows or doors had been disturbed.

Frustrated, Rue stormed over to the piano on which she and Elisabeth had played endless renditions of "Heart and Soul," threw up the cover and hammered out the first few bars of "Shall We Gather at the River?" in challenge.

"Come on!" she shouted over the thundering chords. "Show yourself, damn it! Who are you? *What* are you?"

The answer was the slamming of a door far in the distance.

Rue left the piano and bounded back up the stairs, because the sound had come from that direction. Reaching the sealed door, she grabbed the knob and rattled the panel hard on its hinges, and surprise rushed through her like an electrical shock when it gave way.

Muttering an exclamation, Rue peered through the opening at the charred ruins of a fire. A trembling began in the cores of her knees as she looked at blackened timbers that shouldn't have been there.

It was a moment before she could gather her wits enough to step back from the door, leaving it agape, and dash wildly down the front stairs. She went hurtling out through the front door and plunged around to the side, only to see the screened sun porch just where it had always been, with no sign of the burned section.

Barely able to breathe, Rue circled the house once, then raced back inside and up the stairs. The door was still open, and beyond it lay another time or another dimension.

"Elisabeth!" Rue shouted, gripping the sooty doorjamb and staring down through the ruins.

A little girl in a pinafore and old-fashioned, pinchy black shoes appeared in the overgrown grass, shading her eyes with a small, grubby hand as she looked up at Rue. "You a witch like her?" the child called, her tone cordial and unruffled.

Rue's heartbeat was so loud that it was thrumming in her ears. She stepped back, then forward, then back again. She stumbled blindly into her room and pulled on jeans, a T-shirt, socks and sneakers, not taking the time to brush her sleep-tangled hair, and she was climbing deftly down through the ruins before she had a moment to consider the consequences.

The child, who had been so brave at a distance, was now backing away, stumbling in her effort to escape, her freckles standing out on her pale face, her eyes enormous.

Great, Rue thought, half-hysterically, *now I'm scaring small children.*

"Please don't run away," she managed to choke out. "I'm not going to hurt you."

The girl appeared to be weighing Rue's words, and it seemed that some of the fear had left her face. In the next instant, however, a woman came running around the corner of the house, shrieking and flapping her apron at Rue as though to shoo her away like a chicken.

"Don't you dare touch that child!" she screeched, and Rue recognized her as the drab soul she'd glimpsed in the parlor mirror the night before, wiping the piano keys.

Rue had withstood much more daunting efforts at intimidation during her travels as a reporter. She held her ground, her hands resting on her hips, her mind cataloging material so rapidly that she was barely aware of the process. The realization that Elisabeth had been *right* about the necklace and the door in the upstairs hallway and that she was near to finding her, was as exhilarating as a skydive.

"Where did you come from?" the plain woman demanded, thrusting the child slightly behind her.

Rue didn't even consider trying to explain. In the first place, no one would believe her, and in the second, she didn't understand what was going on herself. "Back there," she said, cocking a thumb toward the open doorway above. That was when she noticed that her hands and the knees of her jeans were covered with soot from the climb down through the timbers. "I'm looking for my cousin Elisabeth."

"She ain't around," was the grudging, somewhat

huffy reply. The woman glanced down at the little girl and gave her a tentative shove toward the road. "You run along now, Vera. I saw Farley riding toward your place just a little while ago. If you meet up with him, tell him he ought to come on over here and have a talk with this lady."

Vera assessed Rue with uncommonly shrewd eyes—she couldn't have been older than eight or nine—then scampered away through the deep grass.

Rue took a step closer to the woman, even though she was beginning to feel like running back to her own safe world, the one she understood. "Do you know Elisabeth McCartney?" she pressed.

The drudge twisted her calico apron between strong, work-reddened fingers, and her eyes strayed over Rue's clothes and wildly tousled hair with unconcealed and fearful disapproval. "I never heard of nobody by that name," she said.

Rue didn't believe that for a moment, but she was conscious of a strange and sudden urgency, an instinct that warned her to tread lightly, at least for the time being. "You haven't seen the last of me," she said, and then she climbed back up through the charred beams to the doorway, hoping her own world would be waiting for her on the other side. "I'll be back."

Her exit was drained of all drama when she wriggled over the threshold and found herself on a hard wooden floor decorated with a hideous Persian runner. The hallway in the modern-day house was carpeted.

"Oh, no," she groaned, just lying there for a moment, trying to think what to do. The curtain in time that had permitted her to pass between one century and the other had closed, and she had no way of knowing when—or if—it would ever open again.

It was just possible that she was trapped in this rerun of *Gunsmoke*—permanently.

"Damn," she groaned, getting to her feet and running her hands down the sooty denim of her jeans. When she'd managed to stop shaking, Rue approached one of the series of photographs lining the wall and looked up into the dour face of an old man with a bushy white beard and a look of fanatical righteousness about him. "I sure hope *you're* not hanging around here somewhere," she muttered.

Next, she cautiously opened the door of the room she'd slept in the night before—only it wasn't the same. All the furniture was obviously antique, yet it looked new. Rue backed out and proceeded along the hallway, her sense of fascinated uneasiness growing with every passing moment.

"Through the looking glass," she murmured to herself. "Any minute now, I should meet a talking rabbit with a pocket watch and a waistcoat."

"Or a United States marshal," said a deep male voice.

Rue whirled, light-headed with surprise, and watched in disbelief as a tall, broad-shouldered cowboy with a badge pinned to his vest mounted the last of the front stairs to stand in the hall. His rumpled brown hair was a touch too long, his turquoise eyes were narrowed with suspicion, and he was badly in need of a shave.

This guy was straight out of the late movie, but his personal magnetism was strictly high-tech.

"What's your name?" he asked in that gravelly voice of his.

Rue couldn't help thinking what a hit this guy would be in the average singles' bar. Not only was he good-looking, in a rough, tough sort of way, he had macho down to an art form. "Rue Claridge," she said, just a little too heartily, extending one hand in friendly greeting.

The marshal glanced at her hand, but failed to offer his own. "You make a habit of prowling around in other people's houses?" he asked. His marvelous eyes widened as he took in her jeans, T-shirt and sneakers.

"I'm looking for my cousin Elisabeth." Rue's smile was a rigid curve, and she clung to it like someone dangling over the edge of a steep cliff. "I have reason to believe she might be in…these here parts."

The lawman set his rifle carefully against the wall, and Rue gulped. His expression was dubious. "Who are you?" he demanded again, folding his powerful arms. Afternoon sunlight streamed in through the open door to nowhere, and Rue could smell charred wood.

"I told you, my name is Rue Claridge, and I'm looking for my cousin, Elisabeth McCartney." Rue held up one hand to indicate a height comparable to her own. "She's a very pretty blonde, with big, bluish green eyes and a gentle manner."

The marshal's eyebrows drew together. "Lizzie?"

Rue shrugged. She'd never known Elisabeth to call herself Lizzie, but then, she hadn't visited another century, either. "She wrote me that she was in love with a man named Jonathan Fortner."

At this, the peace officer smiled, and his craggy face was transformed. Rue felt a modicum of comfort for the first time since she'd stepped over the threshold. "They're gone to San Francisco, Jon and Lizzie are," he said. "Got married a few months back, right after her trial was over."

Rue took a step closer to the marshal, one eyebrow raised, the peculiarities and implications of her situation temporarily forgotten. "Trial?"

"It's a long story." The splendid eyes swept over her clothes again and narrowed once more. "Where the devil did you get those duds?"

Rue drew in a deep breath and expelled it, making tendrils of her hair float for a few moments. "I come from another—place. What's your name, anyhow?"

"Farley Haynes," the cowboy answered.

Privately, Rue thought it was the dumbest handle she'd ever heard, but she was in no position to rile the man. "Well, Mr. Haynes," she said brightly, "I am sorry that you had to come all the way out here for nothing. The thing is, I know Elisabeth—Lizzie—would want me to stay right here in this house."

Haynes plunked his battered old hat back onto his head and regarded Rue from under the brim. "She never mentioned a cousin," he said. "Maybe you'd better come to town with me and answer a few more questions."

Rue's first impulse was to dig in her heels, but she was an inveterate journalist, and despite the fact that her head was still spinning from the shock of sudden transport from one time to another, she was fiercely curious about this place.

"What year is this, anyway?" she asked, not realizing how odd the question sounded until it was already out of her mouth.

The lawman's right hand cupped her elbow lightly as he ushered Rue down the front stairs. In his left, he carried the rifle with unnerving expertise. "It's 1892," he answered, giving her a sidelong look, probably wondering if he should slap the cuffs on her wrists. "The month is October."

"I suppose you're wondering why I didn't know that." Rue chatted on as the marshal escorted her out through the front door. There was a big sorrel gelding waiting beyond the whitewashed gate. "The fact is, I've—I've had a fever."

"You look healthy enough to me," Haynes responded, and just the timbre of his voice set some chord to vibrating deep inside Rue. He opened the gate and nodded for her to go through it ahead of him.

She took comfort from the presence of the horse; she'd always loved the animals, and some of the happiest times of her life had been spent in the saddle at Ribbon Creek. "Hello, big fella," she said, patting the gelding's sweaty neck.

In the next instant, Rue was grabbed around the waist and hoisted up into the saddle. Before she could react in any way, Marshal Haynes had thrust his rifle into the leather scabbard, stuck one booted foot in the stirrup and swung up behind her.

Rue felt seismic repercussions move up her spine in response.

"Am I under arrest?" she asked. He reached around her to grasp the reins, and again Rue was disturbed by the powerful contraction within her. Cowboy fantasies were one thing, she reminded herself, but this was a trip into the Twilight Zone, and she had an awful feeling her ticket was stamped "one-way." She'd never been on an assignment where it was more important to keep her wits about her.

"That depends," the marshal said, the words rumbling against her nape, "on whether or not you can explain how you came to be wearing Mrs. Fortner's necklace."

Leather creaked as Rue turned to look up into that rugged face, her mind racing in search of an explanation. "My—our aunt gave us each a necklace like this," she lied, her fingers straying to the filigree pendant. The piece was definitely an original, with a history. "Elis—Lizzie's probably wearing hers."

Farley looked skeptical to say the least, but he let the topic drop for the moment. "I don't mind telling you," he said, "that the Presbyterians are going to be riled up some when they get a gander at those clothes of yours. It isn't proper for a lady to wear trousers."

Rue might have been amused by his remarks if it hadn't been for the panic that was rising inside her. Nothing in her fairly wide experience had prepared her for being thrust unceremoniously into 1892, after all. "I don't have anything else to wear," she said in an uncharacteristically small voice, and then she sank her teeth into her lower lip, gripped the pommel of Marshal Haynes's saddle in both hands and held on for dear life, even though she was an experienced rider.

After a bumpy, dusty trip over the unpaved country road that led to town—its counterpart in Rue's time was paved—they reached Pine River. The place had gone into rewind while she wasn't looking. There were saloons with swinging doors, and a big saw in the lumber mill beside the river screamed and flung sawdust into the air. People walked along board sidewalks and rode in buggies and wagons. Rue couldn't help gaping at them.

Marshal Haynes lifted her down from the horse before she had a chance to tell him she didn't need his help, and he gave her an almost imperceptible push toward the sidewalk. Bronze script on the window of the nearest building proclaimed, Pine River Jailhouse. Farley Haynes, Marshal.

Bravely, Rue resigned herself to the possibility of a stretch behind bars. Much as she wanted to see the twenty-first century again, she'd changed her mind about leaving 1892 right away—she meant to stick around until Elisabeth came back. Despite those glowing letters, Rue wanted to know her cousin was all right before she put this parallel universe—or whatever it was—behind her.

"Do you believe in ghosts, Farley?" she asked companionably, once they were inside and the marshal had opened a little gate in the railing that separated his desk and cabinet and wood stove from the single jail cell.

"No, ma'am," he answered with a sigh, hanging his disreputable hat on a hook by the door and laying his rifle down on the cluttered surface of the desk. Once again, his gaze passed over her clothes, troubled and quick. "But I do believe there are some strange things going on in this world that wouldn't be too easy to explain."

Rue tucked her hands into the hip pockets of her jeans and looked at the wanted posters on the wall behind Farley's desk. They should have been yellow and cracked with age, but instead they were new and only slightly crumpled. A collection of archaic rifles filled a gun cabinet, their nickel barrels and wooden stocks gleaming with a high shine that belied their age.

"You won't get an argument from me," Rue finally replied.

Chapter 2

Rue took in the crude jail cell, the potbellied stove with a coffeepot and a kettle crowding the top, the black, iron key ring hanging on a peg behind the desk. Her gaze swung to the marshal's face, and she gestured toward the barred room at the back of the building.

"If I'm under arrest, Marshal," she said matter-of-factly, "I'd like to know exactly what I'm being charged with."

The peace officer sighed, hanging his ancient canvas coat from a tarnished brass rack. "Well, miss, we could start with trespassing." He gestured toward a chair pushed back against the short railing that surrounded the immediate office area. "Sit down and tell me who you are and what you were doing snooping around Dr. Fortner's house that way."

Rue was feeling a little weak, a rare occurrence for her. She pulled the chair closer to the desk and sat, pushing her tousled hair back from her face. "I told you. My name is Rue Claridge," she replied patiently. "Dr. Fortner's wife is my cousin, and I was looking for her. That's all."

The turquoise gaze, sharp with intelligence, rested on the gold pendant at the base of Rue's throat, causing the pulse beneath to make a strange, sudden leap. "I believe you said Mrs. Fortner has a necklace just like that one."

Rue swallowed. She was very good at sidestepping issues she didn't want to discuss, but when it came to telling an outright lie, she hadn't even attained amateur status. "Y-yes," she managed to say. Her earlier shock at finding herself in another century was thawing now, becoming low-grade panic. Was it possible that she'd stumbled into Elisabeth's nervous breakdown, or was she having a separate one, all her own?

The marshal's jawline tightened under a shadow of beard. His strong, sun-browned fingers were interlaced over his middle as he leaned back in his creaky desk chair. "How do you account for those clothes you're wearing?"

She took a deep, quivering breath. "Where I come from, lots of women dress like this."

Marshal Haynes arched one eyebrow. "And where

is that?" There was an indulgent tone in his voice that made Rue want to knuckle his head.

Rue thought fast. "Montana. I have a ranch over there."

Farley scratched the back of his neck with an idleness Rue perceived as entirely false. Although his lackadaisical manner belied the fact, she sensed a certain lethal energy about him, an immense physical and emotional power barely restrained. Before she could stop it, Rue's mind had made the jump to wondering what it would be like to be held and caressed by this man.

Just the idea gave her a feeling of horrified delight.

"Doesn't your husband mind having his wife go around dressed like a common cowhand?" he asked evenly.

Color flooded Rue's face, but she held her temper carefully in check. Marshal Haynes's attitude toward women was unacceptable, but he was a man of his time and all attempts to convert him to modern thinking would surely be wasted.

"I don't have a husband." She thought she saw a flicker of reaction in the incredible eyes.

"Your daddy, then?"

Rue drew a deep breath and let it out slowly. "I'm not close to my family," she said sweetly. For all practical intents and purposes, the statement was true. Rue's parents had been divorced years before, going their separate ways. Her mother was probably holed up in some fancy spa somewhere, getting ready for the ski season, and her father's last post-card had been sent from Monaco. "I'm on my own. Except for Elisabeth, of course."

The marshal studied her for a long moment, look-ing pensive now, and then leaned forward in his chair. "Yes. Elisabeth Fortner."

"Right," Rue agreed, her head spinning. Noth-ing in her eventful past had prepared her for this particular situation. Somehow, she'd missed Time Travel 101 in college, and the Nostalgia Channel mostly covered the 1940s.

She sighed to herself. If she'd been sent back to the big-band era, maybe she would have known how to act.

"I'm going to let you go for now," Haynes an-nounced thoughtfully. "But if you get into any trou-ble, ma'am, you'll have me to contend with."

A number of wisecracks came to the forefront of Rue's mind, but she valiantly held them back. "I'll just…go now," she said awkwardly, before racing out of the jailhouse onto the street.

The screech of the mill saw hurt her ears, and she hurried in the opposite direction. It would take a good forty-five minutes to walk back to the house in the country, and by the looks of the sky, the sun would be setting soon.

As she was passing the Hang-Dog Saloon, a shrill cry from above made Rue stop and look up.

Two prostitutes were leaning up against a weath-ered railing, their seedy-looking satin dresses glow-ing in the late-afternoon sun. "Where'd you get them pants?" the one in blue inquired, just before spitting tobacco into the street.

The redhead beside her, who was wearing a truly ugly pea green gown, giggled as though her friend had said something incredibly clever.

"You know, Red," Rue replied, shading her eyes with one hand as she looked up, and choosing to ignore both the question and the tobacco juice, "you really ought to have your colors done. That shade of green is definitely unbecoming."

The prostitutes looked at each other, then turned and flounced away from the railing, disappearing into the noisy saloon.

The conversation had not been a total loss, Rue decided, looking down at her jeans, sneakers and T-shirt. There was no telling how long she'd have to stay in this backward century, and her modern clothes would be a real hindrance.

She turned and spotted a store across the street, displaying gingham dresses, bridles and wooden buckets behind its fly-speckled front window. "'And bring your Visa card,'" she muttered to herself, "'because they *don't* take American Express.'"

Rue carefully made her way over, avoiding road apples, mud puddles and two passing wagons.

On the wooden sidewalk in front of the mercantile, she stood squinting, trying to see through the dirty glass. The red-and-white gingham dress on display in the window looked more suited to Dorothy of *The Wizard of Oz* fame, with its silly collar and big, flouncy bow at the back. The garment's only saving grace was that it looked as though it would probably fit.

Talking to herself was a habit Rue had acquired because she'd spent so much time alone researching and polishing her stories. "Maybe I can get a pair of ruby slippers, too," she murmured, walking resolutely toward the store's entrance. "Then I could just click my heels together and voilà, Toto, we're back in Kansas."

A pleasant-looking woman with gray hair and soft blue eyes beamed at Rue as she entered. The smile faded to an expression of chagrined consternation, however, as the old lady took in Rue's jeans and T-shirt.

"May I help you?" the lady asked, sounding as though she doubted very much that anybody could.

Rue was dizzied by the sheer reality of the place, the woman, the circumstances in which she found herself. A fly bounced helplessly against a window, buzzing in bewilderment the whole time, and Rue felt empathy for it. "That checked dress in the window," she began, her voice coming out hoarse. "How much is it?"

The fragile blue gaze swept over Rue once again, worriedly. "Why, it's fifty cents, child."

For a moment, Rue was delighted. Fifty cents. No problem.

Then she realized she hadn't brought any money with her. Even if she had, all the bills and currency would have looked suspiciously different from what was being circulated in the 1890s, and she would undoubtedly have found herself back in Farley Haynes's custody, post haste.

Rue smiled her most winning smile, the one that had gotten her into so many press conferences and out of so many tight spots. "Just put it on my account, please," she said. Rue possessed considerable bravado, but the strain of the day was beginning to tell.

The store mistress raised delicate eyebrows and cleared her throat. "Do I know you?"

Another glance at the dress—it only added insult to injury that the thing was so relentlessly ugly— gave Rue the impetus to answer, "No. My name is Rue...*Miss* Rue Claridge, and I'm Elisabeth Fortner's cousin. Perhaps you could put the dress on her husband's account?"

The woman sniffed. Clearly, in mentioning the good doctor, Rue had touched a nerve. "Jonathan Fortner ought to have his head examined, marrying a strange woman the way he did. There were odd doings in that house!"

Normally Rue would have been defensive, since she tended to get touchy where Elisabeth was concerned, but she couldn't help thinking how peculiar her cousin must have seemed to these people. Bethie was a quiet sort, but her ideas and attitudes were strictly modern, and she must surely have rubbed more than one person the wrong way.

Rue focused on the block of cheese sitting on the counter, watching as two flies explored the hard, yellow rind. "What kind of odd doings?" she asked, too much the reporter to let such an opportunity pass.

The storekeeper seemed to forget that Rue was a suspicious type, new in town and wearing clothes more suited, as Farley had said, to a cowhand. Leaning forward, she whispered confidentially, "That woman would simply appear and disappear at will. Not a few of us think she's a witch and that justice would have been better served if she'd been hanged after that trial of hers!"

For a moment, the fundamentals of winning friends and influencing people slipped Rue's mind. "Don't be silly—there're no such things as witches." She lowered her voice and, having dispatched with superstition, hurried on to her main concern. "Elisabeth was put on trial and might have been hanged? For what?"

The other woman was in a state of offense, probably because one of her pet theories had just been ridiculed. "For a time, it looked as though she'd murdered not only Dr. Fortner, but his young daughter, Trista, as well, by setting that blaze." She paused, clearly befuddled. "Then they came back. Just magically reappeared out of the ruins of that burned house."

Rue was nodding to herself. She didn't know the rules of this time-travel game, but it didn't take a MENSA membership to figure out how Bethie's husband and the little girl had probably escaped the fire. No doubt they'd fled over the threshold into the future, then had trouble returning. Or perhaps time didn't pass at the same rate here as it did there....

It seemed to Rue that Aunt Verity had claimed

the necklace's magic was unpredictable, waning and waxing under mysterious rules of its own. Elisabeth had mentioned nothing like that in her letters, however.

Rue brought herself back to the matter at hand—buying the dress. "Dr. Fortner must be a man of responsibility, coming back from the great beyond like that. It would naturally follow that his credit would be good."

The storekeeper went pale, then pursed her lips and sighed, "I'm sorry. Dr. Fortner is, indeed, a trusted and valued customer, but I cannot add merchandise to his account without his permission. Besides, there's no telling when he and that bride of his will return from California."

The woman was nondescript and diminutive, and yet Rue knew she'd be wasting her time to argue. She'd met third-world leaders with more flexible outlooks on life. "Okay," she said with a sigh. She'd just have to check the house and see if Elisabeth had left any clothes or money behind. Provided she couldn't get back into her own time, that is.

Rue offered a polite goodbye, only too aware that she might be stuck on this side of 1900 indefinitely.

Although she power walked most of the way home—this drew stares from the drivers of passing buggies and wagons—it was quite dark when Rue arrived. She let herself in through the kitchen door, relieved to find that the housekeeper had left for the day.

After stumbling around in the darkness for a

while, Rue found matches and lit the kerosene lamp in the middle of the table.

The weak light flickered over a fire-damaged kitchen, made livable by someone's hard work. There was an old-fashioned icebox, a pump handle at the sink and a big cookstove with shiny chrome trim.

Bethie actually wanted to stay in this place, Rue reflected, marveling. Her cousin would develop biceps just getting enough water to make the morning coffee, and she'd probably have to chop and carry wood, too. Then there would be the washing and the ironing and the cooking. And childbirth at its most natural, with nothing for the pain except maybe a bullet to bite on.

All this for the mysterious Dr. Jonathan Fortner.

"No man is worth it, Bethie," Rue protested to the empty room, but Farley Haynes did swagger to mind, and his image was so vivid, she could almost catch the scent of his skin and hair.

Desperately hungry all of a sudden, she ransacked the icebox, helping herself to milk so creamy it had golden streaks on top, and half a cold, boiled potato. When she'd eaten, she took the lamp and headed upstairs, leaving the other rooms to explore later.

She'd had quite enough adventure for one day.

In the second floor hallway, Rue looked at the blackened door and knew without even touching the knob that she would find nothing but more ruins on the other side. Maybe she'd be able to get back to her own century, but it wasn't going to happen that night.

Reaching the master bedroom, Rue approached

the tall armoire first. It soon became apparent that Bethie hadn't left much behind, certainly nothing Rue could wear, and if there was a cache of money, it wasn't hidden in that room.

Finally, exhausted, Rue washed as best she could, stripped off her clothes and crawled into the big bed.

Farley didn't make a habit of turning up in ladies' bedrooms of a morning, though he'd awakened in more than a few. There was just something about this particular woman that drew him with a force nearly as strong as his will, and it wasn't just that she wore trousers and claimed to be Lizzie Fortner's kin.

Her honey-colored hair, shorter than most women wore but still reaching to her shoulders, tumbled across the white pillow, catching the early sunlight, and her skin, visible to her armpits, where the sheet stopped, was a creamy golden peach. Her dark eyelashes lay on her cheeks like the wings of some small bird, and her breathing, even and untroubled, twisted Farley's senses up tight as the spring of a cheap watch.

He swallowed hard. Rue Claridge might be telling the truth, he thought, at least about being related to Mrs. Fortner. God knew, she was strange enough, with her trousers and her funny way of talking.

"Miss Claridge?" he said after clearing his throat. He wanted to wriggle her toe, but decided everything south of where the sheet stopped was out of his jurisdiction. "Rue!"

She sat bolt upright in bed and, to Farley's guarded relief and vast disappointment, held the top sheet firmly against her bosom.

Farley Haynes was standing at the foot of the bed, his hands resting on his hips, his handsome head cocked to one side.

Rue sat up hastily, insulted and alarmed and strangely aroused all at once, and wrenched the sheets from her collarbone to her chin.

"I sure hope you're making yourself at home and all," Farley said, and the expression in his eyes was wry in spite of his folksy drawl. He wasn't fooling Rue; this guy was about as slow moving and countrified as a New York politician.

Although the marshal hadn't touched her, Rue had the oddest sensation of impact, as though she'd been hauled against his chest, with just the sheet between them. "What are you doing here?" she demanded furiously when she found her voice at last. She felt the ornate headboard press against her bare back and bottom.

He arched one eyebrow and folded his arms. "I could ask the same question of you, little lady."

Enough was enough. Nobody was going to call Rue Claridge "honey," "sweetie" or "little lady" and get away with it, no matter *what* century they came from.

"Don't call me 'little' anything!" Rue snapped. "I'm a grown woman and a self-supporting professional, and I won't be patronized!"

This time, both the intruder's eyebrows rose, then knit together into a frown. "You sure are a temperamental filly," Farley allowed. "And mouthy as hell, too."

"Get out of here!" Rue shouted.

Idly, Farley drew up a rocking chair and sat. Then he rubbed his stubbly chin, his eyes narrowed thoughtfully. "You said you were a professional before. Question is, a professional what?"

Rue was still clutching the covers to her throat, and she was breathing hard, as though she'd just finished a marathon. If she hadn't been afraid to let go of the bedclothes with even one hand, she would have snatched up the small crockery pitcher on the nightstand and hurled it at his head.

"You would never understand," she answered haughtily. "Now it's my turn to ask a question, Marshal. What the *hell* are you doing in my bedroom?"

"This isn't your bedroom," the lawman pointed out quietly. "It's Jon Fortner's. And I'm here because Miss Ellen came to town and reported a prowler on the premises."

Rue gave an outraged sigh. The housekeeper had apparently entered the room, seen an unwelcome guest sleeping there and marched herself into Pine River to demand legal action. "Hellfire and spit," Rue snapped. "Why didn't she drag Judge Judy out here, too?"

Farley's frown deepened to bewilderment. "There's no judge by that name around these parts," he said. "And I wish you'd stop talking like that. If the Presbyterians hear you, they'll be right put out about it."

Catching herself just before she would have exploded into frustrated hysterics, Rue sucked in a deep breath and held it until a measure of calm came over her. "All right," she said finally, in a reasonable tone. "I will try not to stir up the Presbyterians. I promise. The point is, now you've investigated and you've seen that I'm not a trespasser, but a member of the family. I have a right to be here, Marshal, but, frankly, you don't. Now if you would please leave."

Farley sat forward in his chair, turning the brim of his battered, sweat-stained hat in nimble brown fingers. "Until I get word back from San Francisco that it's all right for you to stay here, ma'am, I'm afraid you'll have to put up at one of the boarding-houses in town."

Rue would have agreed to practically anything just to get him to leave the room. The painful truth was, Marshal Farley Haynes made places deep inside her thrum and pulse in response to some hidden dynamic of his personality. That was terrifying because she'd never felt anything like it before.

"Whatever you say," she replied with a lift of her chin. Innocuous as they were, the words came out sounding defiant. "Just leave this room, please. Immediately."

She thought she saw a twinkle in Farley's gem-bright eyes. He stood up with an exaggerated effort and, to Rue's horror, walked to the head of the bed and stood looking down at her.

"No husband and no daddy," he reflected sagely. "Little wonder your manners are so sorry." With that, he cupped one hand under her chin, then bent over and kissed her, just as straightforwardly as if he were shaking her hand.

To Rue's further mortification, instead of pushing him away, as her acutely trained left brain told her to do, she rose higher on her knees and thrust herself into the kiss. It was soft and warm at first, then Farley touched the seam of her mouth with his tongue and she opened to him, like a night orchid worshiping the moon. He took utter and complete command before suddenly stepping back.

"I expect you to be settled somewhere else by nightfall," he said gruffly. To his credit, he didn't avert his eyes, but he didn't look any happier about what he'd just done than Rue was.

"Get out," she breathed.

Farley settled his hat on his head, touched the brim in a mockingly cordial way and strolled from the room.

Rue sent her pillow flying after him, because he was so insufferable. Because he'd had the unmitigated gall not only to come into her bedroom, but to kiss her. Because her insides were still colliding like carnival rides gone berserk.

Later, ignoring Ellen, who was watchful and patently disapproving, Rue fetched a ladder from the barn and set it against the burned side of the house.

At least, she thought, looking down at her jeans and T-shirt, she was dressed for climbing.

She still wanted to find Elisabeth and make sure her cousin was all right, but there were things she'd need to sustain herself in this primitive era. She intended to return to her century, buy some suitable clothes from a costume place or a theater troupe, and pick up some old currency at a coin shop. Then she'd return, purchase a ticket on a train or boat headed south and see for herself that Bethie was happy and well.

It was an excellent plan, all in all, except that when Rue reached the top of the ladder and opened the charred door, nothing happened. She knew by the runner on the hallway floor and the pictures on the wall that she was still in 1892, even though she was wearing the necklace and wishing as hard as she could.

Obviously, one couldn't go back and forth on a whim.

Rue climbed down the ladder in disgust, finally, and stood in the deep grass, dusting her soot-blackened hands off on the legs of her jeans. "Damn it, Bethie," she muttered, "you'd better have a good reason for putting me through this!"

In the meantime, whether Elisabeth had a viable excuse for being in the wrong century or not, Rue had to make the best of her circumstances. She needed to find a way to fit in—and fast—before the locals decided *she* was a witch.

Ellen had draped a rug over the clothesline and

was busily beating it with something that resembled a snowshoe. Occasionally she glanced warily in Rue's direction, as though expecting to be turned into a crow at any moment.

Rue wedged her hands into the hip pockets of her jeans and mentally ruled out all possibility of searching Elisabeth's house for money while the housekeeper was around. There was only one way to get the funds she needed, and if she didn't get busy, she might find herself spending the night in somebody's barn.

Or the Pine River jailhouse.

The idea of being behind bars went against her grain. Rue had once done a brief stint in a minimum-security women's prison for refusing to reveal a source to a grand jury, but this would obviously be different.

Rue headed for the road, walking backward so she could look at the house and "remember" how it *would* look in another hundred-plus years. A part of her still expected to wake up on the couch in Aunt Verity's front parlor and discover this whole experience had been nothing more than a dream.

Reaching Pine River, Rue headed straight for the Hang-Dog Saloon, though she did have the discretion to make her way around to the alley and go in the back door.

In a smoky little room in the rear of the building, Rue found exactly what she'd hoped for, exactly what a thousand TV Westerns had conditioned her to expect. Four drunk men were seated around a rickety table, playing poker.

At the sight of a woman entering this inner sanctum, especially one wearing pants, the cardplayers stared. A man sporting a dusty stovepipe hat went so far as to let the unlit stogie fall from between his teeth, and the fat one with garters on his sleeves folded his cards and threw them in.

"What the hell...?"

After swallowing hard, Rue peeled off her digital watch and tossed it into the center of the table. "I'd like to play, if you fellas don't mind," she said, sounding much bolder than she felt.

The man in the stovepipe hat had apparently recovered from the shock of seeing the wrong woman in the wrong place; he picked up the wristwatch and studied it with a solemn frown. "Never seen nothin' like this here," he told his colleagues.

Being one of those people who believe that great forces come to the aid of the bold, Rue drew up a chair and sat down between a long-haired gunfighter type in a canvas duster and the hefty guy with the garters.

"Deal me in," she said brightly.

"Where'd you get this thing?" asked the one in the high hat.

"K mart," Rue answered, reaching for the battered deck lying in the middle of the table. She thought of bumper stickers she'd seen in her own time and couldn't help grinning. "My other watch is a Rolex," she added.

Stovepipe looked at her in consternation and opened his mouth to protest, but when Rue shuffled the cards deftly from one hand to the other without dropping a single one, he pressed his lips together.

The gunfighter whistled. "Son of a— Tarnation, ma'am. Where'd you learn to do that?"

Rue was warming to the game, as well as the conversation. "On board Air Force One, about three years ago. A Secret Serviceman taught me."

Stovepipe and Garters looked at each other in pure bewilderment.

"I say the lady plays," said the gunslinger.

Nobody argued, perhaps because Quickdraw was wearing a mean-looking forty-five low on his hip.

Rue dealt with a skill born of years of practice— her grandfather had taught her to play five-card draw back in Montana when she was six years old, and she'd been winning matchsticks, watches, ballpoint pens and pocket change ever since.

Rue had taken several pots, made up mostly of coins, though she had raked in a couple of oversize nineteenth-century dollar bills, in this game when the prostitute in the pea green dress came rustling in.

The woman's painted mouth fell open when she saw Rue sitting at the table, actually playing poker with the men, and her kohl-lined eyes widened. She set a fresh bottle of whiskey down on the table with an irate thump.

"Be quiet, Sissy," Quickdraw said, talking around the matchstick he was holding between his teeth. "This here is serious poker."

Sissy's eyes looked, as Aunt Verity would have said, like two burn holes in a blanket, and Rue felt a stab of pity for her. God knew, nineteenth-century life was hard enough for respectable women. It would be even rougher for ladies of the evening.

Quickdraw picked up Rue's watch, which was lying next to her stack of winnings, and held it up for Sissy's inspection. "You bring me good luck, little sugar girl, and I'll give you this for a trinket."

"I think I may throw up," Rue murmured under her breath.

"What'd you say?" Stovepipe demanded, sounding a little testy. Losing at poker clearly didn't sit well with him.

Rue offered the same smile she would have used to cajole the president of the United States into answering a tough question at a press conference, and replied, "I said I'm sure glad I showed up."

Sissy tossed the watch back to the table, glared at Rue for a moment, then turned and sashayed out of the room.

Rue was secretly relieved and turned all her concentration on the matter at hand. She had enough winnings to buy that horrible gingham dress and rent herself a room at the boardinghouse; now all she needed to do was ease out of the game without making her companions angry.

She yawned expansively.

Garters gave her a quelling look, clearly not ready to give up on the evening, and the game went on. And on.

It was starting to get embarrassing the way Rue kept winning, when all of a sudden the inner door to the saloon crashed open. There, filling the doorway like some fugitive from a Louis L'Amour novel, was Farley Haynes.

Finding Rue with five cards in her hand and a stack of coins in front of her, he swore. Sissy peered around his broad shoulder and smiled, just to let Rue know she'd been the one to bring about her impending downfall.

"Game's over," Farley said in that gruff voice, and none of the players took exception to the announcement. In fact, except for Rue, they all scattered, muttering various excuses and hasty pleasantries as they rushed out.

Rue stood and began stuffing her winnings into the pockets of her jeans. "Don't get your mustache in a wringer, Marshal," she said. "I've got what I came for and now I'm leaving."

Farley shook his head in quiet, angry wonderment and gestured toward the door with one hand. "Come along with me, Miss Claridge. You're under arrest."

Chapter 3

Farley Haynes set his jaw, took Miss Rue Claridge by the elbow and hauled her toward the door. He prided himself on being a patient man, slow to wrath, as the Good Book said, but this woman tried his forbearance beyond all reasonable measure. Furthermore, he just flat didn't like the sick-calf feeling he got whenever he looked at her.

"Now, just a minute, Marshal," Miss Claridge snapped, trying to pull free of his grasp. "You haven't read me my rights!"

Farley tightened his grip, but he was careful not to bruise that soft flesh of hers. He didn't hold with manhandling a lady—not even one who barely measured up to the term when it came to comportment.

To his way of thinking, Rue Claridge added up just fine as far as appearances went.

"What rights?" he demanded as they reached the shadowy alley behind the saloon. He had the damnedest, most unmarshal-like urge to drag Rue against his chest and kiss her, right then and there, and that scared the molasses out of him. The thought of kissing somebody in pants had never so much as crossed Farley's mind before, and he hoped to God it never would again.

"Forget it," she said, and her disdainful tone nettled Farley sorely. "It's pretty clear that around this town, I don't *have* any rights. I hope you're enjoying this, because it won't be long until you find yourself dealing with the likes of Susan B. Anthony!"

"Who?" Farley hadn't been this vexed since the year he was twelve, when Becky Hinehammer had called him a coward for refusing to walk the ridgepole on the schoolhouse roof. His pride had driven him to prove her wrong, and he'd gotten a broken collarbone for his trouble, along with a memorable blistering from his pa, once he'd healed up properly, for doing such a damn-fool thing in the first place.

He propelled Miss Claridge out of the alley and onto the main street of town. Pine River was relatively quiet that night.

They reached the jailhouse, and Farley pushed the front door open, then escorted his captive straight back to the jail's only cell.

Once his saucy prisoner was secured, Farley hung his hat on a peg next to the door and put away his rifle. It didn't occur to him to unstrap his gun belt; that was something he did only when it was time to stretch out for the night. Even then, he liked to have his .45 within easy reach.

He found a spare enamel mug, wiped it out with an old dish towel snatched from a nail behind the potbellied stove, and poured coffee. Then he carried the steaming brew to the cell and handed it through the bars to Miss Claridge. "What kind of name is Rue?" he asked, honestly puzzled.

This woman was full of mysteries, and he found himself wanting to solve them one by one.

His guest blew on the coffee, took a cautious sip and made a face. At least she was womanly enough to mind her manners. Farley had half expected her to slurp up the brew like an old mule skinner and maybe spit a mouthful into the corner. Instead, she came right back with, "What kind of name is Farley?"

If she wasn't going to give a direct answer, neither was he. "You're a snippy little piece, aren't you?"

Rue smiled, revealing a good, solid set of very white teeth. Folk wisdom said a woman lost a tooth for every child she bore, but Farley figured this gal would probably still have a mouthful even if she gave birth to a dozen babies.

"And *you're* lucky I know you're calling me 'a piece' in the old-fashioned sense of the word," she said pleasantly. "Because if you meant it the way men mean it where—when—I come from, I'd throw this wretched stuff you call coffee all over you."

Farley didn't back away; he wouldn't let himself

be intimidated by a smudged little spitfire in britches. "I reckon I've figured out why your folks gave you that silly name," he said. "They knew someday some poor man would rue the day you were ever born."

A flush climbed Rue's cheeks, and Farley reflected that her skin was as fine as her teeth. She was downright pretty, if a little less voluptuous than he'd have preferred—or would be, if anybody ever took the time to clean her up.

Considering that task made one side of Farley's mouth twitch in a fleeting grin.

He saw her blush again, then lift the mug to her mouth with both hands and take a healthy swig.

"God, I can't believe I'm actually drinking this sludge!" she spat out just a moment later. "What did you do, boil down a vat of axle grease?"

Farley turned away to hide another grin, sighing as he pretended to straighten the papers on his desk. "The Presbyterians are surely going to have their hands full getting *you* back on the straight and narrow," he allowed.

Rue stared at Farley's broad, muscular back and swallowed. She was exhausted and confused and, since she hadn't had anything to eat in over a century, hungry. She kept expecting to wake up, even though she knew this situation was all too real.

She sat on the edge of the cell's one cot, which boasted a thin, bare mattress and a gray woolen blanket that looked as though it could have belonged to the poorest private in General Lee's rebel army.

"Did you ever get around to having your supper?" Farley's voice was gruff, but there was something oddly comforting about the deep, resonating timbre of it.

Rue didn't look at him; there were tears in her eyes, and she was too proud to let them show. "No," she answered.

Farley's tone remained gentle, and Rue knew he had moved closer. "It's late, but I'll see if I can't raise Bessie over at the Hang-Dog and get her to fix you something."

Rue was still too stricken to speak; she just nodded.

Only when the marshal had left the jailhouse on his errand of mercy did Rue allow herself a loud sniffle. She stood and gripped the bars in both hands.

Maybe because she was tired, she actually hoped, for a few fleeting moments, that the key would be hanging from a peg within stretching distance on her cell, like in a TV Western.

In this case, fact was not stranger than fiction— there was no key in sight.

She began to pace, muttering to herself. If she ever got out of this, she'd write a book about it, tell the world. Appear on TV.

Rue stopped, the nail of her index finger caught between her teeth. Who would ever believe her, besides Elisabeth?

She sat on the edge of the cot again and drew deep breaths until she felt a little less like screaming in frustration and panic.

Half an hour had passed, by the old clock facing Farley's messy desk, when the marshal returned carrying a basket covered with a blue-and-white checkered napkin.

Rue's stomach rumbled audibly and, to cover her embarrassment at that, she said defiantly, "You were foolish to leave me unattended, Marshal. I might very well have escaped."

He chuckled, extracted the coveted key from the pocket of his rough spun trousers and unlocked the cell door. "Is that so, Miss Spitfire? Then why didn't you?"

She narrowed her eyes. "Don't be so damn cocky," she warned. "For all you know, I might be part of a gang. Why, twenty or thirty outlaws might ride in here and dynamite this place."

Farley set the basket down and moseyed out of the cell, as unconcerned as if his prisoner were an addlepated old lady. Rue was vaguely insulted that the lawman didn't consider her more dangerous.

"Shut up and eat your supper," he said, not unkindly.

Rue plopped down on the edge of the cot again. Farley had set the basket on the only other piece of furniture in the cell, a rickety old stool, and she pulled that close.

There was cold roast venison in the basket, along with a couple of hard flour-and-water biscuits and an apple.

Rue ate greedily, but the whole time she watched Farley out of the corner of one eye. He was doing paperwork at the desk, by the light of a flickering kerosene lamp.

"Aren't you ever going home?" she inquired when she'd consumed every scrap of the food.

Farley didn't look up. "I've got a little place out. back," he said. "You'd better get some sleep, Miss Claridge. Likely as not, you'll have the ladies of the town to deal with come morning. They'll want to take you on as a personal mission."

Rue let her forehead rest against an icy bar and sighed. "Great."

When Farley finally raised his eyes and saw that Rue was still standing there staring at him, he put down his pencil. "Am I keeping you awake?"

"It's just…" Rue paused, swallowed, started again. "Well, I'd like to wash up, that's all. And maybe brush my teeth." *In my own bathroom, thank you. In my own wonderful, crazy, modern world.*

Farley stretched, then brought a large kettle from a cabinet near the stove. "I guess you'll just have to rinse and spit, since the town of Pine River doesn't provide toothbrushes, but I can heat up some wash water for you."

He disappeared through a rear door, returning minutes later with the kettle, which he set on the stove top.

Rue bit her lower lip. It was bad enough that the marshal expected her to bathe in that oversize bird cage he called a cell. How clean could a girl get with two quarts of water?

"This is a clear violation of the Geneva Convention," she said.

Farley looked at her over one sturdy shoulder, shook his head in obvious consternation and went back to his desk. "If you hadn't told me you and Lizzie Fortner were kinfolk, I'd have guessed it anyway. Both of you talk like you're from somewhere a long ways from here."

Rue sagged against the cell door and closed her eyes for a moment. "So far away you couldn't begin to comprehend it, cowboy," she muttered.

Farley's deep voice contained a note of distracted humor. "Since I didn't quite make out what you just said, I'm going to assume it was something kindly," he told her without looking up from those fascinating papers of his.

"Don't you have something waiting for you at home—a dog or a goldfish or something?" Rue asked. She didn't know which she was more desperate for—a little privacy or the simple comfort of ordinary conversation.

The marshal sighed and laid down his nibbed pen. His wooden chair creaked under his weight as he leaned back. "I live alone," he said, sounding beleaguered and a little smug in the bargain.

"Oh." Rue felt a flash of bittersweet relief at this announcement, though she would have given up her trust fund rather than admit the fact. Earlier, she'd experienced a dizzying sense of impact, even though Farley wasn't touching her, and now she was painfully aware of the lean hardness of his frame and the easy masculine grace with which he moved.

It was damn ironic that being around Jeff Wilson had never had this effect on her. Maybe if it had, she would have a couple of kids and a real home by now, in addition to the career she loved.

"You must be pretty ambitious," she blurted out. The sound of heat surging through the water in the kettle filled the quiet room. "Do you often work late?"

Farley put down his pen again and scratched the nape of his neck before emitting an exasperated sigh. "I don't plan on spending my life as a lawman," he replied with a measured politeness that clearly told Rue he wished she'd shut up and let him get on with whatever he was doing. "I've been saving for a ranch ever since I got out of the army. I mean to raise cattle and horses."

At last, Rue thought. Common ground.

"I have a ranch," she announced. "Over in Montana."

"So you said," Farley replied. It was plain enough that, to him, Rue's claim was just another wild story. He got up and crossed the room to test the water he'd been heating. "Guess this is ready," he said.

Rue narrowed her eyes as he came toward the cell, carrying the kettle by its black iron handle, fingers protected from the steam by the same rumpled dish towel he'd used to wipe out the mug earlier.

"I'm not planning to strip down and lather up in

front of you, Marshal," she warned, standing back as he unlocked the cell door and came in.

He laughed, and the sound was unexpectedly rich. "That would be quite a show," he said.

Rue wasn't sure she appreciated his amusement. She just glared at him.

Farley set the kettle down in the cell, then went out and locked the door again. He handed Rue a rough towel and a cloth through the bars, then ambled over to collect his hat and canvas duster.

"Good night, Miss Claridge." With that, he blew out the kerosene lantern on his desk, plunging the room into darkness except for the thin beams of moonlight coming in through the few windows.

It was remarkable how lonely and scared Rue felt once he'd closed and locked the front door of the jail-house. Up until then, she'd have sworn she wanted him to go.

She waited until she was reasonably sure she wouldn't be interrupted before hastily stripping. Shivering there in that cramped little cell, Rue washed in the now-tepid water Farley had brought, then put her clothes back on. After wrapping herself in the Civil War blanket, she lay down on the cot and closed her eyes.

Although Rue fully expected the worst bout of insomnia ever, she fell asleep with all the hesitation of a rock dropping to the bottom of a deep pond. She awakened to a faceful of bright sunlight and the de-licious smell and cheerful sizzle of bacon frying.

At first, Rue thought she was home at Ribbon

Creek, with her granddaddy cooking breakfast in the ranch house kitchen. Then it all come back to her.

It was 1892 and she was in jail, and even if she managed to get back to her own time, no one was ever, *ever* going to believe her accounts of what had happened to her.

She would definitely write a novel. A movie would inevitably follow. Kate Winslet could play Rue, and they could probably get George Clooney for Farley's role....

Rue rose from the bed and immediately shifted from one foot to the other and back again.

"'Morning," Farley said with a companionable smile. He was standing beside the stove, turning the thick strips of pork in a cast-iron skillet.

"I have to go to the bathroom," Rue told him impatiently. "And don't you dare offer me a chamber pot!"

The marshal's white teeth flashed beneath his manly mustache. Expertly, he took the skillet off the heat, setting it on a trivet atop a nearby bookshelf, then ambled over to face Rue through the bars.

"Don't try anything," he warned, gesturing for Rue to precede him into freedom.

She stepped over the grubby threshold, concentrating on appreciating the sweet luxury of liberty, however brief it might be.

The marshal ushered her outside and around the back of the small building. Behind it was a small, unpainted cabin, and beyond that was an outhouse.

Rue wrinkled her nose at the smell, but she was in no position to be discriminating.

She went inside and, peering through the little moon some facetious soul had carved in the door, saw Farley standing guard a few feet away, arms folded.

When they were back in the jailhouse, he gave her soap and a basin of water to wash in before setting the bacon on to finish cooking. Rue felt a little better after that, though she longed for a shower, a shampoo and clean clothes.

"I suppose you'll be releasing me this morning," she said after Farley had brought her a metal plate containing three perfectly fried slices of bacon, a dry biscuit and an egg so huge, it could have been laid by Big Bird's mother. "After all, if playing poker were a crime, you'd have to arrest Stovepipe and Garters and Quickdraw."

Farley, who was perched on the edge of his desk, consuming his breakfast, laughed. Then he chewed a bite of bacon with such thoroughness that Rue grew impatient.

Finally, he responded. "I reckon you're referring to Harry and Micah and Jim-Roy, and you're partly right. It isn't against the law for *them* to play poker, but Pine River has an ordinance about women entering into unseemly behavior." Farley paused, watching unperturbed as Rue's face turned neon pink with fury. "You not only entered in, Miss Claridge—you set up housekeeping and planted corn."

"That's the most ridiculous thing I've ever heard!"

Rue thought about flinging her plate through the bars like a Frisbee and beaning Farley Haynes, but she hadn't finished her breakfast and she was wildly hungry. "It's downright discriminatory!"

Farley went to the stove and speared himself another slab of bacon from the skillet. "Nevertheless," he went on, "I can't ask the good citizens of this town to support you forever."

"If you'd just wire Elisabeth in San Francisco—"

"Nobody's heard from Jon and Lizzie," Farley interrupted. "They were in such a hurry to get started on their honeymoon, they didn't bother to tell anybody where they were going to stay once they got to California. They weren't planning to return until Jon's hand has healed and he's ready to start doctoring again."

Rue finished her breakfast with regret. Although loaded with fat and cholesterol, the food had tasted great. "People have mentioned a little girl. Did they take her with them?"

Farley nodded. "Yes, ma'am. Looks like we'll just have to wait until Jon decides to write a letter to somebody around here. When he left, he wasn't thinking of much of anything besides Lizzie."

After handing her empty plate through the bars, Rue folded her arms and sighed. "They're really in love, huh?"

The marshal's blue eyes sparkled. "You might say that. Being within twelve feet of those two is like being locked up in a room full of lightning."

Rue took comfort in the idea that this whole nightmare might not have been for nothing. If Bethie was really happy and truly in love with the country doctor she'd married, well, that at least gave the situation some meaning.

"I understand there was a fire and that nobody really knows how Dr. Fortner and his little girl escaped."

Farley stacked his plate and Rue's neatly on the trivet and poured the bacon grease from the frying pan into a crockery jar. "That's right. Of course, what's important is, they're alive. There are a lot of goings-on in this world that don't lend themselves to reasoning out."

"Amen," agreed Rue, thinking of her own experiences.

After fetching a bucket of water from outside, Farley put another kettle on to heat.

"You are going to give back my poker winnings, aren't you?" Rue asked nervously. She needed that money to buy some acceptable clothes and pay for a room. Provided she could find someone willing to rent her one, that is.

Farley took a mean-looking razor from his desk drawer, along with a shaving mug and a brush. "It'd serve you right if I didn't," he said calmly, studying his reflection in a cracked mirror affixed to the wall near the stove. "But I'll turn the money over to you as soon as I decide to let you go."

Rue's temper simmered at his blithely officious attitude, but she held her tongue. It was a technique she usually remembered after a conflagration, not before.

She watched, oddly fascinated, when Farley poured water from the kettle into a basin and splashed his face. Then, after moistening his shaving brush, he turned the bristles in the mug and lathered his beard.

Presently, he began using the straight razor with what seemed to Rue to be extraordinary skill.

The whole process was decidedly masculine, and it had a very curious—and disturbing—effect on Rue. Every graceful motion of his hands, every turn of his head, was like a caress; it was as though Farley were removing her clothes and taking the time to explore each new part of her as he bared it. And that odd feeling that she'd just collided with a solid object was back, too; she gripped the bars tightly to hold herself up.

When Farley gave her a sidelong look and grinned, she felt as though the bones in her pelvis had turned to warm wax.

Rue had spent a lot of time on a ranch, and she'd traveled and met people, read hundreds of books, watched all sorts of movies, so she had a pretty fundamental understanding of what was happening in her body. What she *didn't* comprehend was exactly what it would be like to make love, because that was something she hadn't gotten around to doing quite yet. It wasn't that she was scared or even especially noble—she just hadn't found the right man.

Farley finished shaving, humming a little tune all the while, rinsed his face and dried it with the towel draped around his neck.

The jailhouse door opened, and Rue noticed that Farley's hand flashed with instinctive speed and grace to the handle of the six-gun riding low on his hip.

His fingers relaxed when a big woman dressed in black bombazine entered. Her eyes narrowed in her beefy face when she caught sight of the prisoner. Two other ladies in equally somber dress wedged themselves in behind her.

"Something tells me the Presbyterians have arrived," Rue murmured.

"Worse," Farley whispered. "These ladies head up the Pine River Society for the Protection of Widows and Orphans, and they're really mean."

The trio stared at Rue, their mouths dropping open as they took in her jeans, sneakers and T-shirt.

"Poor misguided soul," one visitor said, raising bent fingers to her mouth in consternation and pity.

"Trousers!" breathed another.

The heavy woman whirled on Farley, and Rue noticed that a muscle twitched under his right eye.

"This is an outrage!" the lady thundered, as though he were somehow to blame for Rue's existence. "Where on earth did she get those dreadful clothes?"

"I can speak for myself," Rue said firmly, and the other two women gasped, evidently at her audacity. "This is called a T-shirt," Rue went on, indicating the garment in question, "and these are jeans. I know none of you are used to seeing a woman dressed the way I am, but the fact is, these clothes are really quite practical, when you think about it."

"Well, I never!" avowed the leader of the pack.

Rue's mouth twitched. "Never what?" she inquired sweetly.

Farley rolled his eyes, but offered no comment. It was plain that, although he wasn't really intimidated by these women, he wasn't anxious to cross them, either.

"Are you a saloon woman?" demanded the leader of the moral invasion. The moment the words were out of her mouth, she drew her lips into a tight line and retreated a step, no doubt concerned that sin might prove contagious.

Rue smiled. "No, Miss— What was your name, please?"

"My name is *Mrs.* Gifford," that good lady snapped.

Holding one hand out through the bars, Rue smiled again, winningly. "I'm very glad to meet you, Mrs. Gifford. My name is Rue Claridge, and I'm definitely not a 'saloon woman.'" She dropped her voice to a confidential whisper. "Just between you and me, I think I'm probably overqualified for that kind of work."

Mrs. Gifford turned away and gathered her bombazine-clad troops into a huddle. While the conference went on, Rue stood biting her lower lip and wondering whether or not Farley would turn her over to these people. She thought she'd rather take her chances with a lynch mob, if given the choice.

Farley scratched the back of his neck and sighed. Judging from his body language, Rue was pretty sure he wanted to let her go and get on with the daily business of being a living, breathing antique.

Finally, Mrs. Gifford approached the cell again. "There will be no more prancing up and down the street in trousers and no more poker playing," she decreed firmly.

Under any other circumstances, Rue would have defended her right to dress and gamble as she liked, but she wasn't about to risk getting herself into still more trouble. For all she knew, *Mr.* Gifford was a judge with the power to lock her away in some grim prison.

"No more poker playing," Rue conceded in a purposely meek voice. "As for the—trousers, I promise I won't wear them any farther than the general store. I mean to go straight over there and buy a dress as soon as the marshal here lets me out of the pokey."

The delegation put their heads together for another consultation. After several minutes, Mrs. Gifford announced, "Rowena will walk down to the mercantile and purchase the dress," she said, indicating one of the other women.

"Great," Rue responded, shifting her gaze to the marshal. "Will you give Rowena fifty cents from my winnings so I can get out of here?" If the Society tried to make her go with them, she'd make a break for it.

Rowena, who was painfully thin, her mousy brown hair pulled back tightly enough to tilt her eyes, swallowed visibly and backed up when Farley held out the money.

"Poker winnings," she said in horror. "My hands will never touch filthy lucre!"

Now it was Rue who rolled her eyes.

"*I'll* get the dress," Farley bit out furiously, grabbing his hat from its peg and putting on his long canvas duster. A moment later, the door slammed behind him.

The church women stared at Rue, as though expecting her to turn into a raven and fly out through the barred window.

Thank God I didn't land in seventeenth-century Salem, Rue thought wryly. *I'd surely be in the stocks by now, or dangling at the end of a rope.*

Basically a gregarious type, Rue couldn't resist another attempt at conversation, even though she knew the effort was probably futile. "So," she said, smiling the way she did when she wanted to put an interviewee at ease, "what do you do with yourselves every day, besides cooking and cleaning and tracking down sinners?"

Chapter 4

When Farley returned from his mission to the general store, looking tight jawed and grim, he opened the cell door and handed a wrapped bundle to Rue.

Rue's fiery, defiant gaze swept over Mrs. Gifford and her cronies, as well as the marshal, as she accepted the package. "If you people think I'm going to change clothes with the four of you standing there gawking at me, you're mistaken," she said crisply.

Farley seemed only too happy to leave, although the Society hesitated a few moments before trooping out after him.

If she hadn't been so frazzled, Rue would have laughed out loud at the sheer ugliness of that red-and-white gingham dress. As it happened, she just buttoned herself into the thing, tied the sash at the back and tried with all her might to hold on to her sense of humor.

When the others returned, Farley slid his turquoise gaze over Rue in an assessing fashion, and she thought she saw the corner of his mouth twitch. The ladies, however, were plainly not amused.

"Just let me out of here before I go crazy!" Rue muttered.

Farley unlocked the cell again and stepped back, holding the door wide. In that moment, an odd thought struck Rue: she would miss being in close contact with the marshal.

Their hands brushed as he extended the rest of her poker winnings, and Rue felt as though she'd just thrust a hairpin into a light socket.

"I'll try to stay out of trouble," she said. All of a sudden, her throat felt tight, and she had to force the words past her vocal cords.

Farley grinned, showing those movie-cowboy teeth of his. "You do that," he replied.

Rue swallowed and went around him, shaken. She'd been in an earthquake once, in South America, and the inner sensation had been much like what she was feeling now. It was weird, but then, so was everything else that had happened to her after she crossed that threshold and left the familiar world on the other side.

The Society allowed her to leave the jailhouse without interference, but the looks the women gave her were as cool and disapproving as before. It was plain they expected Rue to go forth in sin.

Once she was outside, under a pastel blue sky laced with white clouds, Rue felt a little stronger and more confident. The air was fresh and bracing, though tinged with the scent of manure from the road. Rue's naturally buoyant spirits rose.

She set out for the house in the country, determined to take another crack at returning to her own time. Not by any stretch of the imagination had she given up on finding Elisabeth and hearing her cousin tell her face-to-face that she was truly happy, but Rue needed time to regroup.

She figured a couple of slices of pepperoni pizza with black olives and extra cheese, followed by a long, hot bath, wouldn't hurt her thinking processes, either.

Soon Rue had left the screeching of the mill saw and the tinny music and raucous laughter of the saloons behind. Every step made her more painfully conscious of the growing distance between her and Farley, and that puzzled her. The lawman definitely wasn't her type, and besides…talk about a generation gap!

When Rue finally reached Aunt Verity's house, she stood at the white picket fence for a few moments, gazing up at the structure.

Even with its fire-scarred side, the place looked innocent, just sitting there in the bright October sunshine. No one would have guessed, by casual observation, that this unassuming Victorian house was enchanted or bewitched or whatever it was.

Rue drew a deep breath, let it out in a rush and

opened the gate. With her other hand, she touched the necklace at her throat and fervently wished to be home.

The gate creaked as she closed it behind her. Rue proceeded boldly up the front walk and knocked at the door.

When the crabby housekeeper didn't answer, Rue simply turned the knob and stepped inside. *Remarkable,* she thought, shaking her head. Bethie and her new husband were off in California and the maid had probably left for the day, and yet the place was unlocked.

"Hello?" Rue inquired with a pleasantry that was at least partially feigned. She didn't like Ellen and would prefer not to encounter her.

There was no answer, no sound except for the loud ticking of a clock somewhere nearby.

Rue raised her voice a little. "Hello! Anybody here?"

Again, no answer.

Rue hoisted the skirts of her horrible gingham dress so she wouldn't break her neck and bounded up the front stairway. In the upper hall, she stood facing the burned door for a moment, then pushed it open and climbed awkwardly out onto a charred beam, praying it would hold her weight.

The antique necklace seemed to burn where it rested against her skin. Clutching the blackened doorjamb in both hands and closing her eyes, Rue whispered, "Let me go home. *Please,* let me go home."

A moment later, she summoned all her courage and thrust herself over the threshold and into the house.

When she felt modern carpeting beneath her fingers, jubilation rushed through Rue's spirit, though there was a thin brushstroke of sorrow, too. She might never see her cousin Elisabeth again.

Or Farley.

Rue scrambled to her feet and gave a shout of delight because she was back in the land of indoor plumbing, fast food and credit cards. Looking down at the red-and-white dress, with its long skirts and puffy sleeves, she realized the gown was tangible proof that she actually had been to 1892. No one else would be convinced, but Rue didn't care about that; it was enough that *she* knew she wasn't losing her mind.

After phoning the one restaurant in Pine River that not only sold but delivered pizza, Rue stripped off the dress, took a luxurious bath and put on khaki slacks and a white sweater. She was blow-drying her hair when the doorbell rang.

Snatching some money off the top of her bureau, Rue hurried downstairs to answer.

The pizza delivery person, a young man with an outstandingly good complexion, was standing on the porch, looking uneasy. Rue smiled, wondering what stories he'd heard about the house.

"Thanks," she said, holding out a bill.

The boy surrendered the pizza, but looked at the

money in confusion. "What country is this from?" he asked.

Rue could smell the delicious aromas rising through the box, and she was impatient to be alone with her food. "This one," she replied a little abruptly.

Then Rue's eyes fell on the bill and she realized she'd tried to pay for the pizza with some of her 1892 poker winnings. The mistake had been a natural one; just the other day, she'd left some money on her dresser. Apparently, she'd automatically done the same with these bills.

"I'm a collector," she said, snatching back the bill. "Just a second and I'll get you something a little more...current."

With that, Rue reluctantly left the pizza on the hall table and hurried upstairs. When she returned, she paid the delivery boy with modern currency and a smile.

The young man thanked her and hurried back down the walk and through the front gate to his economy car. He kept glancing back over one shoulder, as though he expected to find that the house had moved a foot closer to the road while he wasn't looking.

Rue smiled and closed the door.

In the kitchen, she consumed two slices of pizza and put the rest into the refrigerator for later—or earlier. In this house, time had a way of getting turned around.

On one level, Rue felt grindingly tired, as though she could crawl into bed and sleep for two weeks without so much as a quiver of her eyelids. On another, however, she was restless and frustrated.

As a newswoman, Rue especially hated not knowing the whole story. She wanted to find her cousin, and she wanted to uncover the secret of this house. If there was one thing Rue was sure of, it was that the human race lived in a cause-and-effect universe and there was some concrete, measurable reason for the phenomenon she and Elisabeth had experienced.

She found her purse and the keys to her Land Rover and smiled to herself as she carefully locked the front door. Maybe the dead bolt would keep out burglars and vandals, but here all the action tended to be on the *inside*.

Rue drove into town, past the library and the courthouse and the supermarket, marveling. It had only been that morning—and yet, it had *not* been— that the marshal's office and the general store and the Hang-Dog Saloon had stood in their places. The road, rutted and dusty and dappled with manure in Farley's time was now paved and relatively clean.

Only when she reached the churchyard did Rue realize she'd intended to come there all along. She parked by a neatly painted wooden fence and walked past the old-fashioned clapboard church to the cemetery beyond.

The place was a historical monument—there were people buried here who had been born back East in the late seventeen hundreds.

Rue paused briefly by Aunt Verity's headstone, crouching to pull a few weeds, then went on to the oldest section. Almost immediately, she found the Fortner plot, a collection of graves surrounded by a low, iron fence.

She opened the little gate, which creaked on rusty hinges, and stepped inside.

Jonathan Fortner's grave was in the center and beside his stone was another one, marked Elisabeth Fortner. Rue felt tears sting her eyes; maybe Bethie was still alive in that other dimension, but she was long dead in this one. So were her husband and all her children.

After she'd recovered from the shock of standing beside Bethie's grave, Rue studied the other stones. Sons, daughters, sons-in-law and daughters-in-law, even grandchildren, most of whom had lived to adulthood, were buried there. Obviously, Jonathan and Elisabeth's union had been a very fruitful one, and that consoled Rue a little. More than anything else, her cousin had wanted a lot of children.

When Rue turned, she was startled to see a handsome young man crouched by the metal gate, oiling the creaky hinges. He smiled, and something about the expression was jarringly familiar.

"Friend of the family?" he asked pleasantly. Rue had him pegged for the kind of kid who had played the lead in all the high school drama productions and taken the prettiest girl in his class to the prom.

Rue allowed herself a slight smile. "You might say that. And you?"

"Jonathan and Elisabeth Fortner were my great-great-grandparents," he said, rising to his feet. He looked nothing like Bethie, this tall young man with his dark hair and eyes, and yet his words struck a note of truth deep inside Rue.

For a moment, she was completely speechless. It seemed that every time she managed to come to terms with one element of this time-travel business, another aspect presented itself.

Rue summoned up a smile and offered her hand. "I guess you could say Bethie—Elisabeth—was my great-great-cousin. My name is Rue Claridge."

"Michael Blake," he replied, clasping her fingers firmly.

Rue searched her memory, but she couldn't recall Aunt Verity ever mentioning this branch of the family. "Do you live in Pine River, Michael?"

He shook his head and, once again, Rue felt a charge of recognition. "Seattle—I go to the university. I just like to come out here once in a while and—well—I don't know exactly how to explain it. It's like there's this unseen connection and I'm one of the links. I guess this is my way of telling them— and myself—that I haven't broken the chain."

Rue only nodded; she was thinking of the overwhelming significance a simple decision or random happenstance could have. If Bethie hadn't stumbled into that other dimension or whatever it was, then Michael would probably never have existed. In fact, just a few months before, when Elisabeth had not yet stepped over the threshold to meet and fall in love with her country doctor, there had surely been no

Michael Blake. That would explain why Aunt Verity had never talked about him or his family.

On the other hand, Michael had grown to youthful manhood; he had a life, a history. He was as solid and real as anyone she'd ever met.

Rue's head was spinning.

"Are you all right?" Michael asked, firmly taking her elbow and helping her to a nearby bench. "You look pale."

Rue sat down gratefully and rubbed her right temple with a shaking hand. "I'm fine," she said hastily. "Honestly."

"I could get you some water...."

"No," Rue protested. "I'm okay. Really."

Michael brought a small black notebook from his jacket pocket, along with a stub of a pencil. "My grandmother would really like to meet you, since you're a shirttail relation and everything. She lives with my mom and dad in Seattle. Why don't you give her a call sometime?"

Rue grinned at the ease with which he invited a total stranger into the inner circle of the family, but then that was the sort of thing kids did. "Thanks, Michael."

He wedged one hand into the pocket of his jacket, holding the can of spray lubricant in the other. "Well, I guess I'd better be getting back to the city. Nice meeting you."

"Nice meeting you," Rue said hoarsely, looking away. *Did you think about what it means to change history, Bethie?* she thought. *I know I never did.*

Michael had long-since driven away in a small blue sports car when Rue finally rose from the bench and went to stand beside her cousin's grave once again.

"Maybe I should just leave it all alone," she murmured as a shower of gold, crimson and chocolate-colored leaves floated down onto the little plot from the surrounding maple trees. "Maybe it would be better to walk away and pretend I believe the official explanation for your disappearance, Bethie. But I just can't do it. Even though I know I could stir up ripples that might be felt all the way into this century, I have to hear you say, in person, that you want to stay there. I have to look into your eyes and know that you understand your decision."

And I have to see Farley Haynes again.

The stray, ragtag thought trailed in after the others, and Rue immediately evicted it from her mind. For all practical intents and purposes, Farley was just a figment of her imagination, she reminded herself, little more than a character she'd seen in a movie or read about in a book.

The idea left a keen, biting sense of loneliness in its wake, but Rue was determined to accept the fact and get on with her life.

Of course, before she could do that, she had to see Bethie just once more.

Instead of going home, Rue drove into Seattle.

She visited a coin shop first, where she purchased an expensive selection of bills and coins issued between 1880 and 1892. After that, Rue visited a dusty little secondhand store tucked away in an alley behind a delicatessen, and bought herself a graceful ivory gown with tatting on the cuffs and collar, and a waist-length capelet to match. A little searching unearthed a pair of brown, high-button shoes and a parasol.

Rue coughed as the shop's proprietress shook out the ancient garment and prepared to wrap it. "Is this a theatrical costume, or was it a part of a real wardrobe?"

The other woman smiled wistfully. "I suspect this gown came from a camphor trunk in someone's attic, since it's in relatively good condition. If you'll look closely at the handwork, you'll see it's made to last."

"Is it washable?"

"I wouldn't try that. The fabric is terribly old; water or dry-cleaning solution might dissolve the fibers."

Rue nodded, feeling fond of that romantic old relic of a dress already, and hoping she could make it hold together long enough to get back to 1892, have a couple of practical calico dresses made and find Elisabeth. Between her poker winnings and the old currency she'd purchased at the coin shop, Rue figured she'd have enough money to catch a boat or a train to San Francisco, where Elisabeth and Jonathan were supposed to have gone.

As Rue was driving back to Pine River, a light rain began to fall. She found a classical station on the car radio—Rue's musical tastes covered the full range, but on that particular night, Mozart had the greatest appeal.

It truly startled her to realize, just as she reached the outskirts of Pine River, that there were tears on her face.

Rue rarely cried, not because she was in any way above it, but because she'd long ago learned that weeping solved nothing. In fact, it usually just complicated matters.

Nevertheless, her cheeks seemed as wet as the windshield, and her feelings were an odd, explosive tangle. Methodically, she began to separate them.

Meeting Michael Blake had given her a shattering sense of the gossamer threads that link the past with the present and the future. If for some reason Elisabeth changed her mind about staying in 1892 and following through with the new destiny she'd created for herself by making that choice, Michael and a lot of other people would simply be obliterated.

To make matters worse, the problem wouldn't stop with Michael's generation. Whole branches of the family tree that might have lived and loved, laughed and cried, would never come into being at all.

Rue's hands began to tremble so badly that she had to pull over to the side of the road and sit with her forehead resting against the steering wheel.

Finally, after several minutes, she was able to drive on, but she was still crying, and there were more feelings to be faced and dealt with.

Next came the most prickly fact of all, the one Rue could no longer deny: she was lonely. From an emotional standpoint, she sometimes felt as though everyone on the planet had stepped into a parallel dimension. She could see them and hear their voices, but they seemed somehow inaccessible, forever out of reach.

Only her grandfather, Aunt Verity and Elisabeth had been able to reach through the invisible barrier to touch her, and now they were all gone.

Rue sniffled. There was one positive aspect to this experience she and Elisabeth shared, however: it opened the door to all sorts of possibilities. Maybe the philosophers and poets were right and she *would* see her loved ones again someday. Maybe Aunt Verity and Gramps were carrying on happy lives in some other time and place, just as Elisabeth seemed to be.

It was all too mystical for a pragmatic mind like Rue's.

Darkness had fallen by the time she reached home but, as always, the atmosphere of the house was friendly.

After carefully hanging up the dress she'd purchased and setting the high-button shoes side by side on the floor of the armoire, Rue went downstairs and made supper: a grilled cheese sandwich and a cup of microwave soup.

She was too tired and overwrought to think clearly or make further plans. After a warm bath, Rue crawled into bed, read two chapters of a political biography and promptly drifted off to sleep.

In the early hours of the morning, Rue dreamed she was back in Afghanistan, hiding out in the basement of a hotel with several other news people and trying not to flinch every time a bomb exploded. She forcibly woke herself from the nightmare, but the loud noises continued.

Rue's fingers immediately rushed to the necklace at her throat. Once again, the pendant felt warm, almost hot, to the touch. And the predawn air reverberated with gunshots.

Muttering, Rue tossed back the covers and stumbled through the hallway to the sealed door. Sure enough, it opened when she turned the knob, and now she could hear drunken male laughter and the nervous whinnying of horses on the road, though the thick darkness prevented her from seeing anything.

There was more shooting, and Rue cringed. Obviously, a few of the boys where whooping it up, as they used to say on TV, and that made her furious. Someone could be shot!

She gripped the sooty sides of the doorframe and yelled, "Hey, you guys! Knock it off before you hurt somebody!"

Surprisingly, an immediate silence fell. Rue listened for a moment, smiled and closed the door. True, she had unfinished business in 1892, but she wasn't going to attend to it in her nightgown.

There was no point in trying to go back to sleep, thanks to the James Gang. Rue set up her laptop at the kitchen table and brewed a cup of herbal tea in the microwave. Then she sat down, her toes hooked behind the rung of her chair, and began tapping out an account of the things that had happened to her.

Like Bethie with her letters, Rue felt a fundamental need to record her experiences with an orderly succession of words.

Rue had been writing steadily for over half an hour, and the first thin light was flowing in through the window above the sink, when suddenly the keyboard vanished from beneath her fingertips.

Rue looked up, stunned to see that the room had changed completely. Dr. Fortner's cast-iron cookstove stood near the back door. There was no tile, only rough wood flooring, and the wooden icebox had returned, along with the bulky pump handle and the clunky metal sink.

Just as quickly, the modern kitchen appeared. The computer keyboard materialized in front of Rue, and the sleek appliances stood in their customary places.

Rue swallowed hard, remembering the time she'd been standing in the front parlor, looking into the mirror above the mantel. The room had altered that day, too, and she'd even caught a glimpse of a woman dusting a piano.

These experiences gave new credence to Aunt Verity's hazy theory that the necklace had a mind of its own.

She sat back in her chair, pressing her palms to her cheeks, half expecting to find she had a raging fever. Instead, her face felt cool.

After a few moments spent gathering her composure, Rue got out Elisabeth's letters and read them again, carefully, word by word. Not once did Bethie mention seeing a room change; she'd gone back and forth between the present and the past all right, but only by way of the threshold upstairs.

Clearly, the common denominator was the necklace.

Rue rubbed the antique pendant thoughtfully between her thumb and forefinger. She, unlike her cousin, had twice caught glimpses of that other world while just going about her business. Did that mean the invisible passageway between the two eras was changing, expanding? If that were the case, it might also shrink just as unpredictably, or disappear entirely.

Forever.

Rue sighed and shoved splayed fingers through her hair, then began pounding at the keys of her computer again, rushing to record everything. She had always believed that reality was a solid, measurable thing, but there was something going on in and around the house that superceded all the normal rules.

There were no more incidents that day, and Rue spent the time resting and making preparations to return to old-time Pine River. She carefully aired and pressed the fragile dress she'd bought, watched a bit of television and made herself a tuna sandwich for lunch.

Then on a foray into the dusty attic, she found one of Aunt Verity's many caches of unique jewelry and helped herself to a brooch and set of tarnished, sterling combs.

Later, in her bedroom, she put on the dress and sat at the vanity table, putting her hair up and learning to use the combs strategically. When she'd mastered the technique, Rue sat looking at her reflection for a long time, liking the wistful, romantic image she made.

The faintly musty scent of the fabric was a subtle reminder, however, that she and the garment belonged to two distinctly different times.

Carefully, Rue unpinned her hair, took off the dress and got back into her jeans and sweatshirt. She felt a strong draw to 1892, but she wasn't quite ready to go back. She needed to gather all her internal forces and make this trip count.

Just to make certain there wouldn't be any unscheduled visits to the Outer Limits, Rue unclasped the necklace and carefully placed it inside an alabaster box on the vanity. She wondered briefly if the pendant was capable of slipping back and forth between then and now all on its own.

That concept caused Rue a case of keen, if momentary, panic. She reached for the necklace, drew back her hand, reached again. Finally, she turned purposefully and walked away, determined not to be held hostage by a chunk of antique gold on a chain.

The pull of the necklace was strong, though, and Rue had to leave the house to keep away from it.

She decided to call on the Buzbee sisters, the two spinsters who lived on the other side of the road, and find out if they could shed any light on the situation.

Roberta Buzbee, a plain and angular woman, greeted Rue at the door. She seemed pleased to have company and, after explaining that her sister was "indisposed," invited Rue in for tea.

They sat in the front parlor before a blazing applewood fire. It was a cozy room, except for the shrunken head prominently displayed on top of the piano. Rue didn't ask how the sisters had come to acquire the memento because she was pretty sure Miss Roberta would tell her. In detail.

"Have there been any developments in the search for your cousin Elisabeth?" Miss Roberta asked. The sisters had been among the first people Rue had spoken with when she'd arrived in Pine River and begun to look for Bethie, and she knew they'd never bought the official theories.

Rue shrugged and avoided the older woman's gaze for a moment, wishing she dared admit the truth. The situation was simply too delicate. "I'm going to find her," she said, and all the considerable certainty she possessed was contained in those words. "No matter what it takes, no matter what I have to do, I'm going to see Bethie and make sure she's okay."

Miss Roberta nodded primly and took a graceful sip of her tea.

Rue cleared her throat softly and began again. "Miss Roberta, have other people disappeared from that house? Temporarily or permanently?"

The other woman looked distinctly uncomfortable. "Not just that. People have *appeared,* too," she confided. "Folks in old-timey clothes, mostly."

This was new to Rue; she scooted to the edge of her chair. "Like who?" she asked, wide-eyed.

"Well, there was a woman—never liked her. Verity took her under her wing, though, and she finally left town. Once in a while, Sister and I catch sight of a buggy that comes along and turns in at your driveway. And there's another woman who can be seen hanging out clothes on a fine spring morning."

Ellen, Rue thought. Lizzie's housekeeper. "Ghosts?" Rue asked, to keep the spinster talking.

Miss Roberta clucked her tongue. "Oh, my, no. There aren't any such things—just places where the curtain between our time and theirs has worn a little thin, that's all. Time's all of a piece, Sister and I believe, like a big tapestry. Would you like some lemon cookies? I just baked them this morning."

Rue loved homemade sweets, no matter how agitated her state of mind might be, and she eagerly agreed.

While her hostess was in the kitchen, though, Rue was restless. She picked up a small book that was lying on the coffee table—the title, *My Life in Old Pine River,* suggested the subject was local history. She began thumbing through page after page of old pictures in the center of the book.

Rue's heart twisted when she came across a photograph of Elisabeth standing with the townsfolk in front of a new-looking covered bridge, a slight and mysterious smile curving her lips.

Chapter 5

Seeing an impossibly old photograph of Elisabeth left Rue shaken. Even though she knew from personal experience that time travel was possible, the mysteries of it all still boggled her mind.

"Is something wrong, dear?" Miss Roberta asked as she appeared in the doorway with the promised cookies. "You look as though you wouldn't trust your knees to hold you up."

Rue sighed and rubbed her temple. "This picture…"

Miss Roberta put the platter of cookies down on the coffee table and bent to look at the book in Rue's lap.

Even as she acted, Rue knew discretion would have been a better course than valor, but she was tired of being the only one who knew. She needed the understanding and support of another human being.

She tapped the page lightly with an index finger, and when she spoke, her voice was thready and hoarse. "This woman, standing here by the bridge... this is Elisabeth."

The spinster perched gracefully on the arm of the sofa, took the volume from Rue and raised it for a closer view. "My land, that does *look* like Elisabeth. I've been through this book a thousand times.... This little girl sitting on the big rock by the stream grew up to be our mother...but I swear I've never noticed this woman. Well, well, well. What do you make of that?"

"What, indeed?" Rue murmured, longing to take an aspirin.

Miss Roberta was pensive. "Maybe she was an ancestor of yours. That would account for the resemblance. What I can't understand is how something so obvious could have escaped my attention."

Rue accepted the book when it was offered and scrutinized the picture again. The woman standing in that crowd was definitely Elisabeth herself, not just someone who resembled her, and the handsome, dark-haired man at her side was probably Jonathan Fortner.

Rue smiled, though she could just as easily have cried, so fragile were her emotions. Elisabeth and Jonathan looked right together.

"Next thing you know," Miss Roberta said irritably, "we'll have our pictures on the front of those dreadful newspapers they sell at the supermarket, and all because of that troublesome old house of Verity's."

Lowering her head for a moment to hide her smile, Rue nodded. She suspected the neighbor woman secretly hoped an explosion of notoriety would thrust the boundaries of Pine River outward, thus bringing some excitement to an otherwise humdrum town.

Rue ate a cookie and finished her tea, but only to be polite. Now that she'd seen the photograph of Elisabeth, she was more anxious than ever to make contact with her cousin. Bethie looked happy in that old picture, but that didn't mean she wasn't in over her head in some way. After all, during her marriage to Ian McCartney, Elisabeth had put a brave face on things, but she'd also been miserable for the duration.

Dr. Fortner looked like a hard-headed, autocratic type, though there was no denying he was a formidable hunk, and the male sex had virtually ruled the world in the nineteenth century. Maybe the good doctor was dominating Elisabeth in some way, forcing her to stay when she really wanted to come back to her own time.

Just the idea made Rue's blood simmer. Nobody, but *nobody* was allowed to mistreat Elisabeth.

When she could leave without seeming hasty, Rue thanked Miss Roberta for the cookies and tea, and set out for the other side of the road. By that time, it was already getting dark, and a crisp autumn wind was stirring the flame-colored trees.

Reaching the house, Rue built a fire and then carefully assembled all the items she'd purchased for her journey back to 1892—the dress, the brown high-button shoes, the musty, fragile old money, the silver combs.

Since she hadn't bought stockings, Rue made a concession and wore panty hose. She put on a bra, too, because there were certain comforts she just wasn't willing to sacrifice, even for the sake of authenticity. Besides, nobody in 1892 was going to get a look at her underwear, anyway.

Once she'd donned the dress—she had to suck in her stomach and fasten the buttons in front, then turn the gown around again and put her hands through the armholes—Rue did up her hair. Then, reluctantly, wishing she could wear her sneakers as she had before, she slipped her feet into the pinchy-toed shoes.

She folded the money she'd bought in the coin shop, along with the funds she'd won in the poker game, and tucked the bundle securely into her bodice. The hated red-and-white gingham dress was carefully folded into a neon pink designer sports bag, along with a toothbrush and toothpaste, a paperback book, a bottle of aspirin and some snack-size candy bars.

Once she was seated at the kitchen table, the bag perched on her lap, Rue put on the necklace and waited. A sense of urgent excitement buzzed in her stomach, and she was certain something was about to happen.

Rue sat waiting for so long that she finally unzipped the bag and brought out the novel. She was halfway through chapter two when suddenly the necklace started to vibrate subtly and the light changed, dimming until she could barely see.

The first thing Rue was aware of after that was an incredibly bad smell. The second was the moon shape cut out of the crude wooden door in front of her.

Realizing she'd landed in somebody's outhouse, Rue bolted to her feet, sending the book and the sports bag tumbling to the floor. *"Yuk,"* she grumbled, snatching up her belongings again and then turning the loosely nailed piece of wood that served as a primitive lock and bolting out into the sunlight.

An elderly cowboy touched his hat and smiled at her, and the gaps between his teeth made Rue think of a string of Christmas-tree lights with some of the bulbs burned out. "No hurry, ma'am," he said. "I can wait."

Rue's face throbbed with the heat of embarrassment. It was disconcerting enough to be flung back and forth between two different centuries. Landing helter-skelter in somebody's privy was adding insult to injury.

She hurried past a line of laundry flapping in the breeze, not recognizing the house in front of her or the ones on either side, possessed by an entirely new fear. Maybe she wasn't in 1892, or even in Pine River, for that matter.

Rue's hand tightened on the handle of her bag. Reaching a side gate in the white picket fence, she opened it and stepped out onto a wooden sidewalk.

She glanced wildly up and down the street, looking for anything familiar.

She swayed slightly, so great was her relief when she saw Farley come out of a saloon and amble toward her, holding his rifle casually in one hand. With his free hand, he pushed his hat back a notch, and the sigh he gave was one of exasperation.

"You're back," he said.

Rue wrinkled her nose. "How long was I gone?"

Farley's marvelous turquoise eyes narrowed as he studied her. "How long were you…what the Sam Hill are you talking about?"

"An hour?" Rue shrugged and smiled charmingly, pleased that she was confusing Marshal Haynes. He deserved it for being so arrogant. "Two hours? A week?"

"I haven't seen you in about four days." He frowned, and his expression was pensive now. "I figured you'd gone back to your folks or something."

Rue wanted to ask if he'd missed her, but she couldn't quite bring herself to take the risk. "I've been…around," she said, holding out the skirts of the gown she'd bought especially for this trip. "Like my dress?"

Farley wasn't looking at her outfit, however. He was staring at the blindlingly pink bag she was carrying. "That's the damnedest colored satchel I've ever seen," he muttered, reaching out to touch the material. "Where did you get that?"

"Nordstrom," Rue answered with a slight grin. "It's a store in Seattle." Obviously, she couldn't go into much more detail. As it was, if Farley went looking for the place in the Seattle *he* knew, he'd never find it.

"Where are you staying?" he asked suspiciously.

Much as Rue enjoyed Farley's company, she had no desire to do another stretch in his jail. She looked around, biting her lip, and fortunately caught sight of a sign swinging from the lowest branch of an elm tree in a yard down the street. "There," she said. "At Mrs. Fielding's Rooming House."

Farley sighed again. "That's interesting," he commented at some length, "because Geneva Fielding only takes in gentleman boarders, as a rule."

Rue bit her lower lip. "Okay, so I lied," she blurted out in a furious whisper. "If I'd told you the truth, you wouldn't have believed me. I don't *have* a place to stay, since you won't let me set foot inside Elisabeth's house, but you don't need to worry. I'm not going to loiter or anything. I plan to buy a ticket on the next stagecoach out of town."

The marshal raised one eyebrow. "That so? There won't be one leaving for nearly a week."

"Damn!" Rue ground out. If it weren't for the inconvenience this news was bound to cause her, she would have laughed at the expression of shock on Farley's face. She set the bag on the sidewalk and placed her hands on her hips. "Now I suppose you're going to say it's illegal for a lady to swear and I'm under arrest!"

One corner of Farley's mouth twitched almost imperceptibly. "It's true enough that a lady can't cuss on the street and still be within the law. Thing is, I'm not sure whether that ordinance could cover *you* or not."

Rue opened her mouth, closed it again. As a child, she'd been a tomboy, and as an adult, she'd thought more in terms of being a woman than a lady. It hurt that Farley wasn't sure how to classify her.

He allowed her a smile so brief it might have been nothing more than a mirage, then took her elbow in his free hand. "Miss Ella Sinclair takes in roomers now and again. Do you still have that poker money you won the other night?"

It was a moment before Rue could speak, since a series of small shocks was still jolting through her system from the place where Farley was touching her. "Ah...er...yes, I have a little money." She swallowed hard, awed at the cataclysmic shifts taking place in the deepest, most private passages of her spirit. Farley began to walk purposefully onward, and Rue hurried to keep up. "I've got to be careful, though, because I don't know how much I'll need for train fare to San Francisco."

"It'll cost you about seventy-five cents to go from here to Seattle by stage. As for the train ticket, that'll be considerably more."

Mentally, Rue was counting the currency tucked into her bodice, but she kept having to start over because of the distracting sensations Farley's grip on her elbow was causing. She figured she probably had enough money for the trip, provided she skimped on meals and didn't run into any emergencies.

"Is there a place around here where a woman can

get a job?" she asked. Farley stopped in front of a narrow blue house with a white weather vane on the roof.

His look was one of wry annoyance as he cocked his thumb back toward the main part of town. "Sure. They're always looking for dancing girls at the Hang-Dog Saloon."

"Very funny," Rue whispered, stepping away from him. "I'll have you know that I'm a trained journalist, with a college education...."

Farley grinned. He plainly knew full well that what he was going to say would infuriate Rue, and so did she...long moments before he actually spoke. "I guess that's where your kinfolks went wrong. Sending you to college, I mean. That's probably how you got all those muddleheaded ideas you're always spouting."

After telling herself silently that it would be immature to stomp on the man's instep, Rue managed to reply in a relatively moderate tone of voice. "It would serve you right if I told you *exactly* where I got all my 'crazy ideas,' Mr. Haynes. However, since you'd almost certainly be too boneheaded to absorb the information, I won't bother." She opened the gate latch. "Goodbye."

Farley was right beside Rue as she strode up the flagstone walk. "You'll need me to vouch for you," he said, his eyes laughing at her even though his sensual mouth was somber. "Even that might not be enough, given the reputation you've made for yourself in this town by wearing pants, playing poker and getting yourself thrown into jail."

Before Rue could answer, the front door of the house swung open and a woman appeared. She was tall, with blue eyes and thin, blond hair, and she wore a paisley shawl pulled tightly around her shoulders. Her smile was tremulous and hopeful—and it was entirely for Farley.

A laughable stab of jealousy knifed through Rue, but she didn't feel at all amused.

Farley touched his hat brim in a courtly way. "Miss Ella, this is…er…a friend of mine. Miss Rue Claridge." Rue didn't miss the fact that he'd remembered her last name, though she had no idea what conclusions to draw from the discovery. "She needs a place to stay, just until the stage pulls out on Tuesday."

Miss Ella folded her arms and assessed Rue with disapproving eyes, and her nostrils flared slightly in rebellion. "I'm sorry, Farley." Her voice was irritatingly shrill. "I don't have a single room left."

"Then I guess she'll just have to stay at my place," Farley said, resigned. With that, he took hold of Rue's elbow again and propelled her back toward the gate.

Miss Ella took only a few moments to weigh the implications of that. The hard leather heels of her shoes clicked purposefully against the floorboards of the porch as she hurried after Farley and Rue. "Wait!" she warbled. "There is Mama's old sewing room…. It's just a matter of moving out a few trunks and the like."

Rue smiled to herself, though in some ways she'd found the idea of being Farley's houseguest appealing.

Farley winked at her, causing Rue's heart to go into arrest for at least five beats, before turning to look back at Miss Ella. "That's very kind of you," he said cordially.

For the first time, it occurred to Rue that Farley Haynes was a well-spoken man, for a small-town, nineteenth-century marshal. Silly questions boiled up in her heart and rose into her mind like vapor, and Rue was grateful that he'd be going on about his business soon. Hopefully before she made a complete fool of herself.

Sure enough, he escorted the ladies only as far as the porch, then tugged at his hat brim, muttered a polite farewell and left.

Rue felt as though she'd been abandoned on a distant planet.

The look in Miss Ella's eyes was not a friendly one as the woman opened the front door and swept into the thin, blue house.

Rue followed, lugging her pink bag. By that time, sleeping in somebody's barn sounded a shade more inviting than rooming with Miss Ella Sinclair.

"That'll be one dollar in advance," the spinster said, holding out one hand, palm up.

Pulling her money from her bodice embarrassed Rue, but she did it defiantly all the same, to let the landlady know she wasn't intimidated. "Here," she said, peeling off a bill.

"Thank you," Miss Ella replied crisply. "I'll just go and ready up that room I mentioned." With that, she swept off, leaving Rue standing awkwardly in the front parlor, still holding her bag.

The landlady returned in a surprisingly short time for someone who'd allegedly had to move trunks out of a sewing room. Of course, Rue knew there had never been a shortage of beds in this house in the first place; Miss Sinclair was smitten with Farley, and she didn't want him taking in a female boarder.

Rue's quarters turned out to be a closet-size room wedged underneath the stairway. There was very little light and even less air. Someone had made a disastrous attempt at decoration, papering the place with hideous red cabbage roses against a pea green background. It looked as though a child had stood on the threshold and pitched overripe tomatoes at the walls.

"Dinner is at seven," Miss Ella announced. "Please be prompt, because Papa is always ravenous when he returns from a day at the bank."

Rue nodded and set her bag on the foot of the narrow cot she'd be sleeping on every night until the stagecoach came through and she could be off to Seattle. It hardly looked more comfortable than the bed in Pine River's solitary jail cell.

"Thank you." Rue rushed on without thinking, and the instant the question was out of her mouth, she regretted it. "Where's the bathroom?"

"There's a chamber pot underneath the bed," the landlady answered with a puzzled frown. "And as for bathing, well, each boarder is assigned one particular night when he can bathe in the kitchen. Yours will be…" She paused, tapping her mouth with one finger as she considered. "Thursday."

Rue sat down on the edge of the cot with a forlorn sigh. She didn't mind being in the wrong century, she didn't even mind boarding in a house where she wasn't wanted, but not being able to take a shower every day was practically unbearable.

Miss Ella waggled her fingers in farewell and went out, closing the squeaky door behind her.

Rue got out her paperback book, stretched out on the lumpy cot and sighed. She'd stayed in worse places, though most of them had been in third-world countries.

Somewhere between chapters four and five, Rue dozed off. When she awakened, she had a headache and cramps in all her muscles, and she was clutching her sports bag like some pitiful orphan abandoned at Ellis Island.

Since crying wasn't a workable method of operation, she got up, poured tepid water from a chipped pitcher into a mismatched bowl and splashed her face. After that, she opened the window a crack and took a few deep breaths.

Soon Rue was feeling better. She ferreted out the supply of candy bars tucked away in her bag and ate a single piece, then decided to brave Miss Sinclair's parlor. She would borrow a cloak, if she could, and go out for a walk before dinner.

The landlady was nowhere to be found, as it happened, but a young woman who introduced herself as Miss Alice McCall volunteered a long woolen cape. Gratefully, Rue wrapped herself against the evening chill and went out.

There were no streetlights in this incarnation of Pine River, and certainly no neon signs. The blue-gray color of television screens didn't flicker beyond the windows, but oil lanterns sent out a wavering glow.

A crushing wave of loneliness washed over Rue, a bruising awareness that the lights behind those thick panes of glass didn't shine for her.

She was a stranger here.

In the center of town, the golden glimmer of lamps spiced with bawdy piano tunes spilled out of the saloon windows into the streets. Rue was drawn not by the drinking and the ugliness, but by the light and music.

The sudden flare of a match startled her, and she jumped. Farley was leaning against the outer wall of the feed and grain, his trusty rifle beside him, smoking a thin brown cigar.

"Looking for a poker game?" he inquired dryly.

Rue tossed her head to let him know just how much contempt she had for his question, then gestured toward the cigar. "Those things will kill you," she said. She didn't really expect to turn Farley from his wicked ways; she just wanted to make conversation for a few minutes.

He chuckled and shook his head. "You have an opinion on just about everything, it seems to me."

Rue sighed. It wasn't the first time someone had called her opinionated, and it probably wouldn't be the last. "There are worse things," she said, drawing her borrowed cloak more tightly around her. She hoped she would catch up with Elisabeth before too long, because she didn't have the clothes for cold weather.

"I can't deny that," Farley confessed good-naturedly. He started walking along the board sidewalk, and Rue just naturally strolled along beside him.

"Miss Sinclair is—what did you people call it?— oh, yes. She's sweet on you, Marshal. She's set her cap for you."

Now it was Farley who sighed. "Umm," he said.

"Typical male answer," Rue replied briskly. "Who are you, Farley? Where did you go to school?"

His boots made a rhythmic and somehow comforting sound on the wooden walk as he moved along, keeping a thoughtful silence. Finally, he countered, "Why do you want to know?"

"I'm just curious," Rue said. They'd reached the end of the main street, and Farley crossed the road and started back the other way, the ever-present rifle in his hand. "You're educated, and that isn't all that common in the old…in the West."

Farley laughed, and the sound was low and rich. The smell of his cigar was faint and somehow a comfort in the strangeness of that time and place. "My pa was a hard-scrabble farmer in Kansas," he said, "and my ma never got beyond the fourth grade in school, but she loved books, and she taught me to read from the Bible and the *Farmer's Almanac*. Once in Texas, I herded cattle for a man who must have had two hundred books in his house, and he let me borrow as many as I could carry." Farley paused, smiling as he remembered. "I stayed on with that outfit for three years, even though the money wasn't for spit, and I read every damn one of those books."

Rue felt a swell of admiration, along with the usual jangling this man always caused in her nervous system. And she wished she could take him by the hand and show him the library her grandfather had built up on the ranch in Montana. "Awesome," she said.

"Awesome," Farley echoed. They were passing one of the saloons, and he glanced in over the swinging doors, apparently just making sure all was well with the warm-beer set. "I've never heard that word used that way."

Rue smiled. "Kids say 'awesome' in…Seattle." It was true enough. They just weren't saying it *yet*. "I'm impressed, Farley. That you've read so many books, I mean."

"If you ever want to borrow any," he said with an endearing combination of modesty and shyness Rue had never dreamed he was capable of, "just let me know. I've got some good ones."

They had reached the residential part of town, and Rue knew seven o'clock must be getting close. "Thanks," she said, lightly touching Farley's arm. "I might do that."

The instant her fingers made contact with the hard muscles of his forearm, Rue knew she'd made a mistake. The ground seemed to tremble beneath her feet, and she felt more than slightly dizzy.

When Farley leaned his rifle against a building and gripped the sides of her waist to steady her, the whole situation immediately got worse. He gave a strangled groan and bent his head to kiss her.

His tongue touched either side of her mouth, then the seam between her lips. She opened to him as she had never done for another man, and he took full advantage of her surrender.

Much to Rue's chagrin, it was Farley who finally broke away. He gripped her shoulders and held her at a distance, breathing hard and muttering an occasional curse word.

"I'll see you back to the Sinclair place," he said after a long time.

Rue was shaken and achy, wanting the marshal of Pine River as she had never in her life wanted a man before. "Farley, what's wrong?" she asked miserably.

He took her elbow and started hustling her along the walk. "Nothing. You're leaving for Seattle on Tuesday and I'm staying here to start a ranch. Let's remember that."

For the first time, Rue fully understood how Elisabeth could care enough about a man to give up every comfort and convenience of the twenty-first century. Her own attraction to Farley Haynes had just reached a frightening pitch.

She swallowed. "I guess you'll marry someone

like Miss Sinclair, once you're ready to settle down. A man out here needs a wife."

Farley didn't look at her. "I guess so," he said, and his voice sounded gruff. They'd reached the Sinclair's front gate, and he reached down to unfasten the latch. "In the future, Miss Claridge," he said tightly, "it might be a good idea if you didn't go out walking after dark. It's not safe or proper, and the good people of the town don't set much store by it."

Rue was riding an internal roller coaster, had been ever since Farley had kissed her, and she'd exhausted her supply of sensible remarks. "Good night," she said, turning and rushing toward the house.

The Sinclairs and their boarders were just sitting down to supper, and Rue joined them only because she was famished. This was one night when she would definitely have preferred room service.

"What do you do, Miss Claridge?" the head of the household asked pleasantly. He was a tall, heavy man with slate gray hair and a rather bulbous red nose. "For a living, I mean?"

His daughter smiled slyly and lowered her eyes, obviously certain that the new boarder was about to make a fool of herself.

"I'm an heiress," Rue said. The statement was true; it was just that her money was in another dimension, stamped with dates that would be nothing but science fiction to these people. "My family has a ranch in Montana."

"What brings you to Pine River, Miss Claridge?"

asked the young woman who had loaned Rue her cloak earlier.

"I came to see my cousin, Elisabeth Fortner."

Mr. Sinclair put down his fork, frowning, but his daughter did not look at all surprised. Of course, Rue would have been the subject of much female conjecture in the dull little town.

"Jonathan's wife?" Mr. Sinclair inquired, frowning heavily. "The woman we tried for murder?"

"Yes," Rue answered. "The woman you tried... and acquitted."

Pointing out Elisabeth's innocence of any crime didn't seem to lighten the mood at the table. It was as though being accused had been enough to taint not only Bethie, but all who came before and all who could come after.

Once again, Rue wondered how happy her cousin could expect to be in this town. Probably the memory of Elisabeth McCartney Fortner's murder trial would live on long after Bethie herself was gone, and time would undoubtedly alter the verdict.

"More chicken and dumplings, Miss Claridge?" cooed Miss Sinclair with particular malice.

Rue's stomach had suddenly closed itself off, refusing to accept so much as one more forkful of food. "No, thank you," she said. Then she excused herself from the table, carried her dishes into the kitchen and took refuge in her room under the stairway.

After making a reluctant trip to the privy behind the house—Rue refused to use the chamber pot under any circumstances—she washed and brushed her teeth, then climbed into bed. There was one lamp burning on the bedside stand, but the oil was so low that reading was out of the question.

Rue turned down the wick until the room was in darkness, then lay back on her pillow, thinking about Farley and the way she'd felt when he kissed her. She raised one hand to her chest, amazed at the way her heart was pounding against her breastbone, and that was when she made the frightful discovery.

The necklace was gone.

Chapter 6

Rue bounded out of bed, lit the lamp and tore through her sheets and blankets in a panic. There was no sign of the necklace.

Only too aware that she would be trapped in this backward century if she didn't find the antique pendant, she sank to her knees and went over every inch of the floor.

Rue was rifling through her sports bag when the last of the lamp oil gave out and the tiny room went dark. For a long moment, she just knelt there on the splintery wood, breathing hard and fighting a compulsion to scream hysterically.

Finally, reason prevailed. She couldn't retrace her steps through town until morning. Flashlights hadn't been invented yet and, besides, if Farley caught her out prowling the sidewalks at that hour, he'd probably toss her back in jail just on general principle.

Lying very still, Rue forced herself to concentrate on her breathing until she was calmer. Soon her heartbeat had slowed to its regular rate and the urge to rush wildly around Pine River upending things in search of the missing necklace had abated slightly. For all her self-control, Rue didn't manage to sleep that night.

Finally the sun peeked over the blue-green, timber-carpeted hills, and Rue bolted out of her room like a rubber-tipped dart shot from a popgun. She'd long since washed, dressed and brushed her teeth.

She went over every step she'd taken the day before, hoping to find the necklace wedged between one of the boards in the sidewalk or lying beside the Sinclairs' gate or on the path to the privy. After a full morning of searching, however, Rue still had no necklace, and she was pretty forlorn.

In a last-ditch effort, she made her way to Farley's office. The front door was propped open with a rusty coffee can filled with ordinary speckled rocks.

"Hello?" Rue called, peering around the frame.

Farley was just hanging his hat on its customary peg, and a large, rumpled-looking man was snoring away on the cot in the cell.

When Farley smiled in recognition, Rue felt as if two of the floorboards had suddenly switched places beneath her feet. "Good day, Miss Claridge," the marshal said.

He acted as though he hadn't kissed her the night

before, and Rue decided to go along with the pretense.

She stepped into the room reluctantly, torn between approaching the marshal and bolting down the sidewalk in utter terror. Rue hadn't felt this awkward around a guy since junior high. "I wonder if you would mind checking your lost-and-found department for my necklace," she said, sounding as prim as Miss Ella Sinclair or one of the Society.

Farley's dark eyebrows knit together for a moment, then he went to the stove and reached for the handle of the coffeepot. "We've never seen the need for a lost-and-found department here in Pine River," he said with a good-natured patience that nonetheless rankled. "Folks pretty much know what belongs to them and what doesn't."

Rue sagged a little. "Then no one has reported finding a gold necklace?"

Farley studied her sympathetically and shook his head. "Coffee?"

Rue had never been a frail woman, but these were stressful circumstances, and she knew a dose of Farley's high-octane brew would probably turn her stomach inside out. "No, thanks," she said distractedly. "Did you know it's been proven that caffeine aggravates P.M.S.?"

"What aggravates what?"

"Never mind." Rue turned to go, muttering. "I've got to find that necklace...."

There was nowhere else to look, however, so Rue returned to the Sinclair house. The place was empty and, since she'd probably missed lunch, Rue headed for her room. As she was opening the door, a distraught, feminine moan drifted down the stairway.

Holding the skirts of her secondhand dress, Rue swept around the newel post and up the stairs. The sound was coming from beneath the first door on the right. She knocked lightly. "Hello? Are you all right in there?"

"Yes." The answer was a fitful groan.

Rue opened the door a crack and saw Alice McCall lying on a narrow bed in her chemise. A crude hot-water bottle lay on the lower part of her stomach.

"Cramps?" Rue inquired.

"It's the curse," Alice replied, whispering the words as though confessing to some great sin.

Remembering the aspirin in her bag, Rue said, "I think I can help you. I'll be right back." She raced downstairs to her room to fetch the miracle drug she'd brought from her own century and then, after pausing in the kitchen to battle the pump for a glass of water, returned to Alice's room.

The poor girl was pale as death, and her wispy, reddish blond hair was limp with perspiration.

She looked at the pair of white tablets in Rue's palm and squinted. "Pills?"

"They're magic," Rue promised with a teasing lilt to her voice. Aspirin would probably work wonders for someone who had never taken it before. "Just swallow them and you'll see."

Alice hesitated only a moment. Then she took

the tablets and washed them down, one by one, with delicate sips of water.

"Would you like me to fix you a cup of tea?" Rue asked.

"You're very kind, but, no," Alice responded, her face still pinched with pain. It would be a while before the aspirin worked.

Rue sat down at the foot of the bed, since there was no chair, and took in the small, tidy room at a glance. Although Alice's bedroom had a window and the wallpaper was actually tasteful, the place was as sparsely furnished as a monk's cell. Two dresses hung on pegs on the wall, one for everyday and one for Sundays and special occasions. Over the bureau, with its four shallow drawers, was a mirror made of watery greenish glass. A rickety washstand held the requisite pitcher and bowl.

Above the bed was a calendar, clearly marked 1892, with a maudlin picture of two scantily clad children huddling close in a blizzard. The month of October was on display, and the twenty-third was circled in a wreath of pencil lines.

"Is your birthday coming up?" Rue asked, knowing Alice had seen her glance at the calendar.

Alice smiled wanly. "No. That's the day of the Fall Dance at the schoolhouse."

Rue wondered if Alice, like Miss Ella Sinclair, was sweet on Marshal Haynes. The idea took a little of the sparkle off her charitable mood. "Are you hoping to dance with anybody special?"

Color was beginning to return to Alice's cheeks,

though Rue couldn't be sure whether that was due to the aspirin or the prospect of spending time with that special someone. "Jeffrey Hollis," she confided. "He works at the mill."

"Are the two of you dating?"

Alice looked puzzled. "Dating?"

"Courting," Rue corrected herself.

Alice laughed softly. "*I* am definitely courting Jeffrey," she replied, "but I think somebody will have to tell him that he's supposed to be courting me in return." She lay back on the pillow, her lashes fluttering against her cheeks, and then, without further adieu, she floated off to sleep.

Rue covered her newfound friend with a plaid woolen blanket and sneaked out of the room. Back in her own quarters, she ate another candy bar, read two more chapters of her book, and closed her eyes to meditate on the problem of the lost necklace.

Mentally, she retraced every step she'd taken the day before, from the moment she'd found herself in a stranger's privy until she lay down in bed and realized the pendant was gone. And again the chilling thought came to her that that weird, spooky piece of jewelry might have taken to traveling through time all on its own.

Rue squeezed her eyes shut and dragged in a series of slow, deep breaths in an effort to keep her cool, all the while feeling like a one-woman riot.

If she got stuck in this place, she vowed silently, she would pay Elisabeth back by moving into her house like a poor relation. She would stay for fifty years and consciously work at getting more eccentric with every passing day.

Rue brought herself up short. She refused to worry about the future or about the missing necklace. It was time to stop thinking about problems and start looking for solutions.

The first order of business was to find Elisabeth. Once she'd done that, once she knew for a fact that her cousin really wanted to stay in the Victorian era, she could worry about getting home. Or about making a life for herself right there in old Pine River.

With Farley.

She imagined cooking for him, pressing his shirts, washing his back.

The images stirred hormones Rue hadn't even known she had, and a schoolgirl flush rolled from her toes to the roots of her hair in a single crimson wave.

Good grief! she thought, bolting upright on the cot. *Cooking? Ironing?* Washing his back? *What's happening to me? I'm regressing at warp speed!*

Rue sighed and rose from the bed. Lying around in her room in the middle of the day was a waste of daylight. She would check on Alice, then go out and retrace her steps again. Maybe she would find the necklace, or maybe some earthshaking idea would come to her.

Miss McCall was still sleeping, and some of the color had returned to her cheeks, so Rue knew the aspirin was doing its work. She closed the door of Alice's room carefully and turned toward the front stairway.

Mr. Sinclair was standing there, barring her way, a worrisome smile on his face. He was a portly man, with gray hair, shrewd brown eyes, florid cheeks and a somewhat bulbous nose.

"Miss Claridge," he said, as though Rue might have forgotten her name and he was generous enough to enlighten her.

Rue retreated a step, feeling uneasy. She'd seen that look in a man's eyes many times during her travels, and she knew the banker had decided to make a pass. "Good afternoon," she said warily, with a little nod.

"Exploring the house?" He crooned the words, and somehow that was more unnerving than if he'd shouted them.

Rue raised her chin a notch, still keeping her distance. "Of course not," she said with cool politeness.

"Your room is on the first floor, I believe." Sinclair's eyes never linked with hers all the while he was speaking. Instead, his gaze drifted over her hair, her throat, her shoulders and then her breasts.

"I was looking in on Miss McCall," Rue said, folding her arms to hide at least one part of her anatomy from his perusal. "She's suffering from—feminine complaints."

In the next instant, the master of the house reached out with one beefy hand and took hold of Rue's jaw. While his grip was not painful, it was definitely an affront, and she immediately tried to twist free.

"Now, now," Sinclair murmured, as though soothing a fractious child, "don't run away. I wouldn't want to have to tell Farley I caught you going through my personal belongings and get you thrown back into jail."

Rue felt the blood drain from her face. This kind of bore was easy enough to deal with in her own time, but just then the year was 1892 and Sinclair was probably among the most influential men in town. "What do you want?" she asked, hoping she was wrong.

She wasn't.

He ran a sausage-size thumb over her mouth. "Just an hour of your time, Miss Claridge. That's all."

Rue thrust herself away from him. "I wouldn't give you a *moment*," she ground out, "let alone an hour!"

Smiling genially, Sinclair hooked his thumbs in his vest pockets. "That's a pity. More jail time will surely ruin what little is left of your reputation."

Rue inched backward toward the stairway leading down to the kitchen. "I'll deny everything. And Farley will believe me, too!" She wasn't too sure about that last part, but she wanted to keep Sinclair distracted until she was out of lunging distance.

His bushy eyebrows rose in mocking amusement. "Silly child. What the marshal believes doesn't amount to a hill of beans. Not against the say-so of a man who controls everybody's finances."

Knowing she had reached the stairs, Rue whirled and raced down them. She snatched her bag from the little room she had occupied so briefly and fled out the front door.

Now, for all practical intents and purposes, she was homeless. She couldn't go back to her own century because she'd lost the necklace, and since Farley would probably take Sinclair's word over hers, arrest was no doubt imminent.

Much as Rue enjoyed Farley's company, she wasn't about to be locked up again. One stretch in the hoosegow on trumped up charges was more than enough; she had no intention of serving another.

Even so, Rue was forced to admit to herself that she was drawn to Farley's quiet strength. She made her way through the deep grass behind the mercantile and the Hang-Dog Saloon, stopping now and then to crouch down when she heard voices. After nearly half an hour of evasion tactics, she reached the little barn behind the marshal's house and slipped inside.

Farley's horse, a big roan gelding, nickered companionably from its stall.

"At least somebody around here likes me," Rue said, looking around the small structure and deciding the loft would make the best hiding place.

After letting out a long sigh, she tossed her bag up and then climbed the rickety ladder—not an easy task in a long skirt.

The hay in the loft was sweet smelling, and afternoon sunlight flooded in through a gap in the roof. Rue sat cross-legged and automatically unzipped the side flap on her bag, since that was where she had hidden her money.

The currency, like Aunt Verity's necklace, had vanished.

Rue gave a little cry of frustration and fell backward into the hay. A few minutes later, she checked
the main compartment of the bag, but nothing was
missing. Evidently the thief—possibly even Sinclair
himself—had stumbled upon the money first and
been content with that.

Despite her fury, Rue had to smile, wondering
what the robber would have made of her miniature
candy bars and other modern inventions.

Following that, she took the advice her grandfather had given her long ago and quietly accepted
the fact that she was in big trouble. As much as she
would like things to be different, the reality was
that her money was gone, one of Pine River's most
prominent citizens planned to accuse her of stealing,
and she'd lost the only means she'd had of returning to her own time. Only when she'd faced these
problems squarely would solutions begin to present
themselves.

At least, she *hoped* solutions would begin to present themselves. Nothing came to her right away.

The sun was setting and crickets were harmo-
nizing in the quack grass outside the barn when she
heard sounds below and rolled over to peer through
a crack between the floorboards of the loft.

Farley was there. He filled a feedbag and slipped
it over the gelding's head, then began currying the
animal. The graceful play of the muscles in the marshal's back and shoulders did odd things to Rue's
heartbeat, but she couldn't help watching him work.

The lawman caught her completely off guard

when he suddenly whirled, drew his pistol and pointed it at the underside of the loft.

"All right, just come down from there," he ordered. "And keep your hands where I can see them."

Some days, Rue reflected dismally, it just didn't pay to get out of bed.

"Don't shoot, Marshal," she said. "It's only me, Rue Claridge, Pine River's Most Wanted."

When Rue peered over the top of the ladder, Farley was just sliding his pistol back into its holster. He'd hung his hat on a peg on the wall, and his attractively rumpled brown hair glimmered even in the fading light. "What the hell are you doing up there?" he demanded, setting his hands on his hips.

Rue sighed and swung her legs over the side of the loft, gripping the pink sports bag in one hand. "Holding, of course. When Mr. Sinclair put the moves on me, I told him to get lost, and he said he'd have you arrest me...."

Farley scratched his head, obviously impatient and puzzled.

Rue tossed her bag to the floor and then climbed resignedly down the ladder to face her fate. "Here." She held out her hands, wrists together. "Handcuff me."

The marshal looked sternly down his nose at Rue. "You've gone and gotten yourself thrown out of the only boardinghouse that would have you?"

Sudden color pulsed in Rue's cheeks. "Didn't you hear a word I've said? Sinclair wanted me to—to be intimate with him. I refused, of course, and he said he'd have me arrested for robbing his house."

Farley's turquoise eyes narrowed. "Let's see that satchel," he said brusquely.

Rue resented the invasion of privacy, but she also knew she had no real choice, so she handed over the bag.

The marshal turned it end over end, trying to find the opening, and Rue finally reached out and pulled back the zipper herself.

Farley stared at the small mechanism as though it were a bug under a microscope. "What the—"

"It's called a zipper," Rue said with a sigh. "They won't be invented for another twenty-five or thirty years, so don't bother looking for them in your favorite store."

Now Farley studied Rue with the same thoroughness as he'd examined the zipper on her neon pink bag. "You don't talk like anybody I've ever known before, except for Mrs. Fortner, of course. Where did you come from?" he asked quietly.

Rue folded her arms. She might as well tell the truth, she decided, since nobody was going to believe her anyway. "The future. I came from the twenty-first century." She snatched the bag from his hands, suddenly anxious to convince him, to have one person on the face of the earth know what was happening to her. "Here," she said, pulling the paperback spy novel out and thrusting it in Farley's face. "Look. Did you ever see a book like this before, with a soft cover? And read the copyright date."

Farley turned the book in his hands, clearly amazed by the bright red cover and the gold-foil lettering spelling out the title and the author's name.

"Nobody can come from the future," he insisted stubbornly, but Rue could see that the paperback puzzled him.

"I did," she said. After setting the bag down, she politely took the book, opened it to the copyright page and held it out again. "There. Read that."

Farley took in the printed words, then raised baffled eyes to Rue's face. "It's a trick," he said.

"How could it be?" Rue demanded, growing impatient even though she'd known she would never convince him. "Paperback books and zippers don't exist in 1892, Farley!"

"You could have gotten those things at some fancy science exhibition in St. Louis or Chicago or somewhere." Clearly, Farley meant to stand his intellectual ground, even though it was eroding under his feet. "All I know is, it's got to be some kind of hoax."

Rue rolled her eyes. Then she bent and pulled out one of her precious snack-size candy bars. "How about this?" she challenged, holding out the morsel. "Did I get this at an exhibition, too?"

Farley frowned, examining the wrapper.

"You have to tear off the paper," Rue prompted. "Then you eat what's inside."

Farley looked suspicious, but intrigued, also. He tore away the paper, letting it drift to the floor.

Rue picked the litter up and crumpled it on one hand, while Farley carried the candy bar over to the doorway and studied it in the last light. The look of consternation on his face was amusing, even under the circumstances.

"Go ahead, Farley," she urged. "Take a bite."

The marshal glanced at her again, then nibbled cautiously at one end of the chocolate bar. After a moment, he smiled. "I'll be damned," he muttered, then consumed the rest of the candy. "Got any more of those?"

"Yes," Rue answered, thrusting out her chin, "but I'm not going to let you wolf them down. Especially not when you're about to arrest me for something I didn't do."

"I'm not going to arrest you," Farley replied reasonably, looking at Rue with curious amusement. "We've only got one jail cell here in Pine River, as you know, and it's already occupied. I'll just have to give you my bed and bunk out here in the barn until you get on that stage next Tuesday."

Rue didn't protest, nor did she turn the conversation back to the reality of time travel. Farley was still telling himself he was the victim of some elaborate prank, no doubt, but at least she had the satisfaction of knowing she'd planted the seed of possibility in his mind. Maybe after some rumination, he'd begin to take the idea seriously.

It the meantime, they were clearly going to pretend nothing out of the ordinary was going on.

If someone had to sleep in the barn, Rue reasoned, better Farley than she. She lowered her eyes.

"There's a problem with my leaving on the stage," she confessed. "Somebody snitched all my money."

Farley sighed. "With luck like yours, it's purely a wonder you ever managed to win at poker the other night," he said, gesturing toward the door. "Come on, Miss Rue. Let's go in and rustle up some supper. We'll figure out what to do with you later."

Rue picked up her bag, straightened her shoulders and preceded him through the doorway of the barn. An inky twilight was working its way down the timbered hills toward them, and there was a bite in the air.

The inside of Farley's log cabin was cozy and surprisingly neat. Books lined one whole wall, from roof to floor, and a stone fireplace faced the door. An attached lean-to housed a small kitchen area, and Rue suspected the tattered blanket hanging from the ceiling hid Farley's bed.

She went to stand beside the fireplace, hoping the warmth would dispel the sweet shivers that suddenly overtook her. She had a peculiar sense, all of a sudden, of being a piece on some great celestial board game, and she'd just been moved within easy reach of both victory and defeat.

"Hungry?" Farley asked, clattering metal against metal in the lean-to kitchen.

"Starved," Rue said, too tired, confused and frustrated for any more deep thought. She'd missed both breakfast and lunch, and the candy bars weren't taking up the slack.

Farley came out of the lean-to. "The stew'll be

warmed up in a few minutes," he said. As he went around the cabin lighting kerosene lamps, he seemed uncharacteristically nervous.

Rue, on the other hand, felt totally safe. "So you're a cook as well as a reader," she said, wanting to hear him talk because she liked the sound of his voice, liked knowing he was there.

He grinned and shook his head. "No, ma'am," he replied. "My food is provided as a part of my wages, like this cabin. The ladies of the town take turns cooking for me."

The thought made Rue violently jealous, and that was when she realized the horrible truth. Somehow, she'd fallen in love with Farley Haynes.

Talk about Mr. Wrong.

"Oh," she said finally.

Farley shook his head and crouched to add wood to the fire. "Maybe you shouldn't stand so close," he said, and his voice was suddenly hoarse. "Ladies have been known to catch their skirts afire doing that."

Rue moved away to look at Farley's collection of books, and her voice shook when she spoke. "Have you really read all these?"

"Most of them more than once," Farley replied. She heard him retreat into the lean-to, then he called to her to join him. "Stew's warm," he said.

After drawing a deep breath, raising her chin and pushing back her shoulders, Rue marched into the tiny kitchen.

Farley had set a place for her at the small, round

table, and there was a lantern flickering on a shelf nearby. The atmosphere was cozy.

He ladled stew into two bowls, set a loaf of hard bread on a platter and sat down across from her.

Once she'd taken several bites of the stew, which was delicious, Rue was a little less shaky, both inwardly and outwardly. She smiled at Farlcy. "This is quite a place you've got here."

"Thank you," Farley replied, "but I'll be glad when I can take up ranching and let somebody else wear my badge."

A bittersweet sadness touched Rue's heart. "Have you got a place picked out?" she asked, breaking off a piece of bread.

Farley nodded. "There's a half section for sale north of town. I've almost got enough for the down payment, and the First Federal Bank is going to give me a mortgage."

"Mr. Sinclair's bank," Rue murmured, feeling less festive.

Farley was chewing, and he waited until he'd swallowed to answer. "That's right."

An autumn wind tested the glass in the windows, and Rue was doubly glad Farley had taken her in. "If there was any justice in this world, you'd go right over there and arrest that old lecher right this minute for sexual harassment."

A modest flush tinted Farley's weathered cheekbones. "He hasn't broken the law, Rue. And that means he can't be arrested."

"Why?" Rue demanded, only vaguely registering

the fact that Farley had called her by her first name. "Because he's a man? Because he's a banker? I was innocent of any crime, and that didn't keep you from slapping *me* behind bars."

"I've never slapped a woman in my life," Farley snapped, looking outraged.

Rue sat back in her chair, her eyes brimming with tears she was too proud to shed. "It's hopeless," she said. "Absolutely hopeless. You and I speak different languages, Farley Haynes."

"I would have sworn we were both talking English," he responded, reaching calmly for his glass of water.

"I give up!" Rue cried, flinging out her hands.

Farley reached for her bowl and carried it to the stove. "What you need," he said, "is some more stew."

Rue watched him with a hunger she would have been too embarrassed even to write about in the privacy of her journal, and she swallowed hard. "Stew," she said. "Right."

Chapter 7

The stew was remarkably good, hot and savory and fresh, and Rue consumed the second helping without quibbling. She was fiercely hungry, and the food eased her low-grade headache and the shaky feeling that invariably overtook her when she failed to eat regular meals.

After supper, Farley heated water on the stove, and Rue insisted on washing the dishes. It was fun, sort of like playing house in an antique store.

The lean-to was a small place, though, and when Farley poured himself a cup of coffee and then lingered at the table, flipping thoughtfully through a stack of papers, Rue was more painfully conscious of his presence than ever. She tried not to think about him, but it was an impossibility. He seemed to fill

the little room to its corners with his size, his un-
compromising masculinity and the sheer strength
of his personality.

In Rue's opinion, the effect on her nerves, her
muscles and her most-secret parts was all out of proportion to the circumstances, strange as they were.
She felt like a human volcano; lava was burning and
bubbling in the farthest reaches of her body and her
spirit. Simple things like drying the chipped crockery bowls they'd eaten from and setting them on
the shelves took on the significance of epic poetry.

She was wrestling with the enormous enamel coffeepot, trying to pour herself a cupful, when she felt
Farley looming behind her. He displaced her grip on
the pot's handle and filled her cup.

He was only standing at her back, it was nothing
more dramatic than that, yet Rue felt a devastating
charge radiate from his body to hers. In the next
moment, the invisible field, woven of lantern light,
cosmic mystery, half-forgotten dreams and stardust
enfolded her, and she sagged backward against Farley's steely stomach and chest.

Farley made no sound. He simply took the cup
from Rue's hand, set it on the stove and closed his
strong arms lightly around her waist. For all that she
had never been in such trouble, even on her most
memorable assignments as a journalist, Rue felt as
though she'd stumbled upon some magical sanctuary where nothing and no one could ever hurt her.

In the meantime, the seismic tumult was building
inside Rue, gaining force moment by moment. She

knew the inevitable eruption would be more than physical; it would be an upheaval of the soul, as well. And she wanted it despite the danger.

Presently—whether a minute or an hour passed, Rue could not have said—Farley raised his hands slowly, gently, to weigh her breasts. When his thumbs moved over her nipples, making them harden and strain against the fabric of her dress, Rue groaned and tilted her head back against his shoulder.

He touched his lips to her temple, warming the delicate flesh there, and then he bent his head slightly to nibble the side of her neck. Rue would have throttled any other man for taking such liberties, but her need for Farley had sneaked up on her, and it was already so pervasive that she couldn't tell where the craving stopped and her own being began.

When he lifted her into his arms, Rue's logical left brain finally struggled to the surface and gurgled out a protest, but it was too late. The fanciful right side of her brain was hearing rapturous symphonies, and the notes drowned out all other sounds.

Farley carried her out of the kitchen—Rue was vaguely aware of the fire as they passed the hearth—then he took her behind the blanket that served as a curtain. There was a look of grim resignation on his face as he laid her on the neatly made bed and stood gazing down at her for a long moment. It was as if he thought she'd cast a spell over him and he was trying to work out some way to break it.

She couldn't tell him that she was under an enchantment, too, that she had never done anything like this before. All she could do was lie there, all but the most primitive essence of her identity seared away by the heat of her desire, needing him. Waiting.

He took off her funny, old-fashioned shoes and tossed them aside, then began unbuttoning her dress. Only when she lay completely naked on his bed, totally vulnerable, did he speak.

"God help me," he said in a raw whisper, "I've wanted to see you like this since that day I found you wandering in Doc Fortner's house. I've wanted to touch you...."

Rue took his hand in hers, emboldened by the turquoise fire in his eyes and the frantic fever in her own spirit, and pressed his palm and fingers to her breast. "Touch me," she said softly, and the words were both a plea and an affirmation.

Farley complied for a long, torturously delicious interval, then while Rue waited in sweet agony, he withdrew. She watched, dazed, as he removed his clothes.

His body had the stealth and prowess of a stalking panther as he stretched out beside her on the rough, woolen blanket that served as a bedspread. Then he kissed her, first caressing her lips with his, then commanding her mouth to open for the entrance of his tongue.

The conquest was a triumphant one, far more potent than any ordinary kiss. Rue's body arched beside Farley on the bed, and he reached beneath her to cup her bottom in one hand and press her close against his thighs and the solid demand of his manhood.

She was afraid when she felt him, terrified of his size and power, and yet this knowledge did nothing to stem the furious tide of her passion.

Farley kissed Rue, again and again, all the while caressing and shaping her with his hands, until she was in a virtual delirium of need. Perspiration shimmered on every inch of her flesh, and tendrils of her hair clung wetly to her neck and temples.

At last, Farley positioned himself between her legs, then put his hands under her shoulder blades and raised her breasts for conquering. When he captured one eager nipple with his mouth, Rue cried out in despairing surrender, begging him to take her.

For all her travels, for all her reading and her sophistication, when Farley entered her, Rue was startled. There was pain, and it lingered, but it was also promptly overshadowed by a consuming, joyous rage made up of heavenly light and dragon's fire.

Rue pressed her hands to Farley's back, and the play of his muscles under her palms was as much a part of their lovemaking as the ferocious rhythm of joining and parting that was even then transforming them both.

For all the breathless promise of the past half hour or so, when Rue finally achieved satisfaction, she was all but swept away by the force of it. She strained beneath Farley in wild, glorious and totally involuntary spasms, her teeth clenched against the shouts of triumph rattling in the back of her throat. She was just settling back to the bed, breathless and disoriented, when Farley clasped her bottom hard in his hands, pressed her tightly against him and made a series of deep, abrupt thrusts. To Rue's surprise, she reached another climax when Farley had his; her release was a soft, languid implosion, like a blessing on the tempest that had preceded it.

When he'd finally spent the last of his energy, Farley collapsed beside Rue, his breathing hard and raspy. She pressed her face into the taut, moist flesh on his shoulder, at once hiding from her lover and seeking him out.

"I knew it would be like that," Farley muttered after they'd lain entwined for a long time, listening to the beating of each other's hearts, the crackle of the fire and the night sounds of the lively timber town beyond the cabin walls.

Rue's eyes filled with tears, but she wasn't mourning the time before, when she and Farley had been innocent of each other. No matter what happened, whether she lived the rest of her life with this man or without him, in this century or another, she'd given herself truly and totally to Farley Haynes, and she would never forget the splendor of it.

"I thought it was a lie," she finally confessed. "What people said about making love, I mean. I never knew—until now."

Farley sighed and raised his head to look through her eyes, as though they were clear as windowpanes, and straight into her soul. He kissed her forehead and then rested his scratchy chin where his lips had just touched. "I'm sorry," he said, his voice low and hoarse. "I offered you safe haven here, and then I took advantage."

Rue had just been transported to a whole other plane of womanhood, and the journey had had just as great an impact on her senses and emotions as being tossed from one time period to another. She was incapable, for the moment, of working out whether Farley's apology was appropriate or not. "It's not as though you threw me down on the bed and forced me," she pointed out, loving the feel of his back, supple skin over firm muscles. "I wanted you."

Farley drew back to search her eyes again, and the gesture made her feel more naked than she had earlier when he'd methodically relieved her of her clothes. "You are the most forward-thinking female I have ever encountered," he said somberly, but then a grin broke over his face. "I think I like that about you."

Rue swallowed, and her ability to think in rational terms was beginning to dissipate like fog in bright sunshine. Farley was joined to her, and he was getting hard again, and she didn't want him to leave her. "Stay inside me, Farley. Please."

Bracing himself by pressing his hands on the mattress on either side of her, Farley began to move slowly. "I'll find out the truth about you," he said, his words growing short and breathy as he increased his pace, "if it's the last thing I ever do."

Pressing her shoulders deep into the feather pillows and tilting her head back in magnificent surrender, Rue gasped out, "I'd love to tell you—I'd love to show you the place I came from...." And from that moment on, Rue was beyond speaking.

Farley dipped his head to lave one of her distended nipples with his tongue. His attentions were merciless and thorough, and soon Rue was pitching under him like a wild mare trying to shake off a rider.

Once that session had ended, Rue cuddled against Farley's side—his rib cage had about as much flexibility as the staves of a wooden barrel—and promptly drifted off to sleep. When she awakened, the blanket that separated the bed from the rest of the cabin was framed in silvery moonlight and Farley's side of the mattress was empty.

Rue scrambled off the bed, found one of Farley's shirts hanging from a peg in the wall and shoved her arms through the sleeves. The clock on the plain, board mantel over the fireplace read 3:17 and despite the fact that she had no claim on the marshal's time, a sense of alarm crowded her throat.

Obviously, Farley had gone out for some reason—maybe there had been shouts or a frantic knock at the door or even shots fired, and she'd been too drunk on lovemaking to hear. In fact, she hadn't even noticed when Farley left.

Rue's imagination tripped into overdrive. She'd seen enough Clint Eastwood movies to know what awful things could happen to a lone lawman. The difference was that now she wouldn't be able to toss away her popcorn box, fish her car keys out of her purse and go home to an apartment filled with modern conveniences. This was the real thing, and she just happened to be hopelessly in love with the peace officer in question.

On some level, Rue had known from the moment she met Farley that something significant was going to happen between them. But she hadn't expected the event to be on a par with the destruction of the dinosaurs or the formation of the Grand Canyon.

Rue groped her way into the lean-to kitchen, blinded by her emotions rather than a lack of light, and looked at herself in Farley's shaving mirror. Except that her hair was tangled and she was wearing a man's shirt, she seemed unchanged. Inside, however, Rue was wholly different; she'd been converted, not into someone else, but into a better, richer and more genuine version of herself.

Trembling, Rue poured a cup of coffee from the pot on the stove and sank into one of the two chairs at the table. Since it had been sitting on the heat for hours, the brew was black as coal oil and only slightly more palatable. Rue figured there was probably enough caffeine in the stuff to keep her awake well into the next century—be it the twentieth or the twenty-first—but she took a second sip anyway.

Through the closed windows and thin walls of Farley's house, Rue could hear the sounds of laughter and bad piano music and an ongoing argument between a man and a woman. She was overwhelmingly relieved when the door opened and the marshal himself walked in.

He set his rifle in the corner, hung his hat and long canvas duster on their pegs and then began unfastening his gun belt. All the time, he watched Rue in the dim, icy glow of the moonlight.

Rue didn't want to express her relief at seeing him; she didn't have the right. "I hope I didn't keep you from your work," she said with as much dignity as a person wearing only a man's shirt and a glow of satisfaction can be expected to summon up.

Farley didn't answer. He simply came to the table, took Rue's hand and brought her to her feet. He took her back to the bedside, and she crawled under the covers, her heart turning to vapor and then gathering in her throat like a summer storm taking shape on the horizon.

She watched as Farley took off his clothes for the second time that night, more shaken than before by his magnificence and quiet grace.

He stretched out beside her under the blankets and with a few deft motions of one hand, relieved her of the long shirt she wore. Having done that, Farley curved one arm around Rue and arranged her close against his side, her head resting on his shoulder.

Farley did not make love to Rue; instead, he simply held her, sheltering her in his solidity and strength. For Rue, the experience was, in its own way, just as momentous as full surrender had been earlier. The simple intimacy met fundamental needs that had not only been unsatisfied before, but unrecognized.

Rue slept soundly that night and awakened with the first light of dawn, when Farley gently displaced her to get out of bed.

"What do I do now?" Rue asked softly. Sadly. "I can't stay here. The whole town will know if I do."

"The whole town already knows," Farley answered, pulling on a pair of dark trousers and disappearing around the edge of the blanket curtain. "There aren't many secrets in a place like Pine River."

Rue slipped under the covers with a groan of mortification, but she could still hear the clatter and clink of stove lids, the working of a pump handle, the opening and closing of a door.

Presently, the smell and sounds of sizzling bacon filled the air, along with the aroma of fresh coffee. Rue got up, struggled back into her clothes and peered around the blanket.

She could see Farley in the lean-to, standing at the stove. The sight of him, with his hair wetted down and combed, a meat fork in one hand, filled her with a tenderness so keen that it was painful.

Rue approached hesitantly. For the first time in her life, she didn't know what to say.

Farley turned a strip of bacon in the black skillet and ran his turquoise eyes companionably over her length. For an instant, Rue was beneath him again, in the throes of complete physical and spiritual communion, and the sensation left her disconcerted.

The marshal made short work of her poetic mood. "If you're sore," he said, "I've got some balm out in the barn."

Rue sighed. This was the same man who had evoked such violently beautiful responses from her the night before and had later held her snugly against his side, making no demands. Now he was offering her the same medicine he would use on a cow or a horse.

"Thanks," she answered belatedly, "but I'll be fine."

Farley shrugged, took two plates down from a shelf and began dishing up breakfast.

"Interesting," she murmured thoughtfully, pulling back a chair.

He set a plate filled with fried food in front her. "What's interesting?"

"You," Rue reflected. "You're a nineteenth-century male, and here you are cooking for a woman. Even waiting table."

Farley arched an eyebrow. "It's that or risk letting you do the cooking," he replied.

Rue laughed, but her amusement faded as daylight strengthened the thin glow of the lanterns and reality settled in around her. It was morning now; the enchanted night was over and she was stranded in the wrong century, with the wrong man.

"Farley, what am I going to do?" she asked again. "My money is gone, I don't have anywhere to stay and it's beginning to look like my cousin and her husband are going to make their home in San Francisco and never contact anybody in Pine River again."

"Jon and Lizzie will come back when they're ready," Farley said with certainty. "And you can stay here with me."

"Oh, right," Rue snapped, irritated not with Farley for making the suggestion, but with herself for wanting to go on sharing his life and his bed for as long as possible. "The good women of Pine River will love that."

Farley grinned. "No, they won't."

"You're being pretty cocky right now," Rue pointed out, annoyed, "but the truth is, you're afraid of those women, Farley Haynes. They have the power to make both our lives miserable, and you know it."

Farley's smile tightened to a look of grim obstinance, and Rue wondered hopefully if the night before had worked some ancient, fundamental magic in the deepest parts of his being, the way it had in hers.

"Those old hens will just have to do their scratching and pecking in somebody else's dooryard," he said.

"What the devil is that supposed to mean?" Rue countered, reaching for another slice of crispy bacon. The man made love with the expertise of a bard taking up the pen, and he had some pretty modern attitudes, but sometimes he talked in cowboy riddles.

Farley got up to refill his coffee mug and Rue's. "Hell," he grumbled, "even the prissy Eastern lieutenants and captains I knew in the army didn't boss a man around the way those old biddies do."

Rue stifled a giggle, but said nothing.

Farley came back to the table, set their mugs down and shook an index finger at her. "Mind you don't take to carrying on the way they do, because I won't put up with it."

Rue swallowed, unsure how to react. On the one

hand, it was an affront, Farley's presuming to issue orders that way. On the other, though she would have chewed one of Aunt Verity's antique crystal door-knobs before admitting as much to him, she liked the gentle forcefulness of his manner. Here, at last, was a person as strong as she was.

"I don't see where my actions are any concern of yours," she finally managed to say.

He sighed and shook his head, as though marveling that someone so simpleminded could have reached adulthood without being seriously injured in the process. "After last night," Farley told her, making an insulting effort at clarity as he spoke, "there's nothing we can do but get married."

Rue wouldn't have been more stunned if he'd thrown his food all over her. *"Married?"* she squeaked. In that instant, she realized that it was the dearest, most secret wish of her heart to marry Farley Haynes. At the same time, she knew she'd have to be demented even to entertain the idea.

Okay, so she loved Farley, she thought. He didn't feel the same way toward her; in mentioning marriage, he was probably just following the code of the West, or something like that. And there was still the matter of their coming from two different centuries, two different *worlds*. To love Farley, to stay in this time with him, would be to give up everything she knew and much of what she was.

Rue was a strong woman, and that was both her blessing and her curse. Not even for Farley and a lifetime of the tempestuous dances he'd taught her in the night just past could she give up her own identity. She was of another time; she was a journalist, a person with many more bridges to cross, both professionally and personally.

Of course, if she did marry the marshal, she would have a place to stay until she made contact with her cousin, found the necklace and returned to her own century. Farley would undoubtedly make thorough love to her practically every night, and the mere prospect of that brought all Rue's feminine forces to a state of hypersensitivity.

"I'll send somebody over to the next town for the justice of the peace," Farley said, as if the matter had been settled.

"Now just a minute," Rue protested, thumping the tabletop lightly with one fist. "I haven't said yes to your proposal, if you can call it that. It just so happens that I don't want to get married—I don't even plan to stay around here, once I've seen my cousin."

Farley looked untroubled by this announcement. "What if we made a baby last night?" he asked, figuratively pulling the rug out from under Rue's feet. "I don't think things are any different in Seattle or Boston or wherever it is you really come from. Life is damn near impossible for an unmarried woman with a child."

Rue laid both her hands to her stomach. Nature might very well be knitting a tiny being in the warm safety of her womb. She was filled with wanting and fear. "Oh, my God," she whispered.

Farley stood and carried his plate to the sink. Then

he came back to the table, stood beside Rue's chair and bent to simultaneously taste her lips and rub her lower abdomen with one hand. "If there's no baby inside you now," he said huskily, "I'll put one there when I get back."

A hot shiver shook Rue; she was amazed anew at the depths of the passion this man could rouse in her with a few words and caresses. "When will that be?"

He nibbled at her lower lip before answering. "About noon, if nothing goes wrong," he said. Then he walked away to strap on his gun belt, reload his pistol and shrug into his duster. Farley put on his battered hat and reached for his rifle in a smooth, practiced motion. "Try to stay out of trouble until I can get you married," he urged, grinning slightly. Then he opened the door and left.

Rue was restless, and the choices confronting her seemed overwhelming. Go or stay. Love or pretend to be indifferent. Follow her heart or her head. Laugh or cry.

More to keep herself busy than because she was a devotee of neatness, Rue heated water on the cookstove, washed the dishes, wiped off the table and swept the floor. Following that, she made the bed. It was while she was doing that that she found the stash.

Her foot caught on a loose floorboard as she was plumping the pillows, and she crouched to press the plank back into place. The same curiosity that had made her such a good journalist made her a very bad houseguest; Rue couldn't resist peeking underneath.

A cigar box was tucked away in the small, dark

place, and Rue lifted the lid to find a respectable collection of five-dollar gold pieces. This money, surely, was meant to be the down payment on Farley's ranch.

Kneeling now, Rue set the box on the side of the bed and studied one of the coins. Where she came from, the small, ornate bit of gold would be worth far more than five dollars, but here it was ordinary money.

Carefully, Rue closed the lid and set the box back in its place. If Farley had been anyone but who he was, she might have taken that money, used it to get to San Francisco, but she couldn't steal his dreams.

The best thing to do was look for the necklace.

The day was chilly, and Rue wished for a shawl as she walked along the sidewalks of Pine River, searching for the lost piece of jewelry that was her only link with the world she knew.

She searched all morning without any luck, and her shoulders were sagging with discouragement when she started toward Farley's office. Hopefully, since he was willing to give her a baby, he might also offer lunch.

As she was passing Ella Sinclair's boarding house, Rue realized there was one place she hadn't looked— the outhouse she'd materialized in. Her heart started to pound. She wasn't sure which one it was, but she knew it was in this neighborhood.

Lifting her skirts, Rue dashed around the house she'd been passing, avoiding manure and mud in the yard as best she could, and hurtled herself into the outhouse she found there, but to no avail—the necklace wasn't there. She began to run through backyards, entering and searching each outhouse she came to. So intent was she on finding the lost necklace that she was barely aware of the rumbles of consternation, shock and amusement around her.

When she spotted her pendant caught between two boards—thank the Lord—she let out a shriek of delighted triumph and snatched it up.

In practically the same instant, a strong arm curved around her from behind, and Rue was yanked backward against an impervious chest. She knew by the quivering in her spirit and the straightforward method of operation that she'd been apprehended by Farley Haynes. Again.

"I was only getting my necklace," she told him, wriggling to get free. "I lost it in the back of this wagon the other day, when I hitched a ride into town."

With his free arm, Farley swept off his hat and wiped his forehead with his sleeve. "That's just fine," he drawled, obviously furious. "Now I suggest you start apologizing to these people you've been disturbing."

Rue wanted to laugh and to cry, she was so relieved at finding the necklace. She dropped it into her skirt pocket. "Anything you say, Marshal," she responded sweetly. "Are we still getting married?"

The question stirred a buzz in the crowd that had gathered, and Rue was amused. Farley had just assumed she was up to no good, plundering the good citizens' outhouses for heaven only knew what scurrilous purpose, and she wouldn't have put it past him to arrest her. Therefore, in her opinion, a little embarrassment served him right, because after the previous night's activities, he should have trusted her more.

"Yes," he said as grimly as a judge pronouncing a death sentence.

Rue smiled all the while as she offered her apology to the crowd, every once in a while reaching into her pocket to make sure the necklace was there. She could not yet return to her own time because she hadn't found Elisabeth, but the door was no longer closed to her, and that was the important thing.

Chapter 8

Some thoughtful citizen had brought fried chicken, biscuits and gravy for Farley's lunch, and he shared the feast with the solitary prisoner and Rue. The marshal's eyes were narrowed, however, as he regarded her across the surface of his messy desk.

"I thought I told you to stay out of trouble," he said.

Rue's cheeks pulsed a little as she thought of the episode. "I was only looking for my necklace, Farley," she answered reasonably. She took a bite from a crispy fried chicken leg and chewed thoroughly before going on. "If you had any idea how important that pendant really is, you wouldn't make such a big deal about a little disturbance."

Farley's frown deepened. He took another piece

of chicken from the lunch basket, which was lined with a blue-and-white cotton napkin. "I know ladies like their trinkets," he allowed. "My mother had a brooch made of marcasite and jet that she wouldn't have parted with to save her own scalp. But I have a feeling this necklace of yours is important for some other reason."

He was remarkably astute, Rue thought, but she wasn't about to explain the necklace's peculiar power—mainly because she didn't begin to understand it herself.

She reached into her pocket and touched the twisted chain, and that was when she felt the strange warning vibration. By instinct, she realized that the pendant was up to its old tricks again; she was about to be sent helter-skelter into some other part of history, and not necessarily the one she belonged in, either.

No, she thought desperately, *not now. Not without saying goodbye....*

The room seemed to waver and shift, like a reflection in old bottle glass. Glimpses of the orchard behind Aunt Verity's house were superimposed over the stove, the bars in the cell door, Farley himself. Rue wrenched her hand from her pocket and the visions faded instantly, along with the sense of an impending spiritual earthquake.

She gripped the edge of Farley's desk with both hands, swaying slightly with mingled sickness and relief.

Farley immediately jumped up to bring her a dipperful of cold well water from the bucket near the stove.

"Are you sick?" he demanded. "Do you want me to go and get the doc?"

Rue smiled thinly and squeezed her eyes shut for a moment, still trying to regain her equilibrium. "Yes. Find Dr. Jonathan Fortner, please," she joked. "And his wife Elisabeth, while you're at it."

Farley crouched beside her chair, looking up into her face with troubled eyes, eyes of such a beautiful Arizona turquoise that it hurt Rue's heart to return their gaze. "What just happened here?" he demanded quietly.

I almost left you, Rue answered in stricken silence.

"Rue," Farley insisted, setting the empty dipper on the desk and holding both her hands in his. "Are you suffering from some sickness of the head? Is that your big secret? Did you run away from one of those mental hospitals?"

Rue laughed, a little hysterically, but with genuine amusement. She could answer only one of his questions with an unequivocal no. The other two he would have to take on trust. She shook her head. "I didn't escape from an asylum, Farley," she said softly.

She could see by his face that he believed her, maybe only because he wanted to, and that was the biggest relief she'd had since finding the necklace in the outhouse.

"I sent for the justice of the peace," he said. "He'll be here in a few hours."

Rue had never, in all her life, had to deal with such a degree of temptation. She wanted so much to marry Farley, to have the right to share his joys and sorrows, his table and his bed, but to vow eternal fidelity when she fully intended to return to her own time as soon as possible would be unthinkable. She would simply disappear, and Farley would be left to wonder, to the end of his days, what had become of her.

"We can't," she said.

"We will," he replied, rising and walking away to hang the dipper on its nail near the bucket.

Nothing was resolved when, fifteen minutes later, Rue left the jailhouse. Since she had nowhere in particular to go, she set out for the house in the country where all this had begun. She meant to find a tree in the orchard, climb up as high as she could and sit there and think, her back to the rough trunk, the way she'd done as a child, in a time far in the future.

She was surprised to find a fancy carriage in the yard next to the farmhouse. There was lots of bustle and activity; a little girl ran full tilt, first in one direction, then another, her small arms outspread in a child's joy at simply existing. A handsome, dark-haired man was taking bags and satchels from the vehicle's boot....

It was only then that the belated realization struck Rue.

Elisabeth was back from San Francisco.

A tearful joy filled her. She struggled with the latch on the front gate, grew impatient and vaulted over the low fence, catching her skirts on the pickets. "Bethie!" she cried in breathless, exultant frustration; even though she had not yet caught sight of her cousin, she knew she was there somewhere.

Sure enough, Elisabeth came bursting through the doorway of one of the outbuildings at the sound of Rue's voice. She heedlessly dropped the crock she was carrying to the ground, and her blond hair tumbled around her shoulders as she ran.

"Rue!" she shrieked, laughing and sobbing the name. "Rue!"

Rue was dimly aware of the man and the little girl looking on in confusion, but she could only think of Elisabeth in those moments. Elisabeth, her best friend, her only real family.

"Bethie," Rue said, and then the two women were embracing and weeping, as women have always done, and probably will do, when meaningful separations end.

Finally, Bethie gripped Rue's upper arms in hands that had been strengthened by life in simpler but more physically demanding times, her blue-green eyes shimmering with tears, her face bright with joy.

"What are you doing here?" she wanted to know.

Rue laughed even as she wiped her cheek with one palm. "I sort of stumbled onto the place, the way I suspect you did," she confessed. "Once I got here, I was determined to find you, to make sure you were all right."

"I'm more than all right," Elisabeth answered,

touching her stomach. "I never thought it was possible to be so happy, Rue. I'm going to have a baby."

The man and the child gravitated toward the two cousins while Rue was absorbing this news. She felt a pang of jealousy, which surprised her, and she even went so far as to hope she was pregnant herself—which was ridiculous, because that could only complicate matters.

"This is my husband, Jonathan," Elisabeth said, and her skin took on the lustrous glow of a fine pearl as she introduced him. The child, who was as lovely as her father was handsome, huddled against Bethie's side and smiled shyly up at Rue. "And this is Miss Trista Fortner," Elisabeth added, as proudly as if she'd somehow produced the little girl herself, just that very moment. "Jonathan, Trista, I'd like you to meet my cousin Rue."

Elisabeth's husband was movie-star gorgeous, in a smooth, urbane way. Farley was just as good-looking, but he was the rugged type, exactly the kind of man Rue had always avoided.

"Hello," Jonathan said. He started to offer his right hand, which was scarred, then shrugged, grinned sheepishly and eased his arm back to his side. Rue recalled Farley saying the doctor had been injured.

Bethie smiled and linked elbows with Rue, marching her double-time toward the house. "I want to hear everything," she told her cousin. *"Everything."*

They sat at the kitchen table, and Rue, hardly knowing where to begin, told the story. She explained that the search had begun after she'd read

Elisabeth's amazing letters about traveling through time, and admitted she'd first thought her cousin needed professional help. Then she'd found the necklace on the floor of the upstairs hallway, she went on, and made the trip herself.

For some reason she didn't fully understand— under normal circumstances Rue would have told Bethie *anything*—she didn't mention the passion she'd developed for Farley Haynes.

Elisabeth told Rue about her honeymoon, blushing intermittently and looking impossibly happy, and explained how Jonathan had hurt his hand. A fire had broken out and, while Farley had dragged Elisabeth out, Jon and Trista had been trapped upstairs. Jon had had the necklace in his possession and he'd escaped with the little girl over the threshold into the future. The flow of time did not run parallel on both sides of the threshold, as Rue had already discovered, and when Dr. Fortner and his child finally managed to return, they'd found Elisabeth on trial for their murder.

Jon had made a dramatic entrance, Elisabeth said, eyes glowing with the memory, thus exonerating her of all charges, and they'd been married that day.

With help from Rue and Trista, Elisabeth began preparing dinner. She did it as naturally as if she'd been born in the nineteenth century. By then, the cousins had begun to speculate about the necklace. Although she couldn't explain why, Elisabeth believed the pendant's magic was different, depending on whose hands it fell into. She cautioned Rue to be careful about her choices.

Lanterns were lit as twilight tumbled silently down around the house and rose past the windows, and Jonathan moved, whistling, between the house and the barn.

"You truly do belong here," Rue marveled to her cousin later that night, when Jonathan had gone out to check on his regular patients and Trista was tucked away in one of the upstairs bedrooms.

Elisabeth nodded, lifting a kerosene lamp from the center of the table and leading the way into the parlor. A cozy fire crackled on the hearth and one other light burned on the mantelpiece. "I never knew it was possible for a woman to love a man the way I love Jonathan," she said softly, and there was a dreamy, faraway expression in her eyes as she gazed out the window toward the barn and the orchard and the covered bridge beyond. "It's like I was never whole before I came here. I felt like the odd woman out in some game of musical chairs—there was never a place for me to sit in that other world. The place is like a dream to me now, and I might even have convinced myself I'd imagined it all if it hadn't been for your appearance."

Rue thought of Farley and wondered if he was worried about her or if he'd even noticed she wasn't around. She sighed. "Don't you ever get scared? I mean, if a thing like this can happen, it changes everything. We're like players in some game, and none of us knows the rules."

Elisabeth turned to meet Rue's eyes. "They say that realizing how little we truly understand is the beginning of wisdom. But I've got a handle on this much—when you love with everything that's inside you, you take a terrible risk. I'm vulnerable in a way I never was before I knew Jonathan and Trista, and, yes, that scares me."

Reaching into her pocket, Rue found the necklace and brought it out, dangling it from her fingers. "Here's your ticket out," she said. "If you don't want to be vulnerable, all you have to do is go back home."

Elisabeth actually recoiled, her blue-green eyes round. "*This* is home," she said. "For heaven's sake, put that thing away before something awful happens."

Rue smiled and hurriedly dropped the pendant back into her pocket. After her experience in the jailhouse at lunchtime, when she'd seen one world taking shape on top of another, she was still a little shy about holding it for too long.

"Then I guess you've decided the risk is worth taking," she said, taking a place on a settee, resting one elbow on the arm and propping her chin in her hand. "Don't you miss it, Bethie? Don't you ever wish you could see a movie or eat frozen yogurt in a mall?"

Elisabeth moved to the fireplace and stood looking down at the fire on the hearth. "I miss hot baths," she said, "and supermarkets and books on tape. I *don't* miss traffic jams, jangling telephones and the probability of one marriage out of two biting the proverbial dust."

"Would you want to go back if it weren't for Jonathan and Trista?"

Bethie thought for a long time before answering, "I'm not sure. Things are difficult here—the old saying about a woman's work never being done certainly holds true—but there's an intensity to life, a *texture,* that I never found in the future. I feel as though I've come home from some long journey of the soul."

Rue sighed. "Well, I guess this completes my mission," she said. "I can go home now."

Elisabeth looked alarmed. "Oh, please say you'll stay for a few days, at least. After all, once you leave..." She paused, lowered her head for a moment, then finished bravely, "Once you leave, we may never see each other again."

"I can't stay," Rue said miserably. She reminded Elisabeth how the power of the necklace seemed to be changing, how she no longer needed to step over the threshold to return to her own century, how she'd seen images of the orchard in the middle of Farley's office that day.

In typical Victorian fashion, Elisabeth laid spread fingers to her bosom. "You're right," she said. "You mustn't take the risk. Do you suppose it's possible for a person to end up in another time period entirely, or another place? Say, medieval England, or Boston during Revolutionary days?"

"I'm the wrong person to ask, Bethie," Rue answered. Her heart was aching at the prospect of leaving her cousin and, she could almost admit it to herself, of leaving Farley. "I don't have any idea what laws govern this crazy situation, or even if there are any. Maybe it's covered by Einstein's Theory of Relativity or something."

Elisabeth's beautiful eyes were glazed with tears. "A day won't go by that I don't think of you," she said. "Oh, Rue, I want you to be as happy as I am. Will you try to go back tonight?"

Rue thought of Farley. "Yes, but there's something I have to do first," she said. She glanced at the clock on the mantel, then at the darkened windows. "Oh, my gosh! I forgot I was supposed to get married!"

"What?"

Rue was hurrying toward the front door. "I wasn't really going to marry Marshal Haynes," she babbled. "He just thought we should because we've slept together and everything." She pulled open the door and would have bolted out into the starry night if Elisabeth hadn't caught her firmly by the arm.

"Now just a minute!" Rue's cousin protested. "You can't just go traipsing off to town through the dark of night! And what's this about your sleeping with Farley?"

Rue sagged against the doorjamb, heedless of the biting chill of the November night, and she began to cry. "I'm in love with him," she whispered brokenly, then sniffled. Her eyes found Elisabeth's worried face in the dim light of the moon and the glow of lanterns from the parlor. "I'm not like you, Elisabeth.

I can't stay here—I can't be happy in a place where there's no UPS, no PBS, no CNN!"

Elisabeth laughed and put an arm around Rue's shoulders. "Come in and sit by the fire. I'll brew us a pot of tea and we'll work out this whole problem."

When Jonathan returned an hour later, Elisabeth and Rue were no closer to a solution. However, the doctor had brought a surprise along with him, a coldly angry Farley Haynes.

"The justice of the peace came and went," Farley said when Jonathan had taken Elisabeth's hand and led her out of the room so that Rue and the marshal were alone. He rested his hands on the sides of her chair, effectively pinning her between his arms.

Rue studied Farley's craggy, handsome face fondly, trying to make a memory that would last for all time. "I'm sorry, Farley," she said, touching his beard-stubbled cheek with one hand. "But I'm not the girl for you, and you wouldn't be happy with me."

Farley set his hands on either side of her waist, stepped back and hauled Rue unceremoniously to her feet. The necklace slipped to the floor, with a *chink* that seemed to echo throughout eternity, and she bent to grab for it. The marshal's hand tightened around her upper arm, as though he thought she might try to escape his hold, and then it happened.

There was a wild spinning effect, as if the parlor were a merry-go-round gone berserk. Colors and shapes collided and meshed. Rue, hurled to the floor, wrapped both arms around Farley's right leg and held on with all her strength to keep from being flung into the void.

"Jumpin' Juniper," Farley said when the wild ride subsided.

Rue couldn't let go of his leg, but she did look around, seeing that while they were still in that same parlor, the furniture was different. There was a TV in the corner with a DVD player on top.

"What the hell just happened here?" Farley whispered. Rue had to admire his cool. She was trembling as she shinnied up his thigh and finally stood on her own two feet.

She wanted to laugh, hysterically, joyously. She was home, and Farley was with her. On the other hand, she would probably never see Elisabeth again, and that made her want to weep.

"You've just aged over a hundred years," Rue said, resting her forehead against Farley's shoulder and almost automatically slipping her hands around his waist. "I've got a lot to show you, Marshal Haynes, but first I'd better give you a little time to absorb the shock."

Farley went to the television set and touched one of the buttons. The head and shoulders of a late-night talk-show host appeared on the screen in an instantaneous flash of light and color.

The marshal recoiled, though only slightly, his wonderful, weathered face crumpled into a frown. "Where's the rest of that fellow?" he demanded. Before Rue could reply, he tapped the screen with his knuckles. "I'll be damned. It's a picture."

Rue set the necklace on the mantelpiece. Suddenly, she was filled with pizza lust and the yearning for a long, hot shower. She went to the telephone and punched out a number.

"One large pepperoni with extra cheese, sausage, green peppers and mushrooms," she said. Then she gave the address and hung up.

Farley had left the television to examine the phone. He picked up the receiver and put it to his ear, as Rue had done, then handed it back. "It's a telephone," she said. "A later version of those big wooden boxes with hand cranks and chrome bells." At his look of puzzlement, Rue added, "I'll explain later. Right now, I'm perishing for pizza." She looked down at her Victorian clothes. "I'd better change or the delivery person will spread a vicious rumor that we're having a costume party."

The marshal, who would certainly have carried off the prize for the most authentic getup at such a gathering, went over to one of the chairs and sank into it. He looked pale beneath his deep tan, and understandably bewildered.

"Where are Mrs. Fortner and the doctor?" he asked. "What happened here?"

"Listen, Farley," Rue said, sitting on the arm of his chair and slipping one arm reassuringly around his shoulders, "it's all pretty complicated, though if you'll remember, I tried to tell you about it before. Anyway, it's going to take a while for you to absorb the fact that this is really happening, let alone process a whole new universe. We just jumped over a hundred years, you and I. Technically, Bethie and Jonathan are long dead. On the other hand, they're alive and well on the other side of some kind of cosmic chasm we don't understand."

"Thanks, Rue. That made everything clear as creek water," Farley said wryly. He was clearly still unnerved, as anyone would have been, but that lethal intelligence of his was stirring, too. Rue could see it in his eyes, hungry, wanting to comprehend everything. "Am I losing my mind?"

"No more so than I am, or Elisabeth. You just crossed from one dimension to another, somehow. All I know is that it has to do with my necklace."

"Good God," Farley sighed, rubbing his chin.

"Now you know how I felt," Rue said, polishing his badge with the sleeve of her dress. After that, she stood again. "Since you're company," she teased, "you can have the first shower."

"The first what?"

Rue laughed and took his hand. "Come on. I'll show you." She led the befuddled lawman up the stairs, along the hallway and into the main bathroom, reserving the one off the master bedroom for herself. There, she gave Farley soap and shampoo and showed him where to find the towels, then adjusted the shower spigots.

Farley's eyes went wide with puzzled amazement, but he was already starting to strip off his clothes when Rue slipped out of the room. She'd gotten only partway down the hall when a shout of stunned annoyance echoed from behind the door.

Thinking she should have explained that one spigot brought forth hot water and one cold, Rue smiled. She hoped it was ice Farley had just doused himself with, and not fire.

In the master bedroom, where all her things were still in the drawers and the closet, Rue had an urge to kneel and kiss the floor. She didn't, however. She just laid out jeans, underwear, socks and a bulky, white sweater, then took a shower.

The doorbell was ringing when she reached the upper hallway, and she heard voices roll up the front stairs.

"Here's the pizza, sir," said a voice, teenage and masculine. "That'll be fifteen dollars and seventy-five cents."

"For one flat box?" Farley boomed. "You'd better take your wares someplace else, boy."

Grinning, Rue hurried down the stairs. Farley was wrapped in a pink chenille bedspread taken from one of the guest bedrooms, and his freshly washed hair was standing up on top of his head.

"It's okay," Rue said quickly. She paid the young man, took the pizza and closed the door. Then looking up at Farley, she started to laugh. With the bedspread draped around him, toga-style, all he needed was a wreath of laurel leaves on his head to make him a very convincing Roman. "Don't tell me, I know. A funny thing happened to you on the way to the forum."

Farley was clearly not amused. "I'm in no mood

for any of your fancy double-talk, woman," he said, glowering.

Rue opened the lid on the pizza box. "Mellow out, Marshal. This will fix you up—prepare to experience one of the best things about modern life." She pried a gooey slice loose and handed it to him. "Go ahead," she urged. "Eat it."

He took a cautious bite, tightened his bedspread toga with a nervous gesture of one hand and took another.

"Good, isn't it?" Rue said, talking with her mouth full.

Farley answered by taking another piece.

Rue had waited too long for this pizza to stand on ceremony. They went into the parlor and sat cross-legged on the floor in front of the empty hearth.

"Bet none of the Pine River ladies ever brought you anything like this for dinner," Rue said smugly.

He lifted a slice to look under it. "Damnedest pancake I've ever seen," he said in all seriousness.

Rue's attention had shifted to the bedspread. "We're going to have to get you some clothes, big fella. I think you're the faded jeans type."

"I've got clothes," Farley protested. Rue hoped he wasn't going to pick now, of all times, to get stubborn.

"Chenille bedspreads have been out of style for a long time," she said. For Farley, the situation was gravely confusing, Rue knew that, but she couldn't help being happy that the two of them hadn't been separated. She would face the lingering pain of saying goodbye to Elisabeth later, and begin learning to live with it. She sighed. "Life is very complicated, Farley."

He glared at her, probably thinking she was a witch or a creature from another planet, that she'd deliberately uprooted him from the world he knew.

"Okay, so maybe that was kind of an obvious statement," Rue conceded. "I can't explain what happened to you, for the simple reason that I don't have the first idea myself. The fact is, you're here now instead of the 1890s, and you can probably go back if you want to just by holding the necklace in one hand." She started to rise to get the pendant from the mantel, but Farley stopped her by grasping her arm.

"Will you go with me?" he asked hoarsely.

Rue hesitated, then shook her head. "I belong here," she said. If she hadn't realized that before, she reflected, traveling back to 1892 had certainly cleared the matter up for her. She had a suspicion Farley belonged, too, because of his insatiable mind and progressive attitudes, but he would have to discover that for himself. It was not something she could decide for him.

Farley swallowed hard, the last slice of pizza forgotten in his hand, and Rue knew he was making a costly decision.

"I ought to go back where I came from," he finally said. "There are things I left undone and people I need to say goodbye to. But, damn it, scared as I am, I want to see this place." Farley gestured toward the TV set. "I want to see what other machines there are and how they work." He reached out from where he sat and touched the dangling cord of a lamp. "And these lanterns. Does the kerosene come in through this wire?"

Rue kissed his forehead. "You've got quite an adventure ahead of you, cowboy."

Farley finished the pizza, thoughtfully examining Rue's jeans and sweater. "I guess women must dress like that here, then?" he inquired, and it was obvious that he didn't wholly approve of the look.

She nodded. "Chinese women have worn pants for centuries," she said. "Here in the United States, the style didn't really catch on until the Second World War."

"There was a war involving the whole world?" Farley's eyes were wide and haunted with the horrible images of such an event.

"There were two," Rue said. "And all of us are praying like crazy that there'll never be a third."

Awkwardly, Farley got to his feet, still carefully clutching the bedspread that preserved his modesty, and started toward the back of the house. "The privy still in the same place?"

Again, Rue laughed. "The outhouse was filled in sometime in the thirties, Farley." She wriggled her fingers to summon him to the downstairs bathroom, showed him how to flush. "There's another one upstairs. I guess you missed it when you took your shower."

He whistled. "That's one fine invention."

"Wait until you see what we can do with computers," she countered, leaving the room and closing the door. She hung up Farley's sheepskin coat, his badge still gleaming on the lapel, and gingerly set his gun belt on top of the highboy in the smaller parlor. Then she dropped his socks, trousers and shirt into the washer. He'd need something to wear while they shopped for contemporary clothes the next day.

By this time, Farley was standing behind her, wearing just a bath towel around his middle now. Obviously, he was feeling a little more comfortable in the circumstances.

"What is that thing doing?" he asked, frowning at the washer.

Rue explained, and Farley grinned at the wonderment of such a thing, flashing his white teeth. He lifted the washer's lid to look inside. The agitator promptly stopped.

Rue closed the lid again and patted the top of the washer's companion appliance. "This is the drier. I'll put your shirt and pants in here after the washer stops, and they'll be ready to wear in less than half an hour."

Farley looked mesmerized. "Will you teach me how to work these things?" he asked.

"Count on it," Rue agreed. She was a firm believer in training a man right in the first place. That way, maybe he wouldn't be dropping socks and wet towels on the bathroom floor and leaving dirty dishes in the kitchen sink.

Upstairs, she gave him a new toothbrush from the supply in the linen closet, along with a tube of paste.

He was standing at the sink in the main bathroom, happily foaming at the mouth when Rue retired to the master bath.

When she came out, Farley was sitting on the edge of the bed, still clad in the towel. Which was almost worse than nothing, because it sent Rue's fertile imagination spinning.

He discovered the switch on the bedside lamp and flipped it on and off three or four times before he was apparently satisfied that the same thing would happen ad infinitum, until either the mechanism wore out or he did.

When Farley turned his eyes to Rue and ran them over her short, cotton nightgown, she knew he'd gone a long way toward adjusting to his situation. He smiled broadly and said, "Hope you don't mind sharing your bed. I'm scared of the dark, and, besides, this was supposed to be our wedding night."

Chapter 9

Rue hesitated in the doorway, fighting a disconcerting urge to fling herself at Farley in unqualified surrender. She'd always found other men highly resistible, no matter how famous or accomplished they might be, but this self-educated nineteenth-century marshal could send her pulse careening out of control with a look, a simple touch or a few audacious words.

"Are you sure it would be wise for us to sleep together?" she finally managed in a thin voice. "After all, we don't exactly know where our relationship is headed."

"Relationship," Farley repeated with a thoughtful frown, stretching out on the bed. At least *he* was comfortable. Rue was a mass of warm aches and quivering contradictions. "That's a peculiar-sounding word. If it means what I think it does, well, I don't believe all of that has to be worked out tonight. Do you?"

Rue ran the tip of her tongue nervously over dry lips. "No, but—"

Farley arched one eyebrow. "But...?" he prompted, not unkindly.

Rue hugged herself and unconsciously took a step closer. "I'm not sure you're going to understand this, being a man, but when we made love, I opened myself up to you in a way that I never had before. There was no place for me to hide, if you know what I mean, and intimacy of that kind—"

He rose, graceful in his bath towel, and came to stand directly in front of her. "Did I hurt you?" he asked.

Rue shook her head. "No," she croaked after a long moment of silence. "It's just that I felt so vulnerable."

Gently, Farley took Rue's hand, raised it to his mouth, brushed the knuckles with his lips. "I'll make you a bargain," he said. "If I'm loving you and you get scared, all you have to do is say stop, and I will. No questions, no arguments."

Gazing into Farley's eyes, Rue knew he was telling the truth. Color pooled in her cheeks. "You know as well as I do," she told him with a rickety smile, "that once you start kissing and touching me, stopping will be the last thing on my mind."

He eased her to the side of the bed, pulled the nightgown off over her head and tossed it aside. Then he feasted on her with his eyes, and that alone made Rue feel desirable and womanly.

Her breasts seemed to swell under Farley's admiring gaze, the nipples protruding, eager. Her thighs felt softer and warmer, as if preparing to cradle his hard weight, and the most secret reaches of her womanhood began a quiet, heated throbbing.

When Farley spread splayed fingers through her freshly combed hair and bent her head back for his kiss, Rue gave an involuntary whimper. She was terrified, and the sensation of his mouth against hers was something like hurtling down the face of Mount Rainier on a runaway toboggan.

Rue felt Farley's towel fall away as he gripped her bottom, raised her slightly and pressed her against him, never slackening the kiss. Most of her wits had already deserted her, but she knew somehow that Farley was afraid, too, as she had been when she'd suddenly found herself in an alien century. He needed her comfort as he might never need it again, and if Rue hadn't already been incredibly turned on, that knowledge alone would have done the trick.

Passion made her bold. Farley broke the kiss with a gasp of surprised pleasure when she closed her hand around his manhood and instinctively began a fiery massage. Finally, Rue knelt and took him into her mouth, and his fingers delved into her hair, frantic, worshiping. A low groan rolled beneath the washboard muscles of his stomach before escaping his throat.

Farley allowed Rue to attend him for a long

time—it was amazing, but somehow he was still in charge of their lovemaking, even while she was subjecting him to exquisite rapture. Finally he stopped her, raised her to the bed and gently laid her there.

He said something to her in a low, rumbling voice, and then repaid her thoroughly for the sweet torment she'd given him. He did not bring her to the brink again and again, as Rue had done to him, however. Instead, Farley took her all the way, pursuing her relentlessly, until her heels dug deep into the mattress and her cries of satisfaction echoed off the ceiling.

When at last he took her, Rue didn't expect to have anything left to give. Her own instant, fevered response came as a shock to her, and so did the deep wells of sensation Farley plumbed with every thrust. He was exposing parts of her emotional life, places in her very soul, that had never seen the light.

Afterward, as before, he held Rue close, and her soaring heart returned from the heavens and settled itself inside her like a storm-ruffled bird that has finally found a roosting place. A tear brimmed the lower lashes of Rue's right eye and then zigzagged down her cheek, catching against the callused side of Farley's thumb.

Maybe he knew she didn't need consoling, that she was crying because life was life, because she was so grateful for the steady beat of her heart and the breath in her lungs. In any case, all Farley did was hold her a little tighter.

"It's strange," she said after a very long time, "to think that Elisabeth and Jonathan and Trista are in this house, too, even though we can't see or hear them."

Farley's hand moved idly against her hair, her temple, her cheek. "I'm still trying to figure out that thing you've got downstairs, the box with the pictures inside. There's no point in vexing my poor brain with how many people are traipsing around without us knowing about it."

Rue smiled, spreading her fingers over the coarse patch of hair on Farley's chest. "It's nice, though, to think Bethie and the others are so close by, that they're not actually dead but just in another dimension."

He reached over to cover her lips with an index finger. "I'm not even going to ask what you mean by 'another dimension,'" he said, "because I'm afraid you'll tell me."

She turned over, resting her leg on top of his and curling her foot partway around his ankle. Then she gave one of his nipples a mischievous lick before smiling into his eyes. "There is so much I want to show you, Farley. Like my ranch, for instance."

"Your what?"

"You remember. I told you I had a ranch in Montana."

He chuckled. "I thought you were just pulling my leg about that. How did you come to have your own land?"

"I inherited it from my grandfather. Let's go there, Farley—tomorrow. As soon as we've bought you some new clothes."

Farley stiffened, and his tone, though as quiet as before, had an edge to it. "The duds I've got will do just fine."

Rue sighed. "This is no time to have a fit of male pride, Marshal. Times have changed, and if you go around in those clothes, people will think you're a refugee from a Wild West show."

"I don't accept what I haven't earned," he replied. He'd clamped his jaw with the last word, and even in the thin moonlight Rue could see that his eyes had gone hard as marbles.

"Good," Rue said. "I need a foreman at Ribbon Creek anyway; my lawyers have been complaining about the one I've got ever since Gramps died."

In the next few seconds, it was as though Farley's masculine pride and desire for a ranch had taken on substance even though they remained invisible. Rue could feel them doing battle right there in the room.

"What are you going to do if you don't work for me, Farley?" she pressed quietly. "You're one of the most intelligent men I've ever known, but believe me, you don't have the kind of job skills you'd need to make a decent living in this day and age."

He was quiet for such a long time that Rue feared he'd drifted off to sleep. Finally, however, Farley replied, "Let's go and have a look at this ranch of yours, then."

Rue laid her cheek against his chest, smiled and closed her eyes.

When she awakened in the morning, Farley was sitting in a chair next to the bed, wearing his regular clothes. Although there were pulled threads shriveling the fabric in places, and the pants looked an inch or two shorter, he was still handsome enough to make Rue's heart do a happy little spin.

"I was beginning to think you meant to lay there till the Resurrection," Farley grumbled, and Rue ascertained in that moment that, despite the fact that he'd gotten up comparatively early, the marshal was not a morning person.

"Low blood sugar," Rue diagnosed, tossing back the covers and sitting up. She'd put her nightgown back on during the night, so she didn't feel as self-conscious as she might have otherwise. "Don't let it bother you. I have the exact same problem. If I don't eat regularly—and junk food is worse than nothing—I get crabby, too."

Farley was already at the door. "I don't know what the hell you're talking about, but if you're saying I'm hungry, you're right. I was planning to make breakfast, and I took some wood from the basket by the parlor fireplace, but I'll be damned if I could figure out where to kindle the fire in that kitchen stove of yours."

Rue grinned and preceded him out of the bedroom and down the stairs. "It's not the kind of stove you're used to, Marshal. Remember the cords on the lamp? Most everything in the kitchen works the same way, by electricity." She'd explained the mysteries of that science as best she could the night before, but in a way it was like trying to illustrate their trip through time. Rue couldn't very well clarify things she barely understood herself. "Never fear," she finished. "There's a set of books at the ranch that covers that type of thing—Gramps had a penchant for knowing how things worked."

She crossed the kitchen and opened the refrigerator, knowing ahead of time what she'd find. Nothing edible, except for three green olives floating in a jar. The other stuff had been there when she arrived at the house days—weeks?—before.

Rue opened the freezer and took out a box of toaster waffles. "I'm afraid this will have to hold us until we can get to Steak Heaven out on Highway 18."

Farley watched in consternation as Rue opened the carton, pulled apart the inner wrapper and popped two waffles into the toaster. While they were warming, she scouted out syrup and put two cups of water into the microwave for instant coffee.

"How does this contraption work?" Farley asked, turning to the stove that had so confounded him earlier.

Rue checked the oven on a hunch and found kindling sticks neatly stacked on the middle rack. She struggled not to laugh as she removed them, thanking heaven all the while that Farley had not gone so far as to light a blaze.

"These knobs on the top control everything," she said when she could trust herself to speak. With one arm, she held the applewood while pointing out the dials with her free hand.

Farley listened earnestly to her explanation, then

nodded with a grin. It was plain that he was a quick study; no doubt he would take in information as fast as it could be presented.

They breakfasted on the waffles and coffee, and then Rue hurriedly showered and dressed. She wasn't afraid of her Aunt Verity's house, even after all that had happened to her and to Elisabeth here; she could never have feared that benevolent place. Still, Rue felt an urgency to be gone, a particular fear she didn't like facing.

Perhaps away from here, the necklace would have no power. If it did, however, Farley could disappear at any moment.

Getting the marshal to leave his gun belt behind required some of the fastest talking Rue had ever done, but in the end, she succeeded by promising him access to the big collection of firearms that had belonged to her grandfather.

It was almost noon when she and Farley locked the house and set out. Rue had brought her laptop computer, clothes and personal things, but she'd deliberately left the necklace behind; in its own way, the thing was as dangerous as the marshal's Colt .45.

Farley was fascinated by the Land Rover. He walked around it three or four times before getting in.

Thinking her guest might be interested in seeing how Pine River had developed over the decades since he'd been its marshal, Rue drove him down Main Street, showed him the movie house and the library

and the local police station. She avoided the churchyard without looking too closely at her reasons.

Farley was, of course, amazed by the changes,
and would have insisted on getting out and exploring, Rue was sure, if he hadn't been so fascinated
by their mode of transportation.

He spent the entire ride to Steak Heaven opening and closing the glove compartment, turning the
dials on the radio, switching on the heat, then the
air-conditioning, then the heat again.

"Soon as we get to Ribbon Creek," Rue promised from her position behind the wheel, "I'll teach
you to drive."

Farley beamed at the prospect.

When they reached the restaurant, Farley turned
his attention from the dashboard and stared in
amazement at the crowded parking lot. "Jumpin' Juniper," he said. "Does everybody in this place have
one of these newfangled buggies?"

Rue smiled. "Almost," she answered, "but they
come in all shapes, sizes and colors, as you can see."

Farley paused to inspect a pricey red sports car as
they passed, giving a low whistle of appreciation. It
only went to prove, Rue thought in amusement, that
some things transcend time. Maybe men had always
been fascinated by methods of transportation.

The noise and bustle of the inside of the restaurant made Farley visibly nervous. His face took on
a grim expression, and Rue saw him touch his outer
thigh once or twice while they waited to be seated.

Probably he was unconsciously seeking reassurance that wasn't there—his gun.

"Table for two?" a waitress asked pleasantly.

Farley's turquoise eyes widened as he took in the girl's short skirt, and Rue realized he'd never seen a female show so much leg in public.

"Yes," Rue answered, linking her arm with Farley's and propelling him between the crowded tables as the girl led the way.

"Tarnation," Farley muttered, looking around and seeing that not only other waitresses but customers were dressed in the same way. "If the Presbyterians saw this, they'd be spitting railroad spikes."

Rue chuckled. "Some of these people probably *are* Presbyterians, Farley. This is an accepted way for women to dress."

They reached their booth, and Farley slid into the seat across from Rue, still looking overwhelmed. His eyes narrowed. "It's bad enough to see a woman in pants," he whispered pointedly. "I hope you don't plan on parading around in one of these getups you call a dress, with your knees sticking out. I'm the only one who should see you like that."

Rue rested her plastic-coated menu against her forehead for a moment, hiding her face while she battled amusement and her natural tendency to protest his arbitrary words. Finally, she met his gaze over the steaming cups of coffee between them, and said, "Even if we were married, which we're not, I wouldn't let you tell me what to wear, Farley. That would be like allowing you to tell me how to vote."

He stared at her. "You can vote?"

She sighed and rolled her eyes heavenward. "I can see this is going to be quite a project, acclimatizing you to this century."

The waitress returned, and Rue ordered a club sandwich and a diet cola, since it was lunchtime. Farley, having read his own menu, asked for sausage and eggs. Plainly, the toaster waffles hadn't seemed like breakfast to him.

When the food came, he loaded it down with pepper, except for the toast, and consumed every bite, leaving nothing on his plate but a few streaks of egg yoke.

Rue paid the check with a credit card, and when the cashier handed it back, Farley intercepted and studied the card intently.

"This is money?" he asked, handing the card to Rue as they crossed the parking lot a few minutes later.

"The plastic variety," Rue affirmed with a nod. She stopped and looked up into Farley's wonderful eyes, feeling so much love for him that it was painful. "I know everything seems pretty bewildering," she said gently, "but you're a very intelligent man and you'll figure things out."

He looked the Land Rover over speculatively as they approached. "I'd like to drive now," he announced.

"No way," Rue answered, pulling her keys from the pocket of her jeans. "Cars move a whole lot faster than horses, Farley, and when they collide, people get killed."

Although the marshal looked disappointed, he didn't argue.

Where before his attention had been taken up by the gizmos on the dashboard, now Farley was intent on the other cars, the buildings, the power lines alongside the highway. As they drove toward Seattle, he asked a million questions about the pavement, the road signs, the cars and trucks in the other lanes.

When Seattle itself came into view, with its busy harbor and the picturesque Space Needle, Farley was apparently struck dumb by the sight. He stared intently, as though his eyes couldn't take in enough to suit him, and he kept turning in different directions.

Rue drove through the city, knowing Farley couldn't have absorbed explanations just then, and kept going until they reached a large mall.

She parked and they entered the concourse. Rue still didn't speak because Farley was so busy absorbing the sights and sounds that he probably wouldn't have heard her anyway.

He studied a colorful display in front of a bookstore with an attitude that seemed like reverence to Rue. She was touched by the depth of his wonder, knowing it must be something like what she felt when he made love to her.

Suddenly she wanted to give him the world, show him everything there was to see.

"I remember that you like reading," she said, her voice a little shaky. She proceeded into the store, located the instructional section and found a comprehensive volume on how things work. Then from another shelf, she took a novel set in the twenty-fifth century. It was the only way she could think of to prepare Farley for the fact that human beings could fly now, that a few brave souls had even visited the moon.

Farley watched as she paid. "You can buy books with plastic money?" he asked as they left.

"You can buy almost anything with plastic money," Rue replied, handing him the bag.

They went on to the men's department of one of the big chain stores, and Farley was soon outfitted with jeans, shirts, underwear and socks. He refused to part with his boots, and Rue didn't press the issue.

Soon they were on the freeway again, headed east. Farley alternated between staring out the window and thumbing through the books Rue had bought for him. When he opened one and started to read, she protested.

"You shouldn't read in a moving car, Farley," she said, amazed at how silly she sounded even as she was saying the words. "It'll make you sick."

Farley wet the tip of an index finger, turned a page and read on. "If you can go around with your knees showing in one of those short skirts," he said without even glancing in her direction, "I can read whenever I want to. And I want to."

"Fine," Rue replied, because there was nothing else she could say. She was glad, in a way, that Farley hadn't given in, because his stubborn strength was one of the qualities she loved most. Without looking away from the road, she took a CD from the box between the seats and shoved it into the slot below the radio.

Farley jumped and then lowered the book when Carly Simon's voice filled the Land Rover.

"I think the closest thing you had to this in 1892 was the music box," Rue said without smugness. She knew Farley's curiosity had to be almost overwhelming. "Or maybe a hand organ."

"I'm getting a powerful headache," Farley confessed, rubbing his eyes. "How could so much have happened in just over a hundred years?"

She didn't tell him about automatic-teller machines and laser surgery, out of simple courtesy. "There were many factors involved," she said gently. "A lot of historians think the nation turned a corner during the Civil War. There were other conflicts later. As wretched and horrible as war is, it forced science to advance, in both good ways and bad, because of the awesome needs it creates."

Farley sat up rigidly straight—clearly some dire thought had just occurred to him—and rasped, "The Union—it still stands, doesn't it?"

Rue nodded and reached out to pat his arm reassuringly. "Oh, yes," she said. "There are fifty states now, you know."

"Canada is a state?"

She laughed. "Hardly. Canada is still a great nation in her own right. I was talking about Arizona, Utah, New Mexico, Oklahoma, Alaska and Hawaii."

Farley was quiet.

That evening, they pulled in at a truck stop to buy gas and have supper. Rue showed Farley how to work the gas pump, and his pride in the simple task was touching.

In the bright, busy restaurant adjoining the filling station, Farley consumed a cheeseburger deluxe, fries and a chocolate milk shake. "Anything that good has got to be kissing cousin to original sin," he commented cheerfully, after making short work of the food.

Rue shrugged and smiled slightly. "Only too true," she agreed with regret, deciding to save the nutritional lectures for later.

Farley cleared his throat. "I suppose these folks have filled in their outhouse, too," he said seriously.

Rue laughed, pushed away the last of her own chef's salad, and slid out of the booth. "This way, cowboy," she said. She pointed out the men's room, which was at the end of a long hallway, and paid the bill for their supper.

Farley reappeared shortly, his thick hair damp and finger-combed.

They were cruising along the freeway toward Spokane, a star-dappled sky shining above, before he spoke again.

"I keep thinking I must have gotten hold of some locoweed or something," he said in a low, hoarse voice. "How could this be happening to me?"

Rue understood his feelings well, having experienced the same time-travel process, and she was sympathetic. "You're not crazy, Farley," she said, reaching over to touch his arm briefly. "That much I can promise you. There's something really strange going on here, though, and I owe you an apology for dragging you into it the way I did. I'm sorry."

He turned to her in apparent surprise. "It wasn't your fault."

Rue sighed, keeping a close eye on the road. "If I hadn't attached myself to your leg the way I did when the necklace started acting up again and the room was spinning, you probably wouldn't be here now."

Farley chuckled and gave a rueful shake of his head. "I'd be back there wondering just how a lady could be standing in front of me one moment and gone without a trace the next."

"I think the thing that bothers me the most about this whole situation is not knowing, not being able to pick up a thread of reason and follow it back to its spool, so to speak. I don't like mysteries."

Farley was going through Rue's collection of CDs. "Speaking of mysteries," he marveled, turning a disk over in his hand. "This is the damnedest thing, the way you people can put a voice and a whole bunch of piano players and fiddlers onto a flat circle like this. Back there at that place where we ate, they were selling these things."

"CDs are available almost everywhere. They don't just have music on them, either—you can listen to books and to all sorts of instructional stuff."

Farley grinned. "I saw one back at the truck stop

that interested me," he said. "It was called, *Red-hot Mamas on Wheels*."

Again, Rue laughed. "I didn't say it was all literature, Farley."

"What exactly is a red-hot mama?"

"I'll tell you when you're older."

"I'm thirty-six!"

"And then some," Rue agreed, and this time it was Farley who laughed.

Several hours later, they reached Spokane, and Rue stopped at a large motel, knowing Farley would be uncomfortable with the formality of a city hotel. As it happened, he was pretty Victorian when it came to the subject of sharing rooms.

"It didn't bother you last night!" Rue whispered impatiently. She'd asked for a double, and Farley had immediately objected, wanting two singles. The clerk waited in silence for a decision to be made, fingers poised over the keyboard of his computer, eyebrows raised.

Farley took Rue's hand and hauled her away from the desk. They were partially hidden behind a gigantic jade tree, which only made matters worse, as far as Rue was concerned.

"We're not married!" he ground out.

"Now there's a flash," Rue said, her hands on her hips. "We weren't married *last* night, either!"

"That was different. This is a public place."

Rue sighed. "Like the beds are in the lobby or something." But then she conceded, "Okay, you win. Explaining this is obviously going to be a monumental task, and I'm too tired to tackle the job. We'll compromise." She went back to the desk, credit card in hand, and asked for adjoining rooms.

Her quarters and Farley's were on the second floor, along an outside balcony.

"Good night," she said tightly, after showing Farley how to unlock his door with the plastic card that served as a key. There was an inner door connecting the two rooms, but Rue had promised herself she wouldn't use it. "Don't eat the peanuts or drink the whiskey in the little refrigerator," she warned. "Everything costs about four times what it would anywhere else."

Farley's tired blue eyes were twinkling with humor. "I'm only looking out for your reputation as a lady," he said, plainly referring to their earlier row over shared accommodation.

"I have a reputation as a reporter," Rue replied, folding her arms. "Nobody ever accused me of being a lady."

Farley put down her suitcase and curled his fingers under the waistband of her jeans, pulling her against him with an unceremonious jerk. "Somebody's accusing you of it right now," he argued throatily, and then he gave Rue a long, thorough, lingering kiss that left her trembling. "You're all woman, fiery as a red-hot branding iron, and the way you fuss when I have you, everybody in this place would know what was happening. I don't want that—those gasps and cries and whimpers you give belong to me and me alone."

Rue's face was crimson by that time. She'd heard

much blunter statements—while traveling with other journalists and camera crews, for instance—but this was intimate; it was personal. "Good night," she said again, trying to wrench free of Farley's grasp.

He held on to her waistband, the backs of his fingers teasing the tender flesh of her abdomen, and he kissed her again. When he finally drew back, her knees were so weak, she feared she might have to *crawl* into her room.

"Good night," Farley said. Then he went into his room and closed the door.

Chapter 10

That night, Farley experienced a kind of weariness he'd never had to endure before—not after forced marches in the army or herding cattle across three states or tracking outlaws through the worst kind of terrain. No, it wasn't his body that was worn out—he hadn't done a lick of honest work all day long—it was his mind. His spirit. There was so much to understand, to absorb, and he was bewildered by the onslaught of information that had been coming down on him in a continuous cascade ever since his abrupt arrival in the future.

He moved to toss his hat onto the bed, with its brown striped spread, and stopped himself at the last second. Where he came from, to do that was to invite ill fortune. In this strange place where everything was bigger, brighter and more intense, he hated to think what plain, old, sorry luck might have developed into.

After a little thought, he went to the wardrobe, which was built into the wall, and put his hat on the shelf. The conveniences were right next to that, and he couldn't help marveling at the sleek and shiny bathtub, the sink and commode, the supply of thick, fluffy towels.

Except for Rue, who was just beyond a puny inside door, he was most attracted by the box on the bureau facing the bed. Rue had called the machine a TV, describing it as a shirttail relation to the camera, and Farley found the device wonderfully mystifying.

Facing it, he bent to squint at the buttons arrayed down one side, then touched the one that said Power.

Immediately, a black man with hair as flat as the top of a windswept mesa appeared, smiling in a mighty friendly way. He said something Farley didn't quite catch, and a lot of unseen people laughed.

Farley punched another button and found an imposing-looking fellow standing behind the biggest pulpit he'd ever seen in his life. Beginning to catch on to the system, the marshal pressed still another button.

A lady wearing one of those skimpy dresses appeared, pushing something that might have been a carpet sweeper. There was a block in one side of the window, listing several different figures.

Farley proceeded to the next button, and this time he got a faceful of a bad-natured galoot with a long, red mustache and six-guns as big as he was. He was moving and talking, this noisy little desperado, and yet he wasn't real, like the other TV people had been. He was a *drawing*.

Farley sat down on the end of the mattress, enthralled. Next came a rabbit who walked upright, jabbered like an eager spinster and would do damn near anything for a carrot.

Finally, Farley turned off the machine, removed his boots and stretched out on the bed with a sigh. This century was enough to terrify a body, though he couldn't rightly admit that out loud, being a United States marshal and all.

On the other side of the wall, he heard a deep voice say, "This is CNN," and smiled. A month ago, even a day ago, he'd have torn the place apart, hearing that. He'd have been convinced there was a man in Rue's room, bothering her. Now he knew she was only watching the TV machine.

He imagined her getting ready for bed, brushing her teeth, washing her face, maybe padding around in one of those thin excuses for a nightdress that made his whole body go hard all at once. He could have been in there with her—it was torture knowing that—but he didn't want anybody thinking less of her because she'd shared a room with a man who wasn't her husband. She was too fine for that, too special.

Farley got up after a time, stripped off his clothes and ran himself a bath in the fancy room with the tiles that not only covered the floor but climbed most of the way up the wall. When the tub was full, he tested the steaming water with a toe, yelped in pain, and studied the spigots, belatedly recalling that *H* meant hot and *C* meant cold.

He had scrubbed himself from head to foot and settled into bed with one of the books Rue had bought for him when the ugly contraption on the bedside stand started to make a jangling noise. Farley frowned, staring as though to intimidate it into silence. Then, remembering the brief lecture Rue had given him at her house, he recognized it as a telephone.

He picked up the removable part and heard Rue's voice, tinny and small, saying, "Farley? Farley, are you there?"

He put the device to his ear, decided the cord wasn't supposed to dangle over his eye and cheek, and turned it around. "Rue?"

"Who else would it be?" she teased. "Did I wake you?"

He glowered at the contrivance, part of which still sat on the bedside table. If the TV machine was family to the camera, this thing must be kin to the telegraph. Now that he thought about it, the conclusion seemed obvious. "No," he said. "I wasn't sleeping." Farley liked talking to Rue this way, there was a strange intimacy to it, but he surely would have preferred to have her there in the bed with him. "I was watching that TV box a little while ago."

There was a smile in her voice, though not the kind meant to make a man feel smaller than he should be. "What did you see?"

Farley shook his head, still marveling. "Pictures—drawings—that moved and talked. One was supposed to be a person, but it wasn't."

Rue was quiet for a moment, then she said, again without a trace of condescension in her voice, "That was a cartoon. Artists draw and paint figures, and then they're brought to life by a process called animation. I'll tell you more about it tomorrow."

Farley wasn't sure he was really that interested, not when there were so many other things to puzzle through, but he didn't want to hurt Rue's feelings, so he would listen when the time came. They talked for a few minutes more, then said good-night, and Farley put the talking part of the telephone back where he'd found it.

He'd mastered light switches—to his way of thinking it was diabolical how the damn things were in a different place on every lamp—so he twisted a bit of brass between his fingers and the room became comparatively dark.

He was as exhausted as before, maybe more so, and he yearned, body and soul, for the comfort Rue could give him. He closed his eyes, thinking he surely wouldn't be able to sleep, and he promptly lost consciousness.

He must have rested undisturbed for a few hours, but then the dream was upon him, and it was so real that he felt the texture of the sheets change beneath him, the firmness of the mattress. Indeed, Farley felt the air itself alter, become thinner, harder to breathe.

The traffic sounds from the nearby highway

turned to the twangy notes of saloon pianos, the nickering of horses, the squeaks and moans of wagon wheels.

Farley was back in his own lifetime.

Without Rue.

He let out a bellow, a primitive mixture of shock and protest, and sat bolt upright in bed. His skin was drenched with sweat, and he was gasping for breath, as though he'd been under water the length of the dream.

The dream. Farley wanted to weep with relief, but that, too, was something unbefitting a United States marshal. There was an anxious knock at the door separating his room from Rue's, and then, just as Farley switched on the lamp, Rue burst in.

"Good grief, Farley, are you all right? It sounded like you were being scalped!"

He was embarrassed at being caught in the aftermath of a nightmare, and that made him a little angry. "Do you always barge in on people like that?"

Rue was wearing a white cotton nightdress that barely reached the top of her thighs. Her eyes were narrowed, and her hands were resting on her hips. "I seem to recall asking you a similar question," she said, "when I woke up in the master bedroom at Pine River and found you standing there staring at me." She paused, drew a deep breath and went on, a fetching pink color rising in her cheeks. "Your virtue is in no danger, Farley. I just wanted to make sure you were okay. I mean, you could have slipped in the bathtub or something."

He arched one eyebrow after casting an eye over her nightclothes—there were little bloomers underneath the skimpy gown, with ruffles around the legs—and then her long, slender legs. Lordy, she looked as sweet as a sun-warmed peach.

"Suppose I *had* fallen in the bathtub," he responded huskily, leaning back against the padded headboard and pulling the sheets up to his armpits. One of them had to be modest, and it sure as hell wasn't going to be Rue, not in the getup she had on. "How would you have known?"

She ran impudent eyes over the length of his frame. "The walls are thin here, Marshal. And you would have made quite a crash." She folded her arms, thus raising the nightdress higher. "Stop trying to evade the subject and tell me what made you let out a yell like that."

Farley sighed. Now that he'd stalled long enough to regain most of his composure, he figured he could talk about what happened without breaking into a cold sweat. "I dreamed I was back in 1892, that's all," he said.

Rue came and sat on the foot of the bed, cross-legged like an Indian. "Was I there?"

Farley hoped the tremendous vulnerability he was feeling wasn't audible in his voice. "No," he said. "Don't you have a dressing gown you can put on? I can't concentrate with you wearing that skimpy little nightgown."

She gave him a teasing grin. "You'll just have to suffer."

He fussed with his covers for a few moments. He was suffering, all right; it felt like he had a chunk of firewood between his legs. He changed the subject.

"Can one or the other of us be sent back even if that damn necklace is nowhere around?"

Rue's smile faded. She bit her lower lip for a moment. "I don't know, Farley," she said quietly. "When I first found the necklace, I had to be wearing or holding it to travel through time, and I had to pass through a certain doorway in the upstairs hall of my aunt's house. It was the same for Elisabeth. Later, it was as though the two time periods were meshing somehow, and I no longer had to go over the threshold to reach 1892."

"But you always had the necklace?"

She nodded. "Things are obviously changing, though. It seems to me that if people can step backward or forward in time, anything can happen."

Farley had another chill, though this was only a shadow of the one that had gripped him during the nightmare. Maybe he wouldn't be allowed to stay in this crazy, mixed-up century, with this crazy, mixed-up woman. The idea was shattering.

Rue was as vital to him as the blood flowing through his veins, and there was so much he wanted to see, so much he wanted to know.

He moved over and tossed back the covers to make room for her. He hadn't changed his mind about the impropriety of sharing a bed in a public inn, but he needed to sleep with his arms around her.

She switched off the lamp and crawled in beside

him, all warm and soft and fragrant. When she snuggled close, Farley let out an involuntary groan.

Rue smoothed the hair on his chest with a palm. "Let's hope we don't do any time traveling while we're making love," she teased. "We could make an embarrassing landing, like in the horse trough in front of the feed and grain, or on one of the pool tables at the Hang-Dog Saloon. I don't mind telling you, Marshal, the Society would be livid!"

Farley laughed, rolled onto his side and gathered her close with one arm. There was no use in trying to resist her; she was too delicious, too funny, too sweet.

"What am I going to do with you?" he asked in mock despair.

Rue started nibbling at his neck, and murmured, "I have a few suggestions."

When Rue awoke the next morning, Farley was already up. He'd showered and dressed in some of his starchy new clothes, and he was sitting at the requisite round table by the windows, reading *USA Today*. "It seems to me that politicians haven't changed much," he commented without lowering the newspaper.

Rue smiled. She was hypersensitive, but in a pleasant way; the feel of Farley's hands and mouth still lingered on her lips, her throat, her breasts and stomach. "Some things stay the same no matter how much time passes," she replied, sitting up and wrapping her arms around her knees.

He peered at her over the colorful masthead. "I agree," he said solemnly, folding the paper and setting it aside. Having done that, Farley shoved one hand through his gleaming brown hair. "It's wrong for us to—to do what we did last night, Rue. That's something that should be confined to marriage."

Rue would have rolled her eyes if she hadn't known Farley was dead serious. She reached for the telephone and punched the button for room service. "Are you trying to tell me that you were married to every woman you ever slept with?" she inquired reasonably.

"No, ma'am," replied the youthful masculine voice at the other end of the line.

Hot color surged into Rue's face, and she would have hung up in mortification if she hadn't wanted coffee so much. "I wasn't talking to you," she told the room-service clerk with as much dignity as she could manage. Farley had clearly figured out what had happened, and he was chuckling.

Rue glared at him, then spoke into the receiver again, giving the room number and asking for a pot of coffee, fresh fruit and toast.

The moment she hung up, Farley gave a chortle of amusement.

"Well?" Rue demanded, not to be deterred. "*Were* you married to everyone you've ever made love with?"

Farley cleared his throat and reddened slightly. "Of course not. But this is different. A nice woman doesn't—"

Rue interrupted with an imperious upward thrust of one finger and, "Don't you dare say it, Farley Haynes!" She stabbed her own chest with that same digit. "*I* slept with you, and I'm one of the 'nicest women' you'll ever hope to meet!"

"You only did it because I took advantage of you."

"What a crock," Rue muttered, flinging back the covers and standing. "Did I act like I was being taken advantage of?"

"You should have just stayed in your own room," Farley grumbled.

"So now it's my fault?"

The marshal sighed. "I think it would probably be easier to change General Custer's mind about strategy than win an argument with you. Damn it, Rue, what I'm trying to say is, I think we should be married."

Rue sat down on the edge of the bed again. She loved Farley, and she hadn't agreed to marry him in 1892 because she'd known she didn't want to stay in that dark and distant century. This proposal, however, was quite another matter.

"It might be difficult getting a marriage license," she said awkwardly after a long time. "Considering that you have no legal identity."

While Farley was still puzzling that one out, the food arrived. Rue wrapped herself in one of the big shirts they'd bought the day before to let the room-service waiter in and sign the check.

Once they were alone again, she sat at the round

table, feet propped on the edge of the chair, and alternately sipped coffee and nibbled at a banana.

"What do you mean, I don't have a legal identity?" Farley wanted to know. He added two packets of sugar to his coffee and stirred it with a clatter of spoon and china. "Is there a gravestone with my name on it somewhere back there in the long ago?"

A chill made Rue shiver and reach to refill her coffee cup. "I can show you where Elisabeth and Jonathan are buried," she said, not looking at him. "But that's different, because they stayed in the past. You came here."

"So if we find my marker, say around Pine River someplace, that'll mean I'm going back. It would have to."

Rue's head was spinning, but she understood Farley's meaning only too well. Elisabeth had a grave in the present because she'd returned to the past and lived out her life. Coming across Farley's burial place would mean he wasn't going to stay with her, in the here and now, that he was destined to return.

"You're right," she blurted, "we should get married."

A slow smile spread across Farley's rugged face. "What are we going to do about my identity?"

Rue bit her lip, thinking. "We'll have to invent one for you. I know a guy who used to work with the Witness Protection Program—those people can come up with an entire history."

After giving the inevitable explanations, Rue finished her breakfast and took a shower. Farley brought her things from the room next door, so she was able to dress and apply light makeup right away.

They were checked out of the motel and on the road to Montana while the morning was still new.

As they passed out of eastern Washington into Idaho and then Montana, the scenery became steadily more majestic. There were snow-capped mountains, their slopes thick with pine and fir trees, and the sheer expanse of the sky was awe inspiring.

"They call Montana the 'Big Sky Country,'" Rue said, touched by Farley's obvious relief to be back in the kind of unspoiled territory he knew and understood. She'd have to tell him about pollution and the greenhouse effect sooner or later, but this wasn't the time for it.

"Are we almost there? At your ranch, I mean?"

Rue shook her head. "Ribbon Creek is still a few hours away."

They stopped for an early lunch at one of those mom-and-pop hamburger places, and Farley said very little during the meal. He was clearly preoccupied.

"We should have stopped at the cemetery in Pine River," was the first thing he said, much later, when they were rolling down the highway again.

Just thinking of standing in some graveyard reading Farley's name on a tombstone made Rue's eyes burn. "I'll call the church office and ask if you're listed in the registry for the cemetery," she said. Even as Rue spoke the words, she knew—she who had never been a procrastinator—that this was a task she would put off as long as possible.

In the late afternoon, when the sun was about to plunge beneath the western horizon in a grand and glorious splash of crimson and gold, Rue's spirits began to lift.

Roughly forty-five minutes later, the Land Rover was speeding down the long, washboard driveway that led to the ranch house.

Farley had opened the door and gotten out almost before the vehicle came to a stop. Rue knew he was tired of being confined, and he was probably yearning for the sight of something familiar, too.

Soldier, a black-and-white sheepdog, met them in the dooryard, yipping delightedly at Rue's heels and giving Farley the occasional suspicious growl. There were lights gleaming in the kitchen of the big but unpretentious house, and Rue had a sweet, familiar sensation of being drawn into an embrace.

The screen door at the side of the house squeaked, and so did the old voice that called, "Who's that?"

"Wilbur, it's me," Rue answered happily, opening the gate and hurrying along the little flagstone walk that wound around to the big screen porch off the kitchen. "Rue."

Wilbur, who had worked for Rue's grandfather ever since both were young men, gave a cackle of delight. Now that he was elderly, he had the honorary title of caretaker, but he wasn't expected to do any real work. "I'll be ding danged," he said, limping Walter Brennan-style along the walk to stand facing Rue in the glow of the porch light. His rheumy blue eyes found Farley and climbed suspiciously to a face hidden by the shadow of the marshal's hat brim.

"Who might this be?" Wilbur wanted to know and, to his credit, he didn't sound in the least bit intimidated by Farley's size or the aura of strength that seemed to radiate from the core of his being.

"Farley Haynes," the marshal answered, taking off the hat respectfully and offering one hand.

Wilbur studied Farley's face for a long moment, then the still-extended hand. Finally, he put his own palm out for a shake. "Since it ain't none of my business," the old man said, "I won't ask who you are or what your errand is. If Miss Rue here says you're welcome at Ribbon Creek, then you are."

"Thank you," Farley said with that old-fashioned note of courtliness Rue found nearly irresistible. Then he turned and went back to the Land Rover for their things, having learned to open and close the tailgate when they left the motel that morning.

"He gonna be foreman now that Steenbock done quit?" Wilbur inquired in a confidential whisper that probably carried clear to the chicken coop.

Rue looked back at Farley, wishing they could have arrived before sunset. When he got a good look at the ranch, the marshal would think he'd been carried off by angels. "Mr. Haynes is going to be my husband," she said with quiet, incredulous joy. "That means he'll be part owner of the place."

The inside of the house smelled stale and musty, but it was still the same beautiful, homey place Rue remembered. On the ground floor were two parlors—they'd been her grandmother's pride—along with a study, a big, formal dining room, two bathrooms and an enormous kitchen boasting both a wood stove and the modern electric one. Upstairs, above the wide curving staircase, there were five bedrooms, one of which was huge, each with its own bath.

"This looks more like a palace than a ranch house," Farley said a little grimly when they'd made the tour and returned to the kitchen.

Rue took two steaks from the freezer in the big utility room and set them in the microwave to thaw. "This is a working ranch, complete with cattle and horses and the whole bit," she said. "Tomorrow, I'll show you what I mean."

Farley shoved a hand through already-rumpled hair. "What about you? What are you going to do way out here?"

"What I do best," Rue said, taking two big potatoes from a bin and carrying them to the sink. "Write for magazines and newspapers. Of course, I'll have to travel sometimes, but you'll be so busy straightening this place out that you won't even notice I'm gone."

When she looked back over one shoulder and saw Farley's face, Rue regretted speaking flippantly. It was plain that the idea of a traveling wife was not sitting well with the marshal.

She busied herself arranging the thick steaks under the broiler. After that, she stabbed the potatoes with a fork so they wouldn't explode and set them in the microwave.

"Farley, you must have already guessed that I have plenty of money," she said reasonably, bringing plates to the table. "I'm not going to be rushing out of here on assignment before the ink's dry on our marriage license. But I have a career, and eventually I'll want to return to it."

Farley pushed back his chair, found the silverware by a lucky guess and put a place setting by each of the plates. He was a Victorian male in the truest sense of the word, but he didn't seem to be above tasks usually regarded as women's work. Rue had high hopes for him.

"Farley?" She stood behind one of her grandmother's pressed-oak chairs, waiting for his response. Quietly demanding it.

His wonderful turquoise eyes linked with hers, looking weary and baffled. "What if we have a baby?" he asked hoarsely. "A little one needs a mother."

Rue smiled because he'd spoken gently and because the picture filled her with such joy. "I quite agree, Mr. Haynes," she said, yearning to throw her arms around Farley's neck and kiss him soundly. "When we have a child, we'll take care of him or her together," she assured him.

She turned the steaks and wrapped the microwaved potatoes in foil. Soon, Rue and Farley were sitting at the table, like any married couple at the end of a long day, sharing a late supper. Farley ate hungrily of the potatoes and steak, but he politely ignored the canned asparagus Rue had heated on the stove. To him, the vegetable probably looked as though it had been boiled to death.

When they'd finished, they cleaned up the kitchen together.

"Sleepy?" she asked.

Farley's wind-weathered cheeks blushed a dull red. He was going to get stubborn about the marriage thing again, she could tell.

"Look," Rue said with a sigh, "you can have your own room until after the wedding. After that, there will be no more of this Victorian-virgin stuff, understand?"

Farley stared at her for a moment, then smiled. "Absolutely," he agreed, his voice throaty and low.

Rue led the way upstairs. On the second floor, she paused in front of an electrical panel and switched off the downstairs lights. "This will be our room eventually," she said, opening the door to the large master suite with its fireplace and marble hot tub, "so you might as well get used to sleeping here. I'll be just down the hall."

Farley's throat worked visibly as he swallowed and nodded his agreement. Rue wanted him to sleep alone in the big bed, to imagine her sharing that wonderful room with him.

She stood on tiptoe to kiss the cleft in his stubbly chin. "Good night," she said.

"Good night," he replied. The words were rough, grating against each other like rusty hinges.

Rue went down the hall to her own room, whistling softly.

It was comforting to be back where she had sometimes slept as a child. When she was small, she'd spent a lot of time at the ranch, but later, her mother and grandfather had had some sort of falling out. That was why she'd ended up at Aunt Verity's when her parents had finally been divorced.

She unpacked, took a quick bath and climbed into bed. For a long time, Rue lay in the darkness, letting her eyes adjust, remembering. Once, a long time ago, she'd dreamed of living out her whole life on this ranch, marrying, raising her children here. Now it seemed that fantasy was about to come true.

Not that Farley wasn't going to have a hard time adjusting to the idea of having a working wife. He was fiercely proud, and he might never regard the ranch as a true home.

"Stop borrowing trouble," Rue scolded herself in a sleepy whisper. "Farley's always wanted a ranch. You know that."

She tossed restlessly from one side to the other. Then she lay flat on her back and spread her hands over her stomach. *Let there be a baby,* she thought. *Oh, please, let there be a baby.*

Imagining a child with turquoise eyes and unruly brown hair like Farley's made her smile, but her pleasure faded as she remembered his terrible dream the night before. He'd been flung back to his own time without her.

Rue squeezed her eyes closed, trying to shut out

the frightening possibilities that had stalked her into this quiet place. It was hopeless; she knew Farley could disappear at any time, maybe without any help from the necklace. And if that was going to happen, there was a grave somewhere, maybe unmarked, maybe lost, and he would have to lie there eventually, like a vampire hiding from the light.

A tear trickled over Rue's cheekbone to wet the linen pillowcase. Okay, she reasoned, love was a risk. *Life* was a risk, not just for her and Farley, but for everyone. The only thing to do was ante up her heart and play the hand she'd been dealt with as much panache as possible.

Chapter 11

Rue was out of bed with the first crow of Wilbur's pet rooster, but when she reached the kitchen, wearing boots, jeans and a chambray work shirt left behind on her last visit, Farley was already there. He'd built a fire in the wood cookstove and had used Gramps's old enamel pot to brew coffee. He was reading intently from his how-things-work book.

She decided to demonstrate the automatic coffeemaker another time; Farley would have enough to think about, between grasping the ways ranching had changed since the 1890s and dealing with the cowboys. He would not be given their respect and allegiance simply because he was the foreman; he would have to earn them.

Rue kissed the marshal's cleanly shaved cheek

and glanced again at the book he was devouring with such serious concentration. He was studying the inner workings of the combustion engine, and she could almost hear his brain cataloging and sorting the new information.

"'Morning," he said without looking up from the diagram that spanned two pages.

Rue got a cup and went to the stove for coffee. The warmth of the wood fire seemed cozier, somehow, than the kind that flowed through the heat vents from the oil furnace. "Good morning, Mr. Ford."

"Mmm-hmm," Farley said.

Rue was gazing out the window over the sink, watching as big, wispy flakes of November snow began to drift down past the yard light from a gray-shrouded sky. Silently, she marveled that she'd stayed away from the land so long, loving it the way she did. She'd let things go where the ranch was concerned, having her accountants go over the books, but never examining them herself, hiring one foreman after another by long-distance telephone without meeting them, sizing them up.

Sorry, Gramps, she said silently.

Wilbur had bacon and eggs in the refrigerator—he had spent the night in the bunkhouse with the other men now that Rue was back—so she made a high-fat, high-cholesterol and totally delicious breakfast. "We'll have to go into town and stock up on groceries," she said, serving the food. "Then I'll introduce you to the men, and you can choose a horse."

By that time, Farley had finished reading about

car engine motors, but he looked sort of absent-minded, as if he was still digesting facts and sorting ideas. A light went on in his eyes, though. "A horse?" he echoed.

Rue grinned, a slice of crisp bacon in one hand. "Horses are still fundamental to ranching," she said.

"Is this a big spread?"

She told him the acreage, and he whistled in exclamation.

"You raise mostly cattle?"

Rue nodded. "Some horses, too. I'd like to pursue that further, start breeding show stock." She got up and pulled a newspaper clipping she'd spotted earlier from the bulletin board. Wilbur had a habit of saving unusual accounts. "As you can see," she went on, placing the picture of a miniature pony and its trainer next to Farley's plate, "horses come in all shapes and sizes these days."

Farley frowned, studying the photograph. "Tarnation. That little cayoose doesn't even reach the man's belt buckle. Can't be more than two feet high at the withers."

"People breed miniature ponies to show and sell," Rue said, reaching for her coffee. She was prattling, but she didn't care. She enjoyed talking to Farley about anything. "Horses used to be about the size of house cats back in prehistoric times. Did you know that?"

"What good is a two foot horse?" Farley asked practically, letting the history lecture pass without comment. "I don't imagine you could housebreak them like an old lady's pet dog."

Rue laughed. "True enough. And just imagine what it would be like if they jumped up in your lap, the way a cat or a puppy might do." Seeing Farley's consternation, she spoke seriously. "I know in your time every animal had to have a distinct function. Nowadays, people raise all kinds of creatures just because they enjoy it. I know of a woman who raises llamas, for instance, and a man who keeps a little pig as a pet. It even rides in his car."

"You know some strange people," Farley said, and he clearly wasn't kidding.

Rue smiled. "Yes," she agreed. "And the strangest one of all is a United States marshal from 1892."

Farley smiled back, but he was obviously a little tense. He probably felt nervous about meeting the ranch hands; after all, up until then, Rue had been the only modern person he'd had any real dealings with. Now he would have to integrate himself into a world he'd only begun to understand.

Rue touched his hand. "Everything will be fine," she promised. "Hurry up and finish your breakfast, please. I'll show you the horse barn, and then I want to get the grocery shopping out of the way."

After giving her a humorously ironic look, Farley carried his plate to the sink. "Don't nag me, woman," he teased.

Widening her eyes in feigned innocence, Rue chirped, "Me? Nag? Never!"

With a lift of one eyebrow, Farley put on his hat

and the canvas coat he'd been wearing when he and Rue were suddenly hurled into the future. Rue put on a heavy jacket, gloves and a stocking cap, knowing the wind would be ferocious.

The sun had yet to rise, the snow was still coming down, and the cold was keen enough to bite, but Rue's heart brimmed with happiness all the same. Although she hadn't consciously realized the fact before, this ranch was home, and Farley was the man she wanted to share it with.

When they reached the horse barn, the lights were on and one of the hands was helping Wilbur feed and water the valuable geldings and mares. Soldier, the sheepdog, was overseeing the project, and he ran over to bark out a progress report when Rue and Farley appeared.

Farley grinned and affectionately ruffled the animal's ears, one of which was white, the other black. "Good boy," he said.

Rue proceeded along the center of the barn until she came to the stall that held her own mare, Buttermilk. It had been too long since she'd seen the small, yellow horse, and she longed to ride, but there were other things that had to be done first.

She went on to meet Wilbur, who was hobbling toward her.

"Where is that stallion you wrote me about? The one we bought six months ago?"

Wilbur ran his fingers through hair that existed only in his memory. "That would be Lobo. His stall is on the other side of the concrete wall. Had to keep him away from the mares, of course, or he'd tear the place apart."

"Lobo," Rue repeated, well aware of Farley towering behind her. "That's a silly name. You've been watching too many cowboy movies, Wilbur."

The old man winked, not at Rue, but past her right shoulder, at Farley. Obviously Wilbur had pegged the marshal as a kindred soul. "No such thing as too many cowboy movies," he decreed. "Ain't possible. Hell, when the Duke died, those Hollywood folks just stopped making good Westerns altogether."

Rue could feel Farley's questions and his effort to contain them until they were alone again.

"Movies," she said as they rounded the concrete wall Wilbur had mentioned, headed for Lobo's private suite, "are pictures, like on TV, put together to make a story."

"Who's this Duke Wilbur was talking about? I thought we didn't have royalty in America."

Rue grinned, working the heavy latch on the door to the inner stable. "There was a very popular actor called John Wayne. His nickname was the Duke."

Inside his fancy stall, the stallion kicked up a minor fuss. Rue supposed it was some kind of macho thing, a way of letting everybody know he was king of the stables.

"Easy, Lobo," she said automatically.

Farley let out a long, low whistle of admiration as he looked at the magnificent animal through the heavy metal slats of the stall door. "You broke to ride, fella?" he asked, stepping closer.

Rue had been around horses a lot, but she felt as nervous then as she would have if Farley had stood on the threshold of that mysterious doorway in Aunt Verity's house with the necklace in his hand. Either way, he'd have been tempting fate.

"Sure is," Wilbur replied from behind them, before Rue had a chance to answer.

She looked at the horse and then at Farley. "I don't think—"

"Where can I find a saddle?" Farley broke in. The line of his jaw and the expression in his eyes told Rue he would not be dissuaded from riding the stallion.

Wilbur produced the requested tack, along with a bridle and saddle blanket, and Farley opened the stall door and stepped inside, talking quietly to Lobo. Beyond the windows, the snow continued to tumble through the first gray light of morning.

Rue bit her lip and backed up, knowing Farley would never forgive her if she protested further. He was a grown man, he'd probably ridden horses most of his life, and he didn't need mothering.

Wilbur stood back, too, watching closely as Farley slipped the bridle over Lobo's gleaming, ebony head, then saddled the horse with an expertise that made a lump of pride gather in Rue's throat. Finally, he led the animal from the stall and through the outer doorway into the paddock.

Lobo was fitful, nickering and tossing his head and prancing to one side.

"You're sure that stallion is broken to ride?" Rue

asked Wilbur, watching as Farley planted one booted foot in the stirrup and swung himself into the saddle.

"Pretty much," Wilbur answered laconically.

Lobo gave a shriek of outrage at the feel of a man's weight on his back. He set his hind legs, and his coal black flanks quivered as he prepared to rebel. Several of the ranch hands had gathered along the paddock fence to watch.

"Damn it," Rue ground out, "this isn't funny!" She was about to walk up to Lobo and grab hold of his bridle when Wilbur reached out and caught hold of her arm.

"Let the man show what he's made of," he said, and Rue could have sworn those words came not from the mischievous old man beside her, but from her grandfather.

"That's stupid," Rue protested in a furious whisper, even though she knew Wilbur was absolutely right.

Lobo had finished deliberating. He "came unwrapped," as Rue's grandfather used to say, bucking as if he had a twenty pound tomcat burying its claws in his hide.

Farley looked cool and calm. He even spurred the stallion once or twice, just to let Lobo know who was running the show.

Finally, with a disgruntled nicker, the stallion settled down, and permitted Farley to ride him around the paddock once at a trot. The watching ranch hands cheered and whistled, and Rue knew Farley had taken the first step toward making a place for himself at Ribbon Creek.

Farley rode over to the fence and spoke to the men who remained there, and soon he was bending from Lobo's back to shake hands.

Rue gave Wilbur a look fit to scorch steel, then crossed the paddock to speak to Farley. She smiled so that no one, least of all the marshal himself, would get the idea she was trying to boss him around.

"I guess we'd better be getting to town if we're going to get our business done," she said.

Farley nodded and rode toward the stables without protest, dismounting to lead Lobo through the doorway.

The cowboys at the fence greeted Rue pleasantly and then went on about their own tasks. When she stepped inside the stable, Farley had already unsaddled Lobo and was praising the horse in a low voice as he curried him.

"That was some fancy riding, Marshal," she said.

Farley didn't look away from the horse. "This is some pretty fancy stallion," he replied.

Rue nodded and wedged her hands into the pockets of her jacket. "The men seem to like you. I guess you know they'll play some pranks and bait you a little, to see if they can get a rise out of you."

"I know about ranch hands, Rue," he said with gentle amusement in his voice. "Don't worry yourself. The boys and I will get on just fine."

Rue sighed. "Maybe I'm like Wilbur," she said. "Maybe I've seen too many Westerns on TV."

He looked back at her over one shoulder, grinned and shook his head.

"In the movies, the new arrival on the ranch always has to prove himself by showing that he's got the hardest fists and the quickest draw," Rue said a little defensively.

Farley ran those saucy eyes of his over her in a searing sweep. "I haven't seen anybody around this place I couldn't handle," he said. He gave the horse a last wistful look before joining Rue to walk toward the house.

She put a hand on his arm. "Don't worry, Marshal. You'll be back here and in the saddle before you know it."

Since it was a two-mile stretch to the main highway, Rue let Farley drive on the first leg of the journey to town. He swerved right off the road once, and sent the Land Rover barrelling through the creek that had given the ranch its name, whooping like a Rebel soldier leading a raid.

Rue decided he was better at riding horses.

The drive into town took another half an hour. By the time they arrived, the community's one supermarket was open for business.

Even though he'd been to the mall outside Seattle and had driven across three states with Rue, Farley was still stricken mute with amazement when he walked into the market and saw the wide aisles and the colorful, complicated displays of boxes and cans and bottles. He jumped when the sprayers came on over the produce, and his eyes widened when he saw the pyramids of red apples and plump oranges. In the meat department, he stood watching a mechanized cardboard turkey until Rue finally grabbed his sleeve and pulled him away.

When they finally returned to the parking lot to load two bulging cartfuls of food into the back of the Land Rover, the marshal was looking a little dazed. All during the ride home, he kept turning around in the passenger seat and plundering products from the bags. He read the boxes and labels letter by letter, it seemed to Rue, frowning in consternation.

"No wonder you women are getting into so much trouble with your short dresses and all," he finally remarked when they were turning off the highway onto the ranch. "Everything can be cooked in five or ten minutes, and you've got all sorts of contraptions besides, like that washing machine. You've got too much free time."

Rue smiled. "I'm going to let you get by with that chauvinistic observation just this once, since for all practical intents and purposes, you're new in town."

"Chauvinistic?" Farley looked puzzled, but certainly not intimidated.

"It's another word for a hardheaded cowboy from 1892," Rue replied. Then she proceeded to explain the finer points of the definition.

Farley sighed when it was over. "I still think you've got too much free time," he said. He was gazing out at the snow-dusted plains of the ranch, and the longing to escape the confines of the Land Rover was clearly visible in his face.

"I guess you'll want to saddle one of the horses and look the place over on your own," Rue observed, pulling to a stop in front of the house.

He grinned with both relief and anticipation, and the moment they'd taken the grocery bags into the house, he headed for the barn.

Knowing Farley needed private time to acclimatize himself, Rue put away the food, then retired to the study to make some calls. Farley's old-fashioned insistence that they needed to be married had never been far from her mind and, due to her wide travels, she had contacts in virtually every walk of life.

It wasn't long before she'd arranged a legal identity for Farley, complete with a birth certificate, Social Security number, S.A.T. scores and even transcripts from a midwestern college. All the necessary paperwork was on its way by express courier.

Farley hadn't returned by noon, when a new snow began to powder the ground, so Rue made a single serving of vegetable-beef soup and sat by the big, stone fireplace in the parlor, her feet resting on a needlepoint hassock.

Once she was finished eating, Rue immediately became bored. She went to the woodshed and split a pile of pine and fir for the fireplace. She was carrying the first armload into the house when Farley appeared, striding toward her from the direction of the barn.

His smile was as dazzling as sunlight on ice-crusted snow as he wrested the wood from Rue's arms and carefully wiped his feet on the mat outside the back door. Obviously the ride had lifted his spirits and settled some things in his mind, and she found herself envying him the fresh air and freedom.

"At least you haven't come up with a machine to chop wood," he said good-naturedly, carrying his burden through the kitchen after seeing that the box by the cast-iron cookstove was full.

Rue followed, marveling at the intensity of her re-actions to his impressive height, the broad strength of his shoulders, the muscular grace of his arms and legs. "We can get married in a few days," she said, feeling slightly foolish for her eagerness. "The sys-tem recognizes you as a real, flesh-and-blood per-son."

Farley laid the wood on the parlor hearth, pulled aside the screen and squatted to feed the fire. "That sounds like good news," he commented wryly, "though I've got to admit, I can't say I'm entirely sure."

Rue smiled. "Trust me," she said. "The news is good. Are you hungry?"

Farley closed the fireplace screen and stood. "Yes, but I can see to my own stomach, thank you." He went into the kitchen, with Rue right behind him, and took a frozen entrée from the fridge.

Rue watched with amusement as Farley read the instructions, then set the dish inside the microwave and stood staring at the buttons. She showed him how to set the timer and turn on the oven.

He took bread from the old-fashioned metal box on the counter, and his expression was plainly disapproving as he opened the bag and pulled out two slices. "If a man tried to butter *air,* it would hold up better than this stuff," he remarked scornfully, evidently wanting to let Rue know that not everything about the twenty-first century was an improvement over the nineteenth. He held up a slice and peered at Rue through a hole next to the crust. "It's amazing you people aren't downright puny, the way you eat."

Rue laughed and startled Farley by jumping up and flinging her arms around his neck. "I never get tired of listening to you talk, lawman," she said, and her voice came out sounding husky. "Tell me you won't ever change, that you're always going to be Farley Haynes, U.S. Marshal."

He set the bread aside and cupped her chin in one hand. "Everybody changes, Rue," he said quietly, but there was a light in his eyes. She knew he was going to kiss her, and the anticipation was so intense that she felt unsteady and interlocked her fingers at his nape to anchor herself.

The bell on the microwave chimed, and hunger prevailed over passion. Farley stepped gracefully out of Rue's embrace and took his food from the oven.

It was a curious thing, being moved emotionally and spiritually by the plain sight of a man eating spaghetti and meatballs from a cardboard plate, but that was exactly what happened to Rue. Every time she thought she'd explored the depths of her love for this man, she tumbled into some deeper chasm not yet charted, and she was amazed to find that the inner universe was just as vast as the outer one.

Shaken, she tossed her hair back over one shoulder and stood with her hands resting on her hips. "I'm really in trouble here, Farley," she said, only half in jest. "It seems I want to cook for you and wash your clothes and have your babies. We're talking rapid retrograde, as far as women's rights are concerned."

Farley smiled and stabbed a meatball with his fork. "I imagine you'll be able to hold your own just fine," he said, and Rue wondered if he knew how damnably appealing he was, if his charm was deliberate.

That afternoon, while Farley was out somewhere with Wilbur and the dog, Rue dusted off her grandmother's old cookbooks and hunted down a recipe for bread. When the marshal returned, the dough was rising in a big crockery bowl, and the air was still clouded with tiny, white particles.

Farley's turquoise eyes danced as he hung up his hat and gunslinger coat. "Somebody dynamite the flour bin?"

Rue was covered in white dust from head to foot, but, by heaven, those Presbyterians back in 1892 Pine River had nothing on her. As soon as the dough had puffed up for the second time, she would set it in the oven to bake, and Farley would have the kind of bread he was used to eating.

Sort of.

She thought of the vast differences between them, and the very real danger that they might be parted by forces they could neither understand nor control.

All the rigors of past days caught up with her…all of a sudden, and Rue felt some barrier give way inside her.

She was stricken with what women of Farley's generation would have called "melancholia," she guessed, or maybe she was pregnant. The only thing she was certain of was that for the next little while, she wasn't going to be her usual, strong self.

Rue let out a wail of despair, covered her floury face with her floury hands and sobbed. Out on the utility porch, Soldier whined in unison.

Smelling of soap and clean, country snow, Farley came to her and gently pulled her hands down. His mouth quirked at one corner, and his eyes were still shining with humor.

"Stop that crying," he scolded huskily, wiping a tear from her cheekbone with the side of one thumb. "You're going to paste your eyelids together."

"I don't…even know…why I'm…acting like this!" Rue babbled.

Farley kissed her forehead, no doubt leaving lip prints. "You've been through a whole lot lately, and you're all tired out," he said. Then he led her into one of the downstairs bathrooms, ran warm water into the sink and tenderly, carefully washed her face.

The experience in no way resembled lovemaking, and yet the effect was just as profound.

After that, Farley carried her into the parlor, laid her on the big leather sofa and covered her with the lovely plaid throw she'd brought home from a trip to Scotland. She lay sniffling while Farley went to build up the fire.

"This is really unlike me," she whimpered.

"I know," he answered, his voice low and laced with humor. "Just close your eyes and rest awhile, Rue. I'll look after you."

Rue was used to taking care of herself, for the most part. Aunt Verity and Elisabeth had coddled her when she came down with a head cold or the flu, but having a man's sympathy was an entirely new experience. The sensation was decadently delicious, but it was frightening, too. She was afraid that if she laid down her sword even for a little while, it would prove too heavy to lift when the time came to fight new battles.

Chapter 12

Rue hadn't suffered through her bread-baking crisis for nothing. After she'd enjoyed the crackling parlor fire and Farley's pampering for half an hour, she returned to the kitchen and tackled the remainder of the job.

While the loaves were baking, filling the room with a very promising fragrance, Rue put game hens on the portable rotisserie, washed some russet potatoes for baking in the microwave and poured a can of cooked carrots into a saucepan to heat.

Farley had gone out to help with the evening chores, and when he returned, Rue had set the kitchen table with her grandmother's favorite china and silver. She'd exchanged her flour-covered clothes for a set of black lounging pajamas with metallic silver stripes, put on a little makeup and swept up her hair.

When the cold Montana wind blew Farley in, he stood staring at her, at the same time trying unsuccessfully to hang his hat on the peg next to the door. "How soon did you say we'd be getting married?" he asked.

Rue smiled, pleased, and lifted one shoulder. "Three or four days from now, if all goes well." She sighed. "Too bad you're such a prude. Montana nights can get very cold, and it would be nice to have somebody to snuggle with."

Farley was unbuttoning his coat. "Seems to me Montana nights can turn hot even in the middle of a snowstorm," he retorted hoarsely. He walked to the sink, rolling up the sleeves of his shirt as he went, and washed his hands as thoroughly as any surgeon would have done.

Proudly, Rue served the dinner she'd made, and Farley made it obvious that he enjoyed the fare, and even though the bread was a little on the heavy side, he didn't comment.

After eating, they washed and dried the dishes together—Rue never mentioned the shiny, perfectly efficient built-in dishwasher—and they went into the parlor. Rue had hoped for a romantic interlude in front of the fire, but Farley, having apparently absorbed everything in his how-things-work book, had gone to Gramps's bookshelf for another volume. This time, it seemed, he'd decided to investigate the secrets of indoor plumbing.

Resigned, Rue got out her laptop computer, and soon her fingers were flying over the keyboard. It seemed more important than ever to record what had happened to Elisabeth, and to her and Farley because of the strange antique necklace Aunt Verity had left as a legacy.

Rue had written several pages when she realized Farley was watching her. She glanced at him over her shoulder. He was next to her on the couch, holding his place in his book with a thumb. He'd already read nearly half the volume, which was incredible, given the technical nature of the material.

She smiled, reading the questions from his eyes and the furrows in his brow. "This is a computer, Farley. If I were you, I'd make that my next reading project. The modern world runs on these handy little gadgets."

Farley had seen the laptop before, of course, but never while it was running. "Light," he marveled. "You're writing words with *light* instead of ink."

As usual, his wonderment touched Rue deeply. He'd made such a profound difference in her life simply by being who he was, and even though she had been happy and fulfilled before she'd met him, Rue cherished the special texture and substance he gave to her world.

She showed him how to work the keyboard, and she watched with delight as he read from the screen.

All in all, it was a wonderful evening.

In the morning, Farley was up and gone before Rue even opened her eyes. She stumbled in and out of the shower, dressed warmly and went down to the kitchen for coffee. Since Soldier was whimpering on the back porch, she let him in to lie contentedly on the hooked rug in front of the old cookstove.

Farley had left a note on the table, and Rue read it while the water for her instant coffee was heating in the microwave.

Rue,
It might be a long day. The snow is getting deeper, and Wilbur and the others think some of the cattle may be in trouble out on the range. Stay close to the house; folks have been lost in weather like this. Warm regards,
F.H.

"'Warm regards,'" Rue scoffed, turning to the dog, who lifted a single ear—the black one—in polite inquiry. "I give the man my body, and he signs notes 'warm regards.' And this command to stay in the house! What does he think I am? A child? A greenhorn? Next he'll be tying a rope between the back porch and the chicken coop so I don't get lost in the blizzard when I gather the eggs!"

Soldier whimpered and lowered his muzzle to his outstretched paws, eyeing Rue balefully.

"Oh, you're right," she conceded, though not in a generous way. "I'm being silly. Farley is a man of the 1890s, and it's perfectly natural that he sees things from a very different angle."

She went to the window and felt a vague sense of

alarm at the depth of the snow. The drifts reached halfway up the fences and mounded on the sills, and shimmering, pristine flakes were still whirling down from a fitful sky.

Rue drank her coffee, poured herself a bowlful of cereal and began to pace. She was an active person, used to a hectic schedule, and the sense of being trapped in the house made her feel claustrophobic.

She went upstairs and made her bed, and even though she tried to resist, she couldn't. Rue opened the door to the master suite, intending to make Farley's bed, as well, and stopped cold on the threshold.

Farley had already taken care of the task, but that wasn't what troubled Rue so much. A golden chain lay on the bedside table, shimmering in the thin, winter light, and she knew without taking a single step closer it was *the* necklace, the magical, deadly, ticket-through-time necklace she'd purposely left on Aunt Verity's parlor mantel.

Rue sagged against the doorjamb for a moment, one hand cupped over her mouth. The discovery had been as startling as a sudden earthquake, and the implications crashed down on her head with all the weight of timbers shaken loose from their fittings.

Farley knew about the pendant, knew about its power. He could only have brought it along for one reason: he didn't intend to stay in this time with Rue, despite all his pretty talk about their getting married. This was only a cosmic field trip to him; he planned to return to 1892, to his jailhouse and his horse and women who never wore pants!

She started toward the necklace, possessed by a strange, tender spite, fully intending to carry the thing into the master bathroom and flush it. In the end, though, she retreated into the hallway, afraid to touch the pendant for fear that it might send her spiralling into some other period in time.

The distant toot of a horn distracted her, and she was grateful. She ran down the main staircase, one hand trailing along the banister, and bounded out onto the porch without bothering to put on her coat.

A white van had labored up the road from the highway. The logo of an express-courier company was painted brightly on its side, and the driver came cheerfully through the gate in the picket fence and up the unshoveled walk.

"Rue Claridge?" he inquired.

Rue nodded, hugging herself against the cold, her thoughts still on the necklace.

The courier handed her a package and pointed out a line for her signature. "Sure is a nasty day," he said.

Rue had long ago made a personal pledge to fight inanity wherever she encountered it, but she was too distracted to do battle that day. "Yes," she muttered, scrawling her name. "Thank you."

She fled into the house a moment later and tore open the packet. Inside were the papers her somewhat shady acquaintance had assembled for Farley.

Tears filled her eyes, and her throat thickened. Maybe he didn't intend to marry her at all. Or perhaps he'd planned to go through with the ceremony and then blithely return to 1892, leaving his bride behind to cope as best she could....

Soldier was in the kitchen, and he suddenly started to bark. Grateful for the distraction, Rue headed in that direction, the express packet still in her hand.

Through the window in the back door, she saw Wilbur standing on the porch, smiling at her from beneath the brim of his hat. She was surprised, having gotten the impression from Farley's note that the old man had gone out to help with the cattle.

Rue opened the door. "Hi, Wilbur. Got time for a cup of coffee?"

Her grandfather's old friend looked a little wan. "It isn't often that I turn down the opportunity for a chat with a pretty lady," he said, "but the truth is that I'm under the weather today. I wondered if you could pick up my prescription for me, if you were going to town or anything."

Rue took a closer look at the old man. "You come in here and sit down this instant," she ordered in a firm but friendly tone. "Of course, I'll get your medicine, but why didn't you have the store deliver it?"

"Costs extry," said Wilbur, hanging up his hat and slowly working the buttons on his ancient coat. He took a chair at the kitchen table and accepted the coffee Rue brought to him with a philosophical sigh.

"For heaven's sake," she scolded good-naturedly, sitting down with her coffee, "you're not poor, Wilbur." She knew that was true; Gramps had provided well for the faithful employee in his will. "Besides, you can't take it with you."

Wilbur smiled, but his hand trembled as he lifted his cup to his mouth. "You young people gotta spend a nickel or it burns a hole in your pocket."

Rue leaned forward, frowning. "What kind of medicine are you taking, anyway?"

"Just some stuff that jump starts the old ticker," he replied with a sort of blithe weariness.

In the next instant, Wilbur's coffee clattered to the table. Brown liquid stained the cloth, and the old man clutched at his chest, a look of helpless bewilderment contorting his face.

"Oh, my God," Rue gasped, jumping up, rushing to him and grabbing his shoulders. "Wilbur, don't you do this to me! Don't you dare have a heart attack in my kitchen!" Even as she spoke the words, she knew how inane they were, but she couldn't help saying them.

He started to fall forward, making a choking sound in his throat. Soldier hovered nearby, whimpering in concern. Rue gently lowered her friend to the floor and loosened the collar of his shirt—a handmade one, Western cut with pearl snaps—that was probably older than she was.

"Hold on," she said urgently. "I'll have some help out here right away. Just hold on!"

She stumbled to the phone on the wall, punched out 911. Wilbur lay moaning on the floor, while Soldier helpfully licked his face.

"This is Rue Claridge out at Ribbon Creek," she told the young man who answered her call. "A man has collapsed, and I think he's having a heart attack."

"Is he conscious? Breathing?"

Rue glanced nervously toward her patient. "Yes. I think he's in extreme pain."

The operator was reassuringly calm. "We're on our way, Miss Claridge, but the roads are bad and the trip is bound to take some time. Are you trained to administer CPR?"

Rue nodded, then realized that was no help and blurted out, "Yes. Tell the paramedics to hurry, will you? We're in the kitchen of the main house."

"Would you like me to stay on the line with you?"

She looked at Wilbur, and her eyes filled with tears at his fragility. "I'd appreciate that—I think I'd better put some blankets over him, though."

"I'll be right here waiting," the dispatcher answered, and the unruffled normalcy of his tone gave Rue a badly needed dose of courage.

She quickly snatched thick woolen blankets from a chest in one of the downstairs bedrooms and rushed back to the kitchen to cover Wilbur, then rushed back to the phone.

"Should I give him water?"

"No" was the brisk and immediate response on the other end of the line. "Can the patient speak?"

Rue rushed back to the old man's side. He was looking up at her with glassy, frightened eyes, and she found herself smoothing his thin hair back from his forehead. "You'll be all right, Wilbur," she said. "Help is on the way. Can you talk?"

He grimaced with effort, but only an incoherent, helpless sound came from his lips. His hands were still pressed, fingers splayed and clutching, against his chest.

Rue spent the next half hour running back and forth between the telephone and the place where Wilbur lay, but it seemed like much longer to her. When she heard a siren in the distance, she felt like sobbing with relief.

"The cavalry's just about to come over the rise," she told Wilbur. "Hold on."

Farley and the others must have heard the siren, too, for the paramedics had just finished loading their charge into the ambulance when the whole yard seemed to be crowded with horses.

"What happened?" Farley asked, reaching Rue's side first. He was gazing speculatively at the vehicle with the spinning red light. "Is this what was making all that racket?"

Rue linked her arm through his and let her head rest against the outside of his shoulder. She hadn't forgotten that he'd brought the necklace to Ribbon Creek, knowing full well what could happen, but she was still in the throes of the current crisis and unable to pursue the point.

Yet.

"Wilbur came by to ask me to pick up his prescription if I went to town," she said. "After a few minutes, he grabbed his chest—" Emotion overcame her, and Farley held her close against his side.

Life was so uncertain, so damn dangerous, she thought. Here today, gone tomorrow. No guarantees. Catch as catch can.

One of the paramedics slammed the rear doors of the ambulance, then the vehicle was reeling away through the ever-worsening weather. The light flung splashes of crimson onto the snow, and the sound of the siren was like big needles being pushed through Rue's eardrums.

With Farley holding her close, Rue's heart was mended, if only briefly, and she could almost believe he hadn't planned to desert and betray her.

She forced herself to look up into his wonderful, rugged, unreadable face. "Are the cattle all right?"

He nodded, this man she loved, this man she'd hoped to spend her life with. "For the moment. Let's get you back in the house before you start sprouting icicles." With that, he ushered her away toward the warmth and light of the kitchen.

And the danger of the necklace.

Perhaps because she was used to crises, Rue quickly regained her composure. There was no point in worrying about Wilbur until she'd heard something from the hospital, and she wasn't sure how to broach the subject of the antique pendant.

"We can get married now," she said with only a slight tremor in her voice, after showing him the paperwork. They were in the parlor, by the fire, sitting on the raised hearth and drinking hot coffee laced with Irish cream. She watched him closely after making the announcement.

"Today? Tomorrow?"

Rue was heartened by his response, but only a little. "I think there's a three-day waiting period and, of course, it would be foolish to try to get into town today."

Farley grinned. "We could make it if we went on horseback."

Rue's heartbeat quickened, but she sternly reminded herself how sneaky men could be. Words were cheap; it was what a person *did* that counted. "Okay, cowboy," she said testily, thrusting out her chin. "You're on."

Farley looked at his feet and the gleaming hardwood floor immediately surrounding them. "On what?"

"I'm accepting your challenge. We're going to put the Land Rover into four-wheel drive and head for town. Just don't blame me if we get stuck and freeze to death!"

The marshal narrowed his eyes, not in hostility, but in confusion. "Wilbur was just saying the other day that women are odd creatures, and he was right. What the devil's gotten into you, Rue?"

"You kept the necklace!" she cried, surprising herself as much as Farley. "How could you do that? How could you pretend that I meant something to you, that you were planning to stay here with me, when all the time you intended to go back!"

Farley gripped her shoulders and lifted her onto her toes. While the gesture was in no way painful, it was certainly intimidating. "I thought you'd forgotten the damn thing," he said, his eyes darkening from turquoise to an intense blue. "I was trying to help."

Rue longed to believe him, and she felt herself

wavering. "Sure," she threw out. "That's why you didn't mention it."

He closed his eyes for a moment, jawline clamped down tight, and if he wasn't feeling pure frustration, he was doing a good job of projecting that emotion. "It's not every day a man jumps over a hundred years like a square on a checkerboard, Rue. I've been thinking about electricity and gasoline engines and computers and supermarkets and shopping malls—and how much I want to sleep with you again. There just wasn't room in my head for that blasted necklace!"

Rue felt herself sagging, on the inside at least. She wondered, not for the first time, whether this man sapped her strength or nurtured it. She let her forehead rest against his shoulder, and he slipped his arms lightly around her waist and kissed the top of her head.

"Let's hitch up your Land Rover," he said with a smile in his voice. "I think I'd better hurry up and marry you before you decide Wilbur's the man for you."

Rue laughed and cried and finally dried her eyes.

Then she grabbed the false papers proving Farley was a real person, smiling at the irony of that, and the two of them headed for town. The conditions were bad, but the snowplows and gravel trucks were out, and the Land Rover moved easily over the slippery highways.

At the courthouse in Pigeon Ridge, Farley and Rue applied for a marriage license, then went to the town's only restaurant to celebrate. The establishment was called the Roost, to Rue's amusement.

She called the hospital in the next town, while Farley's cheeseburger and her nachos were being made, and asked about Wilbur. He had arrived, the nurse told her, but was still in the emergency room.

Farley was poking the buttons on the fifties-style jukebox at their table, frowning the way he always did when something puzzled him.

Rue smiled, fished a couple of coins out of her wallet and dropped them into the slot. "Push a button," she said.

Farley complied, and a scratchy sound followed, then music. A country-western ballad filled the diner, an old song that would, of course, be totally new to the marshal. He grinned. "CDs," he said triumphantly.

"Close," Rue replied, fearing the strength of the love she felt for this man, the depth and height and breadth of it. She explained about 45-r.p.m. records and jukeboxes while they ate. After the meal, she called the hospital again.

Farley was having a second cup of coffee when she returned. "How is Wilbur?" he asked.

Rue sighed and slid back into the booth. "He's going to make it, thank God. He definitely had a heart attack, but he could live a long time yet, if he takes care of himself. I mean to see that he does."

"If Wilbur were a younger man, I'd be jealous."

Rue smiled at Farley's teasing, knowing he was trying to help her over a slick place, so to speak.

"You should be. A guy like Wilbur can drive a woman mad with passion."

"Can we see him?"

She shook her head. "Not today. He needs to rest."

The trip back to the ranch was even more treacherous than the journey into town. Even with four-wheel drive, the Land Rover fishtailed on the icy highway, and finally Farley braced both hands against the dashboard and let out an involuntary yelp of alarm.

"For heaven's sake, Farley," Rue snapped, managing the steering wheel with a skill her grandfather had taught her, "get a grip!"

He thrust himself backward in the seat and pushed his hat down over his eyes, and Rue knew for certain that it wasn't because he wanted to sleep.

She spared one hand from the wheel just long enough to thump Farley hard in the shoulder. "I suppose you think you could do better!"

He pushed the hat back and glared at her. "Lady, I *know* I could do better."

"This superior, know-it-all attitude is one of the many things I don't like about men!" Rue yelled. She wasn't sure *why* she was yelling; maybe it was the stress inherent in the day's events, the tension of driving on such dangerous roads or frustration because it would be three days before she and Farley could be married and he had suddenly decided he had to be a virgin groom. Then again, it could have been because she'd thought she'd escaped the power of Aunt Verity's necklace, only to find that it had followed her.

Very carefully, she pulled to the side of the road.

"All right, wise guy," she challenged, "you can drive the rest of the way home. But when we're both in the emergency room, shot full of painkillers and wrapped in surgical tape and looking like a couple of fugitives from the King Tut exhibit, don't say I didn't warn you!"

Farley had already unfastened his seat belt, and he was opening the door before Rue even finished speaking. "I don't have the first idea what you're talking about," he said evenly, "but I know a dare when I hear one and, furthermore, I don't care for your tone of voice."

They traded places, Rue grimly certain they'd end up in the ditch before they'd traveled a mile, Farley quiet and determined. Much to Rue's relief and, though she wouldn't admit it, her disappointment, they reached the ranch without incident, and Soldier met them in the yard.

"There's a blizzard blowing in," Farley announced, looking up at the sky before he wrapped one arm around Rue and shuffled her toward the house. Even though the gesture was protective, there was something arrogant and proprietary about it, too.

Within an hour, the power had gone off. Farley built up the fire in the kitchen stove, and Rue lit a couple of kerosene lamps she'd found on the top shelf of the pantry. While she read the book she'd started earlier, Farley went over the account books for the ranch. He made notes, paused periodically to slip into deep thought, then went back to the study for more reports and files.

If Rue hadn't known better, she'd have sworn he was auditing her income tax return.

"I'm sorry," she said.

"About what?" Farley asked without looking up. He was making notes on a pad of paper, and every once in a while, he stopped to touch the tip of the pencil to his tongue.

"For yelling before. It's just that—well—it's the necklace. It's really bugging me."

That made him lay down the pencil and regard her somberly. "'Bugging' you?"

"Troubling. Irritating. Farley, this is no time for a lesson in modern vocabulary. I love you, and I'm afraid. That necklace has the power to separate us."

Farley reached across the table and took her hand in his. For a moment, she really thought he was going to say he loved her, too, she believed she saw the words forming in the motion of his vocal cords. In the end, though, he simply replied, "We're going to be married. I don't know how to make my intentions any plainer, Rue."

She traced his large knuckles with the pad of her thumb. When Farley declared his love, it had to be by his own choice and not because she'd goaded him into it. She suspected, too, that men of his time had an even more difficult time talking about their feelings than the contemporary variety did.

"Okay," she finally responded, "but I'm still scared."

Farley gripped her hand and gently but firmly steered her out of her chair and around the table, then into his lap. "Don't be," he muttered, his lips almost touching hers. "Nothing and no one will hurt you as long as the blood in my veins is still warm."

Rue could certainly vouch for the warmth of the blood in *her* veins. She ached with the need to give pleasure to Farley, and to take it, and when he kissed her, tentatively at first and then with the audacity of a plundering pirate, her whole body caught fire.

"Just tell me," she pleaded breathlessly when Farley finally freed her mouth, "that you won't go back to 1892 without me."

The stillness descended on the room suddenly, with all the slicing, bitter impact of a mountain snowslide. Farley thrust Rue firmly off his lap and onto her feet. "I can't promise that," he said.

Chapter 13

Rue clenched her hands into fists and stood beside the table, staring down into Farley's stubborn, guileless face. "What do you mean, you can't promise you won't go back without me?" The question was a whispery hiss, like the sound of water spilling onto a red-hot griddle.

Farley reached out and pulled her back onto his lap. He splayed his fingers between her shoulder blades, offering slight and awkward comfort. "Rue, I was the marshal of Pine River, and I had responsibilities. People trusted me. One day, I just vanished without a fare-thee-well to anybody. Sooner or later, I have to find a way to let those folks know I'm not lying in some gully with a bullet through my head, that I didn't just ride out one day and desert them. I can't make a new life with you until I've made things right back there."

Rue looked away, but she didn't have the strength to escape his embrace again. The day had been long and stressful, and she was drained. "So I was right in the first place," she said miserably. It wasn't often that Rue wanted to be wrong, but this time she would have given her overdraft privileges at the bank for it. "You brought the necklace to Ribbon Creek because you knew you were going back, just like I said. When you claimed you thought I'd forgotten it, well, that was just a smoke screen."

Farley paused, obviously stuck on the term "smoke screen," then he met Rue's gaze squarely. "I'm not the kind of man the Presbyterians entirely approve of," he confessed in a grave tone of voice, "but there's one thing I'm definitely not, and that's a liar. And if you'll search your memory, you'll find that I never promised to stay here."

Rue was aghast. "We took out a marriage license today," she whispered. "Didn't that mean anything to you? Was it just something to do?"

He laid his strong hands to either side of her face, forcing her to look at him, making her listen. "There's nothing I want more than to be your husband," he said evenly. "Unless you change your mind and call off the wedding, we *will* be married. We'll fill this big house with children, and I think I can even set aside my pride long enough to accept the fact that my place at Ribbon Creek came to me by marriage instead of honest effort. But the longer I talk, the more certain I get that I can't leave that other life unfinished."

Rue was exasperated, even though she could see the merit in his theory only too well. "What are you going to do, Farley?" she demanded, and something in her tone made Soldier whimper fretfully from his place on the hooked rug by the stove. "Grab the necklace, click your heels together, make a dramatic landing in 1892 and tell everybody you're a time traveler now?"

He shook his head. "I wouldn't talk about what really happened with anybody but Jon Fortner or your cousin Elisabeth." He frowned, his brows knitting. "You don't suppose they're in any sort of trouble over our being gone all of a sudden like that, do you? After all, we were in their parlor when we disappeared."

Rue was ashamed to realize that the possibility had never crossed her mind. "I imagine the townspeople think I spirited you away to some den of never-ending iniquity. Besides, Jon and Bethie had no motive for foul play. Jon is—was—your friend, and everybody knew—knows."

Farley didn't look reassured, and Rue was almost sorry she'd ever confronted him about the necklace. It was plain that if he'd had any intention of using the pendant to escape her and an admittedly hectic modern world, he hadn't been consciously aware of the fact. No, the marshal had only begun to seriously consider returning to 1892 to tie up loose ends *after* Rue had reminded him that such a thing was possible.

She laid her head against his shoulder. "Don't try to send me off to bed alone tonight, Marshal, because I'm not stepping out of reaching distance. If I have to attach myself to you like one sticky spoon behind another, I'll do it. And I don't give a damn about your silly ideas about keeping up appearances, either. Everybody within a fifty-mile radius of this ranch thinks we're making mad, passionate love every chance we get."

Farley kissed her forehead. "We'll be married soon enough," he said.

The house was cooling off rapidly, since the furnace wasn't working, and the kitchen was the only logical place to sleep. Rue took one of the lamps and went in search of sleeping bags, making a point of going nowhere near the necklace. She returned sometime later to find Farley still absorbed in paperwork. He reminded her of Abraham Lincoln, sitting there in the light of a single lantern, reading with such solemn concentration.

She built up the fire in the wood stove and spread the sleeping bags within the warm aura surrounding it. "What are you doing?" she asked, sitting cross-legged on the floor to watch him.

He scribbled something onto a yellow legal pad and then glanced at her distractedly. "Doing? Oh, well, I'm just writing up some changes we could make—in the way the ranch is being run, I mean."

Rue was heartened that he was thinking of the

ranch from a long-range perspective, but her fear
of being abandoned hadn't abated. Afraid or not,
though, she was tired, and after brushing her teeth
and washing her face, she stripped to her T-shirt and
stretched out on one of the sleeping bags.

The power outage wasn't bothering Farley a bit;
lantern light and wood fires were normal to him.
Rue wasn't above wishing he were a little spooked
by the encroaching darkness and the incessant howl
of the wind; she would have liked for him to join her
in front of the stove. With his arms around her, she
might have been able to pretend there was no danger, just for a little while.

She yawned and closed her eyes. Sleeping on
the kitchen floor reminded her of other nights, long
ago, when Aunt Verity had sometimes allowed Rue
and Elisabeth to "camp out" on the rug in front of
the parlor fire. They had turned out all the lights,
munched popcorn and scared each other silly with
made-up stories about ghosts and vampires and ram-
paging maniacs—never dreaming that something
with equally mysterious powers, an old-fashioned
pendant on a gold chain, lay hidden away among
their aunt's belongings.

Waiting.

Farley continued to read and work on the rough
outline of his plans for the ranch, but every once in
a while, his gaze strayed to Rue, who lay sleeping in
a bedroll in front of the cookstove. Looking at her
tightened his loins and made barbs catch in the ten-

derest parts of his heart, but he wouldn't let himself approach her.

He sighed and took a cold, bitter sip from his mug, rather than pass Rue to get fresh coffee from the pot on the stove. If he got too close, he knew he'd end up pulling that peculiar-looking nightdress off over her head and making love to her until the sun came up.

The lights flared on just as dawn was about to break, and Farley switched them off so Rue wouldn't be disturbed, then he went upstairs to shower and change clothes. After last night's storm, there would be plenty to do.

As he entered the room he would soon be sharing with Rue, Farley looked at the big, welcoming bed and wondered if he was losing his mind. Rue was so beautiful, and he wanted her so much. Refusing to sleep with her now was like putting the lid back on the bin after the mice had gotten to the potatoes, and he knew she was right in believing that her reputation was long gone. Still, he wanted to offer her a tribute of some sort, and honor was all he had.

The necklace glittered on the nightstand, as if to attract his attention, and he reached for it, then drew back his hand. He'd be returning to 1892, all right, but only long enough to put his affairs in order. Then he would come straight back to Rue. He didn't intend to go before he'd married her, at any rate, nor would he leave without saying goodbye.

He made his way into the bathroom, kicked off his boots and peeled away his clothes. By then he'd figured out the plumbing system, thanks to one of the books he'd found in the study, and when there was no hot water, he knew it was going to take a while for the big heater downstairs to return to the proper temperature.

Resigned, Farley went back to the bed, crawled under the covers because he was naked and the room was still frigidly cold, and immediately felt the fool for being afraid of a little geegaw like that necklace. He reached out and closed his hand over it and, in the next instant, the room rocked from side to side. It was as though somebody had grabbed the earth and yanked it out from under the house like a rug.

Farley felt the firm mattress go feathery soft beneath him, and he bolted upright with a shout. "Rue!" He was sweating, and he could feel his heart thundering against his breastbone, as if seeking a way to escape.

He knew immediately that he was in a different room, in a different house. He could make out blue wallpaper, and the bed, an old four-poster with a tattered canopy, faced in another direction. And those things were the least of his problems.

Not only had Farley landed in a strange bed, there was someone sharing it. At his shout, a plump middle-aged woman in a nightcap let out a shriek loud enough to hasten the Resurrection, bounced off the mattress and snatched up a poker from the nearby hearth.

She continued to scream while Farley frantically clutched the necklace and willed himself back to Rue. The poker was coming toward his head when the mattress turned hard again and the wallpaper changed to paneling. He hadn't had more than two seconds to acclimatize himself when the bedroom door flew open and Rue burst in. She hurled herself over the foot of the bed and scrambled the rest of the way to Farley on her knees, throwing her arms around his neck when she reached him.

"I heard you yell. You saw something, didn't you? Something happened."

Farley tossed the necklace aside and embraced Rue. She was real and solid, thank God. "Yes," he finally rasped when his breathing had slowed to the point where speech was possible. "Yes."

"What?"

"I don't know. A woman with a poker in her hand—"

Rue drew back, her hands resting on the sides of his face, her eyes full of questions. "You're sure you weren't dreaming?"

Farley laughed, though amusement was about the last thing he felt. "I wasn't dreaming. That woman was as real as you are, and she wasn't pleased to find a naked cowboy in her bed, I can tell you that. Another second and she would have changed the shape of my skull."

Rue turned her head, looking at the necklace lying a few feet away on the carpet. "Farley, let's throw the pendant away before something terrible—and irrevocable—happens. Surely the good people of Pine River hired a new marshal, and Jonathan and

Elisabeth *must* have found a way to explain your disappearance."

Farley gathered Rue close and held her, taking comfort from the soft, fragrant, womanly substance of her. "We can't do that, Rue," he reasoned after a long time. "There's no way of predicting what the consequences might be. Suppose somebody found it, a child maybe? No, we've got to hide that pendant and make damn sure it stays put."

She buried her face in his chest, that was all, but the surface of Farley's skin quivered in response, and he felt himself come to attention. "I'm scared," she said, her voice muffled by his flesh.

Farley wanted Rue more than ever, having been separated from her by a wall of time, but he was strong and stubborn, and so were his convictions. The next time he made love to Rue, she would bear his name as well as the weight of his body.

Her hand trailed slowly down over his chest and belly, leaving a sparkling trail of stardust in its wake. Then she captured him boldly.

He groaned in glorious despair. "Damn it, Rue, let go."

She did not obey. "You're bigger and stronger," she teased in a whimpery voice. "But I declare, Marshal, I don't see you trying to wrest yourself free of my sinful attentions."

Farley fully intended to pull her fingers away, but his hands went instead to the sides of her head. With a strangled cry, he kissed her, his tongue invading her mouth, plundering. And still she worked him mercilessly with her hand.

He broke away from the kiss, gasping. "Oh, God, *Rue*—"

She teased his navel with the tip of her tongue. "You promised not to make love to me again until we were married," she said, and he trembled in anticipation, knowing what was going to happen. "I, on the other hand, never said anything of the kind."

Farley felt her moving downward and groaned, but he could not make himself stop her. When Rue took him, he gave a raspy cry of relief and surrendered to her.

Later, Farley left the bed, showered and went about the business of running a ranch. Rue took a pair of tweezers from her makeup case, picked up the necklace, which was still lying on the floor where Farley had thrown it after his unscheduled flight into history, and dropped it gingerly into a big envelope.

She held the envelope by a corner, carrying it downstairs and laying it on the desk in the study. She opened the safe hidden behind her grandmother's bad painting of a bowl of grapes, expecting to find it empty since she had long since gone through all her grandfather's papers. To her surprise, however, there was a thin envelope of white vellum inside, and when she pulled it out, a chill went through her.

The handwriting on the front was old and faded and very familiar, and it read, "Miss Rue Claridge, Ribbon Creek, Montana." There was even a zip code, a fact that might have made Rue smile if she hadn't been so shaken. The date on the postmark was 1892.

She let the other envelope, containing the necklace, drop forgotten to the floor and sank into a chair, her heart stuffed into her throat.

Apparently the letter had been delivered to Gramps, and he'd saved it for her, probably never noticing the postmark or the antiquated ink.

Rue drew in a deep breath and sat up very straight. If the letter had been delivered to the ranch, why hadn't she found it before, when she'd settled Gramps's affairs? Come to that, why was any of this happening at all?

The only explanation Rue could think of was that Farley was going back to 1892 in the near future, if he hadn't done so already. And this was the only way he could contact her, by writing a letter that would be misplaced and passed from person to person for a hundred years.

Fingers trembling, Rue opened the envelope and pulled out a single, thin page. Stinging tears came instantly to her eyes. These words had been written over a century before by a man she'd brazenly made love to only that morning.

My Dearest Rue,

I'm writing this to say goodbye, even though I know my words will be confusing to you when and if you ever lay eyes on them. Maybe you'll not see this page at all, but I don't mind admitting I take some comfort from the writing of it.

I never meant to leave you forever, Rue, especially not on our wedding day; I want you to know that. My love for you is as constant as my breath and my heartbeat, and I will carry that adoration with me into the next world, where the angels will surely envy it.

I have every confidence that if a child is born of our union, you will raise our son or daughter to be strong and full of honor.

I'm staying here at the Pine River house, having been shot last week when there was a robbery at the bank. Oftentimes, I wonder if you're in another room somewhere, just beyond the reach of my eyes and ears.

When last I saw your cousin Lizzie, which was just a little while ago when she came to change my bandages, she was well. She saw that I was writing you and promised to help me think of a way to get the letter to you, and she asked me to give you her deepest regards.

I offer mine as well.

With love forever,

Farley.

Rue folded the letter carefully and tucked it back into the envelope, even though there was a wild fury of panic storming within her. She wanted to scream, to sob, to refuse to accept this fate, but she knew it would be useless.

Farley was going back; the letter was tangible proof of that. And he was dying from the wounds he'd received during the robbery. He hadn't come right out and said that, but she had read the truth between the lines.

She pushed the envelope under the blotter on the desk. She wanted to confront Farley with what she'd discovered, but she couldn't. For one thing, he hadn't done anything wrong; it was his life, and if he wanted to go back to 1892 and throw it away in a gunfight with a pack of outlaws, that was his prerogative. No, Farley wasn't the only one with integrity; Rue had it, too, and in those moments, the quality was her greatest curse.

Rue paced. She could warn him. Maybe if she did that, he would at least avoid stumbling into that bank at the wrong moment and getting himself killed.

Finally she remembered the registry at the graveyard in Pine River, got the number from information and put a call through. After half an hour and a string of hassles that heightened her frustration to new levels, a clerk in the church office finally unearthed an old record book and found Farley's name in it.

"Yes, he's listed here," the woman said pleasantly. "His grave would be out in the old section, under the oak tree. I hope that helps. It might be hard to find otherwise. Not everyone had a stone, you know, and a wooden marker would be long gone."

Rue squeezed her eyes shut, almost overwhelmed by the images that were filling her mind. "Does the record list a cause of death?" she asked, her voice thin.

"Gunshot wound to the chest," the clerk replied

after a pause. "He was attended by Dr. Jonathan Fortner, a man who played quite an important part in the history of Pine River—"

"Thank you," Rue said, unable to bear another word, even though it meant cutting the woman off in the middle of a sentence. Her eyes were awash in tears when she hung up the receiver. Soldier came and leaned against her leg, whining in sympathy.

Rue knew it might be hours until Farley returned, and she couldn't stand to stay in the house, so she went out to the woodshed and split enough firewood to last through a second ice age. When that was done, she started up the Land Rover, Soldier happily occupying the passenger seat, and headed out over roads of glaring ice.

It took an hour to reach the hospital in the next town over from Pigeon Ridge. Leaving the dog in the Land Rover, Rue went inside and bought a card in the small gift shop, then asked to see Wilbur.

He'd spent the night and most of the day in intensive care, a nurse told her, but she supposed one visit would be all right if Rue kept her stay brief.

She found him in Room 447, and although there were three other beds, they were all empty. Wilbur looked small and forlorn, with tubes running into his nose and the veins of both his wrists.

"Hello, Wilbur." Rue set the card on his nightstand, then bent to kiss his forehead.

He looked surprised at his misfortune, and helpless.

Rue blinked back tears and patted his arm.

"That's all right, I know you can't talk right now. I just wanted to stop by and to say hello and tell you not to worry about Soldier. I'm taking good care of him. In fact, he's out in the car right now—it was as close as the nurses would let him get."

Wilbur made a funny noise low in his throat that might have been a chuckle.

"I'd better go," Rue said. "I know you need to rest and, besides, you won't want me hanging around when all your girlfriends come in." She touched his shoulder, then left the room. In a glance backward, she saw him reach awkwardly up to catch hold of the get-well card she'd brought.

For all her activity, Rue had not forgotten Farley's letter for a moment. She circled the thought the way a she wolf might move around a campfire, fascinated but afraid to get too close.

The sun was out when Rue returned to the Land Rover, and the ice seemed to be thawing, but it still took forever to get home, because there were so many accidents along the way. When she and Soldier arrived, Farley and the other men were driving several hundred head of cattle into the big pasture west of the house, where a mountain of hay and troughs of fresh water awaited.

Rue started toward Farley, fully intending to tell him about the letter she'd found in the safe, but the closer she got, the more convinced she became that it would be impossible. She could barely think of being parted from him, let alone talk about it.

She stopped at the fence, listening to the bawling

of the cattle, the yelling and swearing of the cowboys, the neighs and nickers of the horses. In those moments as she stood watching Farley work, she realized how simple the solution really was.

All she had to do was destroy the necklace. Once that was done, there would be no way for Farley to return to 1892 and get himself shot.

He rode over to look down at her, his face reddened by the cold and his mustache fringed with snow. His smile practically set her back on her heels.

"Where have you been?" he asked. He didn't sound annoyed, just curious.

"I went in to see Wilbur at the hospital. He's doing all right." The words brought an image of a wounded Farley to mind, a man dying in another time and place, close enough to touch and yet so far away that even science couldn't measure the distance.

Farley shook his head. "You've got no business driving on these roads."

Rue wanted to weep, but she smiled instead. "Are you jealous, Farley?" she teased, stepping close to Lobo and running a finger down the inside of the marshal's thigh. "Think I'm paying Wilbur too much attention?"

Farley shivered, but Rue knew it wasn't from the cold. He'd loved the game they'd played that morning, and her attempt to remind him of it had been successful. He bent down and exclaimed in a low voice, "You little wanton. I ought to haul you off to the woodshed and blister your bustle!"

"Very kinky," she said, her eyes twinkling even as

tears burned at their edges. Then, before he could ask for the inevitable definition, she turned and walked toward the house.

That night, the power stayed on and the wind didn't blow. Rue and Farley curled up together on the couch in the big parlor and watched television. At least, Farley watched—Rue alternated between thinking about the necklace and about the letter hidden beneath the desk blotter.

Although they didn't make love, Farley seemed to know Rue would not be separated from him, and they shared the large bed in the master bedroom. He held her and for the time being that was enough.

Contrary to her expectations, she slept, and the next thing she knew, Farley was kissing her awake.

"Get up," he said, his breath scented with toothpaste. "Today is our wedding day."

Some words from the letter he didn't know he'd written echoed in Rue's heart. "I never meant to leave you forever, especially not on our wedding day." Unless she did something and soon, she would become Farley's wife and his widow without turning a single page of the calendar in between.

"I love you," she said, because those were the only safe words.

He kissed her lightly and quoted a mouthwash commercial they'd seen the night before. One thing about television, it had an immediate impact.

Rue got out of bed, passed into the bathroom and brushed her teeth. When she came back, Farley was gone.

Panic seized her. With another man, she would only have thought he'd left the room, or maybe the house. Farley might have left the century.

Dressed in jeans and a warm woolen shirt, she raced into the hallway and down the stairs. "Farley!"

He was in the kitchen, calmly sipping coffee, and he smiled at Rue with his eyes as he took in her furious expression. "A body would almost think you'd been left at the altar, the way you carry on when I get out of sight."

Looking up at him, Rue ached. Why did it all have to be so complicated? Other people had problems, sure, but not this kind. "Farley, the necklace—"

"I know where it is," he said calmly. "The safe, behind that painting of the fruit."

Rue paled. "But you couldn't have known the combination."

He had noticed her terror by then, and he reached out with his free hand to caress her jaw. "I found it when I went through the ranch records, Rue," he said quietly. "I checked the safe to see if there were any more reports to go over."

Rue closed her eyes, swayed slightly and was steadied by Farley's firm grip. "But the necklace is still there?" she asked evenly, reasonably. "You didn't move it, did you?"

"No," he answered. "But I want your promise that you won't move it again, either. I need to know where it is, Rue. Now, for the moment, all I want you thinking about is becoming my wife." He bent his head, bewitched her with a soft kiss. "I hope you're planning to wear something pretty, though. I draw the line at a bride wearing trousers."

Chapter 14

Rue struggled to maintain her composure; in all her travels as a reporter, she'd never faced a greater challenge than this one. "Farley," she began reasonably, "you've got to listen. If you go back to 1892, you'll die."

He touched her face. "Everybody dies, darlin'," he answered gently. "Considering that I was born in 1856, I've outlived a number of folks already."

She stepped back, raised her fingertips to her temples. It sounded as if Farley knew what was going to happen to him if he went back to 1892 and that he'd resigned himself to that fate. "You found the letter, too."

"By accident," he said. "I spilled a cup of coffee on the desk, and when I moved the blotter, I came across an envelope with my own handwriting on it. I would have put it aside if it hadn't been for that."

Rue sagged into one of the kitchen chairs. "You'd go back, knowing you were going to be shot by a bank robber and die of the wounds?"

"I have to settle my affairs, Rue. I told you that. And I'm still the marshal of Pine River, as far as I know. God knows, it wasn't a job the town council would be able to foist off on somebody else without a fight. If there's a holdup, I'll have to do whatever I can to intervene. Besides, I've been warned—I'll just be more careful than usual."

Rue felt sick. This was supposed to be one of the happiest days of her life. And she *was* happy, because she wanted the legal and spiritual bond with Farley no matter what lay ahead—or behind—but she was terrified, as well.

Apparently nothing would shake his determination to return to 1892. That left only one avenue open to his distraught bride-to-be.

"I'm going with you, then."

"Rue—"

"I mean, it, Farley," she interrupted, rising so fast that her chair toppled over backward behind her. She didn't pick it up. "I'm not marrying you so we can be apart. We belong together."

He looked at her for a long time, then sighed. "All right," he agreed reluctantly. He kissed her, then left the house without breakfast.

Rue was still inwardly frantic, but fortunately for her, she had things to do. She called the hospital for a progress report on Wilbur, who was doing well, then emailed her mother, who had no doubt moved on from the spa to one of several favorite ski resorts.

"Mother," it read, "I'm marrying at last, so stop telling your friends I'm an old maid. His name is Farley Haynes, and I adore him. Love, Rue."

The message to Rue's father, who might have been anywhere in the world, but could be counted on to check with his answering service in New York on occasion, was even more succinct. "Dad. By the time you get this, I'll be married. Rue."

With those two tasks out of the way, Rue turned all her concentration to the upcoming wedding. She hadn't brought anything suitable for the ceremony—in fact, she didn't *own* anything suitable. But she remembered the line of trunks in the attic, filled with things from all phases of her grandmother's life. When she was younger, she'd worn those lovely, antique garments to play solitary games of dress-up during long visits.

Naturally, the room at the top of the house was dusty, and the thin winter sunlight barely found its way through the dirty panes of glass in the only window. Rue flipped the light switch and the single bulb dangling in the middle of the ceiling flared to life.

This was a friendly place, though cold and a little musty smelling, and Rue smiled as she entered. If there were ghosts here, they were merry ones come to wish the bride well on her wedding day.

After a few moments of standing still, feeling a reverence for the old times and wondering if her grandmother might not be here after all, young and pretty and just beyond the reach of Rue's senses, she approached the row of trunks.

The sturdy old chests had metal trim, tarnished to a dead-brass dullness by the passing of time, and the stickers plastered to their sides were peeling and colorless. Still, Rue could make out the names of a few places—Istanbul, Prague, Bora Bora.

She smiled. Grammie had been quite the traveler in her youth. What had it been like for such an adventurous woman to settle on a remote ranch in Montana?

Rue knelt in front of the first trunk and laid her palms on its dusty lid. She didn't remember her grandmother, though Gramps and Rue's own mother had spoken of her in only the most glowing terms.

She lifted the lid and right on top, wrapped tightly in yellowed tissue paper, was a beautiful pink satin dress. Rue took a few minutes to admire it, to hold the gown to her front and speculate as to whether or not it would fit, then carefully rewrapped it and returned it to the chest.

Time blew past like the wind flying low over the prairies, and Rue was barely aware of its passing. Going through the things her grandmother had so carefully packed away, she found a lovely calf-length dress of ecru lace, with a modest but enticing neckline, a pearl choker, pale satin slippers that were only slightly too small and a lovely, sweeping straw picture hat with a wide rose-colored ribbon for a band and a nosegay of pink and blue flowers for decoration.

Because the chests were lined with camphor, the fragile old clothes smelled only faintly musty. Totally charmed, the threat of Aunt Verity's necklace held at bay for just a little while, Rue carried the treasures down from the attic and hung the dress on the screen porch to air.

Upstairs again, she gave herself a facial, washed her hair and then took a long, hot bath. She was back in the kitchen sipping from a cup of noodle soup, a towel wrapped around her head turban-fashion, when Farley came in.

"Are you hungry?" Rue asked, lowering her eyes. She'd said and done outrageous things in this man's arms, and it wasn't as if he hadn't seen her in considerably less than a bathrobe, but suddenly she felt shy.

"Yes," he answered with a smile in his voice. "But I'm still planning to wait until after some preacher has said the words that make it all right."

Rue blushed. "I was talking about food."

"I wasn't," Farley replied. "Are we getting hitched here, or do we have to go into town?"

She felt another stream of color rush into her cheeks, but since the previous flood probably hadn't subsided yet, it wouldn't be so obvious. She hoped.

"I arranged for a justice of the peace to come out. It was the same day we got our license."

"Where was I?" Farley hung up his hat and coat, then crossed to the refrigerator and opened the door. It was an ordinary thing, and yet Rue pressed the image into her mind like a cherished photograph. Just in case.

She smiled. "You were playing with the drinking fountain," she said.

Farley took the milk carton out, opened it and started to raise it to his mouth. He went to the cupboard for a glass when he saw Rue's warning glare. "I don't have a ring," he said worriedly, "or a fancy suit."

"You're still going to be the best-looking groom who ever said 'I do,'" Rue retorted, taking the carton from his hand.

He squeezed her bottom through the thick terry cloth of her robe when she bent over to return the milk to the fridge. "And after I've said 'I do,'" he teased huskily, "you can bet that I will."

The justice of the peace, who ran a little bait shop at Ponderosa Lake in the summertime, arrived an hour later.

By then, Farley had showered and changed into clean clothes, and Rue had put on makeup, arranged her hair in a loose Gibson-girl style and donned the lovely, gauzy lace dress and the pearl choker.

A couple of the ranch hands came in to serve as witnesses, wearing shiny, ill-fitting suits that had probably been in and out of style several times. One of the old-timers, Charlie, brought along his new digital camera, fully prepared to record the event.

Rue didn't allow herself to think beyond the now; she wanted to cherish every second for its own sake.

Being a civil ceremony, the wedding itself was

short. Even though Rue was trying to measure out the moments and make them last, the whole thing didn't take more than five minutes. When Farley kissed her, the hat tumbled off her head and the flash of Charlie's camera glowed red through her closed eyelids.

Rue would have been content to go right on kissing her husband, but, of course, they weren't alone, so that was impossible. Hope overflowed her heart as she looked up into Farley's tender eyes, and in those golden moments, she found it impossible to believe that time or trouble or even death could ever separate them.

The justice of the peace left as soon as he'd been paid, but the ranch hands stayed for refreshments, since festive occasions were such a rare treat. Sara Lee provided the wedding cake, which had to be thawed out in the microwave, and coffee and soda completed the menu.

When Charlie wasn't eating, he was taking pictures.

Finally, however, one of the other hands elbowed him in the ribs, then cleared his throat pointedly and suggested that they get back to the bunkhouse and change into their working duds. Some of the cowboys started to protest, then caught on and pushed back their chairs, beaming.

Time was more precious now than ever, so Rue didn't urge the hands to stay. Despite her insistence that Farley take her with him when he went back to 1892, she hadn't forgotten that his letter said he'd gone alone—on their wedding day. She was glad when she and her new husband were finally by themselves.

She unbuttoned the top two buttons of Farley's shirt. "No more virginal protests, Farley," she said, sliding her hand under the soft chambray to find and caress a taut masculine nipple. "You're my husband now, and I demand my rights as a wife."

He chuckled, but the sound was raw with other emotions besides amusement. No doubt he, too, was wondering how much of their destiny could be changed, if any. He swept Rue up into his arms and mastered her with a thorough kiss, then carried her to the bedroom.

"You look so beautiful in that dress," he said after setting her on her feet at the foot of the massive bed. "I almost hate to take it off you."

For Rue time no longer stretched into the past and the future, forming a tapestry with no beginning and no end. Nothing and no one existed beyond the walls of that room, and their union would be eternal.

She didn't speak, but simply began unfastening the pearl buttons at the front of her gown, her chin at a high, proud angle, her eyes locked with Farley's, challenging him to resist her.

He couldn't; sweet defeat was plain in his face, and the knowledge made her jubilant.

The dress fell over her hips, and Rue hung it over the back of a chair, then kicked off the tight slippers. She kept stripping until all that was left was the wide, pearl choker at her throat.

Farley's throat worked visibly as he swallowed, looking at her as if he'd never seen a naked woman before. When Rue lifted her arms to unclasp the choker, Farley rasped, "No. Leave it," and she obeyed him.

He began taking off his own clothes, starting with his boots, setting them aside with a neatness that made Rue impatient. She watched with brazen desire as he removed his shirt, unfastened his belt, stepped out of his jeans.

Finally, Farley stood before her wearing only his skin, and he was as incorrigibly, magnificently male as a wild stallion.

He held out a hand to Rue. "Come here, Mrs. Haynes," he said.

It wasn't the time to say she meant to hyphenate both surnames into one; in that bedroom, alone with her mate, no title suited her better than Mrs. Haynes. Rue yearned to give herself to Farley totally.

She went to him and he drew her upward into his kiss, a tall shaman working his treacherous magic. Rue trembled as she felt his hand cup her breast, and she moaned into his mouth as his fingers lightly shaped the nipple.

As Rue's body was pleasured, so was her soul. There was a joy in the depths of her being that overruled all her fears and doubts and furies. She was, while Farley loved her, in step with a dancing universe.

He continued to worship her with words and kisses and caresses while she stood with her head back, lost in glorious surrender. When he knelt to pay the most intimate homage, she gave a soft, throaty sob and burrowed her fingers in his thick hair, holding him close, stroking the back of his head.

Their lovemaking was woven of silver linings plucked from dark clouds, golden ribbons of sunset and lengths of braided rainbow, formed at once of eternity itself and the most fleeting of moments. Farley's and Rue's souls became one spirit and did not exist apart from each other, and this joining sanctified their marriage in a way an official's words could never have done.

There was no room in Rue for any emotions other than soaring happiness and the most intense pleasure, not while she and Farley were still celebrating their wedding. Finally, however, she dropped off to sleep, exhausted, perspiration cooling on her warm flesh.

Farley held Rue for a long time. He'd heard other men talk about love, but he'd never imagined it could be the way it was for him with this woman.

He kissed the top of her head, even though he knew she wasn't awake to feel the touch of his lips, and his eyes stung. Returning to 1892 wasn't really his choice, as he'd implied to Rue earlier, but it was his fate—he knew that in his bones. The letter, penned in his own handwriting, was irrefutable proof of that.

Farley grew restless. If he managed to circumvent destiny, somehow, and stay here with Rue, would the letter stop existing? Would his fate, or anyone's, be altered?

The room was filling with gray twilight, and Farley felt a chill. He eased himself apart from Rue and went into the bathroom, where he took a shower. Then he put on the same clothes he'd worn earlier, because he'd been married in them and because they'd borne a vague hint of Rue's scent. He stood beside the bed for a long time, memorizing the shape of her face, the meter of her breathing, knowing his heart was beating in rhythm with hers, even though he could hear neither.

"I love you," he whispered raggedly. He knew he should wake her, since any parting could be a permanent one, but he turned away. If he looked into her eyes, he would see the reflection of his own despair, and the pain would be beyond bearing.

Downstairs, Farley put on his coat, took the necklace from the safe, left the house and strode toward the barn. Most of the men were in the bunkhouse, since the day's work was over, but he found Charlie puttering around in the barn.

Farley touched the brim of his hat as he passed the man, but he didn't trust himself to speak. He needed to ride, cold as it was, and let the fresh air clear his mind. Maybe then he could figure out some way to change things.

He entered the separate part of the barn where Lobo was stabled, led the big stallion out of his stall and saddled him. The animal nickered and tossed his head, as eager for the open spaces as Farley was, and it was then that a profound, almost mystical bond took shape between the man and the horse.

Farley led Lobo outside, under a full but icy moon, and swung up into the saddle.

"Everything all right, boss?" Charlie inquired. He was leaning against the paddock fence, Soldier at his side, both of them lonely for Wilbur.

Farley looked around him at the land, the kind of land that could soak up a man's blood and sweat and still make him happy. In his mind the ranch would always be Rue's, even if he managed to keep himself from getting shot back in 1892 and found his way home to her. One day, though, the land on either side of Ribbon Creek would belong to their child, if he'd been fortunate enough to sire one, and Farley wanted to guard the place and make it grow almost as much as he wanted to stay with Rue.

He looked toward the big house, adjusted his hat and finally answered the ranch hand's question. In a way. "You'll look out for her if something happens to me?"

"Exactly what is it you're expectin' to happen to you, Mr. Haynes?"

Farley lifted a shoulder. "Maybe nothing." He reined an impatient Lobo toward the south, where the moon spread silver over the snow.

He rode until neither he nor the horse could travel any farther, until he wasn't even sure he was still within the borders of the ranch. He pulled off his gloves and reached into his coat pocket for the thin cigars he loved, but instead of the package, he felt a cold, fragile chain between his fingers.

He'd tried to forget he was carrying the necklace.

"Go on," he muttered hoarsely, glad nobody was there to hear him talking to a trinket. "Do your worst and get it over with!"

Farley held the pendant up, watched the moonlight do a twinkling dance along the length of the chain. He considered flinging it aside into the snow, but he knew now that that would do no good. A force he did not begin to understand had brought the necklace into his life, for good or evil, and that force would not be denied. He had to tie up the loose ends of his old life so that he could live the new one to the fullest.

"Rue." Her name was a ragged, broken whisper on his lips. Once again, his vision blurred, and he wasn't sure whether the necklace was working its bitter magic or if he was finally giving way to the grief dammed up inside him.

Five minutes passed, then ten, while the stallion rested and Farley waited.

When the transition occurred just as the sun came up, it was a subtle one. There was a roaring in Farley's ears, and Lobo fretted and sidestepped beneath him. The power lines and the distant gray ribbon of the highway dissolved into nothingness.

Farley knew without consulting a calendar that he and the horse were back in his own century, and it was a long way back to Pine River from the Big Sky Country.

Still, he dropped the necklace into his pocket and

rode back to the place where the house should have
been, where Rue should have been drinking coffee in a warm kitchen and Soldier should have been
barking. There was nothing except for an abandoned
cabin and a single grave marked with a wooden cross.

Farley took off his hat for a moment, his throat
thick with misery, his heart full of the kind of loneliness that can drive a person to do stupid, reckless things. He lowered his head for a few moments,
struggling with his emotions, and then turned Lobo
west, toward his destiny.

Rue stirred in her marriage bed, dreaming. She
saw Farley riding alone through a winter dawn, his
horse's gleaming onyx coat contrasting starkly with
the pristine snow. Knowing she could never catch up
with her husband, she struggled to awaken instead.

The instant Rue opened her eyes, however, she
knew the nightmare was real and she hadn't escaped
it. She and Farley had said their vows and consum-
mated them, and now he was gone.

A frantic sob tore itself from her throat and she
covered her face with both hands, trying hard to get
a grip on her emotions. Farley was probably downstairs, reading one of his how-to books with one eye
and watching his favorite TV program with the other.

She jumped out of bed, found her robe, pulled it
on and dashed downstairs.

"Farley?"

The parlor fire was out, and the TV screen was
blank.

Rue hurried into the study, but she knew before she reached it that Farley wouldn't be there. His presence had a substance, an impact all its own, and she felt nothing except a rising numbness.

"Oh, God," she prayed, unable to go farther, stumbling through the darkening house to the kitchen.

No fire in the cookstove, no coffee brewing, no Farley reading at the table.

Rue was still in shock, but she could feel her emotions moving underneath the hard layer of control. Soon they would break through and panic would reign.

She continued to entreat heaven as she ran back up the stairs to shower quickly and dress. Her hair was still damp when she followed Farley's boot prints along the path that led to the barn. She nearly collided with Charlie at the gate.

"He's gone," she choked out miserably when the aging man gripped her shoulders to steady her.

"He took Lobo out hours ago," Charlie said, his craggy, ancient face looking worried in the light of the moon. "I'm going to wake the other men so we can saddle up and start lookin' for him soon as the sun's up."

"I'm going with you," Rue insisted, as if anyone had given her cause to argue. "I think we should start right now."

"Mr. Haynes made me swear to look after you," Charlie said stubbornly. "And lettin' you ride out in the dark of night over dangerous ground ain't my idea of keepin' my promise."

Rue's heart stopped for a moment, and she felt her eyes widen. "Farley asked you to take care of me?" The certainty came to her then that they weren't going to find her husband, no matter how long or how thoroughly they searched, but since the realization wasn't one Rue was ready to accept, she pushed it to the back of her mind.

"That's right," Charlie responded with a nod. "Now, you just go back in that house and mind your p's and q's until we can head out. Remember this, too—you won't be a damn bit of good to the man if you've worked yourself up into a tizzy."

Doing fierce battle with a flock of instincts that bade her to do otherwise, Rue obeyed. She walked stiff legged into the house, brewed coffee, drank a cup and then ran to the bathroom to throw up.

That ruled out the idea of breakfast—she would only have been going through the motions anyway— and her knees were too shaky for effective pacing. She took a chair at the kitchen table and laid her head on her arms.

The pinging of her email made her jump a good six inches off her chair, and she snatched the laptop and yelled, "Farley?" before she realized he wasn't very likely to use email.

Even in the face of logic, however, Rue's disappointment was keen when she had a message from her mother.

"'A set of sterling is on its way. What do you know about this man? Is he a fortune hunter? Have they found poor Elisabeth yet? Do write. Love, Mummy.'"

At least the annoyance of her mother's passionate disinterest had put some starch in her knees and she was able to pace for a while.

Rue even drank another cup of coffee, but that proved to be a foolish choice. She was back in the bathroom, in the midst of violent illness, when she heard the back door open and close.

Quickly, Rue rinsed her mouth and washed her face, but when she hurtled into the kitchen, Farley wasn't there. Charlie was, and he stood, hat in hand, looking worried and authoritative, obviously trying to do and say the things Wilbur would have. The crisis had made him younger and stronger, if only for a little while.

Rue didn't speak. She just put on her winter gear and followed him outside. Her mare, Buttermilk, had been saddled, and all the hands were mounted and ready to ride out.

Lobo had left a trail of hoofprints in the hard snow, and they followed it for several miles, their breaths and those of the horses making white clouds in the bitterly cold air.

The tracks led to the middle of a vast clearing, and there they stopped. Rue, who had been riding in front, alongside Charlie and a younger man called Bill, closed her eyes, absorbing the shattering reality that Farley was gone.

Without her.

Recalling the words of Farley's letter, written from his deathbed, Rue reminded herself that he had left her reluctantly. It was that damn code-of-honor thing, the need to finish all his business before he took up something new.

He was gone, and he surely had the necklace, so there was no way to follow him.

The hands were circled around the pattern of tracks in the snow, exclaiming. Naturally, they'd never seen anything like that before. One even speculated that both Farley and his horse had been abducted by aliens, and Rue wondered disconsolately if that theory was really any stranger than the truth.

Reining Buttermilk toward the house, feeling too broken inside even to cry, Rue let the animal take her home. She was aware of the men riding with her, although she didn't look at them even once.

"I'll get the sheriff out here quick as I can, Mrs. Haynes," said one. "Don't you worry. We'll find your bridegroom."

Tears glittered in Rue's eyes, but she kept her chin high. "They won't find him," she managed to say. "Nobody could find him."

"You don't believe that crackpot idea of Buster's about the spaceship and the little green men, do you?" Bill asked.

Rue meant to laugh, but a sob came out inside. "Right now," she said when she could speak, "I don't know what I believe, but I'm sure of one thing— wherever Farley is, that's where I want to be."

The sheriff came, and he called in the state police. All the ruckus attracted reporters from the tabloids. A week passed, and no trace of Farley or the horse was found, and in every supermarket check-out line in the country, the front page of the *National Scoop* screamed, UFO SNATCHES MAN AND STAL-LION, STATE OF MONTANA ON RED ALERT.

If Rue hadn't been in mourning, she would have thought it was all a wonderful joke.

Chapter 15

It took Farley a full week, riding hard, to reach Pine River. Having no money and no gun, he'd lived on what he could scavenge, which wasn't much, considering there was snow on the ground. Lobo, once fat from his winter confinement in the stables at Ribbon Creek, was now sleeker and leaner, the kind of horse a man could depend on.

Folks shouted from the sidewalks and waved from the windows as Farley rode through the center of town, but he not only didn't stop to talk, he didn't even acknowledge them. His whole being was focused on a single objective: getting back to Rue.

As he came abreast of Jon Fortner's office, Farley saw his friend waiting by the hitching rail out front, his arms folded, his gaze steady.

"That's a fine-looking horse, Farley," the doctor said.

The marshal drew back on the reins, dismounted and tethered the stallion to the rail. He needed to talk with Jon, but he feared to start because his emotions were so raw and sore and so close to the surface.

Jonathan came down the steps and laid a reassuring hand to Farley's shoulder. "I've been there, too, remember?" he said, keeping his voice low so the gawking townspeople wouldn't hear. "Come on inside, and I'll pour you a cup of my special medicinal coffee."

For the first time in more than a week, Farley smiled, though he knew the effort was probably somewhat on the puny side. "How about just giving me a cup of medicine with a little coffee in it?"

Rue was lying in bed one night, a month after Farley's dramatic disappearance, when the memory invaded her mind, three-dimensional and in full color.

She saw herself in Pine River, at the churchyard, talking with a dark-haired young man. Michael Blake, that was his name, and he'd said Elisabeth and Jonathan Fortner had been his great-great-grandparents.

Now her heart was pounding like some primitive engine, and the fog of pain and confusion was finally lifting. She heard the young man say cordially, *My grandmother would really like to meet you, since you're a shirttail relation and everything. She lives*

*with my mom and dad in Seattle. Why don't you give
her a call sometime?*

Rue threw back the covers and leapt out of bed.
Michael had written a name and telephone number
on a page from a pocket-size notebook. She squeezed
her eyes shut. Where had she put that piece of paper?

At the same time she was pulling on clothes, Rue
was ransacking her memory. Whenever someone
handed her a business card or anything like that,
she always slipped it into her pocket, and she'd been
wearing a Windbreaker jacket that day....

Her stomach clenched into a painful knot as she
struggled to pursue the recollection further. It was
like trying to chase a rabbit through a blackberry
thicket, but Rue followed tenaciously, because finding Farley and saving him from the bank robber's
bullet was so critically important to her.

"My purse!" she yelled, flipping on the overhead
lights. She snatched her bag from the bureau top and
upended it over the bed, sending pennies and gum
wrappers, credit-card receipts and scruffy tissue all
over. After a feverish search, however, she unzipped
the change pocket and found the paper folded inside.

On it, Michael had written a name, Mrs. Elisabeth
R. Blake, and a telephone number.

Rue reached for the bedside telephone, then
caught sight of the alarm clock and realized it was
four o'clock in the morning, and just three in Seattle.

"Hell," she muttered, wondering how she could
contain herself until a decent hour. Maybe Mrs.

Blake was one of those old ladies who have trouble sleeping, and she was sitting up, working a crossword puzzle or watching one of the cable channels.

Rue's speculations changed nothing. Michael had said his grandmother lived with his parents, and *they* were probably sleeping, with no clue of what a mystery their existence really was.

She went downstairs and made herself a cup of tea, since she could no longer tolerate coffee, a drink she'd once loved. She felt dizzy sometimes, too, and she was cranky as a bear recovering from a root canal, but she attributed these symptoms to the stress she'd been under for nearly a month. Pregnancy was both too wonderful and too terrible a prospect to consider.

Soldier, who had been sleeping on the hooked rug in front of the cookstove, as usual, traipsed over to give Rue a friendly lick on the forearm. Idly, she patted his head and went right on sipping her tea.

Perhaps this delay was a good thing. Rue didn't have any idea what to say to Mrs. Blake once she reached her, but she knew the woman was her only link with Elisabeth and Farley, now that the necklace was gone.

Slowly, the icy gray light grew brighter at the windows. Rue fed Soldier, let him out and wandered back to the study.

The photographs taken at the wedding were there, tucked into a place of honor in a drawer of her grandfather's cherrywood desk. Although it always did her injury to look at them, Rue could no more have ignored those pictures than she could have given up breathing or stilled the meter of her heartbeat.

She flipped through them, smiling even as tears pricked her eyes. Farley with coconut frosting all over his mouth. Herself wearing the gauzy dress from the attic. The bride and groom kissing right after the justice of the peace had pronounced them man and wife....

Rue carefully returned the photos to their envelope, then put on her coat and boots and made her way to the woodshed. She brought back an armload of pitchy pine logs, feeling better because of the effort of wielding the ax.

She made a fire and watched an early-morning news show in the study. When eight o'clock came around, Rue simply could not wait any longer. She sat down at the desk, pulled the telephone close and carefully punched out the number Michael had given her that day in the graveyard.

There were a few vague thumps on the line, then a long ring, then another.

"Blake residence," a pleasant male voice answered.

"My name is Rue Claridge-Haynes," Rue blurted. "I'd like to speak with Mrs. Blake—the senior Mrs. Blake—about some genealogy research I've been doing."

"That would be my mother," the man said. "If you'll wait just a moment...." There was a thumping sound as he laid the receiver down, and Rue chewed a fingernail while she waited.

After what seemed like a long time, though it was probably not more than a minute or two, a woman's voice came on the line, almost drowned out by the racket of an extension being hung up.

"Rue Claridge?"

Rue shoved a hand through her hair. "Yes. Mrs. Blake, I'm calling about—"

"I know what you're calling about," the old lady interrupted, crisply but not unkindly. "I've been waiting all my life for this moment."

"I beg your pardon?"

"My grandmother, Elisabeth Fortner, left something for you under the flyleaf of her Bible."

Rue's heart was hammering. This, she realized, was what she had been subconsciously hoping for. Elisabeth had found a way to reach across time, to send word about herself or Farley.

"Miss Claridge? Are you there?"

"My name is Claridge-Haynes now," Rue said. It sounded totally inane, she knew, but she was in shock. "I'm married." She paused, cleared her throat. "Mrs. Blake, what did my cous—your grandmother leave for me?"

"It's an envelope," Bethie's descendant answered. "A letter, I suppose. I didn't look because Grandmother's instructions said I mustn't. No one but you is to open the packet, and I cannot send it through the mail or by messenger. The note on the front specifically says that you will contact me when the time is right and that I must insist on your coming for it in person."

Rue was practically dizzy with excitement and suspense. "I'm in Montana, Mrs. Blake," Rue said. "But I'll be there as soon as I can."

Mrs. Blake gave Rue an address and told her to call the moment she arrived in Seattle, no matter what time it was. "I'll be waiting by the phone," she finished.

Rue immediately called the nearest airport, but there were no planes available, charter or otherwise, because of the weather. Rue accepted that disappointment. She told Wilbur, who was recuperating at the ranch house under the care of a nurse, that she was leaving and he was boss until further notice, then threw her suitcases into the back of the Land Rover and left.

The storm started out as a light, picturesque skiff of snow, but by the time Rue reached Spokane, it had reached blizzard proportions. She stopped there and forced down a hearty dinner while a man at a service station across the street put chains on her rear tires.

"You shouldn't drive in this, ma'am," he said, when Rue returned from the restaurant and was settling up the bill. "It's a long way to Seattle, and you've gotta go over the mountains. Snoqualmie Pass is probably closed anyway...."

Rue smiled, nodded, got behind the wheel and went right on.

Hours later, she reached the high mountain pass that connected the eastern and western parts of Washington state. Sure enough, traffic was backed up for miles, but the road was closed only to people who didn't have chains on their tires.

On the other side of the mountain range, there was hardly any snow, and a warm, drizzling rain was washing that away.

Just over an hour after that, Rue pulled into the parking lot of a convenience store in the suburbs of Seattle. She called Mrs. Blake, who was awake and waiting, as promised.

After washing her face, combing her hair and brushing her teeth in the rest room, Rue bought a tall cup of hot chocolate and went on.

She found the Blake house with relative ease, but even though her exhausted state made her feel slightly bewitched, Rue wouldn't let herself attribute the fact to anything mystical. She had always had a good sense of direction.

A white-haired old woman with a sweet smile and soft blue eyes came to the door only an instant after Rue rang the bell.

"Rue," she said, and something in the very warp and woof of the woman reminded Rue of Elisabeth and filled her with an aching sense of nostalgia. Bethie's *granddaughter*—how impossible that seemed. "Come in."

"I hope I haven't awakened anyone…."

"Mercy, no," Mrs. Blake said, linking her thin,

age-spotted arm with Rue's and ushering her into a large, tastefully decorated room to the left. "Phillip, my son, is a surgeon, and he's been up and gone for hours. Nadine, my daughter-in-law, is at the health club, swimming, and, of course, Michael lives in one of the dorms at the university now. I pretty much have the place to myself, except for the maid. Won't you sit down?"

Even though she felt sure she would faint any moment, Rue was so tired, she was almost painfully tense. She sat in a graceful Queen Anne chair, upholstered in a pretty blue-and-white floral pattern, and tried to keep calm.

"Would you care for some coffee?" Mrs. Blake inquired, taking a chair facing Rue's and gesturing gracefully toward the silver service on the cocktail table.

Rue shook her head. "No, thank you," she said, and then bit down hard on her lower lip to keep from demanding the envelope Elisabeth had left for her.

"Well, then, there's no sense in dragging this out, even if it is the biggest thing to happen around here since Nadine's friend Phyllis crawled out on the roof during last year's Christmas party and made a world-class fool of herself. She sang twenty-two different show tunes before the fire department got her down, you know, and every note was off key."

Rue smiled and nodded and tapped the arm of the chair with her fingertips.

Mrs. Blake flushed slightly. "I'm sorry, I do get to

running on." She pulled a battered blue vellum envelope from her bag, which was resting on the marble-topped table beside her chair, and held it out to Rue.

Rue forced herself not to snatch it out of Mrs. Blake's fingers. She must have looked calm on the outside, but inside, Rue was suffering an agony of hope. If this was nothing more than a cosmic postcard—"How are you? I am fine. Wish you were here"—the disappointment would be beyond tolerance.

Rue made herself read the faded but familiar lettering on the front of the envelope, and tears filled her eyes. Elisabeth's cryptic instructions were all there, just as Mrs. Blake had relayed them.

Finally, like a child opening a fascinating, fragile present found under the Christmas tree, Rue broke the old wax seal and pulled a single page from inside the envelope.

The necklace did not tumble to her lap, as Rue had hoped it would, but she'd mourn that oversight later. Now, she would read words that had waited over a hundred years for her attention.

My Dearest Rue,
I know you probably expected to find the necklace folded inside this letter, so that you could return here to find Mr. Haynes, but, of course, once you think about it, you'll realize that I couldn't take a chance like that. You and

I know only too well what magic Aunt Verity's pendant is capable of.

If you must find it, I can only tell you to remember that rainy afternoon when we were thirteen and we decided to make a time capsule.

I hate writing this part, knowing what an awful impact it's going to have, but you married Farley, and I think you have a right to the truth, so you can get on with your life. Rue, Farley was shot ten days ago while stopping a robbery, and last night he died of his wounds.

Rue stopped there, fighting to hold on to consciousness while the gracious room swayed around her, then forced herself to go on reading.

There are no words I can say to console you, except that I know Farley loved you desperately, and that his greatest wish was to return to you.

Rue, I told you where to find the necklace because I know I don't have the right to withhold a choice that rightfully belongs to you, but I beg you not to try to return. The power of that pendant is unpredictable, we know that if hardly anything else, and it's dangerous. Anything could happen.

I love you, Cousin, with my whole heart,

and I'm depending on you to do your grieving,
then pull yourself together and go on.
Forever, and with a new understanding of the
word,
Beth

When Rue let the letter crumple to her lap, Mrs.
Blake was ready with a glass of cool water.

"Here, dear, drink this. You look as waxen as a
ghost."

Rue might have smiled under other circumstances.
As it was, she only reached out a trembling hand for
the glass and drank with desperate thirst. Once she
felt a little steadier, she thanked Mrs. Blake, carefully
folded Bethie's letter and tucked it into her purse.

"I can't share it," she confessed softly. "I hope
you understand."

Mrs. Blake's smile was reminiscent of Elisabeth's.
"I won't say I'm not curious, dear," she replied, "but
I understand. There are mysteries aplenty in this life,
and I've learned to accept the fact."

Rue kissed the old lady's cheek lightly. "Thank
you again, Mrs. Blake. And goodbye."

Barely an hour later, Rue was back in Pine River,
her eyes puffy and sore. Alone in the Land Rover,
insulated from a world that couldn't have compre-
hended her pain, Rue had screamed in rage and
grief over her husband's unfair death. Tears had left
acid trails on her cheeks, and her throat was so con-
stricted, she could barely breathe.

Instead of heading for Aunt Verity's house, Rue stopped at the churchyard. She found Farley's grave, under the old oak tree as the clerk in the church office had told her. If there had ever been a stone or a wooden marker, no trace remained.

Rue was mourning a man who'd been dead over a century, and there wasn't even a monument to honor his memory.

The cemetery was cold on that grim winter day, and Rue's strength was almost gone. She turned—she would visit Elisabeth's and Aunt Verity's graves some other day—and made her way back to the muddy Land Rover.

Moving like a person in a voodoo documentary, Rue bought soup and soap and tea and other supplies at Pine River's state-of-the-art supermarket, then drove to the house where all her adventures had begun.

The mail was knee-deep in front of the slot in the door, and there were so many messages on the answering machine that the disk space had run out. Rue didn't play them back. She just put away her groceries, made a bowl of tomato soup and ate without actually tasting a single spoonful.

After rinsing the bowl, she went upstairs, put fresh sheets on one of the beds, took a shower and collapsed. She slept for fourteen hours straight, got up and made herself another bowl of soup, then went back to sleep for another seven.

When she awakened, rested at last, but still numb

with sorrow, Rue took Elisabeth's earlier letters from their hiding place in the rolltop desk in the parlor and read them again.

Her heart began to thump. Time did not necessarily run parallel between then and now, she remembered, with growing excitement. If she found a way back—and the whereabouts of the necklace was teasing the edges of her consciousness even then—she would probably arrive after Farley's shooting. But she could also get there before it happened.

Maybe she could intercede.

She ran to find her purse—she'd discarded it on the floor of the downstairs hallway when she first returned—pulled out the letter Mrs. Blake had kept for her and scanned it.

Her gaze snagged on one particular sentence. "...I can only tell you to remember that rainy afternoon when we were thirteen and we decided to make a time capsule."

Rue yelped in frustration and began to pace. Her memory wasn't good when it came to things like that, though she could reel off statistics and stock prices and phone numbers until her voice gave out.

"Time capsule, time capsule, time capsule." She repeated the words like a litany, hoping they would trigger some rusty catch deep down in her mind.

Suddenly, gloriously, the memory was there.

Rain on a leaky roof. The smell of dam dust and moldy hay. Two adolescent girls, herself and Elisabeth, in the barn loft, talking about the distant future. They'd wanted posterity to know about their lives, so they'd swiped a lidded plastic bowl from Aunt Verity's kitchen and put in things they considered representative of Planet Earth in their time. Lip gloss. Pictures of their favorite rock group, carefully snipped from fan magazines. A candy bar with peanuts and caramel....

Rue hurried through the house and outside, crossing the dead winter grass in long strides. The barn was old and flimsy and should have been torn down years before, but safety was the last thing on Rue's mind as she went inside.

She did test the ladder leading up to the loft, but only in a quick and cursory way. The boards under her feet swayed a little when she reached the top, but that didn't stop her, either. She and Elisabeth had put their time capsule into the creaky framework where the floor and wall met with great ceremony.

"X marks the spot," she said breathlessly when she found the hiding place and knelt to wrench back a board. The whole loft seemed to shimmy at the intrusion, but again Rue was undaunted.

Behind the filthy, weathered board was a dirty plastic container riddled with the tooth marks of some creature that could probably qualify for top billing in a horror movie. Rue tossed the bowl aside without lifting the lid to look inside and peered into the crevice behind it.

At first, she could see nothing but darkness, dirt and spider webs, but after a few moments her vision seemed to sharpen. Well behind the place where her and Elisabeth's treasures had been hidden, a solid-looking shadow lurked in the gloom.

Rue grimaced, reached deep into the unknown and closed her hand around the object. Having found what she sought, she drew back so fast that a splinter or the tip of a nail made a long, shallow gash in her arm.

She paid no attention to the wound; all she could see was the round, rusted tin she held. Once it had held salve, and the distinct possibility that it was nothing more than a stray piece of trash raised panic into Rue's throat like bile.

"Please," she whispered, and it was at once the most sincere and the most succinct prayer she had ever said.

It was hard, and she broke a couple of fingernails, but Rue finally managed to pry off the lid of the tin. Inside, dusty and tarnished and as full of mystery as ever, lay the necklace.

Rue's eyes filled with tears of relief, and she clutched the pendant to her chest. Now, if only the magic would work again.

Nothing happened, so Rue carefully tucked the necklace into the pocket of her jacket. Only then did she notice that the bit of paper lining the salve tin had writing on it.

Carefully, Rue lifted it to the thin light coming in through one of the wide cracks in the barn wall. "I knew you wouldn't listen!" Elisabeth had scrawled.

Rue smiled, dried her eyes with the back of one hand and climbed cautiously down the ladder again.

Inside the house, she laid the necklace on the drainboard beside the kitchen sink and washed it with cotton balls, mild soap and water. When the pendant was clean, she patted it dry with a soft paper towel, draped the chain around her neck and carefully closed the clasp.

She shut her eyes, gripped the edge of the counter and waited. Hoped.

At first, nothing happened, but then a humming sound filled Rue's ears, rising steadily in pitch. The floor buckled and rolled under her feet, and it seemed that she could feel the spin of the earth itself.

Someone screamed and something crashed to the floor.

Rue opened her eyes to see Bethie's housekeeper standing there, aghast and staring, a shattered crockery bowl at her feet. Its contents covered the length of the woman's calico skirts.

"Ellen, for heaven's sake..." a familiar voice complained, and then Elisabeth appeared in the doorway leading to the main parlor. When she saw her cousin, her blue-green eyes widened and her face lit up with a dazzling smile. "Rue!"

"She just came out of nowhere, missus," Ellen blathered. "I'm telling you, I don't know about the goings-on in this house. I just don't know. And now I've got myself a sick headache."

"You'd better go and lie down," Elisabeth told her

gently, but she didn't look at the housekeeper again. She gave Rue a gentle hug.

"Is he dead?" Rue whispered, unable to bear the agony of wondering for another moment.

"Who?" Bethie asked, and her look of puzzlement raised Rue's spirits considerably.

"Farley. Farley Haynes, the marshal." For the first time, the thought occurred to Rue that she might have come back not only before her husband's death, but before he knew her.

"Well, he hasn't been very happy about being separated from you," Elisabeth said with a fond smile, "but people don't usually die of a broken heart. They just *wish* they could."

Farley was alive, and he would know her. Rue's knees literally went slack with relief, and she might have collapsed if Elisabeth hadn't steadied her.

"I've got to go to him right now," she said after a few deep breaths.

"But you're shaken—you need to sit down and have a cup of tea—"

"I need to find my husband!" Rue said. "Is there a horse I can borrow?"

Elisabeth offered no further argument; she knew her cousin too well. "There's a chestnut mare in the barn. Her name is Maisie, and she prefers to be ridden bareback."

Rue hugged her cousin, bade her a good life with Jonathan and raced out the back door, nearly tripping because the steps were different from the ones she was used to. The barn that had been a teetering disaster the last time she entered it was sturdy now, and well maintained.

Quickly, Rue bridled the small mare and swung up onto its back. A woman in pants, riding astride no less, was going to come as yet another shock to the fine people of Pine River, but that could not be helped. The necklace had slipped beneath her shirt; it felt warm against her collarbone, and she was filled with a new and terrifying sense of urgency.

She'd gotten back in time, but just barely. There wasn't a second to lose.

Sure enough, Rue heard the shots just as she and Maisie hit the foot of the town's main street. Rue spurred the animal through the uproar and confusion—everybody was trying to take cover—weaving her way around wagons and buggies and other horses.

Undaunted, Rue rode hell-bent for the bank. If she had to, she would catch that outlaw's bullet herself before she let it strike Farley.

Two men ran out of the bank, their faces, except for their eyes and foreheads, covered by dirty bandannas. It was just like a scene in a John Wayne movie, except that here the bullets were real.

Rue looked frantically for Farley, which was why she was caught completely unprepared when an arm as hard as iron wrenched her off the mare's back and onto another horse. After that, everything was a dizzying blur.

Either she was dreaming, or she was sitting side-saddle behind Farley, clutching his canvas duster with both hands. The magnificent animal carrying them both was Lobo. She felt the swift, skilled movement of the marshal's arm as he drew his .45. Then she heard two shots in rapid succession and felt the recoil in the muscles between Farley's shoulder blades, where her cheek rested. The air seemed thick with the smells of horse manure and burned powder, and Rue figured if she survived this, the first thing she was going to do was vomit.

In that moment, of all moments, she realized she was definitely pregnant.

A brief silence followed. Rue clung to Farley, soaking in the hard strength of his body in front of her. He was alive, and so was she.

He turned his head to look back at her, and although a muscle in his jaw jumped in irritation, Rue could see joy in his eyes. "That was a damn fool thing to do," he bit out. "You could have been killed."

The necklace was searing Rue's skin. She locked her hands together in front of his stomach, determined that even a brand new Big Bang wouldn't blast her loose. "I love you, too, Farley Haynes," she said.

The magic was beginning again; the air was filled with a vibrant silence so noisy that Rue could hear nothing besides her own voice and Farley's heartbeat. She threw back her head and shouted for joy, at the same time tearing the necklace from her throat and flinging it away.

They might land in heaven or in hell. Either way, the die was cast.

"Tarnation," Farley marveled when the spiritual storm subsided. The marshal, Rue and Lobo were square in the middle of the deserted parking lot at Pine River High School. It was twilight, and the wind was chilly, but to Rue, the sky had never looked brighter nor had the air felt warmer.

Farley turned, his beautiful teeth showing in a broad grin. "Well, Mrs. Haynes," he asked, just before he kissed her, "what do we do now?"

It was a long moment before Rue caught her breath. "That's easy, Mr. Haynes," she replied. "We ride off into the sunset."

* * * * *

Dear Reader,

Seth Dalton, the youngest of my three original Cowboys of Cold Creek, was one of those characters I fell in love with from the first moment he showed up on the page. Yes, he was sexy and used it to full advantage, but I could sense a vulnerability in him, too. I knew I needed to find a very special heroine for him, someone who could see past his glib charm to the good, honorable man he was at heart.

Jenny Boyer is new to Pine Gulch, taking the helm as the principal of the elementary school and trying to make a new life for herself and her two children. She has a reputation to protect, and as she finds herself falling for Seth—who has his own reputation as the town's biggest player—she worries how their growing relationship might interfere with her ability to do her job.

I loved writing their story, of family and tenderness and second chances. I love all my Cowboys of Cold Creek, but Seth and Jenny will always have a very special place in my heart!

All my very best,

RaeAnne

DALTON'S UNDOING

USA TODAY Bestselling Author

RaeAnne Thayne

To Jared, for twenty-six wonderful years
filled with joy and laughter and midnight trips
to the store when I run out of printer ink.
I love you dearly!

Chapter 1

Some little punk was stealing his car.

Seth Dalton stood on the sidewalk in front of his mother's house, the puppy leashes in his hand forgotten, and watched three years of sweat, passion and hard work take off down the road with a flash of tail lights and the squeal of rubber.

Son of a bitch.

He stood looking after it for maybe fifteen seconds, trying to comprehend how anybody in Podunk Pine Gulch would have the stones to steal his 1969 Matador red GTO convertible.

Who in town could possibly be stupid enough to dream he could get more than a block or two without somebody sitting up and taking notice that Seth wasn't the one behind the wheel and raising the alarm?

Just how far did the bastard think he would get? Not very, if Seth had anything to say about it. He'd worked too hard on his baby to let some sleazebag drive her away.

"Come on, kids. Fun's over." He jerked the leashes, grateful the dogs weren't in midpee, and dragged the two brindle Australian herder pups up the sidewalk and back into the house.

Inside, the members of his family were crowded around his mother's dining-room table playing one of their cutthroat games of Risk.

Looked like Jake and Maggie were kicking butt. No surprise there, with his middle brother's conniving brain and his wife's military experience. The Dalton clan was in its usual teams, Jake and Maggie against his mother and stepfather, with his oldest brother, Wade, and wife, Caroline, making up the third team.

That was the very reason he'd volunteered to take the puppies out for their business in the first place. It was a little lonely being the solitary player on his side of the table. Usually he teamed up with Natalie—but it was a little disheartening to find his nine-year-old niece made a more cutthroat general than he. She was in the family room watching a DVD with her brothers, anyway.

The only one who looked up from strategizing was his mother.

"Back so soon? That was fast!" Marjorie crooned the words, not to him but to the puppies—or her half of the dynamic duo anyway. She picked up the birthday gift he'd given her and nuzzled the little male pup.

"You're so good. Aren't you so good? Yes, you are. Come give Mommy a birthday kiss."

"Don't have time, sorry," Seth said drily.

He ignored the face she made at him and reached for the keys to Wade's pickup from the breakfast bar.

"I'm taking your truck," he called on his way out the door.

Wade looked up, a frown of concentration on his tough features. "You're what?"

He paused at the door. "Don't have time to explain, but I need your truck. I'll be back. Mom, keep an eye on Lucy for me."

"I just washed that truck," his brother growled. "Don't bring it back all muddy and skanky."

He wasn't even going to dignify that with a response, he decided, as he headed down the stairs. He didn't have the time, even if he could have come up with a sharp response.

Wade's truck rumbled to life, smooth and well-tuned like everything in Seth's oldest brother's life. He threw it in gear and roared off in the direction the punk had taken his car.

If he were stealing a car, which road would he take? Pine Gulch didn't offer a lot of escape routes. Turning south would lead him through the houses and small business district of Pine Gulch. To the east was the rugged western slope of the Teton Mountains, which left him north and west.

He took a chance and opted to head north, where the quiet road stretched past ranches and farms with little traffic to notice someone in a red muscle car.

He ought to just call the police and report the theft.

Chasing after a car thief on his own like this was probably crazy, but he wasn't in the mood to be sensible, not with thirty thousand dollars' worth of sheer horsepower disappearing before his eyes.

He pushed Wade's truck to sixty-five, keeping his eye out in the gathering twilight for any sign of another vehicle.

His efforts were rewarded just a moment later when he followed the curve of the road past Sam Purdy's pond and saw a flash of red up ahead.

His brother's one-ton pickup rumbled as he poured on the juice and accelerated to catch the little bugger.

With its 400-cubic-inch V8 and the three hundred and fifty horses straining under the hood, the GTO could go a hundred and thirty without breaking a sweat. Oddly enough, whoever had boosted it wasn't pushing her harder than maybe forty.

His baby puttered along fifteen miles below the speed limit and Seth had no problem catching up with her, wondering as he did if there was some kind of roving gang of senior-citizen car thieves on the loose he hadn't heard about.

He kept a respectable two-car length between them as the road twisted again. He knew this road and knew that just ahead was a straightaway that ran a couple of miles past farmland with no houses.

He couldn't see any oncoming traffic so he pulled into the other lane as if to pass and drew up alongside his baby, intent on getting a look at the thief.

He *was* a punk, nothing more. The kid behind the wheel was skinny, dark-haired, maybe fifteen, sixteen. He looked over at the big rumbling pickup beside him and he looked scared to death, eyes huge and wild in a narrow face.

Good. He should be, the little dickhead. Seth rolled the window down, wishing he could reach across, pluck the kid out of the car and wring his scrawny little neck.

"Pull over," he shouted through the window, even though he knew the kid wouldn't be able to hear him.

He must have looked like the Grim Reaper, Freddy Kruger and the guy from *The Texas Chainsaw Massacre* all rolled up into one, he realized later, and he should have predicted what happened next. If he'd been thinking straight, he would have handled the whole thing differently and saved himself a hell of a lot of trouble.

Even if the car thief couldn't hear Seth's words, obviously the message got through loud and clear. The kid sent him another wild, scared look and yanked the wheel to the right.

Seth growled out a raw epithet at the hideous sound of metal grinding against metal as the GTO scraped a mile marker post on the right. In reaction, the kid panicked and swerved too hard to the left and Seth groaned as his baby nosedived across the road and landed in an irrigation ditch.

At least it was blessedly empty this time of year.

The sun was just a sliver above the horizon and the November air was cold as Seth hurriedly parked the pickup and rushed to his car to make sure the kid was okay.

He jerked open the door and was petty enough for just a moment to enjoy the way the kid cringed against the seat like he thought Seth was ready to break his neck with his bare hands.

He felt like it, he had to admit. He had no doubt the GTO's paint was scraped all to hell from the run-in with the mile marker post and the left fender looked to be crumpled where she'd hit a concrete gate structure in the ditch.

He held on to his anger while he checked the thief for any sign of injury.

"You okay?" he asked.

"Yeah. I…think so." The boy's voice shook a little but he warily took Seth's hand and climbed out of the car.

Seth revised downward his estimate of the boy's age, figuring him to be no older than thirteen or fourteen. Just old enough to start shaving more than once a month, by the look of it.

He had choppy dark hair worn longer than Hank Dalton would ever have let *his* sons get away with and he was dressed in jeans and a gray hooded sweatshirt about four sizes too big with some logo of a wild-looking music group Seth didn't recognize.

The kid seemed familiar but Seth couldn't immediately place him—odd, since he knew just about every kid in the small community. Maybe he was the son of one of the dozen or so Hollywood types buying up good grazing land for their faux ranches. They tended to stay away from the general population, maybe afraid the down-home friendliness and family-centered values would rub off.

"My mom is gonna kill me," the kid moaned, burying his head in his hands.

"She can stand in line," Seth growled. "You have any idea how much work I've put into this car?"

The kid dropped his hands. Though he still looked terrified, he managed to cover it with a thin veneer of bravado. "You'll be sorry if you mess with me. My grandpa's a lawyer and he'll fry your ass if you try to lay a single hand on me."

Seth couldn't help a short, appreciative laugh even as the pieces clicked into place and he registered who the kid must be and why he had looked familiar.

With a grandfather who was a lawyer, he had to be the son of the new elementary school principal. Boylan. Boyer. Something like that.

He didn't exactly hang around with the elementary-school crowd but Natalie had pointed out her new principal and the woman's two kids one night shortly after school started when he'd taken his niece and nephews out to Stoney's, the pizza place in town.

His grandfather would be Jason Chambers, an attorney who had retired to Pine Gulch for the fishing five or six years back. His daughter had moved out to join him with her kids—no husband that Seth had heard about—when the principal position opened up at the elementary school.

"That lawyer in the family will probably come in handy, kid," he said now.

The punk groaned and his head sagged into his hands once more. "I am so dead."

He wasn't quite sure why but Seth was surprised to feel a few little pangs of sympathy for the kid. He remembered all too well the purgatory of this age. Hormones firing, emotions jerking around wildly. Too much juice and nothing to do with it.

"Am I going to jail?"

"You boosted a car. That's a pretty serious crime. And you're a lousy driver, which is worse, in my book."

"I wasn't going to take her far. You've got to believe me. Just to the reservoir and back, I swear. That's all. When I saw the keys inside, I couldn't resist."

Damn. Had he really left the keys in the ignition? He looked inside and, sure enough, there they were, dangling from the steering column.

How had that happened? He remembered pulling up to his mother's house for her birthday dinner, then rushing out to take care of business when Lucy started to squat on the floor mats. Maybe in all the confusion, he had been in such a hurry to find a patch of grass before his puppy busted her bladder that he'd forgotten his keys.

What kind of idiot left his keys in a ride like this, just begging for the first testosterone-crazed teenager to lift her?

Him. He mentally groaned, grateful at least that the boy hadn't been hurt by their combined stupidity.

"What's your name, kid?"

The boy clamped his teeth together and Seth sighed. "You might as well tell me. I know your last name is Boyer and Jason Chambers is your grandpa. I'll figure out the rest."

"Cole," he muttered after a long pause.

"Come on, Cole. I'll give you a lift to your grandpa's house, then I'll come back and pull her out with one of my brothers."

"I can walk." He hunched his shoulders and shoved his hands in the pocket of his hooded sweatshirt.

"You think I'm going to leave you and your sticky fingers running free out here? What if you happen to find another idiot who's left his keys in his ride? Get in."

Though Cole still looked belligerent, he climbed into the passenger side of the pickup.

Seth had just started to walk around the truck to get in the driver's side when he saw flashing lights behind him.

Instead of driving past, the sheriff's deputy slowed and pulled up behind the GTO. Seth glanced at the boy and saw he'd turned deathly white and his breathing was coming fast enough Seth worried about him hyperventilating.

"Relax, kid," he muttered.

"I am relaxed." He lifted his chin and tried for a cool look that came out looking more like a constipated rabbit.

Seth sighed and closed his door again as he watched the deputy climb out of the vehicle. Before he even saw her face, he knew by the curvy shape that the officer had to be Polly Jardine, the only female deputy in the small sheriff's department.

She dimpled at him, looking not much different than she had in high school—cute and perky and worlds away from his idea of an officer of the law. Though she still looked like she should be shaking her pom-poms at a Friday night football game, he knew she was a tough and dedicated cop.

He imagined she inspired more than a few naughty

fantasies around town involving those handcuffs dangling from her belt. But since her husband was linebacker-huge and also on the sheriff's department—and they were crazy about each other—those fantasies would only ever be that.

"Hey Seth. I thought that was your car. Man! What happened? You take the turn a little too fast?"

His gaze shifted quickly to the boy inside the truck then quickly back to Polly, hoping she hadn't noticed. He found himself strangely reluctant to throw Cole Boyer into the system.

"Something like that," he murmured.

She followed his gaze to the boy and speculation suddenly narrowed her eyes. "You sure that's the whole story?"

He leaned a hip against the truck, tilted his head and gave her a slow smile. "Would I lie to an officer of the law, darlin'?"

"Six ways from Sunday, *darlin'*." Though her words were tart, she smiled in a way that told him she remembered with fondness the few times they'd fooled around under the bleachers before Mitch Jardine moved into town and she had eyes for no one else. "But it's your car. If that's the way you want to play this, I won't argue with you."

"Thanks, Pol. I owe you."

"That's the new principal's kid, isn't it?"

He nodded.

"We've had a few run-ins with him in the few months they've been in town," she said. "Nothing big, breaking curfew, that kind of thing. You sure letting him off is the right thing to do for him? Today a joy-ride, tomorrow a bank robbery."

He didn't know anything except he couldn't bring himself to turn him in.

"For now."

"Let me know if you change your mind. I'm sup-posed to file an accident report but I'll just pretend I didn't see anything."

He nodded and waved goodbye then climbed into the truck. Cole Boyer watched him, his green eyes wary. "Am I going to jail?"

"No. Not today, anyway."

"Friggin' A!"

"Don't be so quick with the celebration there," he warned. "A week or two in juvie is probably going to look pretty damn good by the time your mother and grandfather get through with you. And that doesn't even take into account what you'll have to do to even the score with me."

She was late. As usual.

In one motion, Jenny Boyer shoved on slingbacks and shrugged into her favorite brocade jacket.

"Listen to Grandpa while I'm gone, okay?" she said, head tilted while she thrust a pair of conservative gold hoops into her ears.

"I always do." Morgan, her nine-year-old, going on fifty, sniffed just like a society matron finding some-thing undesirable in her tea. "Cole is the one who doesn't like authority figures."

Didn't she just know it? Jenny sighed. "Well, make sure he listens to Grandpa, too."

Morgan folded her arms and raised an eyebrow. "I'll try, but I don't think he'll pay attention to either me or Grandpa."

Probably not, she conceded. Nobody seemed to be able to get through to Cole. She'd thought moving to Idaho to live with her father would help stabilize her son, at least get him away from the undesirable elements in Seattle who were leading him into all kinds of trouble.

She had hoped his grandfather would give the boy the male role model he had lost with his own father's desertion. So much for that. Though Jason tried, Cole was so angry and bitter at the world—more furious with her now for uprooting him from his friends and moving him to this backwater than he was with his father for moving to another continent.

She glanced at her watch and groaned. The school board meeting started in ten minutes and she was scheduled to give a PowerPoint presentation outlining her efforts to raise the elementary school's performance on standardized testing. This was her first big meeting with the school board and she couldn't afford to blow it.

The therapist she'd gone to after the divorce suggested Jenny's chronic tardiness indicated some form of passive aggression, her way of governing a life that often felt beyond her control.

Jenny just figured she was too busy chasing after her hundreds of constantly spinning plates.

"I've got to run, baby. I'll be home before you go to sleep, I promise." She kissed her on the forehead, wondering as she headed out of her room if she had time to hurry down to the basement to say goodbye to

Cole. No, she decided. Besides her time crunch, any conversation between them these days ended in a fight and she wasn't sure she was up for another one tonight.

"Bye, Dad," she called down the hall as she grabbed her laptop case and her purse. "Thanks for watching them!"

"Don't worry about a thing." Jason Chambers appeared in the doorway, wearing his favorite Ducks Unlimited sweater and jeans that made him look far younger than his sixty-five years. "Give 'em hell."

She mustered a distracted smile, grateful all over again that they'd been able to move past their complicated, stiff relationship of the past and find some measure of peace when she moved to Pine Gulch.

Juggling her bags and her keys, she yanked open the door and rushed out, then gave a shriek when she collided with a solid, warm male.

With a little gasp, Jenny righted herself, registering the muscles in that hard frame that seemed as immovable as the Tetons. "I'm sorry! I didn't see you."

She knew who he was, of course. What woman in Pine Gulch didn't? With that slow, sexy smile and those brilliant blue eyes that seemed to see right into a woman's psyche to all her deepest desires, Seth Dalton was a difficult man to overlook.

Not that she didn't try her best. The youngest Dalton was exactly the kind of man she tried to avoid at all cost. She'd had more than enough, thank you very much, of smooth charmers who swept a woman off her feet with flowers and champagne only to leave her dangling there, hanging by her fingernails when they decide young French pastries are more to their taste.

What earthly reason would Dalton have for showing up at her doorstep? He had no children at her school, he was years past his own education and somehow she couldn't picture him as the type to bake cookies for the PTA fundraiser.

She couldn't think of anything else that would bring him to her door and the clock was ticking.

"May I help you, Mr. Dalton?"

Surprise flickered in those eyes for just a moment, as if he hadn't expected her to know his name. "Just making a delivery."

She frowned, impatient and confused, as he reached around the door out of her view, tugging something forward. No something, someone—someone with a sullen scowl, a baggy sweatshirt and a chip the size of Idaho on his narrow shoulders.

"Cole!"

Beneath her son's customary sulky defiance, she thought she saw something else beneath the attitude, something nervous and on edge.

"What's going on? You're supposed to be down in your room working on geometry!" she exclaimed.

"Geometry blows. I went out."

"You went out," she repeated, frustration and bewilderment and a terrible sense of failure rising in her chest. How could she possibly reach the students at her school when she couldn't manage to find even the tiniest connection to her own son? "Out where? I didn't hear you leave."

"Ever hear of a window?" he sneered. Nothing new there. He had been derisive and mean to her before they ever came to Pine Gulch. He blamed her for everything wrong in his life, from his short stature to Richard's affair and subsequent abandonment.

She was mortified that a stranger had to witness it. She was even more mortified when Seth Dalton raised one of those sexy dark eyebrows and placed a firm hand on Cole's shoulder. "Now, do you really think that's the proper way to address your mother?"

Jenny gave the man a polite smile, wishing him to Hades. "Thank you, Mr. Dalton, for bringing him home, but I believe I can handle things from here."

For some reason, either her words or her tone seemed to amuse him. His mouth quirked up and a masculine dimple appeared in his cheek briefly. "Can you, now? I'm afraid we still have a few matters of business to discuss. May I come in?"

"This isn't a good time. I'm late for a meeting."

"Sorry about that," he drawled, "but I'm afraid you'll have to make time for this."

He didn't wait for permission, just walked through her father's entry into the living room. She had no choice but to follow, noting as she went that Jason and Morgan were nowhere to be seen.

"Cole, you want to tell her what you've been up to?"

Her son crossed his arms, his expression even more belligerent, but again she caught a faint whiff of fear beneath it. Her stomach suddenly twisted with fore-boding.

"What's going on? Cole, what is this about?"

He clamped his mouth shut, freezing her out again, but once more Seth Dalton placed a firm hand on his shoulder.

Cole suddenly seemed to find the carpet endlessly fascinating.

"Istolehisride," he mumbled in one breath and Jenny's heart stopped, hoping she'd heard wrong.

"You *what?*"

Cole finally lifted his gaze to hers. "I took his car, okay? What did he expect? He left the frigging keys in it. I was only going to take it for a mile or two. I figured I'd have it back before he even knew it was gone. But then I crashed…"

"You *what!* Are you hurt? Did you hurt anyone else?"

Cole shook his head. At least he had enough guilty conscience to look slightly ashamed.

"He scraped a mile marker post and front-ended into an irrigation ditch. The only thing damaged was my car."

She sagged into the nearest chair as her career suddenly flashed in front of her eyes. She could almost hear the echo of gossip across shopping carts at De-Loy's, under the hair dryers at the Hairport and over beer at the Bandito.

Did you hear about that new principal's wild boy? She can't control him a lick. That little delinquent stole a car. Crashed it right into a ditch! Seems to me a woman who can't control her own son sure don't belong in that nice office down at the elementary school.

She screwed her eyes shut, wishing this was all some terrible dream, but when she opened them, Seth Dalton was still standing in front of her, as dangerous and sexy as ever.

"I am so sorry, Mr. Dalton. I...don't know what to say. Are you pressing charges?"

She thought she heard Cole make a small sound, but when she glanced at him, he looked as prickly and angry as ever.

"It's going to take me considerable work to fix it."

"We will, of course, cover any damages."

He suddenly sat down on the sofa across from her, crossing his boots at the ankle. "I had something else in mind."

She stiffened. "I'm an elementary school principal, Mr. Dalton. If you're looking for some kind of huge financial settlement, I'm afraid you're off the mark."

"I'm not looking for money." He glanced at Seth. "But I will need another set of hands while I'm doing the repair work. I figured the kid could work off the damages by helping me out with the repair work and around my ranch with my horses until the bodywork is done."

Cole straightened. "I'm no stupid-ass cowboy."

Seth Dalton gave him a measuring look. "No, from here you look like a stupid-ass punk who thinks he's living out some kind of video game. This isn't Grand Theft Auto, kid, where you can always hit the restart button. You broke it, now you're going to help me fix it. Unless you'd rather serve the time, of course."

Cole subsided back into his customary slouch as Jenny considered his proposal. Her gut wanted her to tell him to forget it. She didn't want her son to have anything to do with Pine Gulch's busiest bachelor.

Cole had had enough lousy male role models in his

life—he didn't need a player like Seth teaching him all the wrong things about how to treat a woman.

On the other hand, her son stole the man's car—not only stole it, but wrecked the blasted thing. That he wasn't in police custody right now seemed nothing short of a miracle.

What choice did she have, really? Seth could easily have called the police. Perhaps he should have. Maybe a hard gut check with reality might be just what Cole needed to wake him up, as much as she hated the idea of her son in juvenile detention.

Seth Dalton was being surprisingly decent about this. From what little she knew about him—and she had to admit, most of her biased information came from overheard conversations and breathless comments in the teachers' lounge about his many flirtations—she would have expected him to be hot-tempered and petulant.

Instead, she found him rational, calm, accommodating.

And extremely attractive.

She let out a slow, nervous breath. Was that the reason for her instinctive opposition to the man's reasonable proposal? Because he was sinfully gorgeous, with that thick, dark hair, eyes a stunning, heartbreaking blue and chiseled, tanned features that made him look as though he should be starring in Western movies?

He made her edgy and ill at ease and that alone gave her enough reason to wish for a way to avoid any further acquaintance between them. She was here in Pine Gulch to help her little family find some peace and healing—not to engage in useless, potentially harmful fantasies about a charming, feckless cowboy with impossibly blue eyes and a smile that oozed sex.

"I'll know better after I tow the car out to the ranch and take a look at her but from my initial look, I'd estimate there was about fix or six hundred dollars' damage," he was saying. "The way I figure it, if he worked for me a couple afternoons a week after school and Saturday mornings, we should be clear in a few months. Is that okay with you?"

She looked at Dalton and then at Cole, his arms still crossed belligerently across his chest, as if everyone else in the room was responsible for his troubles but himself.

He disdained everything about Idaho and would probably consider being forced to work on a ranch every bit as much punishment as going to juvenile detention, she thought.

"Yes. That's more than fair. Wouldn't you agree, Cole?"

Her son glared at both of them—and while Jenny felt her own temper kindle in automatic response, Seth met his look with cool challenge and Cole quickly dropped his gaze.

"Whatever," he muttered.

"Thank you," Jenny said again, walking with him to the door. "As tomorrow is Saturday, I'll drive him out to the Cold Creek in the morning. What time?"

"How does eight work for you?"

"We'll be there. I'm very sorry again about this. I can't imagine what he was thinking."

His smile was slow and wide and made her insides

feel as if she'd just done somersaults down a steep, grassy hill.

"He's a teenage boy, so I'd guess he probably wasn't thinking at all. See you in the morning."

Jenny nodded, wondering why that prospect filled her with an odd mix of trepidation and anticipation.

Chapter 2

"This is totally lame," her son muttered the next morning. "Why do I have to give up a whole Saturday?"

Jenny sighed and cast Cole an admonishing glance across the width of her little Toyota SUV. "You prefer the alternative? I can call Mr. Dalton right now and tell him to go ahead and file charges if that's what you'd rather see happen here."

Cole sliced her a glare that told her quite plainly he considered *her* totally lame, too, but he said nothing.

"I don't think it's fair, either," Morgan piped up from the backseat. "Why does Cole always get to do the fun stuff? I want to help with the horses, too. Natalie says the Cold Creek horses are the prettiest, smartest horses anywhere. They've won all kinds of rodeo awards and they sell for *tons* of money. She said her uncle Seth knows more about horses than anybody else in the whole wide *world*."

"Wow. The whole wide world?" Sarcasm dripped from Cole's voice.

Morgan either didn't pick up on it or decided to ignore it. Judging from past experience, Jenny was willing to bet on the latter. Her daughter tended to ignore anything that didn't fit into her vision of the way the world ought to operate.

Even during her frequent hospital stays after bad asthma attacks, she always managed to focus on some silver lining, like a new friend or a particularly kind nurse.

"Yep," she said eagerly now, with as much pride in Seth Dalton as she might have had if he were *her* uncle instead of her best friend's. "People bring their horses to the Cold Creek from all over the place for him to train because he's so good."

"If he knows more than anyone else in the world, why is he stuck here in Buttlick, Idaho?"

Morgan's enthusiasm faded into a frown. "Just because you don't like it here, you don't have to call it mean words."

"I thought that was the name," Cole said with a sneer. "Right next to Hairy Armpitville and across the holler from Cow's Rectum."

"That's enough." Jenny's hands tightened on the steering wheel and she felt familiar stress weigh like a half-ton hay bale on her shoulders. She wasn't at all sure she was going to survive her son's adolescence.

"I hope you treat Mr. Dalton with more respect than you show me or your sister."

"How can I not, since apparently the man knows more about horses than anybody in the whole wide world?" Cole muttered.

Who was this angry stranger in her son's body? she wondered. Whatever happened to her sweet little man who used to love cuddling up with her at bedtime for stories and hugs? Who used to let her blow raspberries on his neck and would run to her classroom after school bubbling over with news of his day?

That sweet boy had been slipping away from her since the year he turned eleven, when Richard had moved out. Through the three ugly years since, he'd pulled deeper and deeper into himself, until now he only emerged on rare occasions.

This obviously wasn't going to be one of them.

Somehow Cole had come to blame her for the separation and divorce. She wasn't sure how or why she had come to bear that burden but the unfairness of it made her want to scream.

She, at least, had been faithful to her marriage vows. Though she hadn't been perfect by any means and had long ago accepted her share of responsibility for the breakup of her marriage, in her heart she knew she had tried to be a good wife.

She had supported Richard through his last years of medical school, residency, internship. She had scrimped and saved throughout their twelve-year marriage to help pay off his student loans, had run the household virtually alone during that time as he worked to establish his career, had tried time and again to bridge the increasing chasm between them as he focused on his practice to the complete exclusion of his family.

She had tried. Not perfectly, she would admit, but she had wanted her marriage to work.

Richard had had other ideas, though. He went to Paris for a conference and met his Giselle and decided family and vows and twelve years of marriage didn't stack up well against a twenty-year-old Frenchwoman with a tight body and pouty lips.

Jenny had long ago come to terms with Richard Boyer's betrayal of her. But she would never forgive him for what his complete abandonment of his family had done to his children. Morgan had stopped crying herself to sleep some time ago and seemed to be adjusting, but Cole carried so much anger inside him he seethed with it.

Lucky her, she seemed to be the only outlet for his rage.

She tried to remember what the therapist she'd seen in Seattle had told her, that Cole only lashed out at her because she was a safe target. Her son knew she wouldn't abandon him like his father, so he focused all the force of his rage toward her.

She still wasn't sure she completely bought into that explanation. Even if she did, she wasn't sure it would make his rebelliousness and unhappiness any more palatable.

With each mile marker, he seemed to sink further into gloom on the seat beside her.

A large timber arch across a gravel side road proudly bore the name of the Cold Creek Land & Cattle Company in cast-iron letters. She slowed the SUV and turned in.

"It won't be so bad," she said, fighting the completely juvenile urge to cross her fingers. "Who knows? You might even enjoy it."

He rolled his eyes. "Cleaning up horse crap? Right. Can't wait."

She sighed, wondering if Seth Dalton had any clue what joy was in store for him today.

The ranch house was shielded from the main road by a long row of trees, which made the first sight of it all the more dramatic. It was perfect for the landscape here, a bold, impressive structure of rock and logs, with the massive peaks of the Tetons as a backdrop.

She'd always considered November a particularly lonely, unattractive month, without October's swirling colors or December's sparkling anticipation. In November, the trees were bleak and bare and everything seemed frost-dead and barren.

The Cold Creek seemed to be an exception. Oh, the gardens out front had been cut down, the beds prepared for winter, but the long rows of weathered fence line and the sheer impressiveness of the house and outbuildings gave a stark beauty to the scene.

Not sure quite where to go to find Seth Dalton, she slowed as she reached the house and then stopped altogether when she saw a figure emerge from an immense barn, carrying a bale of hay by the baling twine.

It wasn't Seth, she realized, but his brother Wade, Natalie's father.

The oldest Dalton brother had two children in her school—Natalie and her younger brother, Tanner. Natalie was a dear, though a little bossy, but Tanner had been in her office on more than one occasion for some mischief or other. He wasn't malicious, just highly energetic.

The few times she had met with Wade Dalton and his wife, Caroline, at various school functions and when having discussions about Tanner's behavior, she'd been struck by the deep vein of happiness she sensed running through the family.

She didn't like to admit she felt envy and regret when she saw two people so obviously in love.

Wade caught sight of them now and smiled, dropping the bale and tipping his hat in a way she still hadn't become accustomed to here in cowboy country.

He didn't look at all surprised to see them as he crossed the yard to her SUV. Seth must have told him the whole story about Cole stealing his brother's car. What must he think of her and her delinquent son? she wondered, her face warming.

He only smiled in welcome. "Ms. Boyer. Kids," he said in that slow drawl she'd noticed before. "Welcome to the Cold Creek."

She couldn't help but smile back. "Thank you. We were supposed to be meeting your brother Seth this morning."

"Right. He mentioned your boy would be coming by to help him. He's up at the horse barn. Just follow the gravel road there another half mile or so and you can't miss it."

"Thank you," she said, wondering how big the ranch must be if the horse barn was a half mile from the main ranch house. The road took them up a slight grade, through a heavy stand of spruce and pines and aspen and then the view opened up and she caught sight of the horse operation.

Two dozen horses grazed in the vast pasture, their coats gleaming in the cool morning sunlight.

Barn seemed a vast understatement for the imposing white-painted structure that dominated the view. It was massive, at least twice as large as the barn they had passed closer to the ranch house, and more horses were in individual corrals off it.

As she pulled up and parked, she caught sight of a small two-story log home behind it. Situated to face the Tetons, the house had one steep gable with a balcony protruding from a window in the center and a wide porch looking out over the view.

She wasn't sure how she knew—maybe the tiny saplings out front that looked like they hadn't been there long—but the house looked new. Everything did, she thought. From the corrals to the vast gleaming barn to the pickup truck parked outside, everything gleamed with prosperity.

She had barely turned off the engine when Seth Dalton walked out of the barn and she had to catch her breath at the picture he made. He was wearing a worn denim jacket and a black cowboy hat. As he moved with that unconscious grace she'd noticed the night before, she saw he also wore figure-hugging jeans that suddenly made her feel jittery and weak-kneed.

The man was entirely too good-looking. She wasn't sure why that observation made her so irritable, but she found herself fighting the urge to shut the SUV door with a little more force than necessary, especially when he aimed that killer grin in her direction.

"Morning. It's a gorgeous one, isn't it?"

She raised a skeptical eyebrow. Clouds hung low over the Tetons and the cold wind felt heavy with the promise of snow.

"If you say so."

He laughed, a low, throaty sound that made her insides flutter, then he turned his attention to Cole, who had climbed out the other side of the vehicle to slouch against the door.

"You ready to work?"

Cole glowered at his benefactor, much to Jenny's chagrin. "Do I have a choice?"

In answer, Dalton just gave him a long, slow look and Jenny was amazed to watch Cole be the first to back down, shifting his gaze to the work boots he'd borrowed from his grandfather.

Before she could say anything, Seth's attention shifted to Morgan, who had climbed out of the back-seat to join them.

"And who are you?"

"I'm Morgan Jeanette Boyer." She spoke with formal precision and held out her hand exactly like a nine-year-old princess greeting her favorite courtier.

A muscle twitched in Seth's cheek but he hid any sign of amusement as he took her hand and shook it. "Pleased to meet you, Miss Boyer. I'm Seth Dalton."

Morgan smiled. "I know. You're my friend Natalie's uncle. She says you have more girlfriends than Colin Farrell."

"Morgan!" Jenny exclaimed hotly, her cheeks fiery.

"What?" her daughter asked, all innocence.

Seth grinned, though Jenny thought she saw a hint of embarrassment behind it.

"Are all those horses your very own?" Morgan asked.

"Actually, most of them aren't. I have six or seven of my own but the rest I guess you could say I share with my family. Plus I'm training a few for other people."

He studied the avid interest in her eyes. "I don't suppose you'd want to have a look around, would you?"

Morgan gave a little jump of excitement. "Yeah! Can I, Mom?"

How could she say no? "I suppose. As long as you're sure we won't be in the way."

"Not at all. I have to show Cole around, anyway. No reason you two can't tag along."

They made a peculiar tour group, she thought as Seth led them inside the barn. It was more arena than stable, she realized. Though stalls ran around the perimeter, most of the space was taken up by a vast, open dirt floor. Handy for year-round training during the Idaho winters, she thought.

As he pointed out various features of the facility, Cole slouched along behind, Morgan asked a million questions and Jenny mainly focused on trying to keep her gaze away from Seth Dalton, difficult though it was.

"Everything looks so new," Jenny commented while Morgan was busy patting a horse and Cole slumped against the fence ringing the arena, looking as though he'd rather be anywhere else on the planet.

"The Cold Creek has been here for five generations,

but the horse operation is pretty new. My brother and I decided a few years ago to diversify. We've always raised and trained our own horses on a limited scale and only for ourselves. We decided a few years ago to expand that part of our operations and try the open market."

"How has it been going?"

"I've got more work than I can handle right now."

"That's a good thing, isn't it?"

"Better than I ever dreamed." His smile was slow and sexy and seemed to suck all the oxygen molecules from the vast structure.

She didn't realize she was staring at it for several seconds, then she quickly shifted her gaze away from his mouth to find him watching her, an odd, glittery look in his blue eyes.

"What's that room?" Morgan asked, shattering the sudden painfully awkward silence.

Seth shifted his attention to her. "That's my office. Come on, I'll show you."

He opened the door to a small room several degrees warmer than the rest of the barn. When he opened the door, an oddly colored puppy blinked at them then jumped up from a blanket on the floor and started yipping a frantic greeting.

"You're finally waking up, sleepyhead?" Seth smiled at the pup. "Come and meet our company."

The puppy sniffed all their shoes in turn and made it as far as Morgan before the girl scooped him up and hugged him tightly. "He's so cute! What's his name?"

"He's a she and her name is Lucy."

"Oh, you are a pretty girl. Yes you are," Morgan

cooed, rubbing noses with the puppy. Jenny felt a pang. Her daughter adored animals of all shapes and sizes and used to constantly beg for a dog or cat of her own, until her pulmonologist in Seattle recommended against it.

"What kind of dog is she?" Cole asked, his first words since they'd arrived at the ranch.

"Australian shepherd. I bought her and her brother at a horse auction in Boise last month. I only meant to buy one for a birthday present for my mother but I couldn't resist Lucy."

"You have sheep, too?" Morgan asked.

"Uh, no." He looked a little embarrassed. "But they work cattle, too, and I figured she can help me when I'm training a horse for cutting."

"Cutting what?" Morgan asked.

"Cutting cattle. That's a term for picking an individual cow or calf out of a herd. A well-trained cutting horse will do all the work for a cowboy. He just has to point out which cow he wants and the horse will separate him out of the rest of the cows."

"Wow! Can your horses do that?"

Instead of being put off my Morgan's relentless questions, Seth seemed charmed by her daughter. "Some of them," he said. "Sometime when you come out I'll give you a demonstration."

"Cool!"

He grinned at Morgan's enthusiasm and Jenny could swear she felt her blasted knees wobble. Oh, the man was dangerous. Entirely too sexy for his own good. She had to get out of there before she dissolved into a brainless puddle of hormones.

"Morgan, you and I had better go. Cole and Mr. Dalton have work to do."

She was pleasantly surprised when Morgan didn't kick up a fuss but followed her out of the barn into the cool November sunshine. Only as they approached the SUV did Jenny pick up on the reason for her daughter's unusual docility.

In just a few seconds, Morgan had turned pale, her breathing wheezy and labored.

She should have expected it from the combination of animal dander, hay and excitement, but the swiftness of the asthma flare-up took her by surprise.

Still, Jenny had learned from grim experience never to go anywhere unprepared. She yanked the door open and lunged for her purse on the floor by the driver's seat. Inside was Morgan's spare inhaler and she quickly, efficiently puffed the medicine into the chamber and handed it to Morgan, then set her on the passenger seat while she drew the medicine into her lungs.

Morgan had that familiar panicky look in her eyes and Jenny spoke softly to calm her, the same nonsense words she always used.

She forgot all about Seth Dalton until he leaned past her into the SUV, big and disconcertingly masculine.

"That's it, honey," Seth said, keeping his own voice low and soothing. "Concentrate on the breathing and all the good air going into your lungs. You're doing great."

After a moment, the rescue medication did its work and the color started to return to her features. The panic in her eyes slowly gave way to the beginnings of relief and Jenny's heart twisted with pain for her child's trials and the courage Morgan wielded against them.

* * *

"Better?" Seth asked after a moment.

The girl nodded and Seth was grateful to see the flare-up seemed to be under control. "I'd tell you to go on back into the barn where it's warmer," he said to Jenny, "but I suspect the hay or the puppy triggered the attack, didn't they?"

Her eyes widened as if surprised he knew anything about asthma. He didn't tell her he could have written the damn book on it.

"That's what I thought," Jenny said. She was starting to lose her tight, in-control look, he saw, and now just looked like a worried mother. "I should have realized they might."

"Why don't we take her into the house over there for a minute until she feels better? This cold can't be the greatest for her lungs."

She looked as if she wanted to argue, but Morgan coughed just then and her mother nodded. "That's probably a good idea."

Seth scooped the girl into his arms easily, and headed for the house with Jenny and Cole following behind him. Morgan still breathed shallowly, her little chest rising and falling quickly as she tried to ease the horrible breathlessness he remembered all too well.

"I hate having asthma," she whispered, her voice far too bitter for a little girl.

He recognized the bitterness, too. He knew just what it felt like to be ten and trapped with a body that didn't work like he wanted it to. He had wanted to be a junior buckaroo rodeo champion, wanted to climb the Tetons by the time he was twelve, wanted to be the star pitcher on the Little League baseball team. Instead, he'd been small and weak and spent far too much time breathing into a lousy tube.

"Sucks, doesn't it?" he answered. "The worst is the one time you forget to take your inhaler somewhere and of course you suddenly you get hit by a flare-up."

She blinked at him and he was struck by how sweet it was to have a child look at him with such trust. "You have it, too?"

He nodded. "I don't have attacks very often now, maybe once or twice a year and they're usually pretty mild. When I was your age, though, it was a different story."

He set her down on his leather sofa and grabbed a blanket for her.

She couldn't seem to get over the fact that he knew what she was going through. "But you're big! You ride horses and everything."

"You can ride horses, too. You just have to watch for your triggers, like I do, and do your best to manage things. When I was a kid, they didn't have some of the newer maintenance meds they have now and we had a tough time finding the best treatment for me but eventually we did. You probably know you never grow out of asthma, but lots of times the symptoms decrease a lot when you get older. That's what happened to me."

"You probably weren't afraid like I am when I have an attack. Cole says I'm a big wussy."

Jenny looked pained by the admission and Seth sent the boy a pointed look. At least Cole had the grace to look embarrassed.

"I was just kidding," the kid mumbled. He needed

a serious attitude adjustment, Seth thought, wondering if he'd been such a punk when he'd gone through his rebellious teens.

"I can't think of anything scarier than not being able to breathe," Seth told Morgan. "People who haven't been through it don't quite understand what it's like, do they? Like you're trapped underwater and somebody's got two fists around your lungs and is squeezing them tight so you can only take a tiny breath at a time."

Morgan nodded her agreement. "I always feel like I'm trapped under a big heavy blanket."

"What's your peak flow?"

She told him and he nodded. "Mine was pretty close to that when I was about your age." He paused and saw the conversation was starting to tire her. "Can I get you a glass of water or some juice?"

She nodded, closing her eyes, and he rose and went into the kitchen to find a glass. Somehow he wasn't surprised when Jenny followed him.

"Thank you." She gave him a quiet smile and he felt an odd little tug in his chest.

"I didn't do anything," he said as he poured a glass of orange juice from the refrigerator.

"You were very kind to her and I appreciate your sharing your own condition with her. It's great for Morgan to talk to adults who have managed to move past their childhood asthma and go on to live successful lives. Thank you," she said again, following it up this time with another small, hesitant smile.

He studied that smile, the way it highlighted the lushness of a mouth that seemed incongruous with her buttoned-down appearance.

What was it about her? She wasn't gorgeous in a Miss Rodeo Idaho kind of way. Not tall and curvy with a brilliant smile and eyes that knew just how to reel a man in.

She was small and compact, probably no bigger than five foot three. He supposed he'd call her cute, with that red-gold hair and her green eyes and the little ski jump of a nose.

Seth couldn't say he had a particular favorite type of woman—he was willing to admit he loved them all—but he usually gravitated toward the kind of women who hung out at the Bandito. The kind in tight jeans and tighter shirts, with big breasts and hungry smiles.

Jenny Boyer was just about the polar opposite of that kind of woman. Cute or not, he probably wouldn't usually take a second look at a woman who looked like a suburban soccer mom, with her tailored tan slacks and her wool blazer. Jenny Boyer was the kind of settled, respectable woman men like him usually tended to avoid.

Yet here they were, and he couldn't seem to keep his eyes off her. She might not be his usual type but he sure liked looking at her.

He frowned a little at the unexpectedness of his attraction to her, then decided to shrug it off. He would never do anything about it. Not with a woman like Jenny Boyer, who had *Complication* written all over her.

Morgan's color was much better when they returned to the living room. She was sitting up bickering with her brother, something he figured was a good sign.

She took the juice from him with a shy smile.

"Cole and I have things to do but you two are welcome to hang out here until Morgan feels better."

"I think I'm all right now," the girl said.

"I should get her home for a nebulizer treatment and to check her peak flow."

"I can carry you back out to the car if you want."

Morgan shook her head. "I can walk. But thanks."

After her daughter was settled in the SUV, Jenny turned to him and to Cole.

"What time shall I come back?" she asked.

He thought of his schedule for the day. "Don't worry about it. I'll be running into town about four. We should be done by then so I'll bring him back and save you a trip. Just take care of Morgan."

"All right. Thank you." She looked at her son as if she wanted to say something more, but she only let out a long breath, slid into her vehicle and drove away.

"So are we going to work on the car or what?" Cole finally addressed him after the SUV pulled away.

If Seth hadn't noticed how concerned the boy had looked during those first few moments of the flare-up, he would probably find him more trouble than he was worth.

"Oh, eventually," he said with a smile that bordered on evil. "First, you've got some stalls to muck. I hope you brought good thick gloves because you're going to need 'em."

Chapter 3

Fourteen was a miserable bitch of an age.

Though more than half his life had passed since that notable year, it felt just as fresh and painful now as Seth watched Cole Boyer shovel manure out of a stall.

Though the kid wasn't tall by any stretch of the imagination, he was gangly and awkward, as if his muscles were still too short to keep up with his longer bones.

Seth remembered those days. He'd been small for his age, too, six inches shorter than most of the other guys in his class, and with asthma to boot. His father's death had been just a few years earlier. And while he hadn't been exactly paralyzed by grief over the bastard, he *had* struggled to figure out his place in the world now that he wasn't Hank Dalton's sickly, sissy-boy youngest son.

He'd been a little prick, too, full of anger and attitude. He had brothers to pound on to help vent some of it, but since fights usually ended with them beating the tar out of him, he tended to shy away from that activity. Eventually, he'd turned some of his excess energy to horses.

He trained his first horse that year, he remembered, a sweet little chestnut mare he'd ridden in the Idaho state high school rodeo finals a few years later.

Yeah, fourteen had been miserable, for the most part. But the next year everything started to come together. Between his fourteenth and fifteenth years, he hit a major growth spurt, the asthma all but disappeared and he gained six inches of height and thirty pounds of muscle, almost as if his body had just been biding its time.

Girls who'd ignored him all his life suddenly sat up and took notice—and he noticed them right back. After that, adolescence became a hell of a lot more fun, though he doubted Jenny Boyer would appreciate him sharing that particular walk down memory lane with her son, no matter how miserable he looked about life right now.

He *should* be miserable, Seth thought. Though he was tempted to turn soft and tell Cole he'd done enough for the day, he only had to think about the damage to his GTO to stiffen his resolve.

A little misery never hurt a kid.

"Can you hurry it up here?" Seth leaned indolently

on the stall railing, mostly because he knew it would piss the kid off.

Sure enough, all he earned for his trouble was a heated glare.

"This isn't exactly easy."

"It's not supposed to be," Seth said.

After three hours, the kid had only mucked out four stalls, with two more to go. The more he shoveled, the grimmer his mood turned, until Seth was pretty sure he was ready to implode.

Tempted as he was to wait for the explosion, he finally took pity on him and reached for another shovel.

Cole gave him a surprised look when Seth joined him in the stall. "I thought I was supposed to be doing this."

"You are. But since I'd like to take a look at the car you trashed sometime today, I figure the only way that's going to happen is if I lend a hand."

"I'm going as fast as I can," Cole muttered.

"I know. If I thought you were slacking, you can bet I'd still be out there watching."

Surprise flickered in eyes the same green as his mother's, but he said nothing. They worked in silence for a few moments, the only sounds the scrape of shovels on concrete, the whickers of the horses around them and Lucy's curious yips as she followed them.

Only after they'd moved onto the last stall did the boy speak. "Why don't you have a real job or something?" he asked, his tone more baffled than hostile.

Seth raised an eyebrow. "You don't think this is real work?"

"Sure. But what kind of loser signs up to shovel horse crap all day?"

Seth laughed. "If this was the only thing I did around here all day, I'd have to agree with you. But I usually leave the grunt work to the hired help while I get to do the fun stuff."

"Like what?"

"Working with the horses. Breeding them, training them."

"Whatever."

"Not a real horse fan?"

"They're big and dumb. How hard could it be to train them?"

"You might be surprised." He scraped another shovel full of sunshine. "I can tell you there's nothing so satisfying as taking a green-broke horse—that means an untrained one—and working with him until he obeys anything you tell him to do without question."

"Whatever," Cole said again, his voice dripping with scorn.

To his surprise, Seth found he was more amused by the kid's attitude than he'd been by anything in a long time. "Come on, I'll show you. Drop your shovel."

Cole didn't need a second invitation. He dropped it with a clatter and followed Seth toward a stall at the end of the row, where his big buckskin Stella waited.

In moments, he had her saddled, then led her outside to one of the corrals where he kept a dozen or so cattle to help with the training.

"Okay, now pick a steer."

"Why?"

He had to laugh at the boy's horrified expression.

"I'm not going to make you ride the thing, I promise. Remember how I was telling Morgan about cutting? Stella's going to cut whatever steer you pick out of the herd for you. Just tell me which one you want her to go after."

"How the hell should I know? They all look the same!"

"You've got a lot to learn, city boy. How about the one in the middle there, with the white face?"

At least the kid had lost his belligerence, though he was looking at Seth like he'd been kicked by a horse one too many times.

"Sure. Get that one."

He gave the commands to Stella then sat back in the saddle and let her do her thing. She was brilliant, as usual. In minutes, she had the white-faced Hereford just where Seth wanted him, away from the herd and heading for the fence where Cole had perched to watch the demonstration.

"There you go. He's all yours," Seth called over the cattle's lowing.

The boy jumped down faster than a bullet at the sight of a half-ton animal heading toward him.

Seth pulled Stella off and let the steer return to the rest of the herd, then led the horse back through the gate.

"So what do you think? She's brilliant, isn't she?"

"You told her what to do."

"Sure. But she did it, didn't she? Without even hesitating. She's a great horse." He slid out of the saddle, then sent the kid a sidelong glance. "You do much riding?"

Cole snorted. "There aren't too many horses on Seattle street corners sitting around waiting to be ridden."

"You don't have that excuse here. Get on."

Before Cole could argue, Seth handed him the reins and hefted him into the saddle.

He looked even smaller than his age up on the big horse, though Seth gave him points for not sliding right back down. With one hand on the bridle, he led them back inside the training facility.

"You probably know the basics, even if you've never ridden before, just from watching TV. Keep a firm hand on the reins, pull them in the direction you want her to go. Above all, have fun."

He let go of the bridle, confident the horse was too well-trained to unseat her rider, no matter how inexperienced.

Sure enough, she started a slow walk around the arena. Cole looked terrified at first, then he gradually started to relax. By the second time around the arena, he even smiled a little, though he bounced in the saddle like a particularly hapless sack of flour.

"I suck, don't I?" he said ruefully as they passed Seth.

Sit up, boy. Or are you too tired *to learn to be a man? You'll never be able to ride the damn thing if you slouch in the saddle like that and gasp like a trout on the end of a frigging hook every time the horse takes a step.*

He pushed away the echo of his father's voice, wondering if he'd been four or five during that particular riding lesson. "You don't suck," he assured Seth. "You just have to learn to move with the rhythm of the horse.

It takes a while to figure it out. For your first time, you're kickin' A."

For one shining instant, Cole looked thrilled at the praise. He must have felt himself smile, though, because he quickly retreated back into his brittle shell.

"Am I done here? My butt's starting to hurt."

Seth sighed as the momentary animation slipped away. He shrugged and held Stella again so Cole could slide down.

"We've got one more stall to finish. Work on that while I take off Stella's saddle."

Cole grimaced but headed back to his shovel.

He couldn't expect to change the kid's attitude with one horseback ride, Seth thought. But maybe the car would do the trick.

He caught his own thoughts and grimaced at himself. Since when was he the do-gooder of Pine Gulch? He had no business even trying to fix this troubled kid's problems. Better just to get his money's worth out of him in labor to compensate for the car damage and leave the attitude-adjusting to his mother.

Saturdays were usually one of her most productive days of the week, away from the office and all the distractions of running an elementary school with four hundred students.

She usually accomplished more in a few hours than she could do in two days at school, between lunch duty and phone calls from concerned parents and dealing with state and federal education regulations.

Today, Jenny couldn't seem to focus on work at all while she waited for Seth Dalton to return with Cole.

After trying for an hour and a half to slog through some paperwork while Morgan rested on the couch next to her in the den watching television, she finally gave it up for a lost cause.

She wasn't worried about Cole. Not precisely. She was more concerned that her belligerent son would forget Seth was doing him a huge favor and instead would vent his unhappiness in all the usual ways.

She couldn't stress about that. Something told her a man like Dalton was more than capable of holding his own against a fourteen-year-old rebel.

He struck her as a man who could handle just about anything. She thought of those strong, capable shoulders and had to suppress a sigh. Why couldn't she seem to get the man off her mind?

She'd had an unwilling fascination for him since the first time she heard his name, long before her son's recklessness brought them into his orbit. It had been a month or so after school started and she'd been in her office after lunch when one of her brand-new teachers, just out of college and still half terrified of her students, stopped in during her prep hour to talk to Marcy, the school secretary.

It hadn't surprised her the two were friends. Marcy was only a few years older than Ashley Barnes, the new kindergarten teacher. Beyond that, she was warm and bubbly, the kind of person who drew everyone to her. Not only was she great at her job but the children adored her and Jenny had learned most of the other teachers did, too.

She hadn't meant to eavesdrop, but her door had been open and she'd been able to hear every word.

"He said he'd call me," Ashley complained. "How stupid was I to believe him?"

Marcy had only laughed. "You're human and you're female. There's not a woman in town who can resist Seth Dalton when he gives that smile of his. Heck, he even has all the old ladies in my grandma's quilting club batting their fake eyelashes at him."

"That night at the Bandito, you'd think I was the only woman in the world," Ashley said, the bitterness in her voice completely at odds with her usual sunny disposition. "He never left my side all night and we danced every single dance. I thought he really liked me."

"I'm sure he did like you that night. But that's the thing about Seth. He lives completely in the moment."

"He's a dog." Ashley sounded close to tears.

"No, he's not. Believe it or not, he's actually a pretty decent guy. He's the first one out on his tractor plowing his neighbors' driveways after a big snowstorm and he always stops to help somebody in trouble. But he was blessed—or cursed, however you want to look at it—with the kind of good looks that make women go a little crazy around him."

"You think I imagined that night?"

"No. Oh, honey, I'm sure you didn't," Marcy had replied in her patient, kind voice. "My friends and I have a theory. We call it Seth Dalton's School of Broncobustin'. If you're lucky to find him turning his attention to you, just climb on and hold on tight. It probably won't last too long, but it will be a hell of a ride."

"I'm not like that!" Ashley had exclaimed. "I never even go to bars. I don't drink. I probably wouldn't even have met him if my roommate hadn't dragged me along that night."

"Which is probably the reason he didn't call you," Marcy pointed out gently. "You're a kindergarten teacher with *Marriage Material* stamped on your forehead. You're sweet and innocent, and you probably have already got names picked out for the four kids you're going to have."

"Is that such a bad thing?"

"Oh, honey, absolutely not. I think it's wonderful, and somewhere out there is someone who is going to love those things about you. But that's not what Seth Dalton is about."

One of the third-graders had come in just then complaining of a stomach ache. Marcy had turned her attention to calling the girl's mother to come get her and Ashley had returned to her class, but not before Jenny had developed a strong dislike for the man under discussion.

It was one of those weird cases where, once she heard a name, she suddenly couldn't seem to escape it: Seth Dalton's kept popping up.

She heard another teacher just before the start of a faculty meeting talk about running into him in the grocery store and how she'd been so flustered just because he'd smiled and asked her how she was that she'd left without half the items on her list.

When they were brainstorming ways to raise money for new library books, someone suggested a bachelor auction and someone else said they'd have enough books to fill every shelf if only they could get Seth Dalton on the auction block.

Now that she'd met him, she certainly understood all the buzz about the man. A woman could forget her own name just from one look out of those blue eyes.

"Are you done with your work?" Morgan asked from her spot on the couch, distracting her from her completely unproductive train of thought.

She closed her laptop and gathered her papers, shoving them back into her briefcase. She had learned long ago how to recognize a lost cause. "For now. Want to watch a DVD or play a game?"

"Sure. You pick."

They were still discussing their options a moment later when she heard the back door open and a moment later her father came in, his cheeks red from the November chill and his arms full of wood to replenish the low supply in the firebox by the woodstove.

"You should let me do that," she chided, upset at herself for being too distracted by thoughts of Seth Dalton to pay attention to her father's activities.

"Why?" Jason looked genuinely surprised.

"I feel guilty sitting here where it's warm and comfortable while you're outside hauling wood."

"I need the exercise. Keeps my joints lubricated."

She had to laugh at that. At sixty-five, her father was more fit than most men half his age. He rode his mountain bike all over town, he fished every chance he got—winter or summer—and his new passion was cross-country skiing.

"Maybe I need the exercise, too."

"And maybe it does my heart good to know I'm still capable of seeing to the comfort of my daughter and granddaughter. You wouldn't want to take that away from an old man, would you?" Jason said, with a twinkle in his eyes and the incontrovertible logic that had made him such a formidable opponent in the courtroom.

She rolled her eyes and was amused to see Morgan copying her gesture.

"Grandpa, you're silly," her daughter said with fondness. "You're not old."

The two of them were kindred spirits and got along like the proverbial house on fire. Coming to Pine Gulch had been the right decision, she thought again. Even if Cole still fought and bucked against it like one of Seth Dalton's horses with a burr under the saddle, the move had been good for all of them.

She couldn't be sorry for it. Morgan and Cole had come to know the grandfather they had been acquainted with only distantly, and in a lot of ways, Jenny felt the same. Jason had been a distant, distracted figure in her life, even before her parents had divorced when she was twelve. Coming here had led to a closer relationship than they'd ever had.

"We're going to watch a DVD. Are you interested? We're debating between a *Harry Potter* or one of the *Lord of the Rings* trilogy."

"Oh, Tolkien. By all means."

They settled on which of the three to see and were watching the opening credits when by some mother's intuition, she heard the low rumble of a truck out front.

"Go ahead and start the movie," she said. "Since I've seen it at least a dozen times, I'm sure I won't be too lost when I come back."

She reached the front door just as Cole hopped down

from a big silver pickup truck. Through the storm door, she studied her son intently. Though he didn't appear to be exactly overflowing with joy, he didn't seem miserable, either, as he headed up the sidewalk to the house.

She wasn't really surprised when Seth climbed out the other side of the truck and followed the boy up to the house. She opened the door for her son, who would probably have walked right by without even a greeting if she hadn't stepped right in his way.

"How did it go?" she asked, fighting the yearning to pull him into her arms for the kind of hug he used to give her all the time.

"My favorite Levi's smell like horse crap."

"I'm sure that will wash out."

"I doubt it," Cole grumbled. "They're probably ruined forever."

"Here's a tip for you," Seth spoke from the doorway with a lazy smile. "Next time you come to the ranch, maybe you shouldn't wear your favorite pair of Levi's."

"If you're going to suggest I buy a pair of Wranglers, I might just have to puke."

"I wouldn't dare," Seth drawled. "Then your favorite pair of Levi's would smell like horse crap and puke."

Cole's snort might have passed for a laugh, but Jenny could not be quite sure.

"Wear whatever you want. But if you take the school bus to the Cold Creek on Tuesday, we might be ready to get into the real work on the car now that we've taken a look at the damage. Bus Fifteen is the one you want to take. Ray Pullman is the driver."

"Right. I need to take a shower."

"Bring your jeans out when you're done so we can wash them," Jenny said.

Cole didn't answer her or even acknowledge her as he headed down the stairs to his bedroom, leaving her alone with Seth.

In part because of embarrassment over her son's rudeness and in part because Seth was so masculine and so blasted attractive, she was intensely aware of him. He seemed to fill up all the available space in the small foyer.

She gave a small huff of annoyance at herself and tried to ignore the scent of him that seemed to surround her, of warm male and sexy aftershave.

"Tell me the truth. How did it really go today? I doubt Cole will tell me much."

"Good. He worked hard at everything I asked him to do and some of it wasn't very appealing. I can't ask for more than that."

She relaxed the fingers she hadn't realized she'd clenched tightly in the pockets of her sweater. "Was he…" her voice trailed off and she couldn't figure out how to ask the question in a way that wouldn't make her sound like a terrible mother.

"Rude and obnoxious? Not much, surprisingly. He digs cars and we spent much of the afternoon working on mine, so everything was cool."

"I can't tell you how relieved that makes me."

"You should probably know I did throw him up on a horse for a few minutes. He actually seemed to enjoy it. Even smiled a few times."

She blinked, trying to imagine her rebellious city-boy "I-hate-everything-country" son on the back of a horse.

"You're sure we're talking about the same kid? He wasn't possessed by alien cowboy pod people?"

Seth laughed, his blue eyes crinkled at the corners, and she could swear she felt warm fingers trickling down her spine just looking at him.

"Not a UFO in sight, I swear."

She shouldn't be here, sharing laughter or anything else with Seth Dalton. With sharp efforts, she broke eye contact. "Thank you for all the trouble you've gone to," she said after an uncomfortable moment. "It would have been less work on your part if you had just turned him over to the authorities."

"I'm getting free labor with my horses and with my car. Not a bad deal. I'm no saint here."

"So they tell me."

Had she really said that aloud? She mentally cringed at her rudeness and Seth looked startled at first, then gave her one of those blasted slow smiles that ought to come with a warning label as long as her arm.

"Who's been talking about me, Ms. Boyer?"

Her nerve endings tingled at his low, amused voice, but she ignored it, turning her own voice prim. "Who hasn't? You're a favorite topic of conversation in Pine Gulch, Mr. Dalton."

He didn't seem bothered by town gossip—or maybe he was just used to it.

Looking for all the world as if he planned to make himself right at home, he leaned a hip against the door frame and crossed his arms across his chest. "That must tell you what a quiet town you've settled in, if nobody in Pine Gulch has anything more interesting to talk about than me. So what's the consensus?"

That you're a major-league player. That you flirt with anything female and have left a swath of broken hearts behind you. That half the women in Teton Valley are in love with you and the other half are in lust.

She *so* didn't want to be having this conversation with him. She thought longingly of the paperwork she'd been putting off all afternoon and would have given just about anything right then to be sitting at her desk filling out federal assessment forms. Anything but this.

"Nothing I'm sure you haven't already heard," she finally said. "You're apparently a busy man."

A purely masculine, absolutely enticing dimple appeared in his cheek briefly then disappeared again. "Yeah, starting a full-fledged horse ranch can take a lot of hours."

He had to know she wasn't talking about his equine endeavors, but she decided she wasn't going to set him straight.

"I'm sure it does," she murmured drily. Dating a different woman every night probably tended to fill up the calendar, too. But not this woman, even if she wasn't four years older than him and the exact opposite of all the tight, perky young things he was probably used to.

She knew all about men like him. She'd been married to one, a man compelled to charm every woman in sight.

She had worked hard to rebuild her heart and her life and her family in the last three years. After a great deal of hard work and self-scrutiny, she had finally become someone she could respect again.

She was a strong, successful woman who loved her work and her family, and she wasn't about to let a man like Seth Dalton knock her on her butt again.

Even if he did make her hormones wake up and sing hallelujah.

"Thank you for taking the time away from your horses to bring Cole back," she said, in what she hoped was a polite but dismissive tone.

He either didn't pick on it or didn't care. "No problem. How's Morgan doing now?"

She didn't want him to be interested in her daughter or for the simple question to remind her just how kind and patient he had been during Morgan's flare-up.

That was the problem with charmers, she supposed. They seemed instinctively to know how to zero in on a woman's weak spot and use that to their advantage. He'd already slipped inside her defenses a little by being so decent about Cole crashing his car. She would have preferred if he ignored Morgan altogether.

How was she to pigeonhole him as a selfish womanizer when he showed such genuine concern for her daughter's welfare?

"She's fine. By the time we returned home, her peak flow was about seventy percent. After we nebulized her, it went up to about eight-five percent."

"Good. I hope the flare-up doesn't discourage you from bringing her out to the ranch again. She's welcome to tag along with Cole anytime. You both are."

She smiled politely, though she had absolutely no intention of taking him up on the invitation. "Thank you. But I'm sure the very last thing you need underfoot—with you being so *busy* and all—is a wheezing nine-year-old girl."

"I'd like to have her back. Both of you. Pretty ladies are always welcome at the Cold Creek."

His smile was designed to reach right into a woman's soul and she felt it clear to her toes. Darn him. No, darn her for this ridiculous crush, the weakness she had for handsome charmers.

She couldn't endure his light flirtation, especially knowing he didn't mean any of it, it was all just a game to him.

He couldn't possibly be seriously interested in a stuffy, overstressed thirty-six-year-old elementary school principal with no chest to speak of and the tiniest bit of gray in her hair that she only managed to hide by the grace of God and a good stylist.

He wasn't interested in her, and he had no business smiling at her as if he were.

"Do you stay up nights thinking of lines or do you just come up with them on the fly?"

He raised an eyebrow, though amusement still lurked in his blue eyes, even in the face of her frontal attack. "Was that a line? I thought I was simply extending an invitation."

She sighed. "Look, you've been incredibly understanding about what Cole did to your car. If I had been in your shoes, I can't imagine I would be nearly so magnanimous. He's going to be working with you to make things right for at least a few months and I suppose we'll see a great deal of each other in that time, so let's get this out of the way."

"I'm all ears."

And sexy smiles and gorgeous eyes and broad shoulders that look like they could carry the weight of the world.

She frowned at herself. "I'm not interested in being charmed," she said bluntly.

"Is that what you think I was doing?"

"Weren't you?" She didn't give him a chance to answer. "I doubt you're even aware of it, it's so ingrained in your nature. The flirting, the slow bedroom smiles. Even if you're not attracted to a woman, something in your blood compels you to conquer her, to find her weaknesses and exploit them until she surrenders to your charm like every other woman."

He gazed at her, obviously taken aback by the sudden attack. She heard her own rudeness and was appalled but couldn't seem to stop the words from gushing out.

All she could think of was Ashley Barnes crying her eyes out when Seth never called her back and Richard murmuring lies and promises while he was already sleeping with another woman and planning to abandon his children.

"It's different if a man is genuinely interested in a woman," she went on. "If he truly wants to know about her, if he might feel some spark of attraction and want to follow up on it. That's one thing. But you're not interested in me. Men like you charm just because you can."

He straightened from the door jamb, a sudden fiery light in his eyes that had her stepping back a pace. "That's quite a scathing indictment, Ms. Boyer, especially since you've known me less than a day. I thought good teachers and principals weren't supposed to rush to snap judgments."

His words gave her pause and she had to wonder what in heaven's name seemed to possess her around him.

"You're right. Absolutely. I'm very sorry. That was completely uncalled-for. I'll make a deal with you. I won't rush to any snap judgments provided you refrain from trying to add me to your list of conquests."

Before he could answer, she held open the door in a pointed dismissal. Cold air rushed in, swirling around her like a malicious fog, but she knew it wouldn't be enough to take care of her hot embarrassment. "Thank you again for bringing Cole home. I'll be sure to send him out to your ranch on the bus Tuesday."

Seth gave her a long, hard look, as if he had much more he wanted to say, but he finally turned around and walked outside.

She closed the door and leaned against it, her hands clenched at her sides.

How had she let him get her so stirred up? He hadn't done anything. Not really. Sure, he'd flirted a little, but she had always been able to handle a mild flirtation. He seemed to push all her buttons—and several she hadn't realized were there.

How on earth was she supposed to face him again after she'd all but accused him of trying to seduce her?

She would simply have to be cool and polite. She would be gracious about what he was doing for her son but distant about everything else. She had no doubt she could keep him at arm's length, especially after she'd just slapped him down so firmly.

Keeping him out of her head was a different matter entirely.

Chapter 4

Seth stood on the porch of Jason Chambers's red-brick rambler, the November evening air sharp with fall, and tried to figure out what the heck had just happened in there.

He wasn't at all used to being on the receiving end of such a blunt dismissal, and he was fairly certain he didn't care for it much. He had only been talking to the woman, just trying to be friendly, and she was treating him like she'd just caught him looking up her skirt.

He wasn't quite sure how to react. He had certainly encountered his share of rejection. It never usually bothered him, not when there were so many other prospects out there.

He had to admit, he just wasn't used to rejection accompanied by such blatant hostility.

He ought to just march right back in there and ask Jenny Boyer what he had done in the course of their short acquaintance to warrant it. He lifted a hand to the doorbell then let it fall again.

No. What would that accomplish, besides making him look foolish? She had the right to her opinions, even if they were completely ridiculous.

Even if you're not attracted to a woman, something in your blood compels you to conquer her, to find her weaknesses and exploit them until she surrenders to your charm like every other woman.

That wasn't true. He didn't need to charm every female he came in contact with. He just happened to be a sociable kind of guy.

Where did she get off forming such a harsh opinion on him when they'd barely met?

More to the point, why did it bug him so much?

It was no big deal, he told himself as the cold wind slapped at him. Better to just forget about Ms. Uptight Jennifer Boyer and head over to the Bandito, where he could find any number of warm, willing women who didn't think he was so objectionable.

His boots thudded on the steps as he headed off the porch toward his truck. He climbed in and started the engine, but for some strange reason couldn't bring himself to drive away from the house just yet, too busy analyzing his own reaction to being flayed alive by a tongue sharper than his best Buck knife.

He ought to be seriously pissed off at the woman and not want anything more to do with her. He was, he told himself.

So why was he somehow even more attracted to her?

He liked curvy women who played up their assets, who wore low-cut blouses and short skirts and towering high heels that made their legs look long and sexy.

His brothers seemed to think that was just another sign that he needed to grow up and get serious about life. He had to wonder what Jake and Wade would say if they knew about this strange attraction for the new elementary school principal.

Yeah, he liked looking at her—the tilt of her chin and the flash of her green eyes and those lush lips that seemed at odds with her starchy appearance.

And she smelled good. He had definitely picked up on that. Her perfume had been soft and sweet, putting all kinds of crazy images in his head of wildflowers and spring mountain rain showers.

And her hair. A man could go a little crazy trying to figure out just how to describe it. It was red, yeah, but not just red. Instead, it was a hundred different shades, from gold to something that reminded him of the first soft brush of color on the maples in fall.

He let out a breath. Oh, he was attracted to her all right. Curiously more so now than he'd been even before he walked inside with Cole.

More than that, he was also intensely curious to know whether he could change her opinion of him.

The challenge of it seemed irresistible suddenly.

He shook his head at himself, wholly aware of the irony. He was sitting here pondering how to change the mind of a woman who thought he was nothing more than a womanizer. That was all fine, except for the reason he wanted to change her mind—because he wanted to seduce her, exactly like the womanizer she thought he was.

He ought to just drive away and leave her alone. But the thought of that was as unappealing as riding a steer. He had to try. Something about her prim, buttoned-down beauty appealed to him more than any woman in longer than he could remember.

He didn't even want to think what insight someone could get into his brain that the first woman to really intrigue him in a long time was the one woman who apparently wanted nothing to do with him.

Was she right, that it was all about the challenge to him?

Maybe.

But what was life without a little challenge?

Jennifer Boyer was a tough nut to crack, Seth thought two weeks later outside the Cold Creek horse barn.

He'd seen her a handful of times since that first evening when he dropped Cole off. Though he'd been tempted to pour on the charm, he decided on a more low-key approach. She told him she wasn't interested in a flirtation and he had a strong feeling she would automatically reject any blatant overtures so instead he had tried to be warm and friendly, carefully suppressing any sign of his increasing attraction.

Whatever he was doing wasn't working. She wasn't interested. Worse, she seemed more distant each time they met than she had the time before. She responded politely enough, all the while looking at him out of those green eyes that he discovered could turn to ice chips in an instant.

He should have given it up for a lost cause a week ago, but the more she pushed him away, the harder he tried to find a foothold. He was determined to change her mind about him, but after two weeks he was beginning to fear it was a lost cause.

The only chink in her hard shell appeared to be Lucy, he had discovered. The stiff, distant principal seemed to melt around his puppy. Her whole demeanor relaxed and her face lit up in a smile that took his breath away.

Though it was no doubt ruthless of him, he had to admit, he flaunted his single advantage without scruple.

He wasn't a stupid man—he always made sure Lucy was awake and nearby, looking her adorable self, whenever he knew Jenny was due to arrive at the ranch with Cole.

If nothing else, Lucy served the purpose of keeping his quarry around a little longer, when he was sure she would otherwise have rushed off in a second. She always seemed to be in a hurry to get somewhere, unless the puppy happened to be around.

He watched her and Morgan now tossing a ball for Lucy. The late-autumn sunlight glinted off that magnificent hair and she looked fresh and soft and beautiful.

He wanted her with a heat that continued to baffle him.

Morgan was the one throwing the ball, so by rights Lucy should have been returning it to her. But she couldn't seem to get the message and kept dropping it at Jennifer's feet, to the amusement of all of them.

"You silly girl. What are we going to do with you?" Jenny said after several repeats of the neat little trick he would have taught the puppy, if only he'd thought of it. She picked Lucy up and brushed noses with her and it was all he could do hide the naked longing he knew must be obvious on his face.

He turned his attention to Morgan instead. "You're really great with her. You ought to think about being a vet."

Morgan beamed at him with none of her mother's reserve. "That's just what I told my teacher I want to be! I wrote a paper about it in school. Me and Natalie both want to be veterinarians."

This was new. Last he heard, his niece wanted to be a rodeo queen, but then he figured Nat would probably change her mind a hundred more times before she even reached middle school.

He tugged at one of her ponytails. "Tell you what. The next time the vet is scheduled to come out to look at my horses for some reason on a weekend or holiday, I'll give you a call and you and Natalie can tag along and watch him. If it's all right with your mom, of course."

Morgan's face lit up, making him feel about a dozen feet tall. Now if only he could get her mother to look at him the same way....

"Oh, please, Mom!" she begged. "It would be so awesome to watch a vet work with real horses. We wouldn't get in the way, I swear."

Jenny didn't look thrilled to be put on the spot.

"We'll have to see," she murmured in that cool, non-committal tone every parent seemed to have perfected.

In his limited experience, a "We'll see" was just the same as a "No" but Morgan didn't seem to see it the same way. She looked ecstatic at the possibility. He wanted to tell her most of the time the vets just came out to give shots, not do anything exciting or dramatic, but he didn't want to spoil it for her.

The girl threw the ball for the puppy one more time just as Cole came out of the garage.

"Finished putting the tools away?" Seth asked.

The boy nodded. "You know, I bet she's looking better now than she ever has, even when she was new."

Seth laughed. "You might be right. I can't imagine the folks in Detroit took as much care building her as we've spent restoring her."

Cole grinned and held up his bandaged index finger, the result of a minor accident with a rough piece of metal. "And we've got the war wounds to prove it."

If Seth hadn't been watching Jenny, he might have missed the raw emotion on her face when she looked at her son.

"How's the work on the car coming?" she asked. Seth opened his mouth to answer but saw her gaze was still trained on her son so he waited for the boy to answer.

"Okay," Cole said. Though he spoke only a single word, his tone wasn't at all his usual surly one.

"Better than okay," Seth corrected. "We've got the minor dings smoothed out and we're waiting for a new headlamp we had to order from a specialty shop back

East. Cole here is kicking butt on smoothing out the scrape on the side."

The boy looked pleased. "It's nothing. I'm only doing what you tell me to do."

"That's just what you're supposed to be doing," he growled. "Now if only I can keep you from throwing in those crappy CDs you call music, we'll get along fine."

"Just because you drive an old car doesn't mean you have to listen to the same music my grandpa does."

"It's blues and classic rock. And good for your grandpa, if he listens to CCR and Bob Seger. Maybe between the two of us, we can teach you to appreciate fine music."

Cole made a gagging sound that sent his sister into the giggles. Seth had to admit, for all his belligerence at first, the kid had warmed to him far easier than his mother had.

Cole Boyer loved cars. No question about it. Every time he walked into the garage to work on the GTO, he became a different kid. It was a physical and emotional change that Seth found fascinating to watch. He lifted his shoulders and stopped the perpetual slouch, he made eye contact more, he climbed out of his attitude and talked and chattered as much as Seth's nephew Tanner.

He glowed while he was working on the GTO and it was one more vivid reminder to Seth of himself. It didn't matter how small he'd been until he was fifteen, that he was wheezy and raspy and weak. Behind the wheel of a hot car, everything was relative.

Cole even seemed to respond to the horses. Every time he came to the ranch, Seth saddled a horse for him to ride a little. At first he hadn't been very enthusiastic about it, but as he gained more confidence in the saddle, that seemed to be changing.

Today Cole had even spurred his horse to a slight lope around the arena and had looked as thrilled by it as a bronc rider the first time he hit eight seconds on the timer.

He had to admit, he liked the kid. He was smart and worked hard. Though he still adopted his tough-guy attitude from time to time, when he relaxed his guard enough to let it slip, he was funny and bright and full of interesting observations about the world around him.

His favorite days of the week were those when Cole came out and helped him around the place—and only part of that had to do with knowing he would probably see Jenny, since she usually drove out to the Cold Creek to pick him up.

"When we have her back to her full glory, we'll all have to take a celebratory drive somewhere," Seth said. "Maybe we can run over to Idaho Falls for dinner or something."

"Can we take Lucy?" Morgan asked.

"If she learns to behave herself and doesn't pee on my floor mats."

Morgan giggled. "She is so cute. I wish we could take her home."

"You should see her with her brother," Seth said. "The two of them are quite a pair."

"Is he bossy, too?" Morgan asked him, with a pointed look at her own brother.

"I think she's the bossy one, but it's hard to tell.

They wrestle and play and get into all kinds of mischief when they're together."

"I bet they're funny," Morgan said.

"Come on, kids," Jenny finally broke in. "I have another school board meeting tonight and I don't want to dump all the chores and homework on Grandpa to supervise."

"Can I throw one more time?" Morgan asked. "I know she'll bring it back to me this time."

An idea sparked in his head as he watched the girl with the puppy—who finally seemed to get it right and dropped the ball at her feet instead of Jenny's.

He discarded it at first as completely out of the question, but it seemed to rattle around in his head as Cole and Morgan were climbing into her little SUV. He didn't want her to feel backed into a corner so he waited until they were settled inside the car, out of earshot, before he spoke.

"Do you have plans tomorrow?"

She looked at him warily. "Why?"

"I know it's still a week before Thanksgiving but my family is getting together tomorrow to go up on some land we've got up in the mountains to cut Christmas trees. We try to do it a little early before the real heavy snows hit. Why don't you all come along? My mother and brothers will be here. I'm sure Mom will bring Linus so Morgan can have the chance to play with both of the puppies."

She blinked, clearly not expecting that kind of invitation from him.

"It's a lot of fun," he pressed, warming to the idea

more and more. "We usually take sleds up and make a big party out of it. The kids would have a great time."

She pursed her lips. "I don't think so. It sounds like a family outing. I wouldn't want to intrude."

"You wouldn't be, I swear. Wade has already invited our vet and his family along and there's always room for a few more. I was up there on our land a month or so ago during round-up and tagged more than a dozen little spruces that would be perfect for Christmas trees. You only have to pick out your favorite and there are plenty to go around. You won't find fresher trees anywhere."

She looked tempted as she gazed up at the mountains. Her eyes softened and her expression turned wistful. What would he have to do to have her turn that kind of expression in his direction?

Right then he would have crawled up that mountain on his knees and ripped a tree out with his bare hands if it would make her look at *him* with those soft green eyes.

"Just think what a great holiday memory that would be for your kids," he pushed, wondering when he'd become so ruthless.

Jenny let out a breath at his words. Blast him. Seth Dalton could sell sunshine in the desert. She had been right about him that day at her father's house. The man knew just the right buttons to push, somehow instinctively finding exactly a woman's weakness and using it against her. How could he possibly know that she dreamed of creating the perfect holiday for her children?

She had such hopes for this year, wishing she could make up for the awful holidays past. The last few had been anything but pleasant as both children had been angry and upset after their father had broken yet more promises to visit.

Even before he'd left for Europe and completely abdicated his responsibility to his family, she'd been on her own most holidays. Richard often chose to work extra shifts during the holidays and Cole and Morgan saw him only sporadically.

Like Chevy Chase in Cole's favorite Christmas movie, she had dreamed about making this year perfect. They were in a new home, with a clean, blank slate for creating family traditions. And wouldn't riding into the mountains for their own tree be a perfect start?

Oh, she was tempted by his offer. Her mind was already conjuring up some Currier & Ives images of sleigh rides and hot cocoa and jingle bells on stamping, snorting horses.

But this particular offer came with some serious strings—attached, unfortunately, to a man she was finding extremely difficult to withstand.

She could feel her resistance to him slipping away every time she was with him and she knew she couldn't just surrender it without a fight. She couldn't afford to fall for a handsome charmer, not now when things were finally starting to go right.

"I don't think so." She put on her most brisk tone, the one she used with recalcitrant students throwing food in the lunch room. "Thank you for the offer, but we couldn't possibly intrude on a family event."

For a long moment he studied her, his head canted

to one side, then he finally sighed. "I know you dislike me, Ms. Boyer—"

"I don't!" she protested instinctively.

"Come on. The kids can't hear us so you don't have to pretend for politeness' sake," he said. "I'm not sure how it happened or why but I always seem to rub you the wrong way. Whatever I did, can't we somehow figure out a way to move past it for one day, just so you can allow Cole and Morgan to participate in something we both know they'll enjoy?"

Oh! How could he make her so angry and so guilty at the same time? He was right, blast him. She wanted so much to say yes. Morgan, at least, would have a wonderful time. Cole would probably say it was all lame, but she had a feeling he would secretly enjoy it, too, especially with Seth around.

The only reason she resisted the invitation was because she wasn't so sure she could resist *him*.

How could she deprive her children of this opportunity to create a lasting memory because of her own weakness?

For two weeks she had been doing her best to keep him out of her head, to pretend cool indifference to him. She tried to convince herself the little hitch in her chest every time she drove onto the Cold Creek was simply a little heartburn from eating school lunch with her students.

She knew it wasn't. Even though he was as polite and friendly and noncharming as she could have asked for, her attraction to him only seemed to blossom.

Somehow—without apparently making any effort at all—Seth seemed to be whittling away at her defenses. The prospect of having to pretend disinterest for an entire day was daunting.

She could do it, she thought. For her children's sake, she could be tough, couldn't she?

"What time?" she finally said.

He grinned with triumph, looking so gorgeous in the thin, fading sunlight that she had to remind herself she was supposed to be resisting him.

"We're probably heading up right after morning chores, maybe around eleven or so. Does that work?"

"It should. Yes."

"Bring your father along if you'd like. He can ride a sled up or my mother and stepfather usually stay behind to hang out."

"All right. Thank you."

"Make sure you dress warmly. It's supposed to snow tonight so we'll have plenty of fresh powder."

She nodded as she slid into her car, wondering as she started the engine if the temperatures would possibly cool enough overnight to keep her unruly hormones in the deep freeze she'd stored them in for the last three years.

Chapter 5

She was a bright, successful woman who was certainly mature enough to know her own mind, Jenny thought the next morning as she drove along freshly plowed roads toward the Cold Creek.

So how had she let Seth Dalton con her into this? Through the long, snowy night, she'd had plenty of time to think through the ramifications of what she'd committed herself and her children to by agreeing to come on this outing today.

An entire day in his company. What had she been thinking?

Easy. Thinking apparently wasn't an activity she excelled at when Seth Dalton was around. The man only had to look at her and her brain cells decided to head to the Bahamas.

However this excursion had come about, she didn't doubt Cole and Morgan—and Jason, when it came to that—would enjoy the day. She had to keep that uppermost in her mind.

It was a beautiful morning, at least. Seth had been right about the snow. Maybe some ranching instinct helped him predict the weather—or maybe he just watched the forecast more assiduously than she did.

He had said they would have fresh snow today. As predicted, three to four inches had dropped on the area during the night, something she learned from her father wasn't at all unusual for mid-to late-November in eastern Idaho.

Everything was gorgeous: fresh and white and lovely. This was the perfect kind of early storm, just enough to cover the ground but not enough to make driving a nightmare.

Not much of one, anyway. Her SUV hit a wet spot suddenly and her wheels lost traction a little but she turned into the skid and quickly regained control.

"That's my girl." Jason smiled. "Watch your mother, Cole. Before much longer, you're going to be driving in these kind of conditions. You should be sure you pay attention now and follow her example."

"Does that mean I have to scream like a girl every time I hit a slick patch?" Cole asked with a smirk.

"Hey! I didn't scream," she exclaimed hotly. "That was simply a loud gasp."

Her father and son shared a conspiratorial look. She didn't mind being the source of their amusement, as long as Cole wasn't brooding in the backseat.

The rest of the drive passed smoothly and she

wanted to think it was a good omen when the sun peeked through the clouds just as they reached the Cold Creek, gleaming off the snow that covered everything from fence lines to barns.

The Daltons' gravel drive had been cleared and sanded and she tried not to imagine Seth out here on a tractor taking care of his family's and his neighbors' driveways.

Why she found that such an appealing image, she couldn't begin to guess. Better to focus on the picture the ranch made as the pale sunlight glittered off the new snow.

She parked behind a silver pickup. Almost as if he'd been standing at the window watching for them, Seth hurried out of the house an instant later to greet them, accompanied by two puppies dancing around his feet.

He made a stunning picture, she had to admit, the strong, masculine figure in a Stetson and ranch coat, surrounded by playful puppies. Her insides gave a quick little shiver that had nothing to do with the weather, and she worried that even the presence of her father and children wouldn't be enough to insulate her from his effect on her.

She let out a breath. She was tough: she could do this. How hard could it be to resist the man for one day?

She received some inkling of the answer to that question when he reached to open the door, his broad, delighted smile somehow outshining the sun.

"You made it! I was afraid the snow might deter you."

She made some murmured reply—she wasn't quite sure what—and was relieved when he turned his attention to the rest of the vehicle's occupants. "Hey, Morgan. Cole. Mr. Chambers."

"Call me Jason," her traitor of a father said.

"Jason, then. Welcome to the Cold Creek. I'm so pleased you're all coming along with us today."

"Is that Lucy's brother?" Morgan asked, climbing out to greet the cavorting dogs.

"Sure is. This is Linus."

"They're so cute!" she exclaimed, giggling as they licked her.

"We're just about ready to go," Seth said. "I was just giving the sleds one more look. Jason, you are more than welcome to come up the mountain with us. Or if you'd prefer, my mom and stepfather and our neighbors, Viv and Guillermo Cruz, are staying behind to sit by the fire and enjoy a fierce game of gin rummy while the rest of us are slaving out in the cold hunting Christmas trees for them."

Jason perked up. "Now that sounds like my idea of fun."

"Come on inside, everyone, and I'll introduce you around."

"Are we going to ride horses to find our Christmas tree?" Morgan asked eagerly.

Seth reached down and tugged the long tail of her fleece stocking cap and something sharp and sweet yanked at Jenny's heart.

"Sorry, sweetheart, but it would take all day to get up to where the trees are on horseback. We usually go after our trees on snowmobiles. It's faster that way. But you and Natalie can maybe ride around the arena later when we come back down the mountain if you'd like."

So much for her Currier & Ives fantasy, Jenny thought wryly. A reality slap was just what she deserved for jumping to romantic conclusions. Noisy, growly snowmobiles didn't quite fit her idea of a perfect holiday, but she supposed they would be more efficient.

She shook her head at own foolishness but followed Seth and the two wrestling puppies up the cleared sidewalk into the large log-and-stone ranch house.

Inside, she was assaulted by warmth and welcome. A fire snapped in a huge river-rock fireplace and the house smelled of apples and cinnamon and the sharp scent of wood smoke. For all its size—the soaring ceilings and the grand wall of windows overlooking the western slope of the Tetons—the house struck her as comfortable instead of pretentious.

"We're just waiting for Jake and Maggie," Seth said. "They had some kind of emergency at the clinic but called a few minutes ago and said they were on their way. They shouldn't be long. Take your coats off out here and come in and meet everyone else."

She complied and spent a moment gathering everyone's coats then handing them to Seth. For a moment their arms brushed and she felt hard strength beneath the heavy fabric of his coat.

She had to hope nobody else—especially Seth—noticed she sucked in her breath at the contact.

Seth gave no indication that he had seen anything amiss as he took their coats and set them over the arm of a big plump armchair.

The kitchen was just as welcoming as the great room but on a smaller scale. Painted a cheery yellow, it was

airy and bright, with crisp white appliances and a huge
pine table overflowing with people.

She was assaulted by noise as everyone seemed to
have something to say at once to welcome the newcomers.

The instant they walked in, Natalie—Morgan's good
friend and daughter to Seth's oldest brother, Wade—
jumped up from her chair with a squeal and ran to
Morgan.

They hugged as if they'd been separated for months
instead of merely overnight, before quickly running
off.

Jason slid right into Natalie's newly vacant chair
and immediately struck up a conversation with a
distinguished-looking gentleman and a woman Jenny
recognized as Marjorie Montgomery, Seth's mother.

That left her and Cole as the odd ones out. For an
awkward moment she and her son stood on the fringe
of the crowd, and she experienced a rare moment of
sympathy for him.

She had always been a little hesitant about meeting
new people, though she had been forced to work hard to
overcome it through nearly fifteen years as an educator.

Cole was a great deal like her in that respect, she
realized suddenly. Perhaps he feigned indifference—
and sometimes even contempt—to hide his own social
discomfort. It was an astonishing revelation.

"Have you met everyone?" Seth asked from behind
her, his breath warm in her ear.

"No. Not really."

He quickly performed introductions to his mother
and stepfather, Quinn. Viviana and Guillermo Cruz

both beamed at her in welcome. Seth introduced the man playing with the puppies Morgan had abandoned for her best friend as the best vet in town, Dave Summers, and his wife, Linda.

"My brother Wade is outside checking the snowmobiles and I told you Jake and Maggie are on their way. I'm not sure where Caroline is."

"Right here."

A voice spoke from behind her and Jenny turned and found Caroline Dalton walking into the kitchen, looking lovely and serene and extremely pregnant.

Jenny had met her at various school functions and knew she was married to Seth's oldest brother, Wade, and was stepmother to Wade's three children from a first marriage Marcy told her had ended with the tragic death of his wife just after the birth of their youngest child.

Caroline had always been friendly and kind, even when her stepson Tanner had been sent to Jenny's office for some mischief or other, and she had to admit she was grateful to see a familiar face.

"Cole, would you like a cookie?" she asked, and Jenny wanted to hug her for including him.

"Sure," he said, reaching for one.

He was just taking a big bite when they heard a commotion in the doorway. Jenny looked over to see a blond girl about Cole's age come into the kitchen holding hands with Tanner and Cody Dalton.

Cole hurried to swallow his cookie, straightening to his full height. He looked both surprised and pleased to see the girl.

"Uh, hey, Miranda," he said, his ears turning pink beneath his snowboarder toque.

She gave him a hesitant smile. "Hi, Cole," she said.

Jenny told herself she was glad her son had someone his own age to hang out with during this outing, though she wasn't sure she was ready to spend the day watching his painfully awkward adolescent interactions with a member of the opposite sex.

"This is Miranda Summers, Dave and Linda's daughter," Caroline said. "She's my lifesaver and watches the kids for me sometimes in the afternoon so I can get some work done."

Marcy—the eternally helpful fount of information that she was—had told her Caroline wrote motivational books and was also a very successful life coach.

Jenny wondered if Caroline Dalton might be able to offer any advice for a woman who seemed destined to be fascinated by the absolutely wrong sort of men.

"We were so thrilled when Seth said he had invited you and your family today," Caroline said with a warm smile that went a long way toward easing Jenny's worries about intruding.

"What a great idea and a wonderful chance for us to get to know you," Caroline went on. "I'm so glad you agreed to come."

"Your brother-in-law can be quite…" Annoying. Bossy. Manipulative. "…persuasive."

Caroline Dalton laughed. "That's an understatement."

"What can I say? It's a gift." Seth grinned, popping one of the cookies in his mouth. "I'm just full of them."

"You're certainly full of something," Caroline countered.

Seth only laughed and patted her abdomen with an easy familiarity that told Jenny they shared a close relationship.

"Don't listen to her, kid." He spoke in the general direction of Caroline's midsection. "A few more months and you can make up your own mind about who's your favorite uncle."

Caroline shook her head but with such affection Jenny wondered for an instant at their relationship.

Just then the outside door opened and Wade Dalton came into the increasingly crowded kitchen, stamping snow off his boots and hanging his Stetson on a hook by the door.

His gaze immediately went to his wife, and she smiled at him with such clear joy that Jenny felt foolish even wondering for an instant about Seth and Caroline.

The other woman was obviously crazy about her husband—and vice versa.

"What are we all waiting for here? The sleds are ready and the sun is shining. I say we get this done."

"Maggie and Jake aren't here yet," Caroline said. "They called a moment ago and said they were on their way."

"We can start suiting up anyway," he said. The veterinarian and his wife rose and started shrugging into heavy parkas.

She managed to wrench Cole's attention from Miranda long enough to drag him back to the ranch great room and their coats. For the next several minutes, they were all busy donning their winter gear—parkas, ski pants, thick gloves.

Jenny had just finished helping Morgan zip her coat when the front door opened, admitting two newcomers.

"You just made it," Seth said with a grin. "We were going to leave without you."

"I'm sure we would have survived the pain," his brother Jake said, his voice dry.

The woman with him—small, dark-haired and graceful as she maneuvered on forearm crutches—gave him a reproving look. "You can always stay here and play cards with the parents and I'll go up with the rest of them. I love cutting our own tree."

"We've got a nice Scotch pine in the backyard. Why couldn't we have saved ourselves the trouble and just cut that one so we could spend the day warm and dry by the fire?"

"Jenny, this complainer is my brother Jake and this beautiful creature is his wife, Maggie," Seth said, kissing the latter on the cheek. "This is Jennifer Boyer, the new principal at Pine Gulch Elementary."

She smiled. "I've met Dr. Dalton. Hello again. And nice to meet you," she added to Maggie, wondering about the crutches everyone else seemed to take in stride.

"Hi," Jake Dalton said. "And hello, Miss Morgan. How's the breathing today?"

"Good. Mom made me do a peak flow test before we left and it was ninety-five."

"Excellent!" He held out a hand for Morgan to high-five, which she did with a giggle.

Jenny had met Dr. Dalton soon after arriving in Pine

Gulch when she had taken Morgan in for a refill of her asthma medication. Morgan had been to see him twice since then and each time, he struck Jenny as a very insightful, very compassionate physician, a combination that didn't always go together, in her experience.

"Maggie, sit down for a minute while you have the chance," he said to his wife.

"I'm fine," she said firmly.

"What's with the sticks?" Seth asked, a rude question, Jenny thought, but Maggie Dalton only made a face at him.

Before she could answer, the others came into the great room from the kitchen and Viviana Cruz caught sight of her daughter and hurried toward her.

The resemblance between them was startling, Jenny saw now they were together. The only significant difference was the hint of gray in Viviana's hair and some fine wrinkles in the corners of her eyes.

"Magdalena. What is this?" she asked, worry in her voice. "Why are you using the crutches today?"

"It is nothing, Mama. I promise. Just a little irritation, that's all. My personal physician insisted. I followed his advice since he tends to get pissy when I don't, but really, I'm fine."

"I don't get pissy," Jake growled. "I get even. Next time you put up a fuss, I'll just hide your prosthesis *and* your crutches and make you hop everywhere."

Jenny stared, stunned that the doctor she had come to respect so much would be so harsh with his wife. She was mortified when Maggie saw her shock and shook her head with a smile.

"He's teasing, Jenny, I promise. He wouldn't dare. I know all his hiding places anyway."

"What's a prosthesis?" Morgan asked, in one of those awkward moments all parents experience when they wish their children weren't so naturally curious.

Maggie Dalton didn't seem to mind. She pulled up her pant leg and Jenny saw her left leg ended just below her knee. "It's just a fancy word for a fake leg."

Morgan looked at the metal and plastic device with fascination. "Wow! Can you do cool stuff with it, like jump over cars and stuff?"

Maggie laughed. "Not yet, but I'm working on it."

Her mother still looked concerned. "If you are hurting, you should stay behind with us."

"No, Mama. I'm fine. I've been looking forward to this all week. I'll be sitting on the snowmobile the whole time, I promise."

Viviana bristled like she wanted to argue but her husband, a quiet, sturdy-looking man, put a hand on her arm and she subsided.

A short time later, everyone was ready and they walked outside in the cold air toward a row of gleaming machines.

Jenny gulped. Was she expected to drive one of these complicated-looking beasts? She knew absolutely nothing about snowmobiles. She wouldn't have the first idea how to even start the thing, forget about taking it up a mountain.

To her relief, Seth turned to Cole as soon as they reached the snowmobiles. "Cole, if I take your sister behind me, do you think you can handle driving one with your mom?"

A silly question to ask a fourteen-year-old obsessed with machines. His eyes lit up brighter than Jenny had seen in a long time.

"Oh, yeah," he said with a grin.

"Is it legal?" she asked warily.

"Absolutely or I wouldn't have suggested it," he assured her. "Let's show you how it works."

For the next few moments, he walked Cole through the steps for operating the snowmobile and even had him drive it twenty yards or so before coming back.

"You're all set," Seth assured him.

"Get on, Mom," Cole said gleefully.

She sent Seth a hesitant look but he gave her a reassuring smile. "He'll be great, I promise. I'll keep an eye on you the whole time."

She climbed on, grabbing tight, and realized everyone else was mounted and ready—even Morgan waited on the back of Seth's snowmobile for her driver.

Seth took a few more moments to give Cole some final instructions and she found herself impressed by both his patience and by his consideration. "We'll be climbing into the mountains but it's all pretty gentle and easy. I'll be right ahead of you and will keep an eye on you, and Dave and Linda will bring up the rear."

He paused and gave Cole a stern look. "No hotdogging, okay? Not with your mom on board."

Cole grimaced but nodded. Seth grinned at them both, then climbed onto his own sled and headed off after the others.

"You ready, Mom?" Cole asked.

She grabbed him tightly around the waist, wondering if Seth had arranged things this way so she could remember the joy and connection of being a team with her son.

"Let's go," she said.

With a little jerk, Cole pulled the snowmobile forward and they were off, following Morgan and Seth up the mountain.

Chapter 6

Seth pulled his snowmobile to a stop and turned around to watch Cole and Jenny's progress up the track through virgin snow Wade had cut with his bigger sled.

"Why are we stopping?" Morgan asked behind him, her voice pitched loud to be heard over the growling engines.

"Just checking on the slowpokes," he told her.

She laughed and lifted her face up to the sunshine. Morgan was a sweet kid, he thought, so appreciative of everything. She treated a simple snowmobile ride into the mountains like it was the grandest adventure of her young life.

He was a little surprised at how much he was enjoying this. When he was trying to figure out sled assignments earlier in the morning, he had instinctively wanted Jenny to ride with him. He was more than ready to ramp things up a level, to make her unable to avoid confronting the physical connection he sensed between them.

What better way than to have her holding tightly to him up and down the mountain? He had spent more than a few pleasant moments fantasizing about having her so close to him for the entire half-hour ride up and back down again.

On further reflection, he'd discarded the idea, appealing as it was. Crowding her physically would only push her away. This arrangement was better.

It was not only more safe to have Morgan with him rather than her inexperienced brother but it also provided the bonus of being able to watch Jenny enjoying a fun, peaceful moment with her son, something he'd figured out early wasn't a frequent occurrence between the two.

He hadn't expected to get such a kick out of Jenny's daughter, but he was discovering he enjoyed having her look at him as though he was some kind of hero.

In talking over the Christmas-tree excursion with Wade, they had decided to sandwich experienced drivers around the teens. Wade and his boy Tanner were riding point with Miranda driving a sled and Natalie riding behind her.

Dave and Linda were just ahead of Seth and Morgan, to keep an eye on the girls. Cole and Jenny were behind him, with Maggie and Jake bringing up the rear on another of the bigger snowmobiles. They also towed the sled that would be used to haul down the Christmas trees.

So far the arrangement seemed to be working. He couldn't remember the last time he'd enjoyed himself so much on the annual Dalton Christmas-Tree Trek. A big part of that came from the vicarious enjoyment he found watching Jenny and her kids.

"Are we almost there?" Morgan asked.

"Not much farther. See that small valley of pines up there about halfway up the mountain? That's where we're headed. It should take us about fifteen more minutes. How are the lungs up this high?"

She took a deep, noisy breath. "Great," she assured him.

He was going to tell her to make sure she let him know if she started having any trouble with her asthma, but just then Cole pulled up alongside him.

"What's the matter?" he called over the noise of the sleds.

"Just checking on you. Everything going okay?"

He nodded. "This is a kick!"

"Jenny? How about you?"

She smiled at him, her cheeks wind-chapped and her color high. She looked so bright and vibrant out in the cold sunshine that he had to fight a fierce desire to tug her off the sled and into his arms.

"It's wonderful! The view from up here is absolutely incredible!"

"It is," he agreed, though he was hard-pressed to drag his gaze away from her excitement.

With effort, he managed to do it and turn back to her son. "Cole, I wanted to show you where to go from here. We're heading for that stand of trees about halfway up there."

"Okay," the boy said. "Though I'm pretty sure I'm capable of following a trail made by four other snow-mobiles."

"I'm sure you are, but sometimes it helps to have the bigger picture about where you're ultimately heading, instead of just following the exhaust of the machine in front of you."

"If I was stupid enough to veer off the trail, you'd all be on me like stink on cheese anyway."

He laughed. "Just so you know where you stand, kid."

Cole made a face at him. "Are we going to ride or are we going to sit around shooting the breeze all day?"

Jake and Maggie pulled up before he could answer. He gave his sister-in-law a careful look but she didn't look to be in terrible pain, even though she had her crutches handy.

He knew Jake would never have let her come along if he worried she might overdo it, so Seth decided he would let his brother worry about his own wife.

"You're blocking the trail," Jake called.

"Yeah, yeah. We're going."

He started his sled again, feeling a curious warmth in his chest when Morgan gripped him tightly.

If he wasn't careful, he could seriously fall for Jenny Boyer's kids, he thought. That would be great if their mother came with them in a package deal but he was afraid things wouldn't work out that way.

This was a stupid idea.

An hour later, Seth wondered how in Hades he was going to make it through an entire day pretending this casual friendship with Jenny when he hungered for far more, especially since she seemed determined to push him away at every turn.

The more time he spent with her, the deeper his fascination for her seemed to run. It baffled and unnerved him. He didn't understand it—he just knew he couldn't seem to keep his eyes off her.

He was blowing all his plans to be cool and detached and to give her the time and space she needed until she was ready for him to kick things up a notch. Things weren't working out that way, mainly because he couldn't force himself to stay away from her.

Though he knew he should have let one of his brothers help her while he cut the trees for his mother and the Cruzes, he still found himself trailing after Jenny and her kids, his chainsaw at the ready as they scoured the stand of evergreens for the perfect tree.

What he really wanted to do was drag her behind the closest trunk and steal any chance to explore that mouth, just so he could see if it could possibly taste as delicious as it looked.

With her two kids along, the possibility of that was fairly remote, he acknowledged. Still, a man could dream.

"This is way more fun than pulling our artificial tree out of storage like we've always done," a pink-cheeked Morgan exclaimed as they trudged through the snow toward the outer edge of the small forest.

He locked away his inappropriate lust and put on an exaggerated expression of horror. "Artificial. Please say it's not so."

Morgan giggled. "Yep."

"Don't tell me it's pink."

Jenny made a face at him. "Of course not. It was a perfectly lovely seven-and-a-half-foot spruce. Green, prelit and very convenient."

"That smells like the petroleum product that it is, no doubt. How can you stand here inhaling this delicious scent into your lungs and even consider having an artificial tree?"

"We gave it to Goodwill when we moved. And we're here now, aren't we, searching for the perfect tree? That has to count for something!"

"I don't know. Somebody who's always had an artificial monstrosity might not recognize the perfect tree even if it reached out a branch and tapped you on the head with it."

She stopped suddenly, so abruptly he almost plowed into her. Her gaze was glued to a blue spruce about eight feet high. Though a yellow ribbon tied to the trunk indicated he'd marked it for thinning, now he couldn't really see anything spectacular about it.

Jenny apparently did. She gave a happy sigh. "This one. I want this one."

He wasn't ready for the search to be over yet. Then they would have to go back and rejoin the rest of his family and he would lose any chance for privacy with her.

"There are still maybe a half dozen marked ones we haven't even looked at yet. Are you sure this is the one?"

"Positive. This one is perfect, don't you guys think?"

Morgan nodded with the same kind of glee as her

mother but Cole only shrugged. "It looks like every other tree we've seen today," he said.

"What are you talking about?" Jenny exclaimed. "This tree has personality! It's wonderful! The color is a far richer green than all the rest and can't you see the way all the branches look so perfect except for that little one there in the back pointing in a different direction?"

"If you say so."

"It's just right. I only wish the school didn't have a fire-code policy against real trees or I'd put it out by the office."

She looked so thrilled, so bubbly and excited, Seth couldn't look away. Her eyes glowed and her nose was red and he couldn't seem to think about anything but tasting that bright smile.

He cleared his throat and made himself focus on the tree instead. "You want it, it's yours. Cole, you want to do the honors?"

The kid eyed the big machine in his hands with unmistakable longing, then he looked away. "You can do it."

He probably didn't know the first thing about running a chainsaw, Seth realized. "It's easy. Come on. I'll walk you through it."

He showed Cole how to fire up the saw, then helped guide him to the right spot on the trunk. Between the two of them, they buzzed through the small trunk in seconds and the tree fell in a flurry of snow. It was a good choice, he thought, one of those he'd marked that were being crowded out by bigger trees.

"How are we going to carry our tree down the mountain now?" Morgan asked.

"Jake is pulling a sled behind his snowmobile. We'll tie them all together on that and he and Maggie will drag them down."

"Is that it?" Cole asked.

"I've got to cut one for my place now. Since you're so good at picking them out, you can help me find mine. With my vaulted ceilings, I've got room for a ten-or twelve-foot one. Think big."

They spent several moments walking through the heavy timber looking at possibilities until Jenny stopped in front of the one he'd actually had in mind for his place all along.

"Kids, your mother is a natural at Christmas-tree hunting. Just think what she must have been suppressing through all those years of artificial trees!"

Again he urged Cole to do the honors, though this time he let the boy handle the saw by himself, keeping a careful watch on him as he did.

"Why don't you go back to the one we cut for your house and carry it down to the snowmobiles while your mom helps me haul this one?" he suggested. "Can you find the way?"

"We can see it from here." Cole pointed down the hill to the sleds gleaming in the pale sunshine. He took off with Morgan following close behind, and finally Seth was alone with Jenny, just as he'd orchestrated.

He hadn't expected her to be looking at him with such a warm smile. "Thank you for this," she said. "You were right, it will be a wonderful memory for Cole and Morgan."

"What about for you?"

Her gaze flashed for just an instant then she looked

away. He saw her swallow and would have given half his horses—and a cow or two, as well—to know what she was thinking.

"I've enjoyed it," she murmured.

"You don't relax enough. You should do it more often."

Her mouth opened, her expression indignant. Instead of the sharp retort he expected, after a moment she closed her mouth and sighed. "You're right. I know you're right but it's not always the easiest thing in the world for me to do with any success."

He dared take a step closer, keeping his hands carefully neutral at his sides. "Why is that, I wonder?"

Her gaze flitted back to his and stayed there a little longer, like a wild bird following a trail of sunflower seeds toward an outstretched hand. "I suppose because so much depends on me. It's hard work being a principal and even harder work being a single mother."

"You do both very well."

"And how would you know that? You don't have children in my school to judge my performance there and you don't have children of your own at home to comment on my mothering."

"You don't have to be a jockey to recognize a great racehorse."

She gave a short laugh. "I don't believe I've ever been compared to a horse before."

He debated backing off now, giving her a chance to regroup, then decided that would be foolish. Better to keep her off balance. He stepped forward again until only a foot or so separated them. From here, he could

smell the fresh, flowery scent of her, an unlikely bea-
con of spring amid the wintry landscape.

She swallowed hard at his nearness but didn't
step back. Instead, her chin lifted. "I don't like to be
crowded, Seth."

For some strange reason, her defiance made him
laugh. "Is that what I was doing?"

"Oh, I have no doubt you know exactly what you're
doing. You're very good at what you do. I certainly
won't deny that."

"What I do?"

"The whole seduction bit. The oh-so-casual touches,
those sexy, intimate smiles. Stepping closer and closer
until I can't focus on anything but you. I imagine most
women probably melt in a big puddle at your feet."

The cynicism in her voice smarted. "But not you?"

"I'm sorry if that stings your pride but I'm just not
interested. I believe I told you that."

"So you did," he agreed. "But are you so sure about
that, Ms. Boyer?"

Against the howl of all his instincts, he stepped
closer again. He watched a tiny pulse jump in her throat
and her breathing seemed to accelerate. The hunger
inside him to taste her threatened to consume him,
to wipe out whatever remained of his self-control and
his sanity.

"Ye-es," she said, though that single word came out
breathy, hushed.

"I think we both know that's not precisely true,"
he murmured. He reached out and gripped the ends of
her scarf in some halfhearted effort to keep her from

fleeing, then leaned down slowly, carefully, anticipation thrumming powerfully inside him.

An instant before his mouth would have at last found hers, some subconscious warning system picked up rustling in the underbrush. He dropped her scarf and stepped back just before Wade walked into their little clearing.

His brother surveyed the scene, his hard blue eyes missing nothing, but he only sent one swift, censorious look in Seth's direction. "Cole and Morgan said you cut a big one for your place. I came to see if you need help hauling it down so we can go back down the mountain. My boys are starting to get restless and I think Cody's ready for a nap."

"Yeah. We're on our way."

What the hell was he doing? Seth wondered as he and Wade hauled the big tree down the slope toward the waiting sleds. He had played that last hand like some damn greenhorn who'd never kissed a girl before. That's what was called jumping the gate before the starting pistol sounded.

She wanted him to back off. Hell, she'd practically *ordered* him to, and he'd ignored her. He had no doubt he would have had her pressed up against one of those trees in another ten seconds if Wade hadn't interrupted.

He didn't like the fact that he'd almost lost it back there, that he'd plunged ahead with something that all his instincts were telling him was a bad idea. It wasn't like him at all. He always, *always,* maintained some control over himself when it came to women.

Jenny Boyer somehow managed to shred that control to bits, like a chainsaw ripping through flimsy cardboard.

Where did he go from here? He didn't want to give up before he'd even enjoyed a tiny taste of that lush mouth, but he might just have to accept the grim reality that some things weren't meant to be.

She wanted him to leave her alone. Maybe that was what he ought to do. Forget about Jennifer Boyer, just as she had insisted, and move on. The thought filled him with an odd kind of restlessness but he didn't see any other choice. If she wasn't interested—or didn't *want* to be interested—he had to respect her boundaries.

He was subdued on the ride back down the mountain and everyone else seemed to be, too. A light snow started falling again and while it looked feathery and lovely when you were safe and dry inside watching it through the window, on a snowmobile, it pelted exposed skin like sharp pebbles. Everyone seemed glad when they reached the Cold Creek again.

At the house, they quickly unloaded the trees from the transport sled. Maggie was looking tired and the kids were cold, so Jake and Wade sent the women and children inside the ranch house to warm up.

While they tied the trees onto the respective vehicles for transport to their destination, Seth drove the Cold Creek snowmobiles into the storage garage and performed postride maintenance checks on them. He was the default mechanic on the ranch, and he liked to think he was the go-to guy when machines broke down.

He had just stowed the last one and was checking

fluid levels on it when Jake showed up in the doorway of the garage.

"I'm about done here," Seth said. "Go ahead inside and check on Maggie."

"She'll be okay."

"What's her deal today, anyway? I haven't seen her use the canes for a long time. She said she was having some irritation. Is everything okay?"

"She's changing pain meds and we're trying to find a good safe combination."

His brother gave him a quiet smile that told wonders about how much he adored his wife. "Don't tell anybody, but we're talking about starting a family and Maggie wants to wean off some of her heavy-duty meds before we give it a serious try."

He felt another of those curious pangs in his chest. Both of his brothers were deliriously happy with their wives and their lives. He was glad for them, he told himself. He just couldn't quite figure out why the life he had always thought was perfect suddenly felt so empty in comparison.

"That's wonderful," he said. "I can't think of two people who would make better parents."

When Jake continued to stand in the doorway watching him, Seth sighed, screwed the oil cap back on the snowmobile and stood up to wait for the lecture he sensed was coming.

He knew that look in his brother's eyes all too well. Wade must have seen more of that encounter with Jenny on the mountain than he thought and sent Jake in to do his dirty work.

"Let's have it, then," he said.

"What?"

"You've got on your bossy-big-brother look. Wade was the one giving me the snake eye all the way down the mountain so how did you get to be the one roped into this?"

Jake leaned against the door frame. "We drew straws and I lost."

"Lucky you."

"Right. That means I get to be the one to ask you what the hell you think you're doing."

He really wasn't in the mood for this, Seth decided. He'd been on the receiving end of these little improving talks all his life from one or both of his brothers. He had to wonder if Wade and Jake would still feel inclined to tell him how to live his life when he was seventy.

Probably.

"I believe I'm putting the sleds away right now. You or Wade have a problem with that?"

"You know we don't. Do what you want with the snowmobiles. But neither of us is too crazy about you tangling up a nice lady like Principal Boyer."

He arched an eyebrow. "Tangling up?"

"You know what I mean. What are you doing here, Seth? She's not your usual bar babe. She's a nice woman with a couple of kids and a retired father and a responsible job. She deserves better."

His brothers sure knew just how to twist the knife in his gut. "Thanks," he snapped. "It's always nice to get a vote of support from my family. Don't hold back, doc. Why don't you tell me what a selfish, irresponsible bastard I am, so we can all go in and have some lunch?"

Jake had always been slow to anger but he also never backed down from a fight. "Oh, screw the poor-me routine. That wasn't what I meant and you know it. I'm not talking about you as a person, I'm referring strictly to your usual playbook with women."

Seth yanked down the seat of the sled so hard he was pretty sure he broke something. "Memorized it, have you?"

"Since you've been sticking to the same game plan since before you were old enough to shave, it's not tough to guess where this is headed."

"And where is that?"

"You wine her, dine her, romance her, take what you want, then move on to the next lovely young thing to cross your path."

"Yeah, yeah. Selfish, irresponsible bastard. I got that part."

"I didn't say that. Most of the time the women you hook up with know what to expect and probably are only after exactly what you're willing to give them. Fine. If you're both consenting adults, no harm no foul. But this is different. Jennifer Boyer isn't one of your Bandito bimbos. She's got kids, Seth, one of them a teenager who looks up to you. From what I hear, Cole has already been abandoned by his father. Don't you think you're only going to reinforce that lousy example of how a man should treat a woman when he watches you walk away from his mother, too?"

"I haven't even kissed the woman!"

"But you want to, don't you?"

"None of your business."

"It's not," Jake agreed. "But I have to point out those

kids already care about you and if you take things where I think you want to, Cole and Morgan are likely to come out of this mighty damn hurt when you get bored and move on."

He hadn't given much thought to their feelings in all this, he realized, with no small amount of shame.

"There's a whole forest full of pretty young trees out there," Jake went on. "Find a different one to scratch your itch on. That's all I'm saying."

"What if I don't want a different one?"

He hadn't meant to say that, but somehow the words slipped out anyway. Jake gave him a long, hard look that made him feel like he was fifteen years old again.

"Maybe for once you ought to try thinking not so much about what *you* want but about what *she* wants, and see how that works out for you."

Before he could come up with some undoubtedly pithy reply, Jake left in that frustrating way of his.

Seth should have been relieved the lecture was over but he couldn't stop thinking about what his brother said. The hell of it was, he was absolutely right.

Jenny wanted nothing to do with him. Though he knew she was attracted to him despite her protests, he wasn't going to crowd her anymore, he decided.

He would still have to see her because of his arrangement with Cole. But after today, he would just be polite and friendly and forget about anything else.

No matter how impossible it suddenly seemed.

Chapter 7

She was going to have a tough time dragging everyone away.

Jenny surveyed her family crowded around the Daltons' big kitchen and tried to remember the last time she'd seen them all enjoying a meal so much. Yes, the food was fabulous—a half-dozen different kinds of soup, hot rolls and a salad bar that rivaled anything in a restaurant—but the company was the most appealing part of this meal.

Morgan and Natalie were giggling at the smaller table brought in for the children. At the breakfast bar, Cole and Miranda were deep in a debate over the best ska band of all time. Even Jason was in his element laughing at something Quinn Montgomery said, down at the other end of the big dining table.

It was noisy and crowded and warm but her family seemed to be thriving. In fact, everyone seemed to be having a wonderful time except for her.

She couldn't seem to relax and allow herself to have fun. The Daltons had been everything kind. She found them all warm and friendly—even Seth's oldest brother, Wade. At first he had seemed gruff and intimidating, but throughout the day he had treated her and the children with nothing but kindness.

Despite the jovial company, she couldn't seem to move past her own awkward discomfort.

She was also painfully aware that everyone at the big table had been divided by couple—so by default she sat next to Seth. She had a hard time focusing on anything else but his nearness throughout the meal, his strong hands and his seductive masculine scent and the heat that seemed to shimmer off him in waves.

She didn't want to be here. She would have preferred sitting at the children's table to enduring this close proximity, especially as Seth had been distant and distracted throughout the meal and seemed to become more so as the meal wore on.

He obviously had second thoughts about inviting her and her family and regretted their de facto pairing.

Despite the fabulous food, her stomach felt hollow and achy and she wanted to disappear. That, in turn, made her angry with herself and more determined to see this dinner through as quickly as possible. At least they were already having dessert so the torture would be over soon.

"This pie is delicious," Caroline Dalton exclaimed

from across the table with her warm smile. "I love the crunchy caramel topping."

Jenny smiled politely as others at the table joined in the praise for the caramel apple pie she'd brought along, one of her very few specialties. But even as she smiled and thanked them all for the compliments, she was aware of Seth next to her setting down his fork as if he were suddenly eating fried motor oil, leaving the rest of his pie uneaten on his plate.

A few moments later, he pushed back his chair and aimed his charming smile around the table at every single person but her.

"Thanks for a delicious meal, everybody, but I've got to run up to the barn."

"Can we go, Uncle Seth?" Natalie asked. "You said maybe we could ride later."

"You could go for a horseback ride, I guess." He paused then looked as if he regretted his words even as he spoke them. "Or Cole could grab one of the snow-mobiles and pull you up the hill behind the barn so you can tube down. If it's all right with your mother, of course."

Natalie, Morgan and Tanner looked ecstatic at the possibility and even Cole and Miranda appeared thrilled.

"Oh, please, Mom!" Morgan begged.

How was she supposed to refuse with all those young eyes looking at her with identical entreaties?

"Thanks," she murmured under her breath to Seth.

He gave a smile that seemed only slightly repentant—but at least he wasn't completely ignoring her the way he'd done since that breathless moment on the mountain when he'd nearly kissed her.

"I suppose, if it's all right with the other parents."

"You all just warmed up," Caroline exclaimed. "Are you sure you want to go back out in the cold?"

The children gave a resounding answer in the affirmative and scrambled up from the chairs to climb back into their cold-weather gear.

Half an hour later, they were being pulled up the hill in turns by Cole on the snowmobile, who appeared to be having the time of his life.

Caroline had volunteered to go with them to keep an eye on the children while the others stayed behind to watch a holiday movie. Though Jenny hadn't wanted to spend another minute with Seth, she had also hated thinking of the pregnant woman standing out in the snow.

"I'll do it," she insisted, so here she sat on a bench overlooking the sledding hill.

At least she didn't have to endure more stilted conversation with Seth. After dragging her into this whole thing, he had been astonishingly quick to disappear.

The minute Cole had the snowmobile tow rope figured out, Seth spent a few moments starting a small fire in a small cast-iron outdoor fireplace nearby, then claimed he had some things to do inside the horse barn that couldn't wait.

She hadn't minded sitting alone watching the children. It gave her a chance again to savor the magnificence of the setting. She found a raw grandeur in the snow-covered landscape with the backdrop of wild, rugged mountains.

Though sunset was still a few hours away, the afternoon sky was already beginning to turn lavender and it had started snowing again, big, fluffy flakes that made her want to catch one on her tongue like the children on her playground.

After a moment, she gave into the temptation and stuck out her tongue. Of course, it was at that instant that Seth walked out of the barn, apparently finished with what had been so urgent.

She jerked her tongue back into her mouth and kept it firmly planted there as he stood at the open doorway watching her. She had to hope he hadn't seen that completely childish impulse, though she had a feeling it was a vain hope.

After a moment he pulled the door closed behind him and approached her, looking solid and dark and almost predatory against the snowy white landscape.

She hated herself for the little flutter in her stomach but couldn't seem to control it.

He sat down beside her on the bench. "Looks like they're having a good time. This was always the perfect sledding hill when we were kids."

She couldn't quite manage to wrap her mind around the image of this wholly masculine man in front of her as a gleeful child sledding down the hillside.

"This is much more fun with deeper snow," he went on. "You'll have to bring Morgan and Cole back in a month or so when the conditions are a little better."

The chances of that were fairly slim, she thought. "I can't believe we're still a week away from Thanksgiving and your mountains have more than two feet of snow."

"Better get used to it. We probably won't see bare earth again until March or April at the earliest. The higher elevations might be two or three months after that."

She shuddered, earning a laugh from him. "Didn't your dad warn you about our winters before you moved down from Seattle?"

"He told me they were on the harsh side but he's promised me the summers make up for it."

He smiled a little, though she thought he was still distant. "That's true enough. My mother always says if you complain about the winter, you don't deserve the summer."

"I guess I should watch my mouth, then."

"Just find a winter sport you enjoy, like ice climbing or cross-country skiing. That tends to give you a completely different perspective on the cold weather."

The idea of that wasn't very appealing, since she figured she was probably about the most unathletic person in town. "Does curling up by the woodstove with a good book count?" she asked.

He grinned. "Sure. And you get bonus points if it's at least a book about winter sports."

"I'll have to dig through Dad's library to see what I can find about hockey or ice fishing," she said with a laugh. "I'm all for coming up with anything to make the winter pass more quickly."

"If you're not much of a cold-weather lover, what brings you to Pine Gulch?" he asked. "I would think a school principal could find work just about anywhere."

"Maybe. But I couldn't find my dad anywhere but here. He loves Pine Gulch. After the divorce, he offered to come live with us in Seattle but I knew he would hate it there. All the friends he made after he retired are here and he's got a rich, fulfilling life. The fishing, the photography, his monthly poker game with his friends in Jackson. I couldn't drag him away from that."

Jenny paused, surprised by her compulsion to confide in him. She wouldn't have thought it possible but Seth could actually be a comfortable conversationalist, if she could put her hormones on hold.

"At the same time, I knew my children needed him. Especially Cole. A boy his age needs strong male role models. Since his father's not in the picture anymore, I had to do something. When the principal position opened up at the elementary school, it seemed like an opportunity I couldn't pass up."

Their situation wasn't perfect, but she couldn't regret moving here. She was trying to do the best she could.

"So that's why you took the job at the elementary school and moved to town?" he asked. "To be near your dad?"

"I had to do something. Cole was in trouble almost all the time in Seattle. I hoped moving him here would steady him a little. Of course, six weeks later, he managed to steal and wreck a classic car," she said wryly.

"He's doing a good job of making it right, though."

"You know, the first month or so after we moved here, I thought I'd made a terrible mistake. These last few weeks have been much better. Whatever you've been doing with Cole, thank you."

Seth raised an eyebrow at her words and she saw surprise flicker in the deep blue of his eyes. "I haven't done anything but put him to work," he answered.

"Maybe that's exactly what he needed. A project to focus on. Or perhaps simply someone taking an interest in him. I don't know what it is, I only know things have improved considerably since he started coming out here. He doesn't seem to hate either me or Idaho as much as he used to."

"I'm glad," he said simply.

They sat in silence for a moment, broken only by the distant shrieks of the children and the snap of the fire in the little stove.

This was nice, she thought. Too nice. She could feel herself slipping under his spell again—and this time she couldn't really blame the man, since he wasn't doing anything but sitting there.

She was relieved when Cole pulled up to them a few moments later, breaking the fragile mood.

"Your turn, Mom," her son said. "Hop on. You can use Morgan's inner tube."

Jenny shook her head vigorously. "No. That's okay. I like my legs unbroken, thanks."

Astride the snowmobile, Cole flapped his arms and made a clucking sound. "Come on. Morgan's gone down six or seven times and she's only nine. Is she tougher than you?"

"Oh, without question."

"Come on," Cole cajoled. "Everybody's having a great time. You can't sit down here the whole time."

"You'll have fun," Seth joined in. "You can count this as your first experiment in winter sports."

She gazed at the two males, so physically dissimilar but so surprisingly alike, then sighed and rose from the bench.

"I'm blaming you when this goes horribly wrong," she told Seth with a laugh as she climbed onto the snowmobile behind her son.

Her smile faded when she realized Seth was staring at her mouth. Awareness bloomed in her stomach and she was almost grateful when Cole gunned the engine and started up the mountainside.

He needed to get out of there.

Fast.

All his lofty intentions were being shot straight to hell the more time he spent with Jenny Boyer.

He watched her on the snowmobile behind her son as the boy climbed to the top of the hill.

Even from here, he could see the tension in her posture. She clearly didn't want to be up there but she was doing it anyway, refusing to let her fears hold her back. He admired that in a woman.

He admired a lot about her. He liked the way her eyes lit up when she talked about her children, he liked the way she seemed to sincerely listen to a person, he liked the way she was willing to laugh at herself.

He let out a heavy breath. What the hell good did it do to count down all the things he liked about her? The grim fact remained that Jake was absolutely right. She deserved somebody better than him, somebody who wasn't always looking around the next bend.

He'd been crazy to come out here again. He should have just holed up in the barn until she was gone, taking her big green eyes and her lush mouth and her sweet-as-sugar smile with her.

From here, he could see her arguing with her children, then a minute later she climbed onto the inner tube. She sat there for a long moment, then nodded to her kids, who gave her a push.

She shrieked then he heard her exclamation turn into a delighted laugh that seemed to reach right through him and tug at his insides.

He should make his escape while he had the chance, he thought. He even turned around and headed for the barn but he'd only made three steps when he heard the laughter cut off into an abrupt scream.

He jerked back around just in time to watch her spiral off the inner tube. The tube went one way and she went the other. To his horror she rolled three, possibly four times, then she lay horribly still about twenty yards from the bottom.

He was already racing up the slope before she came to a stop, his heart pumping like crazy. He reached her just seconds later, astonished by his protective impulses. He wanted to grab her close and hang on tight.

"Jen. Talk to me, sweetheart."

She didn't answer, though he could see her chest rising and falling beneath her winter parka. He unzipped it just as Cole roared up on the snowmobile.

"Go down to the ranch house and get my brother Jake," he told the boy, whose face was as white as the landscape around them. "Hurry."

"Right. Okay."

He gunned the snowmobile and took off down the road and Seth turned his attention back to Jenny.

His brother might be the doctor in the family but years of ranch living and dealing with various mishaps had given Seth a basic knowledge of first aid. He ran his hands over her but couldn't find any broken bones.

By now Miranda, Tanner and the girls had gathered, watching him solemnly as he examined her. Tanner and the younger girls looked terrified and even the normally sensible Miranda seemed anxious.

The snow had kicked up in the last few moments and giant flakes drifted down to settle on her still features, alighting on her eyelashes, in her hair, on the curves of her cheek.

By his estimation, it would take Cole ten minutes or so to ride down to the house, grab Jake and drive back up here. He couldn't bear the idea of Jenny lying out here in the snow all that time.

Besides that, the children needed to be inside where they could get warm. All of them were going to be shocky soon if they didn't go inside.

Making a split-second decision, he scooped Jenny into his arms. Moving her some place warm and dry outweighed the first aid axiom about not moving her, he decided. Jake would probably yell at him, but he knew his brother would have done the same.

"Miranda, I'm taking Ms. Boyer inside. Come with me and take the kids into the kitchen, okay? I've got some cookies and I think there's some hot cocoa mix somewhere in there. Morgan, Nat, I need you two to help Miranda with Tanner."

"What about my mom?" Morgan asked. Her features were pale with fright. He could only hope she didn't have an asthma attack just now since he wasn't sure he could cope with a second crisis.

He gave her what he hoped was a reassuring smile

as he carried Jenny into his house. "She just bumped her head a little when she fell off the inner tube but I'm sure everything's going to be fine. Aren't we lucky to have a doctor so close? Jake will take care of her, I promise."

"Why are her eyes still closed?" she asked as he set her mother down carefully on the couch.

He'd been the one pushing her to go on that tube, he thought with guilt. "Have you ever fallen at the playground and had the wind knocked out of you? That's what happened to your mom."

He took time away from his worry over Jenny to give Morgan a quick, reassuring hug. She seemed to find comfort from it—and so did he. "Go on into the kitchen with the others and as soon as Dr. Jake takes a look at her, you can come back and talk to her, okay?"

"She always stays with me and holds my hand when I'm having a flare-up. Will you stay with her?"

"I'm not going anywhere, honey," he promised.

With one last anxious look, she went into the kitchen and he turned his attention back to Jenny.

She looked so frail against the dark maroon leather of his couch. A moment ago she had been laughing with him and complaining about the weather and now she was so terribly still.

He pulled her coat open and was running a hand over her again, looking more carefully this time for anything out of the ordinary when her eyes fluttered open.

She gazed at him for a long moment, her eyes hazy and baffled, then she blinked and seemed to become more alert by the second.

"Seems like a lot of trouble to go to just so you could cop a cheap feel," she mumbled, her voice hoarse.

Relief flooded through him and he closed his eyes for a moment and said a silent prayer of gratitude. She couldn't be at death's door if she could manage a tart comment like that.

He grinned, fighting the urge to pull her into his arms. "That was just a side benefit. And believe me, it wasn't cheap in the least."

To his surprise, she smiled back, then winced at the movement.

"What hurts, besides your head?"

"What doesn't?" She tried to pull herself to a sitting position.

He shook his head. "Take it easy. I'm not letting you go anywhere so you might as well relax for now."

She obeyed, though he thought her compliance stemmed more from her lack of strength than anything else.

"Nothing seems broken from what I could tell," he told her. "Any acute areas of pain?"

"Only my head. Most of me is just one big ache except my head, which I'm afraid might be ready to fall off."

"It wouldn't surprise me if you've got a concussion. You conked it pretty hard."

She winced. "Graceful, as usual."

Tenderness washed through him and he couldn't prevent himself from picking up her hand. Strictly to warm her cold fingers, he told himself, even as he savored the contact. "It was just your trajectory. You couldn't avoid that rock, no matter what you tried to do. Anybody would have crashed in the same situation."

"Thank you for trying to make me feel better," she murmured.

Her fingers curled in his and a terrifying tenderness seemed to soak through him. "Is it working?"

She made a face. "Not really."

They both shared a small laugh he found oddly intimate and again he had to fight the fierce desire to pull her into his arms.

"Where are my kids?" she asked.

"Morgan's in the kitchen with Miranda and the others and I sent Cole down to the house on the snowmobile for Jake. They should be here in a minute. Matter of fact, if I'm not mistaken, I hear an engine out there right now."

Seth barely had time to pull his hand away from hers before Jake and Cole both burst into the house.

Chapter 8

"I'm sorry about this," Jenny said five minutes later to Jake Dalton as he gave her a careful exam after banishing Seth and Cole from the room. "I feel like such an idiot."

He smiled with the calm competence she'd noticed during Morgan's asthma-related office visits. "Don't worry about it. You're not the first one to ever tumble down that hill. I think all of us have done our share. Seth even broke his collarbone on that hill when he was around Morgan's age. I don't suppose he told you that, did he?"

"No. He didn't mention it."

"He saw some snowboarders on TV and thought he'd like to try it."

"Oh, no," she murmured.

"Exactly. We didn't have any equipment, of course, so he improvised with a piece of plywood he found in the barn. He was lucky he only broke his collarbone."

She smiled, though she really didn't want to talk about Seth Dalton. She couldn't seem to shake the memory of that moment she'd awakened and found him examining her.

In her dazed, half-conscious state, she had come dangerously close to wrapping her arms around him and holding on tight. A million sensations had poured through her as his hand touched her ribs, hungers she barely remembered from the early days of her marriage.

She sighed and Jake Dalton gave her a curious look and pressed harder on her shoulder. "Is that a touchy spot?"

"No. Sorry."

"Well, I can't find anything broken. You've got a nasty goose egg where you fell and I suspect a concussion but I'd like to keep a closer eye on that headache for the next hour or so. I'd like you to rest here for a while so I can monitor your head, okay?"

"I've been such a bother."

"You haven't, I promise. I don't want you driving today so your dad is going to take Morgan and Cole home. I'll come check on you in an hour. If you're feeling better at that point, Seth can drive you home."

"I'm fine now."

"I'm sure you are. But you'll have to humor me, okay? It's a doctor thing." He winked at her. "I wouldn't want you to go home too early and drag me out of my warm, cozy bed in the middle of the night if you have any complications. Just rest, okay?"

Her head threatened to throb right off her shoulders and she was exhausted suddenly. She nodded. Closing her eyes gave some relief from the pain anyway.

She awoke some time later to find the room dark except for the flickering fire and next to it a pool of light from a floor lamp of entwined elk antlers. That glow illuminated an entirely too attractive man sitting in an armchair near the fire, a magazine open across his lap and a puppy stretched out at his feet like a pair of fuzzy slippers.

He looked up suddenly as if sensing her gaze. When he saw her eyes open, he gave a slow, painfully sweet smile, and her heart seemed to skip a beat.

"How's the head?" he asked, his voice a low, seductive whisper in the dimly lit room.

As if she could concentrate on anything but him! She closed her eyes for a moment to gauge her pain level then opened to meet his gaze. "Better, I think. Still a bit sore but I'm sure I'll survive. I can tell you with a fairly high degree of certainty that I won't be in a big hurry to go sledding again anytime soon."

He smiled and she felt that same exhilarating, pulse-pounding, toe-curling sensation she'd experienced on the mountain just before she hit that boulder and ruined the ride.

She pulled herself to a sitting position, ignoring the dozens of little elves hammering wildly in her brain. "Has your brother been back?"

"No. He said he'd be here about six and it's only

quarter to. You were only asleep for forty-five minutes or so."

"I really think I'm fine to leave now. I just want to go home. I'm sure my father and children are worried about me and I've imposed enough on you and your family."

He closed his magazine and set it on the table beside him, giving her a stern look as he did. "You have any older brothers?"

"No. I'm an only child."

"Ah. Then you have no idea the emotional and psychological torment I would endure if I dared ignore my brother's strict instructions and took you home before he had the chance to take a look at your head again. I'm on strict orders here."

"Do you always do what your older brothers tell you?" she asked.

He gave a snort of laughter. "Hardly ever. Just ask them."

His levity vanished as abruptly as it appeared. "But in this case, I'm not going to take any chances. If Jake thinks you should rest until he checks you out again, that's exactly what you're going to do."

"All this fuss for nothing."

"Nothing? You have no idea how awful it was watching you tumble through the air and hit the ground so hard. I've been having flashbacks about it all evening."

She winced. "It was probably quite a sight, wasn't it?"

"I'd give you an eight for form and a ten for creativity. I'm afraid your bumpy landing knocked down your overall score."

She smiled at his teasing. "I suppose I shouldn't be surprised this happened to me. I faced the painful truth a long time ago. I'm hopelessly uncoordinated. I would have been valedictorian of my class except I never learned to serve a lousy volleyball and couldn't manage to bring my sophomore P.E. grade up past a B."

His laughter rang through the room.

"I'm serious. It's not funny. You have no idea how traumatic it can be for a fourteen-year-old girl who can't shoot a basketball or catch a baseball to save her life."

"I understand. Believe me. You're talking to the kid who was always chosen last for dodgeball teams—and always the first one out."

She studied his athletic build, his broad shoulders and muscled chest and pure masculinity. "Okay, now you're out-and-out lying."

"Ask my brothers! I was small for my age and had asthma. Nobody wanted a shrimp who couldn't breathe on their team."

"You're not a shrimp."

He shrugged. "I hit a growth spurt when I was about Cole's age. Before then I was scrawny."

"Let me guess," she said, with a considering look. "You also started lifting weights around that same time."

"I didn't need to. When you work on a cattle ranch, every day is a workout. Once my asthma was mostly under control, I could do more around the ranch. It's amazing how much a kid can bulk up hauling hay and herding cattle."

She tried to picture him a scrawny, sickly boy suddenly getting taller and bulkier. With those chiseled features and those intense blue eyes that seemed to see right into a woman's deepest desires, he had no doubt always been gorgeous. She imagined when he started to putting on muscle and height, every girl in the county probably sat up and took notice of the youngest Dalton brother.

And they'd been noticing him ever since.

She tilted her head to study him, wondering how much of that late development—coupled with his health issues as a child—had affected his psyche.

"Why are you looking at me like that?" he asked.

She would have liked to be the kind of woman who could instantly sling back some sort of witty repartee. She wanted to be quick and funny and self-assured.

With him gazing at her out of those impossibly blue eyes, with a smile hovering around that sinful mouth, with the lingering scent of leather and pine clinging to him, she couldn't seem to think of anything to say but the truth.

"I was just wondering if that was around the time you discovered you were irresistible to women."

As soon as the words escaped her mouth, she wanted to call them back—or at least pound her head against the coffee table three or four times at her own stupidity.

"Irresistible?" He gave a disbelieving laugh. "Not even close. You, for one, seem to be doing an excellent job of resisting me."

"Am I?"

An arrested look flickered across his features and the room suddenly thickened with tension. Her pulse seemed abnormally loud in her ear and every sense seemed exaggerated. As he continued to gaze at her, she became aware of a hundred different sensations she'd barely noticed before—the slick, cool leather of the couch, the nubby blanket he'd thrown over her, the shadows dancing on the wall from the fire's glow.

She was especially aware of Seth, of his hands strong and square-tipped and masculine, of the slight evening shadow along the curve of his jaw, of the sudden intense light in his eyes.

He seemed big and dangerous and ferociously attractive to her and she wanted to tell him she wasn't anywhere *close* to resisting him.

She couldn't say the words but he seemed to sense them anyway. "This is a mistake," he murmured.

"What is?" she asked, wondering why her lungs couldn't seem to hold a breath.

Before the two words were even out, he gave a low kind of groan that sounded as if he'd lost some kind of internal struggle, then he leaned forward and kissed her.

Oh, he was good at this, she thought as his warm mouth slid gently over hers. Any attempt at overt seduction, an intense or passionate embrace, probably would have sent her spiraling into panic and she would have pulled away.

But his kiss was slow, soft as the purest of silk and incredibly erotic. He touched her with nothing but his mouth, but she still felt surrounded by him, consumed by him.

She should stop this, she thought, for her sanity's sake, if nothing else. But his mouth was so warm and tasted of cinnamon and apples and she felt as if she'd been standing out in the cold forever.

How could he think for an instant she had the capacity to resist him? she wondered. With a sigh of surrender that somehow didn't seem at all like defeat, she returned the kiss, splaying one hand across the soft material of his shirt and winding the other around his neck to tangle her fingers in his thick hair.

He was right about this being a bad idea. She knew it, had done nothing but warn herself of the dangers since the day she met him, but she resolved to worry about that later.

She suddenly thought of her assistant Marcy's theory she'd shared with Ashley that day in the office— The Seth Dalton School of Broncbusting. *Just climb on and hold on tight. It probably won't last too long, but it will be a hell of a ride.*

For now, she would just savor the wild punch of adrenaline, she decided, and enjoy the moment.

Calling this a mistake was a bit like calling the Tetons outside his window a couple of pleasant little hills.

Seth tried to catch his breath, wondering how the hell a simple kiss had so quickly twisted out of his control. He'd only meant to steal one small taste of her, just enough so he wouldn't have to wonder anymore. But the moment his mouth met hers, he felt as if he was the one tumbling head over heels down the mountain out there, as if no matter how he tried he couldn't manage to find his footing in the slippery snow.

He supposed in the back of his mind, he'd thought

perhaps they could just share a quick kiss and that would be the end of it. One kiss probably wouldn't have sated his curiosity, but at least it might have been temporarily appeased.

But she had been so soft, so warm and welcoming, and she had given just the tiniest of sighs when he kissed her, and shivered against his mouth.

How could a man resist that?

When she returned his kiss and pulled him closer, he had to use every ounce of strength to keep from pressing her back against the sofa cushions and devouring her. The only way he held himself back was remembering she'd just suffered a head injury and was in no condition for anything more strenuous than a kiss.

When he felt his control fray, he forced himself to pull away, feeling as breathless and lightheaded as he had when he climbed the Grand out there.

In the fire's flickering glow, she looked soft and lovely, like something in one of those watercolors hanging in the Jackson art galleries.

"Have dinner with me tomorrow," he said on impulse. "I know this great place in Idaho Falls."

She gazed at him for several seconds, then she seemed to close up like his mom's flowers at the end of day. She shuttered away all the soft sweetness of her kiss as if it had never been.

"No."

He raised an eyebrow. "Just like that?"

"What else do you need? I know it's probably not a word you're well acquainted with, but I won't have dinner with you. Thank you for asking, though."

He shouldn't have been surprised by the rejection,

but after her response to his kiss, he had hoped perhaps she might have changed her mind about him. Obviously, one kiss was not enough to do the trick.

Perhaps he also should have expected the bitter disappointment, but all this seemed uncomfortably foreign.

The silence stretched between them, awkward and uneasy, until finally he spoke, doing his best to keep his voice cool and unaffected.

"Is that a no because you genuinely don't want to, or a no for some other reason?"

She pulled the blanket around her more tightly. "Does it matter?"

"Yeah." More than it should, he admitted to himself. "Humor me. I'd like to know."

She let out a breath. "All right. I'm attracted to you, Seth. I would be lying if I said otherwise."

He frowned. "And yet you say that like it's a bad thing."

"It *is* a bad thing, at least from my perspective. Or if not a bad thing, precisely, at least an impossibility."

"Why?"

She seemed suddenly fascinated by the flickering of the flames. "I'm in a precarious position here. Surely you can see that."

He tried to make sense of what she was talking about but came up empty. "I guess I'm just a big, stupid cowboy," he said. "Why don't you explain it to me?"

"Pine Gulch is a small town. If we—if *I*—gave in to that attraction, people would know. They would talk."

"You're exaggerating a little, don't you think? Who

would know or care what you might do in your personal life?"

She shook her head. "You're either incredibly naive—which I find rather hard to believe—or you're being disingenuous. Of course people will care! I'm in a position of trust and responsibility, charged with educating their children! And you are..."

Her voice trailed off but not before he felt his defensive hackles rise. Suddenly he felt ten years old again, on the receiving end of one of Hank's more vicious diatribes. "I'm what?"

She shifted on the couch and refused to meet his gaze. "A favorite topic of conversation around here, for one thing."

"I can't help what people say about me."

"Can't you?"

"What's that supposed to mean?"

She closed her eyes for a moment but when she opened them, they seemed more determined than ever to push him away. "You're a player. You never date a woman more than a few times and you've left a trail of broken hearts strewn across the county. By all accounts, your conquests are the stuff of legend and frankly, I'm not interested in becoming one of them."

She was even better than Jake and Wade at twisting the knife. He wondered if his guts were spilling all over the carpet from that particular jab because it sure as hell felt like it.

"I suppose that's clear enough," he said quietly.

Her eyes darkened and he thought he saw regret there, but he couldn't swear to anything. "I can't afford a complication like this, Seth. Not now. It would be career suicide."

He forced a laugh he was far from feeling. "A little dramatic, don't you think? I only invited you to dinner, not to have wild monkey sex on the front lawn of the school during recess."

She flushed but held her ground. "I can't afford it," she repeated. "Surely you can see that. I am perfectly aware that when the school board hired me, some people protested hiring an outsider—and a divorced woman at that. I haven't had time to prove myself yet. If I were to jump into something with you, it will forever define me in the eyes of my faculty and the parents at my school. Those voices who spoke out against hiring me will become a cacophony of protest. I'm trying to build a new life here for me and for my children. I can't risk anything that might threaten that."

He wanted to argue, to find some way around her refusal, but before he could form the torrent of words in his head into anything coherent, the doorbell rang and an instant later, Jake walked into the room without waiting for him to answer it.

Lucy woke up with a start and yipped a welcome.

"Sorry I took a little longer than I'd planned," Jake said, shrugging out of his coat and picking up the puppy. He seemed oblivious to the thick tension in the room, a fact that Seth could only view with gratitude. He was *not* in the mood for another lecture.

On the other hand, he wouldn't mind pounding on something right about now and Jake seemed a convenient target. The only downside to that he could see would be facing the wrath of Magdalena Cruz Dalton, who scared him a whole lot more than her husband.

"Caroline decided she couldn't wait to put her tree up so we were all helping her decorate it and I lost track of time," Jake went on.

"You didn't need to return at all," Jenny said briskly in that prim schoolmarm voice Seth was finding increasingly adorable. "I'm perfectly fine, I promise, and more than ready to go home."

Jake studied her carefully and something in her tone or her features had him shifting his gaze back to Seth, his eyes suddenly hard. Seth stared back, hating that his brother could make him feel as though he was sixteen years old again.

"She slept most of the time and has only been awake for the past fifteen minutes or so." He hadn't meant to sound defensive but he was very afraid that was how his words came out.

Jake met his gaze for a long moment then turned back to Jenny. "Good. Rest is just what I would prescribe for you. I'm going to recommend taking it easy for the next few days. You're going to feel like you've been hit by a bus at first, but that should only last a day or two."

"All right. Something to look forward to, then," she said, making Jake smile.

"Maggie and I will give you a ride home. We're ready to go back into town and can drop you off with no problem."

Seth started to protest that he wanted to stick to the original plan and be the one to take her home. He would sound ridiculous if he did, he realized, so he opted to keep his mouth shut.

"Thank you," she said without looking at Seth. She managed to avoid his gaze the entire time Jake helped her into her parka and led her toward the door.

He thought she might leave without a word but just before she left, she turned around, her eyes shuttered. "Thank you for inviting us today. My children had a wonderful time."

Her children. Not her.

"I'm sorry it had to end on a sour note," he said.

"So am I," she said, her voice low, and they both knew they weren't talking about her tumble down the mountain. "Goodbye."

He stood on the porch, the icy air cutting through his clothes, as Jake led her down the steps to his waiting Durango. For a long time after their taillights disappeared down the hill, he stood in the cold, watching after them and wondering why *he* was the one who felt as though he'd been hit by a bus.

Chapter 9

He hadn't missed her. Not a bit.

That was what he tried to tell himself, anyway.

For two weeks, he and Jenny Boyer had successfully managed to avoid each other. Not exactly an easy task in a community as small as Pine Gulch, Idaho.

Now, as Seth drove Cole home after a Saturday spent in the garage working on the GTO, he wondered if this would be the one time he might catch a glimpse of her—or if she would remain frustratingly elusive.

He might not have physically seen her since the day they went hunting Christmas trees on the Cold Creek, but she had never been far from his thoughts.

It was just because she had rejected him, he told himself. She represented the unattainable, the impossible. So naturally, he couldn't focus on anything but her.

For all that he hadn't been able to stop thinking about her, he wasn't completely sure he was all that eager to see her again, not when he was still nursing his wounds from their last encounter. He tended to veer between anger and hurt at the brutal way she had shoved him away after a kiss that to him had been sweetly magical.

She was definitely avoiding him—that much was obvious. The handful of times Cole had come out to the Cold Creek to work on the car or the horses, he had taken the school bus out and his grandfather had picked him up.

She couldn't run from him forever—and she didn't need to. Her message came through loud and clear. He certainly understood rejection when it reached out and slapped him across the face, though that didn't make it any easier to accept.

Cole wound down his monologue about the work they had done on the GTO when they reached the outskirts of town. "Thanks again for giving me a ride," he said.

"No problem. I needed to pick up some things at the store in town anyway."

The only thing in his house was a bottle of Caroline's strawberry jam and a solitary egg and he was out of laundry soap. But he supposed it was safe to admit deep in the recesses of his heart that he'd offered Cole a ride half hoping he might see the boy's mother.

He was pathetic, he thought. What *was* this obsession with her?

This was a pretty miserable way to spend a Saturday night, listening to a teenage boy talk about cars and thinking about his grocery list—and a woman he couldn't have.

So much for her theory that he was some kind of wild-ass cowboy with nothing on his mind but whiskey and women.

Maybe he ought to drop by the Bandito to shake things up a little before he went grocery shopping. He tried to summon up a little enthusiasm for the idea but the prospect was about as appealing as walking through the grocery store wearing only his Tony Lamas.

Something was seriously wrong with him.

He hadn't avoided the place in the past two weeks, he reminded himself. He had stopped at least two or three times to shoot a little pool, have a couple beers, flirt a little with some pretty girls. But he hadn't enjoyed it much.

Maybe if he tried to enjoy it a little more, expended a little energy and took one of those nice ladies up on their subtle offers, he might not be so edgy and restless, he thought as he drove through the thickening snow. Even as he thought it, he knew he wouldn't.

None of them had soft hair of a hundred different shades and a lush mouth that kept a man up at night.

None of them was Jenny Boyer.

"How much longer before the custom touch-up paint you ordered comes in?" the boy asked.

Seth dragged his mind away from his current dry spell in the romance department and turned his attention to the kid. "They said a week or two. Then all we have to do is give her a couple of coats and we'll be done. Maybe during Christmas break we can take her for a ride, if the weather's not too snowy."

"Yeah. Okay." For all his enthusiasm about working on the GTO, Cole didn't look too thrilled by the idea.

"You've worked hard to pay your debt. I figured when we're done with the touch-up paint, we'll be square. You'll be glad to lift your last shovelfull of horse manure, I'm sure."

"I guess." Cole slumped in the seat and gazed out at the wintry landscape.

He frowned at the almost sullen note of dejection in the boy's voice. Was Cole upset not to be working on the Cold Creek anymore?

He would be sorry to see the last of him. Tinkering with cars had always been a solitary escape for him, but he'd enjoyed having company the last month and Cole had been a different kid when he was working on the GTO, curious and talkative and enthusiastic.

He studied him across the dimly lit truck. "Of course, I wouldn't turn away a hard worker if he wanted to earn a little extra money working with the horses and helping out with the occasional mechanical repair," he said on impulse. "The pay's not the greatest, but you could ride the horses all you want. And in the summer after school gets out, I could probably give you all the hours you wanted to work, provided you would be willing to drive a tractor."

Cole straightened, his features suddenly animated, though he was obviously trying not to show too much excitement. The kid reminded him so much of himself sometimes, watching him was almost painful.

"We'll have to talk to your mom about it," Seth cautioned as he pulled up in front of Jason Chambers's house. "She might prefer you to find an after-school job closer to home."

Cole's enthusiasm wavered a bit but not completely. "We could talk to her now," he suggested. "If you wanted, anyway. I know she must be home since my grandpa went to Jackson Hole yesterday and won't be back until Monday."

Oh, Jenny would love having him show up on her doorstep with an offer like this out of the blue, he thought. But Cole was so eager, he didn't have the heart to refuse.

"Okay," he agreed, anticipation churning through him at knowing he would see her in just a few moments.

He parked his truck in front of the house, noting as he did that the sidewalk and driveway needed shoveling. Three or four inches had fallen since noon and several more were forecast before morning.

"I'll talk to your mother with you, on the condition you help me shovel this snow after we're done."

Cole made a face. "What's the good of shoveling while it's still snowing? Seems a whole lot smarter to wait until it stops and then you only have to do it once."

"Here's a little life lesson for you, kid. I know this is probably your first big storm so you might not have learned this yet. Most jobs are easier to swallow if you take them in small bites. Shoveling four inches of snow three separate times in one storm might seem like a pain in the neck. But trust me on this, it's a whole lot easier than waiting until it's all over and having to work a shovel through two-foot deep drifts."

"Or we could all move somewhere warm so we wouldn't have to worry about shoveling snow."

"What? And miss all this?" Seth opened the door and snow swirled inside, icy and cold. The kid rolled his eyes but climbed out of the passenger side.

Their boots left prints in the snow as they trudged up the sidewalk through the dark night. He could see the dark shape of the Christmas tree they'd cut in the window but the lights hadn't been turned on and neither were the porch lights.

Odd, he thought.

Cole pushed open the front door. "Mom, I'm home," he called. He hit a switch and instantly the tree lit up with hundreds of colorful lights. It was beautiful, decorated with a hodgepodge of ornaments, most of which looked homemade. His favorite kind of tree, Seth thought with satisfaction.

"Mom?" Cole called again.

An instant later, Jenny burst into the room wearing a half-buttoned coat and one glove and holding her car keys in the other hand. She looked frazzled and close to tears.

Her gaze locked on Seth. "Oh, thank heavens! I can't tell you how glad I am to see you."

Seth raised an eyebrow. It wasn't quite the reception he'd expected. He might have made some crack about absence making the heart grow fonder, if she hadn't looked out of her head with worry.

"What's going on?"

"Morgan. She's having a bad flare-up. It's been going on for nearly half an hour and nothing we've tried is helping. I called your brother and he's meeting us at the clinic but I can't get my car started."

"I'll drive you," he said instantly, already moving. "Of course I'll take you! Where is she?"

"In the kitchen."

She led the way and his heart broke when he found Morgan looking terrified and breathing into a nebulizer.

For a moment as he took in her pale features and labored respirations, he was ten years old again, frightened and unable to breathe. He pushed away the ghosts of the past.

"Okay, sweetheart. Asthma-slayers to the rescue here. We're going to get you to Dr. Jake and he'll make everything okay."

He was completely humbled by the absolute and unequivocal trust in her eyes as she nodded.

He scooped her up, blanket and all, and headed back through the house toward the front door and his waiting truck.

After he set Morgan on the seat and fastened her belt, he helped Jenny in after her.

"I've only got three seat belts in my pickup, and I don't dare drive without everyone belted in these road conditions," he said to Cole. "Do you mind staying here?"

"No," he said, looking worried. For all his attitude sometimes, he was just a kid, Seth reminded himself. A boy worried for his sister.

"Don't worry," he said as he went around the truck. "She's tough. Jake will take care of her and she'll be just fine. Meanwhile, your mother and sister would probably appreciate it if they didn't have to trudge through snow to get into the door when we get back."

Cole nodded with a man-to-man kind of look and Seth was pleased to see him already reaching for the snow shovel on the porch.

"I'm very sorry about this," Jenny said as he drove toward the clinic. "I was just about ready to call the ambulance."

"Forget it. We can get her there faster this way, rather than wait for the volunteer paramedics to try to come in to the fire station through the snow."

He had to concentrate on driving for the next few moments as the storm's intensity seemed to increase by the minute. With each passing second, he was aware of Morgan's wheezy struggle to breathe and the huge weight of responsibility pressing down his shoulders.

It gave him some tiny inkling of what parents must go through, this fragile terror at knowing they can sometimes literally hold a child's life in their hands.

When he finally pulled up in front of the clinic, he was sweating through the heavy layers of his coat. He gave a silent prayer of gratitude when he saw Jake's Durango already in the parking lot and all the lights blazing inside.

He scooped Morgan into his arms and headed for the door, shielding her from the snow with his body. His sister-in-law Maggie was the first one to greet them inside, ready with oxygen and a wheelchair. Jake was right behind her, bustling with the calm competence that made everybody in town trust him with their health.

They both looked surprised to see him there but

he didn't waste time in explanations as he set Morgan into the wheelchair then stepped back to let them do their thing.

There was no one on earth he'd rather entrust this sweet little girl to than Jake and Maggie, he thought as he watched them work.

An hour later, Jenny sat beside her daughter's bed in one of the small treatment rooms of the clinic holding Morgan's hand and reading to her from an *American Girl* magazine Seth had found for them in the waiting room while Jake Dalton checked her vitals.

"We seem to be through the worst of it," Jake said now, pulling his stethoscope away from his ears.

"So you think it was her cold that triggered it?" she asked.

"There's a trace of bronchitis there and I'm sure that didn't help anything. My gut tells me it's viral but I'm going to give you some antibiotics anyway, just in case I'm wrong."

"Okay."

"And we'll need to continue the steroid nebulizer treatments every four hours."

"Check."

Jake leaned back against the sink. "Now we have a decision to make and I'm going to leave it up to you. I can ship you to the hospital in Idaho Falls if you would feel better spending the night there."

"Or?"

"I can send you home with a monitor and you can keep an eye on her oxygen levels throughout the night and run the nebulizer treatments on your own. Either way you're probably not going to get any sleep but she might do better in her own bed. If you have problems, I can be at your house in five minutes."

Oh, Jenny absolutely *hated* having to make these decisions on her own. These were the moments she missed having a partner she could count on, someone to lean on during hard times and to help her with these terribly tough calls.

"Are you sure that's wise?" Seth said from the corner. She'd thought he would retreat to the waiting room, but he had stuck around for the whole proceedings, teasing Morgan and asking questions of Maggie and Jake and offering quiet support to Jenny.

She wasn't sure what she would have done without him.

Jake didn't seem upset at the question. "I wouldn't have suggested it as an option if I didn't think she would be fine at home. Since the flare-up is under control, it's probably safer having her in her own bed than trying to transport her through the storm just for observation."

"I want to go home," Morgan said, her voice frail and small. Jenny squeezed her hand, knowing how much her daughter hated hospitals.

"I guess we'll take door number two," she finally said. "I have to think the worst of it has passed."

"I agree. But the only way I'm going to let you take her home is if you promise to call if you have any concerns at all in the night."

Jenny nodded and gave him and Maggie a tired but grateful smile. "Thank you both for meeting us here. I have to confess, one of my biggest worries of moving to a small town so far from a major medical center was finding good care for Morgan's asthma. I never expected to find such wonderful providers in tiny Pine Gulch. I can't tell you what a comfort it is to have you close by."

"You won't find better medical care anywhere," Seth spoke up, his voice gruff. "Pine Gulch is just lucky Jake decided to come home instead of taking one of the big-city offers that came down the pike when he finished medical school. Having an experienced nurse-practitioner like Mag is icing."

His brother looked surprised and touched at the praise, though she thought Seth seemed a little embarrassed after he spoke.

"Well, I'm sorry I had to drag you both out on a night like this."

"It's all part of the job description," Maggie assured her. "Don't give it a thought."

After Jake rounded up an oxygen-saturation monitor, Maggie brought a wheelchair for them to use to transport Morgan out to the truck, but Seth shook his head.

"I've got it," he said, wrapping the little girl in a blanket and lifting her into his arms again.

He had pulled his truck right up to the door so only had to take a few steps through the blowing snow to set her inside carefully.

Jenny's heart seemed to shift and settle as she watched this big, overwhelmingly masculine man take such gentle care with her child. Morgan gave him a sleepy smile as he fastened her seat belt and Jenny had to swallow her sigh.

Her daughter was already crazy about Seth. This little episode wasn't going to do anything to diminish her hero worship. She desperately hoped her daughter wouldn't have her heart broken by another male in her life.

Exhausted by her ordeal, Morgan fell asleep before they even made it out of the parking lot.

Seth drove with native confidence through the miserable conditions. At least a foot had fallen since the storm had started earlier in the evening and most of it was still on the roads, but he hardly seemed to notice it.

At her father's house, she was surprised to see all but a skiff of snow had been cleared from the driveway. She frowned. Who could have done it? She could only hope Jason hadn't driven home in these conditions from Jackson Hole.

Maybe a neighbor, she thought as she followed Seth and Morgan inside. She was discovering people in Pine Gulch took care of each other. It was another reason she desperately wanted to make things work out for them here. She loved being part of a community, a small part of the greater whole.

"Where am I heading?" Seth whispered inside the welcome warmth of the house. Morgan was still sleeping, she saw.

"Her room," she whispered back. "I'll show you."

She led the way to Morgan's room, across the hall from her own and he set her carefully down on the bed.

"Thank you," she murmured, aware of him watching her intently as she hooked up the monitor then drew the quilt up over Morgan's sleeping form.

In the living room, they found Cole waiting for them, trying hard not to look worried.

"How is she?" he asked.

"Better. Good enough that Dr. Dalton seemed to think she'd be all right at home tonight," Jenny said.

She was suddenly exhausted after the last two hours of stress and she could feel an adrenaline crash coming on.

"Good job clearing the walks and the driveway," Seth said.

She stared at her son. "You did that?"

He stuck out his jaw. "Yeah. So?"

She sighed, wondering how she always seemed to say exactly the wrong thing to him. She decided to use actions instead of words and pulled him into a hug. "Thank you."

In a rare and precious gift, he let her hug him for a long moment before he stepped away.

"You're supposed to call Grandpa. He said he can come home if you need him."

"I don't want him driving in this mess. But I also don't want to be stuck here without transportation if Morgan has a relapse."

"You won't be without transportation," Seth put in. "You'll have my truck."

She frowned. "If you leave your truck, what will you use to get back to the Cold Creek?"

"Nothing. Not tonight, anyway. I'm bunking on your couch."

Chapter 10

As he might have expected, Jenny was less than enthusiastic about his declaration.

Sparks seemed to shoot out of her suddenly narrowed eyes and the look she gave him plainly did not bode well for him. She opened her mouth—to flay him alive, no doubt—then cast a look at Cole and closed it again. He had never been so grateful for her son's presence.

"I appreciate the offer," she said tightly, "but that's really not necessary. I'm sure you have plenty of other places you would rather be on a stormy night like tonight."

"Nope," he said, and was astonished to realize it was true.

Something was definitely wrong with him. This was usually his favorite kind of night, stormy and cold, the kind of night designed for cuddling up under a warm quilt with a sweet young thing, putting his mind to work coming up with imaginative ways to keep warm.

Why did that seem so totally unappealing to him right now? He would far rather be here in Jason Chambers's house with a woman who wanted nothing to do with him, sleeping alone on a cold couch.

"Jenny, there's no way under the sun I'm going to leave you alone here tonight and that's the end of it. I would never sleep worrying about Morgan and about you stuck here without wheels in this weather. I don't mind the couch."

The phone rang suddenly in the kitchen and though he looked loath to leave this interesting battlefield, Cole went to answer it.

Jenny cast a quick look through the doorway to make sure her son couldn't overhear, then she spoke in a low voice. "You can't stay here. It's impossible. What would people think if your truck were parked out front all night?"

For one near-disastrous second, he almost laughed, but she seemed so serious, so genuinely distressed, the impulse died, leaving a hollow feeling in his gut.

She wasn't joking. She was so concerned about her reputation, she thought just the sight of his truck parked out front of her house all night would destroy it.

He had no idea what it was like to be a pillar of society—and he wasn't sure he wanted to know, especially if it meant worrying about something that seemed so inconsequential to him.

Did she really think anybody would believe the elementary school principal would invite the town's bad boy over for a night of wild sex while her children were in the house?

He had to admit, the thought of that soft body of hers all warm and cuddly was far too appealing under the circumstances, but he managed to rein in his over-active imagination.

"Nobody's going to be out in this weather to be snooping on the neighbors," he assured her. "All the town busybodies are tucked up in their beds dreaming of catching the mayor's wife shoplifting or something. And if anybody's rude enough to ask, we can just tell them the truth. Or if you don't think that's good enough, we can always tell them I loaned my truck to you when your car broke down."

She didn't look convinced. "It's the ones who *won't* say anything who worry me most. Those are the kinds of whispers that can destroy a reputation in an instant."

He couldn't have said why it bothered him so much that she was so concerned about her precious reputation—or that she seemed so convinced he held the power to completely destroy it.

"You really care about the opinions of some old biddies with nothing better to do than bad-mouth a woman whose only crime is worrying about her sick child?"

"It's not that simple."

"What's your alternative? Dragging your father home from Jackson Hole in this weather? I know you don't want to do that."

"No. There must be some other solution."

"Not that I can see. I'm staying, Jen. You don't know stubborn until you've taken on a Dalton."

She opened her mouth to answer but Cole appeared

in the doorway, looking from one of them to the other out of curious eyes. He held out a black cordless phone. "Grandpa's on the phone again, Mom."

She took it from him and Cole disappeared. A moment later, Seth heard his tread on the stairs and assumed the boy had retreated to his room.

While Jenny was on the phone, Seth took off his coat and hung it on a hall tree in the entryway, then returned to the living room. Jenny'd had the same idea—she'd taken off her hat and scarf and her coat and tossed them over a chair.

"No, Dad. I don't want you to come home," she said, unbuttoning her cardigan to reveal a formfitting forest green turtleneck underneath. She slipped out of the sweater, and Seth slid onto the couch and stretched his legs out in front of him, enjoying himself immensely.

She narrowed her eyes at his comfortable pose. "There's nothing you can do. Nothing *anyone* can do," she added with a pointed look at Seth.

He smiled benignly, wondering how much more she might be planning to take off.

"All right. I'll call you if there's any change, I promise. Yes. Okay. Stay safe. Have fun with your friends and don't lose too much money. I know. You always win. That's why you go. All right. I love you, too, Dad."

She hung up from her father, set the phone on the coffee table and stood gazing at her bright Christmas tree, looking so dejected Seth almost offered to go find a nice, respectable widow with her own snowplow if it would make Jenny feel better about the situation.

After a moment, she straightened her shoulders and faced him. He suddenly wanted more than anything to take that grim look out of her eyes, to make everything okay.

"Your dad is obviously a cardsharp, but how are *you* at poker?" he asked.

She blinked, looking a little disoriented. "Sorry?"

"We're going to be up all night worrying about Morgan and giving her treatments every four hours, but we don't have to be bored. Let's call Cole up to play some cards. What do you say? We can play for pennies or toothpicks or matchsticks or whatever you've got. Unless you think we'd be corrupting the morals of a minor."

Her laugh was abrupt, but he took comfort that it was still a laugh. "Are you kidding? My dad taught him to play blackjack the minute he was old enough to count. He'll wipe the floor with both of us."

"Speak for yourself, ma'am. You've never played cards with me. I don't like to lose."

She sniffed. "I believe I've figured that out by now."

He laughed, glad that he'd been able to distract her, if only for a moment.

Where was her child?

Jenny raced through the halls of an unfamiliar hospital, her way strewn with gurneys and hospital equipment and hallways that led nowhere.

She opened every door but couldn't find Morgan anywhere. Somewhere in this labyrinthian hell was her child, ill and wheezy, but Jenny had no idea where to look. Her baby needed her and she wasn't there for her.

She begged everyone she passed to please help her, but no one answered. No one at all. Finally, when she was nearly wailing with defeat, she headed down one last, crowded hallway, devoid of doors except for one at the very end, lit by a strange orange glow from within.

Her child had to be there, she thought, trying to shove her way past uncaring people who blocked her at every turn. She felt so alone, so utterly forsaken. She was so tired of fighting this battle by herself. All she wanted was to curl up and weep out all her pain and frustration, but she had to find her child.

Suddenly—like a miracle, like the parting of the Red Sea—a path opened up for her through the crowd of people. Someone stood in front of her, someone with shoulders broad enough to carry the weight of all her fears. She couldn't see his face, but her salvation blazed a trail for her and she rushed toward the door. When she reached it, she extended a hand to thank the only person who had helped her.

He turned and gave her a slow, painfully sweet smile and opened the door for her. Somehow she had known it was Seth, she thought, even as she rushed inside to her child, sobbing with relief to find her healthy and whole, her breathing slow and even.

She awoke with a start, disoriented by the strange dream.

She wasn't sure where she was at first, then she realized the orange glow she had dreamed about must have been from the woodstove, where a fire still flickered softly.

She was in her father's den, curled up on the couch. She frowned, trying to remember why she'd fallen asleep there, then the lingering tendrils of her dream wrapped around her again and she drew in a quick breath.

Morgan!

Jenny yanked off the soft knitted afghan she couldn't remember pulling around herself and rose so quickly the room whirled for a moment. She barely waited for the walls to steady before rushing down the hall to her daughter's room, her heart pounding.

All was quiet there. The alarm clock by the bed told Jenny she'd slept longer than she thought—it was nearly quarter after four. How could she have fallen asleep when her daughter needed her?

But no. A quick check told her Morgan was sleeping soundly. The oxygen monitor on her bedside table registered a respectable ninety-four. Not fabulous but not terrible, either.

She let out a low sigh of relief and lifted a trio of stuffed animals from the glider rocker by Morgan's bed so she could take their place.

Her daughter was due for another nebulizer treatment and though Jenny hated to wake her, she knew it was something neither of them could avoid.

Poor little thing, to have to endure so much, she thought, as she poured the medicine into the nebulizer then shook her awake.

"I'm sorry, sweetheart, but you need a treatment."

Morgan groaned but blinked her eyes open blearily, just long enough for Jenny to fit the mask over her nose and mouth and turn on the machine. Medicated air blew into the mask, forcing its way into her daughter's lungs. Morgan hated that part, she knew.

"Do you want me to hold you?" she asked.

Morgan nodded, so Jenny slid into bed with her, cuddling her tight and singing softly to her until the medicine was finished.

She settled Morgan back into bed and was grateful when she closed her eyes and slipped easily back to sleep.

Perhaps because of the silly dream and the remembered terror of not being able to find her, Jenny stood for a long time by her daughter's bed, thinking how very much she loved her. Despite what she sometimes had to endure, Morgan was warm and good-natured. An uncommonly kind child, she often thought.

She couldn't imagine how cold and lonely her life would have been without either of her children.

Cole might be struggling through his teenage years but she wouldn't trade him for anything. As she finally left Morgan's room, she couldn't help thinking of the evening she, Seth and Cole had spent together and she had to smile.

She didn't know how Seth had done it, but somehow in the course of the night while they played Five-Card Stud and Acey-Deucy and Texas Hold 'em, he had returned her funny, sweet son to her.

She knew it was probably fleeting, that in the morning Cole would likely revert to his normal sullen, unhappy self. But for a few hours he had laughed and joked and teased with her and—miracle of miracles— had even seemed to enjoy her company.

Around midnight, Cole had been drooping over his cards so Jenny sent him to bed. She had been loath to say good-night to him, both because she had so en-

joyed her time with him and because she desperately
needed the buffer he provided between her and Seth.

She needn't have worried. While she woke Morgan for her midnight treatment, Seth apparently had
thumbed through her father's DVD collection until he
found an old Alfred Hitchcock movie, one of her favorites.

"I haven't seen this in years," he exclaimed when she
returned to the den after that treatment earlier. "What
do you think? Are you up to watching a movie?"

She had agreed and had tried to stay awake, but the
long, arduous evening of worry and caregiving took its
toll. She didn't think she had made it very far through
the movie.

Now the TV was dark and her unwanted houseguest
was nowhere in sight. Had he gone home? She hurried to the window but there was his big black pickup
truck, looking dark and menacing and incriminating
against the snow.

He must have decided to go to bed. It couldn't have
been too long before she woke up, as the log in the
woodstove still looked fresh and barely burned through.

How long had she been out of it while he sat watching the movie? she wondered. She felt curiously vulnerable knowing she must have slept in front of him.
It was a disconcerting thing to realize another person
might have watched her sleep—especially when that
person was a man she found enormously attractive.

Where was he now? Some hostess she was, whether
or not her guest was an invited one. Perhaps he had
found an empty bed to stretch out on, either in her
room or her father's.

She should at least check to see if he had found somewhere to rest. If her guest was awake, a good hostess should at least ascertain if he needed anything.

Her pulse kicked up as a heated image jumped into her mind of wild kisses and tangled limbs.

No! She only meant a clean towel or a spare toothbrush.

She did her best to push the fiery images away but they haunted her as she paused outside her father's bedroom. No light shone underneath the door but she was still cautious as she pushed it open, only to release a heavy breath when she found an empty bed.

He must have gone to her room, then. Her stomach fluttered as she pictured that long, powerful body stretched out on her bed. Her pillow would smell like him, she thought. Leathery and masculine and delicious.

She stood outside the door, her stomach twisting with nerves. She rolled her eyes at her reaction. This was ridiculous. He was only a man, for heaven's sake. Just a man who was probably snoring up a storm right now.

Still, she felt a little like Pandora lifting the lid of her box as she pushed open her bedroom, then slumped against the door.

He wasn't there, either. Her bed was just as she had left it that morning, the corners neat and the pillow shams aligned.

Completely baffled now, she returned to the kitchen. He had to be *somewhere* in the house. She was about to check if he had somehow managed to find her father's guest room in the basement when she heard a clatter on the other side of the door leading to the garage, then a muffled curse.

For the first time, she noticed a narrow slice of light under the door. She frowned. The garage? What on earth would Seth be doing in the *garage* at four-thirty in the morning?

Shaking her head in confusion, she pushed open the door and shivered as a blast of cold air slapped at her.

She heard whistling first, some tune she couldn't name but that she suspected was on the bawdy side. She followed the sound and nearly tumbled down the two small steps leading into the garage at what she saw.

The hood of her little SUV was open and Seth was bent over fiddling with something under it.

She couldn't seem to take her eyes off him as she tried to process what he was doing. It was hours before dawn and he was out in below-freezing weather in the middle of a blizzard working on her car.

This was the man she thought was an immature womanizer interested in only one thing, the man she wouldn't go to dinner with for fear someone might see them and her job might be threatened, the man she had rejected a dozen different ways.

Why would he do such a thing?

Something seemed to break loose inside of her, something precious and tender and terrifying, and she pressed a hand to her mouth, shaken to her soul.

She must have made some sound because the whistling broke off in midnote and he peered his head around the side of her hood. When he saw her, he gave her one of those heartbreaking smiles of his.

"Hi!" he said cheerfully.

She couldn't think of anything to say, lost in the tumult of emotions washing through her.

At her continued silence, his smile slipped away. "Is everything okay with Morgan? I checked on her a while ago and everything seemed fine, I swear, or I would have woken you."

She had to force herself to speak, if only to allay his worry. "She is. Her oxygen levels are still within normal range and I just gave her another nebulizer treatment. As soon as she finished the last of it, she went right back to sleep, just like she did at midnight."

She didn't trust herself to say anything more just now, too stunned by his actions.

"That's wonderful," he said fervently.

She walked down the steps until she stood only a few feet away from him. "Seth, what are you doing here?"

He gave a little laugh that seemed to run down her spine like a warm caress. "A little self-evident, don't you think?"

"It's four-thirty in the morning! You should be home in bed, not standing in my ice-cold garage monkeying under my hood."

He raised an eyebrow and by the sudden amusement in his eyes, she realized how her words could be taken as a euphemism.

Why did men have to turn so much having to do with automobiles and their maintenance into sexual double entendres? *Lube her chassis, rotate her tires, give the old engine a tune-up.* And of course, all engines were female, the better for them to work their wiles.

To her relief, Seth didn't make any smart remark, though—he just smiled. "It was no big deal. I just didn't want you being stuck here tomorrow if your father doesn't make it back from Jackson because of the weather. Anyway, I'm just about done. Let's see if my monkeying did the trick."

He slid behind the wheel and turned the key he must have found on her key ring in the kitchen. The engine started up instantly, practically purring in the cold garage.

"Of course," she muttered to herself. Just like everything else female the man touched.

Seth slid out with a satisfied smile. "There you go. She's all ready to rock."

Oh, she was in serious trouble.

"What was my problem?" she managed to ask. *Besides this foolish, foolish heart?*

"Corrosion around the battery cables. I only cleaned her up a little with some baking soda and water. But then I saw by the sticker on your windshield you were past due for an oil change and discovered your dad happened to have five quarts of the right grade oil, so I decided to take care of that, too. No big deal."

"It's a very big deal to me," she murmured. She couldn't remember the last time anyone had performed such a gesture for her. Against her will, she thought of the nightmare she'd had just before she awoke, of feeling helpless and alone and terribly frightened. And then he was there, lending her his strength when she had none of her own left.

"I'm just glad you won't be left without a car now,"

he said, wiping his hands on one of the rags from a box her father kept in the corner.

She leaned closer. "You've got a smudge on your face."

"Yeah, I always make a mess when I'm working on a car."

He scrubbed it without success. Without thinking, she took the rag from him and stepped forward, carefully wiping at the small spot of grease just above his jawline.

An instant later, she realized what she was doing and she stopped, mortified. Her gaze slid to his and the sudden heat there seemed to burn through her, setting every nerve ending ablaze.

She swallowed hard and thought she might have whispered his name, but it was lost in the wild firestorm of his kiss.

Chapter 11

His arms wrapped around her, tangling her up in a heat and strength that smelled vaguely of motor oil and sexy male.

She clung tightly to his shirt and slid into the wonder of his kiss. He was so good at it, his mouth teasing and tasting until she couldn't seem to grab hold of a single coherent thought.

A corner of her mind protested that she played a risky game. This was crazy, foolish. A smart woman should be running for all she was worth from the heartbreak he would inevitably leave behind, not reaching out to grab it with both hands.

She knew it, but she couldn't let herself think about that now, when his mouth was so warm and exhilarating, with his hard strength beneath her fingertips, with her heart still reeling from the magnitude of what he had just done for her.

The cold and rather drab garage seemed to disappear. Her SUV, her father's power tools, the snow still whirling outside the window. Nothing existed but the two of them, this man who seemed to know her so well, who somehow reached into her deepest dreams and gave her a reality far more magical than anything she could have imagined.

She felt safe in his arms. It was an odd thought— one she didn't quite understand, considering he was the most dangerous man she'd ever met. At least to her emotions.

At this moment, though, as his mouth explored hers and his arms held her tightly, she felt protected from the cold and storms of life, as if he would safeguard her from any threat.

She didn't know how long the kiss lasted. Time seemed to have no meaning, elastic and malleable. Einstein's theory of relativity held new meaning when a woman found herself in Seth Dalton's arms.

When at last she came up for air, they were both breathing hard and she wondered if she looked as dazed as he did.

"Wow," he said, his voice ragged. "That's one hell of a tip just for cleaning off a little battery corrosion."

She flushed and tried to retreat, but he wouldn't let her, pulling her close until she fitted snugly against him. His heat surrounded her, taking away the chill from the cold garage.

"I should *not* have done that," she murmured, though

with him so close, crowding out all her good sense, it wasn't easy to hang on to all the reasons why.

"If you're looking for me to agree with you on that particular point, I'm afraid you're going to be doomed to disappointment."

What must he think of her? She had been an idiot around him, weak and mercurial, since the day they met. Like now, for instance. She knew she shouldn't be so content in the circle of his arms but she couldn't manage the strength to pull away.

"I have no willpower where you're concerned. I'm sorry."

His arms tightened around her. "Sweetheart, you have nothing to apologize about."

She drew in a deep breath and summoned all her strength so she could force herself to step out of that warm haven. "Yes, I do. I've done nothing but give you mixed signals about what I want since that first day you came to the house with Cole. I tell you I'm not interested, then I attack you like some kind of…of sex-starved divorcée."

That masculine dimple appeared briefly. "Are you?"

Yes. *Oh, yes,* at least where this man was concerned. A few weeks ago she would have laughed at the notion that she could be so hungry. She hadn't had a physical relationship since her divorce, hadn't even considered one until Seth—and hadn't noticed the lack of it.

She had devoted all her energy and time to her children and her career. No man had even tempted her until Seth blew into her life with his sexy smile and his broad shoulders and those eyes that seemed to see right into her deepest desires.

Oh, yes. She was starving and he was like a big, gluttonous, delectable feast.

"You're blushing," he observed.

She felt herself flush even hotter and didn't know how to respond to his teasing.

"I'm trying to apologize for the mixed signals. I'm just…I'm not very good at all of this."

"This?"

"We have this…thing between us. I don't know what to do with it. I thought keeping a safe distance was the answer, but that obviously isn't working."

"No?"

"Even though I know perfectly well you're so bad for me, I can't seem to stop thinking about you."

At her words, something hot and intense sparked in his eyes. Perhaps she ought not have mentioned that last part, she thought nervously.

"Why am I so terrible?" he asked. "Because you think the whole town will start a riot if they should find out the elementary school principal might actually want a life?"

A life was one thing. A torrid affair with the town's hottest bachelor was something else entirely.

"You're out of my league, Seth. Way, way out of my league. I'm like the water boy on a Pop Warner football team and you're the starting quarterback in the Superbowl."

"Sorry, but baseball was my game."

"You know what I mean. I don't even know why you're here. You're a…a *player*. You're sexy and exciting and gorgeous. And I'm just a boring, dumpy thirty-six-year-old elementary school principal who has slept with exactly one man in my entire life."

Oh, she shouldn't have said that, either. His gaze sharpened and she could swear he saw right into her soul.

"Really?" he asked in an interested voice.

She flushed. "That's beside the point. What I'm trying to say is I can't figure any of this out. What do you want from me, Seth? I know perfectly well I'm not your usual type. I'm not beautiful or sexy or exciting. I've never been the kind of person who's always the life of the party. I'm just an ordinary woman, someone a man like you shouldn't even look twice at."

He looked astonished at her blunt self-assessment. "How can you say that with a straight face?"

"Because it's true!"

"I don't think you know yourself very well," he murmured. "And I'm certain you don't know me."

She couldn't argue with that. If she knew him, perhaps he wouldn't baffle her so completely.

"You seem to think I'm some rowdy cowboy with nothing on my mind but carving notches on some imaginary bedpost," he went on. "I'll admit, I have a bit of a reputation. Some of it earned, I'm sorry to say, but most of it exaggerated."

He was quiet for a moment, and then he gave her a solemn look, more serious than she'd ever seen from him. "But you know, there's more to me than whatever reputation I might have."

She wrapped her arms around herself, struck by his words. He was right. How unfair had she been to him, to hang everything on some whispered gossip over-heard in her office?

He was more than what people said about him. She only had to look at what he had done for her little family in the last month to see the truth of that.

He had been wonderful to Cole, patient and kind and understanding when most other men would have ranted and raved and pressed charges, more concerned about the damages to their prize automobile than about a troubled boy.

And Morgan adored him. He had shown extraordinary gentleness and rare perception to her daughter, and for that she would never be able to thank him enough. If nothing else, he'd shown her daughter it was possible to move past the frustrating limitations of asthma to have a successful, rewarding life as an adult.

She thought of his steady strength during Morgan's flare-up. They had all been so frightened, but Seth hadn't hesitated for an instant, had stepped into the breach and helped them all find their way through it.

If she needed further confirmation there were deeper levels to him than the world might see, she only had to look at his relationship with his family. The Daltons were a close and loving group and he seemed crazy about them all.

He had no problems hugging his mother in public, he plainly adored his niece and nephews, he was passionate about his horses.

And he had been willing to come out to a cold garage in the middle of a stormy winter night to fix her car so she wouldn't be stranded.

She hadn't wanted to see all those good things about

him, she realized. It was far easier to use his wild reputation as a shield to keep him away—and to keep her heart safe.

Continuing to focus on that one aspect of him was doing both of them an injustice.

"I know there's more to you," she finally admitted. "Perhaps that's why I can't stop thinking about you."

At her low words, a soft and tender warmth stole through him and he couldn't seem to stop looking at her in the dim light of the garage.

How could she actually say she wasn't beautiful? Just now, with her mouth swollen and her eyes still heavy-lidded from their kiss, he had never seen such a stunning sight. She looked rumpled and warm and he wanted her with a ferocity that astonished him.

For now, he contented himself with simply reaching for her hand. "I don't know if this helps anything," he finally said, "but I can't stop thinking about you, either. This sounds crazy, I know, but somehow I missed you these last few weeks. You told me to back off and I've tried to respect that. But I couldn't get you out of my head."

Her hand trembled in his. "How could you miss me? You don't even know me. Not really."

"I don't know the answer to that, I just know it's true. I'd like to know you, Jenny. Just as I'm more than my wild reputation, you're more than the boring, ordinary educator you see in the mirror. I know you are. You're beautiful and smart and funny."

She looked as if she wanted to protest but he didn't give her the chance. "I think we owe each other the chance to see beyond the surface."

"Seth—"

"Have dinner with me. Just one date. That's all I'm asking," he pressed. "One evening without all this tension and conflict that doesn't have to be there. There's this great restaurant I know in Jackson Hole. Neutral territory. We won't see anybody we know and we can talk and laugh and enjoy each other's company. I'll even promise to keep my hands to myself, if that's what it will take."

It just might be the toughest promise he ever had to keep, he thought, but he could handle it if it offered him the chance to bust through all her roadblocks.

She slipped her hand from his and wrapped her arms around herself. His heart sank and he braced himself for one more rejection from her, knowing somehow this one would hurt worse than all the others combined after that tender kiss they had just shared.

He saw the indecision in her eyes, then her gaze shifted from him to her car for just a moment. He had no idea what she saw there, but when she looked back, he was stunned to see the uncertainty replaced by something soft and warm, something that left him breathless.

"All right. Yes. I'll go to dinner with you."

He wasn't at all prepared for the raw emotion that coursed through him at her words—a tangle of joy and relief and elation. It left him more than a little uneasy, but he resolved not to worry about that now.

How had things come to this?

Ten days later, just a week before Christmas, Jenny pulled out the roast chicken to check it one final time. The skin looked perfect, crisp and golden, and the

whole kitchen was redolent with delicious smells—
fresh rolls, creamy mashed potatoes and the succu-
lent chicken.

"Does this look right?" Morgan asked from the
kitchen island where she was drizzling chocolate syrup
across the cheesecake she'd made earlier in the day.

"Delicious," she assured her daughter, who unfortunately had inherited her somewhat less-than-gourmet
skills in the kitchen.

"Do you think Seth will like it?"

"Will like what?" the man in question asked from
the doorway and her heart gave its customary foolish
little leap.

She really needed to have a talk with her father
about letting Seth into the house without giving her
some kind of warning so she could brace herself for
his impact on her.

How was it possible he was more gorgeous every
time she saw him? she wondered. Tonight he wore
faded jeans, worn boots and a burgundy fisherman's
sweater that made her mouth water. Throw in that
heartbreaking smile and the sweet little puppy cavorting around his legs and it was no wonder she had no
defenses against him.

She cleared her throat. "Hi," she said.

His smile widened and she wondered how he could
consume every oxygen particle just by walking into
a room.

"Hi." His greeting encompassed both of them, but
the light in his eyes was entirely for her, she knew,
though she didn't understand it and couldn't quite believe it.

"What will I like?"

"Morgan made you a dessert," Jenny said. "She's a little worried you won't like it."

"You made that?"

He walked closer, bringing with him the clean, masculine scent of his aftershave. He smelled far better than anything she'd fixed for dinner and all she wanted to do was devour him.

She forced herself to take several deep, cleansing breaths to calm down as Morgan nodded with a grimace.

"It's kind of uneven," her daughter admitted. "I was hoping the chocolate syrup would hide it."

"Are you kidding? It looks like something out of a magazine. I hope nobody else is hungry because I just might have to eat that whole thing all by myself."

Morgan giggled, her eyes glowing. Jenny knew she must look the same.

How had things come to this? She had no willpower where the man was concerned.

What had started out as one simple dinner invitation to one of the more exclusive Jackson Hole restaurants had somehow slid into a regular event in the last ten days.

She had seen him nearly every day since the night he'd helped with Morgan's flare-up and fixed her car. They had gone to dinner twice in Jackson Hole, had taken the kids to a movie in Idaho Falls one day, had taken a drive to Mesa Falls to watch the spectacular show of water thrusting through ice.

They'd even gone for a snowy moonlit horseback ride on the ranch—which might have been romantic if they hadn't had both Natalie and Morgan along, chattering all the way.

It was after that horseback ride two nights before when they'd been sipping hot cocoa by his soaring Christmas tree that she'd taken the huge step of asking him to dinner.

She hadn't meant to—had actually been working up to telling him she couldn't see him anymore. But the invitation had slipped from her subconscious to her tongue before she knew it.

She couldn't take it back, especially when he had looked so delighted. It was the first time she had initiated a social encounter between them and she knew he must have realized that fact as well as she did.

As wonderful as she had to admit these ten days had been, she wasn't quite sure where things stood between them. Despite the wild heat of that night in the garage, they hadn't shared anything like that since. He was true to his word, she had discovered. When he said he would keep his hands to himself, he meant exactly that.

Though he was attentive and courteous, any physical contact between them was casual—a hand on her arm to help her over an icy patch, fingers casually laced through hers in a darkened theater as they watched a movie, a barely-there good-night kiss when he dropped her off after dinner.

If he meant to drive her crazy with lust, he was certainly succeeding. She was a quivering mass of hormones when he was around.

They couldn't keep on like this.

The thought crawled through her mind again, stark and depressing. Seeing him was accomplishing nothing except giving her this wild hunger for something she knew she couldn't have.

"Anything I can do?" Seth asked.

She pushed away the thought for now and mustered a smile. "I think we're there, aren't we, Morgan?"

Her daughter nodded.

"We only have to take the food into the dining room."

"I can't even begin to tell you how delicious everything looks," he murmured, and her whole body seemed to shiver and sigh. He was looking at *her* and not the dinner she'd spent so much time preparing.

"Here," she said abruptly, thrusting a dish to him. "You can carry in the bird."

He grinned as if he knew exactly his effect on her, but took the tray from her and headed out of the kitchen.

After he left, Jenny turned to find Morgan watching, a curious light in her eyes. Her daughter waited about ten seconds before she spoke in a voice pitched low. "Are you going to marry Seth?"

The bowl of mashed potatoes slipped from Jenny's suddenly nerveless fingers and she had to scramble to keep them from splattering all over the kitchen floor.

"No! Wherever did you get that idea?"

"You like him though, don't you?"

Heaven spare her from nine-year-old girls who saw entirely too much. "I...yes. Of course I do. But that's a far cry from marrying him, honey. We're only friends."

Morgan digested that, looking a little disappointed. "I just wanted you to know I wouldn't mind. I don't think Cole would, either. He's a lot nicer when Seth is around."

"Okay. Um, good to know." This wasn't a conversation she wanted to have right now, with Seth just on the other side of that wall. She could only pray he didn't come back in.

"Natalie says it's pretty cool having a stepparent. Mrs. Dalton is way nice to her and fixes her hair and everything."

"You already have someone to fix your hair," she pointed out, hoping to distract her. "Me!"

"I know. But I don't have someone to teach me how to ride horses or who knows what I feel like when my asthma flares." Morgan was quiet for a moment. "You laugh a lot more when Seth is here. So if you want to marry him, I wouldn't mind."

Her daughter picked up the cheesecake she put such effort into and carried it out of the kitchen.

When she left, Jenny pressed a hand to her mouth. Oh, she needed to put a stop to this. She should have realized how Morgan would construe the fragile beginnings of whatever this was with Seth. He was the only man she had spent any time with socially since the divorce, so it was logical for Morgan to jump to the wrong conclusion.

Shaking him loose was going to hurt.

The knowledge left a cold knot in her stomach. It would hurt, but not as much as they would all hurt if she let things continue as they were.

He wasn't serious about her. She still didn't know why exactly he seemed to want to spend so much time with her, but she knew he couldn't possibly have anything lasting in mind.

"Are we eating or are we going to sit here looking at all this pretty food all night?" her father called from the dining room.

"I'm coming. Sorry."

She let out a breath, then grabbed the rolls and the salad. Tonight. She had to find some way to tell him this had to be the end of it.

No matter how much she loved being with him, how the whole world seemed more vivid and wonderful whenever he was near, she had to stop indulging herself before her children opened their hearts and their lives to him any further.

And before she did the same.

Chapter 12

Forty-five minutes later, she was no closer to figuring out how she was going to force herself to end something that seemed so perfect—though with each passing moment, she knew she had no choice.

Seth set down his fork with a sigh of satisfaction. "Ladies, that was just about the best dinner I've had in longer than I can remember. Especially the cheesecake."

Morgan beamed, clearly smitten. "It's my mom's recipe. I just followed the directions."

"Even though you had a great recipe to start with, you were the one who did such a good job following it. But kudos to your mom, too."

"I can't really take credit," Jenny protested. "I always just use the recipe that comes on the cream cheese package—nothing very original, I'm afraid."

He laughed. "Enough of this humility! Will somebody please accept the compliment?"

"I will," Cole offered with a grin.

Everyone laughed, since Cole had had absolutely nothing to do with the cheesecake except eating a hefty slice.

As the laughter faded, Jenny looked around the table, a bittersweet pang in her chest. Her children would be hurt when Seth stopped coming around. Would Cole and Morgan understand why she had to send him packing? Or would they blame her for it?

"I need to move after that big meal," Seth said with a smile. "Anybody feel like taking a walk? I figured we could walk the few blocks to downtown and judge for ourselves which house ought to win the town's holiday lighting contest."

"I want to!" Morgan exclaimed.

Cole shrugged but didn't seem opposed to the idea. Or if he was, at least he didn't roll his eyes or say it blew.

"Jen? Jason? What about you two?"

"I have to finish the dishes," Jenny stalled, despising herself for her cowardice.

She had yet to go anywhere in town with Seth where others might see them together.

Though she knew they always stood the chance of running into someone from Pine Gulch in Jackson or Idaho Falls, she'd convinced herself the likelihood of that was slim.

On the other hand, even if someone *did* see them tonight as they walked through town, what would be the harm in enjoying the holiday sights with him accompanied by the rest of her family?

Her father slid his chair back from the table and started to clear away dishes. "You all go have some fun. I'll clean up."

"The kitchen's a disaster," she said. "You know what a mess I make when I cook."

Her dad only smiled. "Well, you *are* the only person I know who can dirty three or four pans just boiling water for pasta. But I think I'm up to the task. Go on."

He used that implacable "don't argue" voice and she sighed. She could have used a little backup, but she didn't think she would find it from her father. At least not in this instance.

Though she wouldn't have expected it, Seth had managed to charm even Jason, quite a feat, since her father had disliked Richard from the start.

The two of them talked about fishing, cars, even politics. After one of their trips to Jackson for dinner, her father had let her know in a subtle way that he thought Seth was a good man.

She didn't have the kind of relationship with her father where she could spill all her own angst to him—all the reasons she knew Seth was bad for her—so after a stunned moment, she had just thanked him for watching Morgan and Cole for her and gone to bed.

No, she couldn't expect any aid from that quarter.

"All right," she said now. "Thanks. I just need to grab my coat."

It wouldn't be so bad, she decided. If she could find a quiet moment while Morgan and Cole were distracted, perhaps on this snowy, moonlit walk, she might be able somehow to find the opportunity—and the strength—to talk to Seth.

Fifteen minutes later, bundled against the cold wind blowing down off the mountains, they walked out into the night, Lucy in the lead, scampering a short way ahead of them.

People in Pine Gulch took their holiday lighting seriously, she had learned the last few weeks. Nearly every house had some kind of holiday decoration, from a string of basic colored lights framing a window to more elaborate displays of reindeer and Santas and full-size nativities.

All the holiday spirit gave the little town a quiet, magical air on a winter evening. They seemed to be the only ones outside and their boots left tracks in the skiff of new snow covering the quiet streets as they walked toward the small downtown.

Seth walked at Morgan's side, easily matching his long-legged stride to her much shorter one, while Jenny walked beside Cole, grateful her son had come along.

The town had its own light display at the small park next to her elementary school and that was their ultimate destination.

Here, the trees were lit with what seemed like millions of tiny multicolored twinkling lights. They were lovely, Jenny thought, though the rest of the display looked as if had been added to piece by piece over the years. A trio of illuminated carolers stood next to a plastic snowman of a different style and size and across the sidewalk from a couple of giant nutcrackers.

Lucy's leash suddenly slipped out of Morgan's hand and the puppy took advantage of the unexpected freedom to race across the park toward the play equipment, her leash dragging through the snow.

"Oh, no!" Morgan exclaimed.

"Don't just stand there like an idiot," Cole snapped. "Go get her."

Seth didn't even say anything, he just raised an eyebrow at the teen. That always seemed to be enough to remind Cole to stow the attitude. This time was no different. After a second, Cole huffed out a breath and went after his sister and the recalcitrant puppy.

As soon as they were out of earshot, Jenny was painfully aware this was the private moment she'd been seeking. She was trying to figure out the right words when Seth spoke.

"What's wrong?" he asked.

She opened her mouth to tell him the truth but the words seemed to catch in her throat. "What makes you think something's wrong?" she stalled.

"You haven't said more than a few words at a time all night. Is something on your mind?"

It was exactly the kind of opening she needed and she knew couldn't put this off anymore, no matter how hard it was. She might not have a better opportunity all night. A careful glance at her children told her they had caught the puppy and were busy watching her scamper through snowdrifts as tall as she was.

Between the three of them, they were making enough racket that anything she might say to Seth wouldn't be overheard.

She released a puff of condensation on a heavy breath. "Yes, actually. Something is on my mind. Seth, I…we can't do this again."

In the colored glow from the lights, she thought she saw some strange emotion leap into his eyes, almost like panic, but it was gone so quickly she thought she must have been mistaken.

"Yeah, you're right," he said after a moment. "We can see the Christmas lights better this way, up close and personal, but it's just too darn cold. Next time we'll take a car so we can cover more ground."

"You know that's not what I mean." She sighed. "This has been wonderful. It has. But—"

Her words ended in a shriek as something cold and wet suddenly exploded in her face.

She brushed snow off and scowled at her offspring, who both surveyed her with expressions so innocent they could have belonged to the angels in the town's crèche.

Even Lucy gazed at her, her little head cocked and her eyes soft and limpid as if butter wouldn't melt in her mouth. Morgan and Cole's innocent looks lasted only seconds before they busted out laughing.

"Oh! That was so not funny!" she exclaimed.

"Don't worry, Jen." Seth bent down for a handful of snow. "I've got your back."

He lobbed the snowball—but instead of aiming it toward her kids, the man she knew perfectly well had been a star baseball pitcher miscalculated by a mile and threw it at her instead, where it thudded against the back of her coat.

Of course, this set Morgan and Cole into more hysterics.

She rounded on him, her glare promising retribution. "I think you are missing the intent of that particular phrase."

Any response he might have made was lost by another snowball, this one launched by Cole, that landed exactly in the center of his chest.

"Kid, that was a big mistake," Seth said, though she didn't miss the glee in his eyes.

From then on, it was full-out war. She took cover behind the plastic snowman and had the satisfaction of hitting both Cole and Seth with solid lobs.

With maternal consideration, she took pity on Morgan, but her daughter repaid her kindness with a sneak attack to her flank. While Jenny was busy evading a concerted attack from the males, Morgan must have skulked along the shrubs until she was just behind her mother, where she had an unobstructed shot. She took full advantage of it, then raced back for cover.

After fifteen minutes or so, Seth finally raised the white flag—or in this case a tan flag, one of his gloves.

"Okay. Enough. Enough!" He stood up. "We're all going to freeze out here if we keep this up. I say we call it a draw and head back to your house for hot chocolate."

As if they had all perfectly choreographed it, she, Morgan and Cole each launched snowballs at him simultaneously, hitting him from every direction while Lucy barked with delight and danced around his feet.

Seth looked down at the dripping mess on his coat and shook his head with a rueful grin. "Remind me not to take on the Boyer clan again unless I have better reinforcements than an Australian shepherd pup."

His laughing gaze met Jenny's, the colored lights

gleaming in his eyes. She stared at him and suddenly felt as if an entire truckload of snow had just been dumped on her head.

There in the city park on a cold December night, the truth washed over her stronger than an avalanche, and she had to grab the plastic snowman just to keep upright.

This wasn't just a casual attraction, something she could walk away from without any lasting ramifications.

She was in love with him.

She shivered, chilled right down to her bones, and she couldn't seem to catch her breath.

Oh, how could she have let this happen? She knew he wasn't good for her. From the very beginning, she had told herself he would break her heart but these last few weeks had been so wonderful, she had completely ignored all the warning signs and plunged straight ahead anyway.

And now look what a mess she'd created!

She was in love with a completely inappropriate man, a man who had probably never had a serious relationship in his life.

The gaping maw of heartache beckoned her. She could see it as clearly as if it were in front of her outlined in bright, blinking Christmas lights. Of what use was it to know just what was in store for her, she wondered, since she was suddenly terrified it was far too late to do anything about it?

"I'm cold, Mom. Can we go home?" Morgan's voice jerked her out of her stupor and she somehow managed to catch her breath again.

"Of course, honey. Let's go," she said, forcing a smile that felt like it was made of thin, crackly ice.

They covered the few blocks toward her father's house quickly as the cold wind cut through their snow-dampened clothes like a chainsaw.

When they reached the house, both kids rushed to their respective rooms to change into dry clothes.

Jason was probably in his den—she could hear the TV going—but he didn't come out to greet her and for the first time in a long time, the silence between her and Seth seemed awkward.

He cast a look at the door, looking suddenly anxious to leave. Why? she wondered nervously. He couldn't suspect her feelings, could he?

She cleared her throat. "Would you like to put on something dry from my father's closet?"

"No. I'll just run the truck's heater full-blast on my way home and I'll be dry soon enough."

"Are you sure?"

"Yeah. I'll be fine."

Again they slipped into that awkward silence. Here was where she should tell him she couldn't see him again, she thought. She opened her mouth but he cut her off so abruptly she almost wondered if it was deliberate.

"Thanks again for dinner. It was really delicious," he said.

"Um, you're welcome. Seth—"

"What are you doing tomorrow?"

She blinked, wondering at his apparent urgency. "I don't know. I have a faculty thing Sunday, but tomorrow I just need to take care of some last-minute shopping for the kids. The last Saturday before Christmas is the biggest shopping day of the year, did you know that? A lot of people think it's the day after Thanksgiving but it's not."

She was babbling, she realized, but she couldn't seem to rein in her unruly tongue. Filling up the space with the inconsequential and mundane only delayed the inevitable, she told herself.

"Shopping is on my agenda, too," Seth said, then smiled suddenly, though she thought it looked a little strained. "You know, I could sure use your help."

"My help?"

"I'm not having much luck this year shopping for my brothers' wives or for Natalie and I'm running out of time. I could use a woman's perspective, you know?"

This from the man who seemed to know far more than most women about what they wanted?

"I was planning to head into Jackson Hole," he went on. "Maybe check out some of the galleries. We ought to save gas and go together. What do you think?"

She didn't think he really wanted to know the grim thoughts running through her mind—that she should run far away from him, that she should make this their last goodbye, that her heart was already bracing itself for the pain.

But, oh, she wanted to say yes. One more time. That was all she craved. A few more hours to spend with him. She would go shopping with him in Jackson and store up one last day of priceless memories and then she would have to break things off.

"All right," she said before she changed her mind.

Again he had an odd reaction. Something like relief flickered in his blue eyes.

"I'll pick you up at nine. Does that work?"

At her nod, he stepped forward for the kind of hurried kiss she'd come to expect from him at the end of the night.

She wanted to curl her hands into his parka and hold him tight for a real kiss, the kind they'd shared that night in the garage, the kind she dreamed about at night. But she knew she couldn't, not in her father's entryway with Jason just down the hall, where her children could come running in at any moment.

"Good night," he said, giving her that slow, sexy smile that curled her toes, then he walked out into the night.

She closed the door behind him and leaned against it. She was weak. Weak and stupid and doomed.

The next morning, Seth climbed back into his pickup after dropping Lucy off with Quinn and Marjorie for a play day with her brother.

Her delight at the prospect of a full day of cavorting with another puppy hadn't quite been enough to prevent her from giving him a reproachful look when he headed for the door without her.

He had withstood her canine wiles, though, not wanting anything—not even his adorable but energetic puppy—to get in the way of what he was hoping would be a perfect day.

Even the weather was cooperating. It was a gorgeous Teton Valley day, the kind they ought to put on travel brochures. The inch or two of new snow from the night before sparkled in the brilliant sunshine and the sky was a bright, stunning blue.

He drove the few blocks from his mom's house to Jenny's, his stomach jumping with anticipation. He wasn't sure he liked the jittery feeling in his gut. It was just a date, after all. Nothing to get so worked up about.

He had been telling himself that all morning while he fed and watered the horses and hurried through the rest of his chores, but he couldn't seem to escape the conclusion that he had to make everything about their time together unforgettable, so incredible she wouldn't be able to bring herself to end things.

He wasn't an idiot. He knew damn well she'd been about to break things off with him the night before while they'd been walking through the town square.

He had seen it in her expressive green eyes, that moment of resignation and resolve, and he'd known a moment of sheer, blind panic before the kids had unknowingly bailed him out by starting their snow-ball war.

She had agreed to go with him today, though. The way he saw it, he had one last chance to change her mind.

He had to. He didn't even want to think about the alternative. He didn't understand any of this, he just knew he couldn't bear imagining his world without her and the kids in it.

These last few weeks with her had been incredible. He'd never been so fascinated with a woman before. Obsessed, even. He thought about her all the time and he couldn't wait until the next time he would see her.

If she asked him why, he had to admit he wasn't

sure he could put a finger on it. It was a hundred different things—the way she pursed her lips when she was concentrating on something, the tenderness in her eyes when she looked at her kids, the little tremble she tried to hide whenever he happened to touch her, even in the most casual way.

She was smart and funny and beautiful, and she had this quiet strength about her he found soothing and incredibly addictive.

He was also amazed how she seemed to bring out the best in everybody around her—even him. When he was with her, he felt like a better man, somebody kind and good and decent.

He wasn't ready to lose all that. Not yet. Maybe after the holidays, though even the thought of that left him with a cold knot in his chest.

He pushed away his nerves as pulled into her driveway. Today he wouldn't think about goodbyes. The sun was shining, the day was perfect, and he would spend the rest of their time together showing her all the reasons she needed him.

"Please! I just want to go home," Jenny practically wailed ten hours later. The bruise around her eye looked dark and ugly—almost as miserable as the blizzard that swirled around his pickup.

"I'm real sorry, ma'am," the highway patrolman at the roadblock to the canyon between Jackson and Pine Gulch leaned across Seth in the driver's seat to say to Jenny in a patient voice, "but I'm afraid nobody's getting through this canyon right now. Between the storm and that jackknifed big rig, the canyon's going to be closed anywhere from three to four more hours. Maybe longer. This is one heck of a nasty storm, coming out of nowhere like it did. It's shut down this whole region and we're recommending that people who don't have to travel stay put until it lets up."

She let out a little sound that sounded suspiciously like a sob. The frazzled highway patrolman gave Seth a dark look before turning back to Jenny.

"I wish I could give you a better option but right now I'm afraid you folks are going to have to turn around and head back into town and find a place to wait out the storm until we open the canyon again. The Aspen is a pretty nice place."

"No!" Jenny and Seth both said sharply.

The patrolman looked a bit taken aback by their vehemence, but there was a long line of cars behind them at the roadblock trying to get through the canyon and Seth knew the man had other frustrated motorists to deal with.

"There are other restaurants in town. You can try to find a hotel room, too. That might be your best bet."

"Thank you for your help," Seth said grimly. "We'll figure something out."

The man waved them on and Seth rolled up his window and turned his truck around to head back into Jackson Hole.

Jenny stared out the windshield, her features stony, and his hands tightened on the steering wheel.

He had screwed up everything. The way things were going, he would be lucky if she ever talked to him again.

He should have paid more attention to the weather,

but he had been working so hard to make sure she had an unforgettable time, he hadn't given the gathering clouds much thought.

If he had just paid a little attention to the warning signs, he would have left two hours ago before the storm that forecasters had said would be just a little skiff decided to hit with a vengeance.

They would have made it through the canyon before the semi jackknifed and they would have been home by now. Maybe Jenny would have been basking in the glow of a wonderful day instead of sitting beside him, her features stiff as if she'd been turned to ice by the storm.

How had things taken such a wrong turn? he wondered. He still couldn't quite figure it out.

For much of the day, everything had gone so well, just as he'd planned. Jackson at Christmas was an exciting, dynamic town, bustling with skiers and shoppers and tourists. He and Jenny had had a great time combing through the trendy little stores and galleries to find last-minute gifts for the rest of the people on their respective lists.

With Jenny's help, he had found the perfect gifts for the important women in his life. He'd already bought his mother and Quinn a gift so he didn't need to worry about them.

For Maggie, he bought a matted and framed photograph of a field of mountain wildflowers in the middle of a rainstorm, their hues rich and dramatic. Caroline's gift was some whimsical handmade wind chimes to go with her collection on the Cold Creek patio, and for Natalie, Jenny had steered him to a set of earrings shaped like horses.

Jenny had already bought most of the gifts for her children and just needed some last-minute things. He helped her pick out a wool sweater for her father that would definitely turn some sweet older lady's head.

For Morgan she bought a whole basket full of books and a pair of earrings just like the set he'd bought for Nat and she finally gave in and bought Cole the snowboard he'd been hinting not so subtly about.

Just as Seth had dreamed, Jenny had glowed through most of the day. She had laughed more than he ever remembered and she had touched him often, taking his arm while they walked, touching him to make a point, even slipping her hand through his as they stood looking at some of the gallery offerings.

And then Cherry Mendenhall had ruined everything.

No. Though it would be easier to blame the other woman, he knew the responsibility for the disaster of the rest of the day rested squarely on his own shoulders.

If only he had paid attention to the weather and left two hours earlier. If only he had picked a different restaurant for their early dinner. Beyond that, if only he'd walked away a few years ago when Cherry had come over to his table at the Cowboy Bar after a business meeting, all tight jeans and pouty lips.

But he hadn't walked away. In fact, idiot that he was, he had invited trouble to sit right down and have herself a drink.

He hadn't really been looking to start anything that night two years ago, but Cherry had been more than enthusiastic, five feet nine inches of warm, curvy, willing woman.

They'd both been a little tipsy—only he hadn't realized until much later that was more the norm than the exception for her. They'd danced, they'd flirted, and to his everlasting regret now, they'd ended up taking the party back to his hotel room.

He'd thought she just wanted a good time and he'd looked her up a few more times when he was in Jackson, but he quickly discovered he'd badly misjudged her.

Suddenly the fun-loving party girl turned clingy and emotional and started calling him all the time, so much so he finally had to change his cell phone number.

He should have handled things far differently. The decent thing would have been to sit her down and try to explain that they were obviously after different things. But he'd been right in the middle of building the training arena, up to his ears in details, and hadn't had time for that kind of complication. It had seemed easier just to ignore her and hope she would just go away.

The whole situation with her hadn't been one of his better moments and he was ashamed of himself for it all over again.

When he and Jenny walked into the Aspen for a late lunch and he'd seen Cherry sitting at the bar, he'd just about turned around and walked back out again.

He should have, even at the risk of Jenny thinking he was crazy, but he had figured nearly two years had passed since he'd even spoken to the woman. She couldn't hold a grudge that long, no matter how stupid he'd been over the whole thing. And besides, she probably wouldn't even remember him.

That had been mistake number 421 in this whole thing.

They'd been seated immediately, at a secluded booth near the fireplace with a spectacular view overlooking the ski resort. Everything had been going so well— they ordered and sat talking about their holiday plans and watching the skiers. When he'd stretched a casual arm across the top of the booth, Jenny had cuddled closer and he couldn't remember ever feeling so happy.

And then Cherry had passed their table on the way to the ladies' room.

From there, their whole magical day went straight to hell.

She'd caught sight of him snuggling there with Jenny and instead of making a polite retreat as he might have hoped, she marched right over to their table and started spewing all kinds of ugliness at him. He couldn't remember most of it, but he was pretty sure *rat bastard* had been about the mildest thing she'd called him.

He had done his best to calm her down, aware of the increasing attention they were drawing from others in the restaurant and of Jenny sitting horrified beside him.

When she turned on Jenny, though, calling her his latest stupid bitch, Seth's patience wore out. He stood up, thinking he would lead Cherry somewhere more private where he could try to calm her down and at least apologize to her for the lousy way he'd treated her. But when he reached for her arm, she went berserk and swung at him.

Unfortunately, she missed—and somehow hit Jenny instead.

From there, the whole episode turned into a farce. Cherry had instantly burst into hysterical sobs—and Jenny had been the one to sit her down at their booth, have the waiter bring her coffee and comfort her while Seth had stood there feeling like the world's biggest idiot.

"I just loved him so much!" Cherry had sobbed and Jenny had hugged her.

"I know, honey. I know," she murmured, giving him a censorious look out of her good eye across the table.

It turned out Cherry had only been at the restaurant waiting for her roommate's shift in the kitchen to be over so she could get a ride home. After a few more painfully miserable moments while they both commiserated about men in general and him in particular, the other woman came out, gave Seth another dirty look and led Cherry away, along with any chance he had of convincing Jenny he was more than his reputation.

Neither of them touched their food. He tried to explain but Jenny hadn't been in any kind of mood to listen as he tried to convince her he wasn't the jackass he appeared—though right about now, even *he* wasn't so sure about that.

He'd finally given up, paid their check and walked outside, only to discover that while they'd been preoccupied inside the Aspen, a blizzard had hit with a vengeance rivaling only the proverbial scorned woman.

He sighed now as they reached the outskirts of town, wondering at what point he might have been able to salvage the disaster.

He was all those things Cherry had called him and more and he didn't deserve a woman like Jenny.

He pulled into the snow-covered parking lot of the grocery store. "So what do you want to do? We can find somewhere to wait around for the pass to open in three or four hours or we can take our chances and drive down through Kemmerer and back up through Star Valley."

"How long would that take us?" she asked, still without looking at him.

"In this weather, about six hours."

She looked close to tears but didn't say anything.

"Or, like the trooper suggested, we could try to find a hotel room somewhere for the night and head home in the morning. That's probably our safest alternative."

She looked miserable at the idea of spending even another second in his company. Her eye had swollen almost shut and around all that color, her face was pale and withdrawn.

"All right," she finally said.

"We probably won't have an easy time finding a room," he was compelled to warn her. "Between the holidays and the ski season, Jackson hotels are usually pretty full this time of year. I'll give it my best shot but it might take me a while."

"We have all night, don't we?" she said.

Two hours ago, the prospect of a night with her would have had his imagination overheating with all the sensual possibilities.

Now he thought he'd almost rather walk barefoot over the pass in this blizzard than have to sit by all night and watch her slip further away from him.

Chapter 13

Barely an hour later, Jenny sat ensconced in a plump armchair pulled up to a crackling fire.

"I'm sorry to do this to you, Dad," she said into her cell phone, "but the storm came up out of nowhere. How is it there?"

"We've got a couple inches but it looks like more is on the way. If this keeps up, you're going to think it never stops snowing around here."

"Does it?" she asked.

"Sure. Round about June." Her dad laughed and Jenny wished she had the capacity to find anything amusing right about now. Her sense of humor seemed to have deserted her.

"Seth talked about trying to push our way through as soon as they open the pass again but even under the best-case scenario, we probably wouldn't make it home until two or three in the morning."

"There's no sense in that. Just stay put. We'll be fine. Morgan and I are watching a great kung fu movie and Cole is on the computer instant-messaging his friends back in Seattle. Are you sure you're okay?"

With a sigh, Jenny looked around the beautiful three-room suite with its massive king-size canopy bed, the matching robes hanging on a hook by the bathroom, the soft rug in front of the fireplace.

Trust Seth to come up with the only room left in town—the honeymoon suite of an elegant bed-and-breakfast she had heard touted as one of the ten most romantic small inns in the West.

She couldn't speak for the rest of the place but the honeymoon suite just screamed romance. Everything about it—from the matching armchairs to the huge whirlpool tub—was designed with lovers in mind.

How on earth was she supposed to be able to resist Seth Dalton under these circumstances?

"I'm fine," she finally lied to her father. Black eye notwithstanding, she reminded herself firmly.

If she had trouble remembering why she needed to keep her distance from Seth, she only needed to find a mirror. That vivid, iridescent shiner ought to do the trick.

"Don't let Cole I.M. all night. He should be off by ten. If he gives you any trouble about it, call me and I'll set him straight."

"We'll be fine. You just stay warm."

At that moment, she heard the key turn in the lock and Seth came in carrying the ice bucket. His reflection in the window looked big and male and gorgeous, and she knew without a doubt keeping warm was definitely not going to be the problem.

"Thanks again," she said to her father. "I'll see you in the morning."

"Don't forget your faculty party."

She winced, wondering if she could find enough makeup in all of Pine Gulch to camouflage her black eye to all her teachers.

"That doesn't even start until six tomorrow night so we should have plenty of time to make it back."

She said her goodbyes to her father and hung up as Seth set the ice bucket down on the dresser.

"Everything okay at home?" he asked.

"Fine. Dad's got everything under control. I shouldn't worry."

His smile didn't quite reach his eyes. "But you're a mother and that's what you do."

"I suppose."

He sat down in the armchair next to her and she wondered how the elegant romance of the room only seemed to make him that much more dangerously male.

"You're lucky you've got your father to help you with Cole and Morgan," he said.

"Moving here has worked out well in that regard."

"But not in others?"

If she had stayed in Seattle, she would have been safe. She wouldn't be trapped here in a romantic inn trying to fight her attraction to a man who would dump a woman without even telling her.

"This is a nice room your friend was able to find

for us," she said instead. "I guess it helps to know the manager."

She hadn't missed the familiarity between the two when they checked in and she had to wonder if there were any females in the three-state region Seth *didn't* know.

"Yeah, Sierra's great. She grew up in Pine Gulch before she moved to the big time here in Jackson. We've been friends forever."

More than friends at some point, unless Jenny missed her guess, but she decided not to press it. She really didn't want to know anyway.

"Are you hungry?" he asked. "You didn't eat much at dinner."

"I'm fine," she said.

He lapsed into silence and she was acutely aware of him and the long evening stretching out ahead of them.

"Oh, I almost forgot. Along with spare toiletries, Sierra gave me a couple of cold packs from the hotel first aid kit for your eye."

He grabbed one from the dresser, popped it to activate the chemicals, then held it out to her.

Their hands brushed as she took it from him and despite everything, her whole body seemed to sigh a welcome at his nearness.

"Thank you," Jenny murmured, grateful for the slap of cold as she held it to her eye. "I'm sure she must have wondered why I look as though I just went ten rounds with a prizefighter."

He lifted a shoulder in a shrug. "I told her the truth. That you stepped in the way of a punch aimed at me. She didn't seem to find that hard to believe at all."

"You mentioned the vengeful ex-lover, I assume."

He winced. "I did. For some reason, she *really* didn't find that part hard to believe."

Despite her best intentions not to let him charm her, a smile slipped out at his rueful tone.

Regret clouded the pure blue of his eyes as he looked at her holding the ice pack to her eye. "Jenny, I have to tell you again how sorry I am that all this happened. Cherry, the storm, all of it. I wanted today to be perfect for you, but as usual, I've only succeeded in making a mess of everything."

He looked so earnestly miserable that she could feel a little more of her resolve erode away like the sea nibbling at the sand.

"Why did you want everything to be perfect?" she asked.

He said nothing for several moments, then he sighed. "I didn't want you to break things off with me. That's what you planned to do last night, wasn't it?"

She stared. How had he figured it out? "You are entirely too good at reading women."

"No. Just you."

His words seemed to hang in the air between them. She wanted to protest that he didn't know her at all, but she knew it would be an outright lie. He just might know her better than anybody else ever had, something she found terrifying.

"Why, though? That's what I can't quite figure out," he went on. "Why were you all set to push me away? I could understand if you never wanted to see me again after the disaster of today. Any woman would probably feel the same. But before this, I thought things were going well. You seemed happy. I know I was happy. Did I completely misread things?"

He looked so bewildered she had to fight the urge to reach across the space between them and grab his hand.

Physical contact between them right now was not a good idea. In fact, if she were smart, she would probably lock herself in the bathroom all night until the snow cleared and she could be safely back in Pine Gulch.

How could she tell him that all the reasons she'd been compelled to end things with him had just crystallized into the form of that poor, misguided girl in the restaurant?

Cherry Mendenhall was *Jenny,* with a little more time and few more drinks under her belt. Oh, she wanted to think she would never throw a drunken scene in a restaurant over him but she would *want* to and that seemed just as demoralizing.

When he moved on to his next conquest—as she had absolutely no doubt he would—he would leave her heart scraped raw and she would be as devastated and lost as Cherry.

"They were going well," she finally said.

"So why were you putting on the brakes?"

She couldn't tell him the truth so she avoided the subject. "You can't honestly tell me your heart would have been broken if you didn't see me anymore, Seth."

"Oh, can't I?" he murmured, his eyes an intense blue in the dancing firelight.

She studied him for a long moment, her heart pounding, then reality intruded and she shook her head, forcing a smile. "Your reputation doesn't do you justice. You almost had me believing you."

"Screw my reputation!" He rose and towered over her suddenly, all the easy amiability gone from his posture, reminding her again that a big, dangerous man lurked beneath all the smiles and flirtation.

"Screw my reputation," he repeated. "Just for one second, forget everything you might have heard about me from mean-hearted people who ought to just keep their frigging mouths shut. If today hadn't happened with Cherry and you'd never heard any of the gossip— if you only had to judge me on the man you've come to know this last month—would you still be so damn cynical and judgmental? Or would you at least be open to the possibility that I might care about you?"

Her answer seemed important to him in a way she couldn't understand so she pondered it.

"I don't know," she finally had to admit. "I'm not the best judge of character when it comes to men."

"You don't think you can trust your own instincts, just because your ex was a bastard and messed around on you?"

She flushed. "Who told you that?"

The anger seemed to leave him as suddenly as it appeared and he slid back into the armchair, looking tired somehow.

"Cole. One day when we were working on the car, he told me his dad walked out on you for his twenty-year-old girlfriend. He abandoned all of you to move to Europe with her. Cole calls him Dick the Prick, by the way. Sounds pretty apt, from what he's told me."

A startled laugh escaped her. Oh, Richard would hate that. "It's apt. Believe me."

She had never heard Cole say anything derogatory

about his father and she couldn't quite fathom him telling Seth all that. From the way Cole had treated her since Richard had moved to France, she had been certain he blamed her for his father's defection. What was it about Seth that made Cole trust him with the truth? Her son had opened up to this man in a way he hadn't to the family therapist they'd seen after the divorce, or to her, or to his grandfather.

She didn't understand it, but she could only be grateful for the comfort it gave her to know that perhaps her son didn't hate her after all.

"Until the day Richard told me he was leaving, I had no idea he was cheating on me. I was completely oblivious. I thought I had the perfect life, the perfect marriage. You wouldn't believe how smug and self-righteous I was. I even used to give relationship advice to my friends! And all the time, my husband was sleeping with another woman."

"You think that automatically makes you a lousy judge of character? Because you made one mistake? Because you didn't know your husband was cheating? Maybe he was just a master manipulator."

She definitely could see that now, but at the time she'd been completely oblivious to it. What if Seth was doing the same thing to her and she was too blind to see it?

"Maybe you are, too. How do I know you're not cut from the same cloth, that you won't say anything, do anything, to charm your way into a woman's bed?"

She regretted her words as soon as she said them, especially when his eyes darkened with some emotion that looked suspiciously like hurt. "Is that really what you think?"

"I don't want to think that," she whispered. "When I'm with you, I want to believe every word you tell me. It's when I step back that all the doubts crowd in and I can't understand what we're doing here. Why would a man like you even want to be with me?"

His laugh sounded raspy and rough. "You have no idea what you do to me, do you?"

She blinked, then her heart seemed to flutter when he stood up and pulled her to her feet as well.

"Fine," he growled. "I'll show you."

He kissed her and the heat in it scorched her right to her bare toes. She curled them into the carpet and just held on, swept into the firestorm he stirred inside her.

After those first fiery moments that left her nerve endings ablaze, he gentled the kiss and his mouth was achingly tender.

"I want you, Jenny," he said softly against her mouth, sending tiny ripples of need through her. "But if this was only about sex, I could have done something about it weeks ago."

Though she felt boneless and weak from his kiss, somehow she marshaled enough strength to give him a skeptical look. "You're so sure about that?"

In answer, he kissed her again, until her hands wrapped around his neck and she had to hold on tight to keep from melting onto the carpet.

"Pretty sure, yeah," he murmured, with a supreme confidence she couldn't deny, given the evidence she had just provided him.

"You tremble every time I touch you. Did you know

that? Even if I just happen to brush up against you when we're walking somewhere. That's an incredibly arousing thing for a man, to know he has that kind of effect on a woman."

Her face burned. She thought she had hid her reaction so well. It was the height of humiliation to learn he'd known all along.

But his eyes were anything but gloating. "You have no idea how hard it's been for me to keep my hands off you these last few weeks. If this had just been about getting you into bed, we would have been there a long time ago. But if nothing else, that alone should tell you that you mean more to me than that. I haven't pushed you. I've been patient and low-key and noble, while I've been burning up from the inside out."

"Seth—"

Whatever she wanted to say was lost against his mouth when he kissed her again, this time with a slow and gentle tenderness that made her eyes burn with emotion.

"I care about you, Jenny. Not just you but Morgan and Cole, too. There's something between us. Something I've never known before, something I don't quite know what to do with. You scare the hell out of me and that alone ought to tell you this is different than anything I've ever experienced. I've never been afraid of any woman. Well, not since Agnes Arbuckle, my junior-high English teacher."

She smiled, trying to imagine him sitting in a classroom giving book reports and learning to diagram sentences.

"You scare me, too," she murmured, but she defied her own words by tugging him closer and kissing him.

Despite everything, in his arms she felt safe from the storms outside, from the howling wind of her own uncertainties and the lashing, pounding ice crystals of self-doubt.

They stood for a long time wrapped around each other while the fire sparked and hissed. All those tender, frightening emotions of that night in her garage came rushing back and she was helpless against them.

She wasn't sure how—everything seemed a blur but his mouth and his hands and his strength—but somehow they ended up in the bedroom of their suite.

He lowered her to the mattress of the canopy bed, and she shivered as his big, powerful body pressed her into the thick, fluffy comforter. Next to all his hard muscles, she felt small and feminine and wanted.

He gazed at her in the glow from the firelight, his eyes glittering, then he kissed her again and she surrendered to the magic.

He trailed kisses down her neck and she moaned, writhing as he unerringly found every one of her most sensitive spots—and a few she'd never realized were there.

"You smell so good." His voice was rough and aroused. "There's this meadow up in the high country where we take our cattle. In early summer it explodes with wildflowers. Lupine, columbine, Queen Anne's lace. A hundred different colors. There's nothing I love more than riding a horse across it just after a rainstorm, when everything smells fresh and sweet and gorgeous."

He trailed kisses to the V-neck of her sweater, then

up the other side again. "Every time I'm near you, I feel like it's June and I'm standing in the middle of that meadow with the sun warm on my face."

Oh, he was good. Everything inside her seemed to stretch and purr and she finally had to slide her mouth to his, just to stop the unbearably seductive flow of his words.

For long moments, they touched and kissed and explored, until she was breathless, trembling with need.

Finally, when she wasn't sure she could bear any more, Seth rolled onto his back, breathing hard.

"We're going to have to stop here, sweetheart. After a month of foreplay, I'm just about at the limit of my self-control where you're concerned."

She shifted her head on the pillow and studied him, those gorgeous eyes hazy with need, those sculpted, masculine features that made her ache just looking at him.

"Stop it," he ordered darkly.

"What?"

"Looking at me like that. You're not making this easier. Sometimes it's hell trying to do the right thing."

He was right. They should stop teasing each other before they passed the point of no return.

She knew making love would be a mistake right now, that she would have to face a mountain of regrets in the morning.

But this might be her only chance with him. Despite his tender words, she knew she couldn't hang on to him for long. Soon enough, she would return to real life. To parent-teacher conferences and doctor appointments and the responsibilities that sometimes seemed more than she could bear.

But for now they were here alone together, sheltered from the storm in this romantic room.

She wanted to live. For once, she wanted to throw caution into the teeth of that blizzard and grab hold of her dreams.

She smiled and reached to touch his face, her fingers curving along his jaw. "Why don't we just stop trying, then?"

He gazed at her for a long, charged heartbeat and she thought for a moment he would be noble and walk away. Then he made a low, aroused sound and kissed her with a ferocity that took her breath away.

He'd been holding all this back, she realized, stunned to her soul as he nipped and tasted.

The hunger rose inside her and she needed closer contact between them. With fingers that trembled, she worked the buttons of his shirt, until all those hard muscles were bared to her hot gaze and her exploring fingers. She smoothed a hand over his chest and was stunned by the rapid pulse of his heart.

He let her touch and explore him for a long time. Finally, his eyes heavy-lidded, he pushed her back against the pillows and pulled off her sweater in one smooth motion, leaving her only in her bra and slacks.

She had to wonder if some subconscious yearning for just this had compelled her to wear something besides her usual no-nonsense white underclothes. Instead, she had picked a pair of black tap pants and a matching lacy bra. She could only be glad for the instinct when his eyes darkened.

"Well, well," he said, his voice low, rough. "Who would have guessed the elementary school principal likes naughty underwear? I think there are hidden depths to you, Ms. Boyer."

She could feel herself blush and cursed her redhead's skin, especially when so much was exposed.

He didn't seem to mind. "You have the most incredible skin I've ever seen," he murmured, then his mouth dipped to the V of her bra. "Pale and creamy, like fresh, warm milk. Except when you blush, then it makes me think of strawberries. Plump, juicy strawberries melting in my mouth."

"I get sunburned just walking to the mailbox. It's a redhead's curse."

She completely forgot her train of thought—why she could possibly think her complexion woes might be of interest to anyone—when his hands reached the front clasp of her bra and he slid the lingerie away from her body.

Suddenly she wasn't convinced this was such a good idea.

Why hadn't she thought this through a little better? Sexy lingerie could only take her so far in situations like this.

She was thirty-six years old and had given birth to two children, one now a teenager. Her stomach hadn't been flat for fourteen years and right about the time she hit thirty, she'd started needing underwires in her bras.

That blasted self-doubt suddenly came rushing back and she wanted to yank the comforter over her. She couldn't compare very favorably to all the sweet young things he was used to.

She braced herself to meet his gaze, suddenly afraid of what she would see there.

She wasn't prepared for the blazing tenderness in his eyes, for the heat and the hunger that seared her.

For a moment, something stunned, almost over-whelmed, flickered in his eyes and she would have given anything to know what he was thinking. He didn't say anything to assuage her curiosity, just continued to gaze at her until she couldn't bear it anymore.

She pulled him to her and lost herself in the storm.

A long time later, after he had divested them both of the rest of their clothing and they had teased and tasted until they were both trembling with need, he framed her face in his hands and kissed her with more of that aching tenderness.

She wrapped her arms around him and held on, their gazes locked, as he entered her. Her entire body seemed to sigh a welcome and she arched to meet him.

"You scare the hell out of me," he repeated softly.

"What?" she teased on a moan, feeling more powerful than she ever had in her life. "A big strong man like you afraid of a little thing like me?"

He repaid her by thrusting deeper until she felt every muscle inside her contract. With one more arch of his body, she climaxed suddenly and wildly, gasping his name as wave after wave of sensation poured over her.

His mouth found hers and his kiss was fierce and possessive as he swallowed the rest of her cries. He gave her only seconds to recover before he thrust into her again. To her astonishment, her body rose instantly to meet him again.

His breathing was ragged as he reached between

their bodies and touched her. She exploded again in a hot fireburst of sparks and this time he followed her, his mouth hard on hers as he found release.

He awoke in the night to find himself in a strange bed with a warm woman in his arms and the smell of rain-washed wildflowers surrounding him.

Jenny.

They were snuggled together like spoons, her sweet little derriere pressed against him and his arm resting across a very convenient portion of her anatomy.

He shifted on the pillow so he could see her, that wispy red-gold hair, the delicate line of her jaw, her creamy skin that tasted every bit as delicious as it looked.

A strange tenderness welled up in his chest like the hot springs in the high country above the Cold Creek.

He wasn't used to this complete sense of rightness he experienced with her in his arms.

It was odd for him. He'd always been a little uncomfortable spending the entire night with a woman and was usually pretty good at finding excuses to go home before this particular stage in the game.

But he couldn't imagine a single place on earth he would rather be at this moment than right here with the snow still drifting down outside and Jenny warm and soft in his arms.

She was still asleep. He could feel her breasts rise and fall in an even rhythm against his arm, and he tightened his hold, astonished at the contentment pouring through him.

Was this what his brothers woke to every morning?

If so, he wondered how the hell either of them managed to climb out of bed at all.

He'd been with his share of women. More than his share, probably, if truth be told. Right now, he saw all those other encounters for what they were. A desperate, pathetic search for exactly this kind of tenderness, for the close connection he and Jenny had shared.

Everything that had come before seemed suddenly tawdry and cheap and he was ashamed of himself for thinking those quick encounters could ever make him happy.

They might have offered momentary pleasure—he couldn't deny that—but it was like the tiny glow from a birthday candle compared to the million-watt floodlights of joy burning in him with Jenny in his arms.

He didn't have a name for all the emotions pouring through him. He suspected what they might be, but he wasn't sure he was quite ready to admit to them yet.

His arms tightened around her again, and at the movement, she stirred.

"Sorry," he murmured in her ear. "I didn't mean to wake you."

"Is everything okay?" she asked, her voice rough from sleep.

He kissed the long, slender column of her neck and felt that slow, astonishing tremble.

"Oh, much better than okay. Everything is perfect."

Chapter 14

Jenny wasn't sure how many times they made love in the night. She couldn't seem to get enough of this wild heat between them.

This was probably number four. Or maybe five. She wasn't sure, she just knew she had awakened some time before to find sunlight streaming through the window and Seth beside her, his face shadowed with stubble and a certain warmth in his eyes she'd come to know well in the night.

"Looks like the storm's stopped," he said.

They would have to leave soon, she knew, but for now the man she loved with a fierceness that shocked her was here in her arms, and she wasn't ready to let him go.

She kissed him, her hands tracing the hard planes

of chest then heading south. She was enjoying the anticipation curling through her—the way his stomach muscles contracted as she touched him—when suddenly her cell phone went off.

During a bored moment a few weeks ago, Morgan had programmed it to play a vocal version of Jingle Bells for the ringtone and they both stared at it as the merry little tune chirped through the room.

"I should get that," she finally said when the singers had sung the first verse and started jingling all the way.

"Do you have to?" He kissed the spot just below her ear he had somehow discovered drove her crazy and she groaned.

She had a wild urge to abandon good sense and let the thing ring, but already that world she feared so much was intruding on their haven. She was a woman with responsibilities and she couldn't just throw them out the window—no matter how much she might want to.

With a deep, regretful sigh, she reached for her phone on the bedside table. "It might be Dad or one of the kids. I have to see."

He sighed and slid away slightly, though he stayed far too close for her to keep a coherent thought.

She didn't recognize the incoming number but she answered it anyway, hoping the caller couldn't hear that ragged edge to her voice.

"Hello?"

There was a pause for three or four seconds. "Jen? Is that you?" she finally heard and her heart sank as she recognized Marcy Weller's voice.

She sat up, pulling the sheets around her.

"Hi Marcy. How are you?"

Her assistant gave a crazed-sounding laugh. "Oh, just dandy. I'm only in charge of planning a dinner party for fifty people in ten hours and the caterer has to pick today of all days to go flaky on me."

The faculty party. She hadn't given it a thought since the day before. How much power did Seth hold over her if he could make her completely forget something she'd been obsessing about for weeks?

In an effort to shore up the sagging morale at the school and to try yet again to make a connection with her staff—some of whom were still resentful the school board had brought in an outsider—she'd decided to dig into her own savings to throw a party for the faculty and staff at the school. Marcy had offered her parents' large, elegant house as the venue since they were traveling during the holidays.

Her vivacious assistant had taken over the party planning, handling all the details and leaving Jenny only to worry.

Which she'd forgotten to do for the last twenty-four hours.

She gathered her thoughts and tried to sound professional and composed. "What do you mean? What's wrong with Allen?"

"Not him. His stupid wife," Marcy exclaimed. "Candy went into labor three weeks early, can you believe it? How can she do this to us? Where are we supposed to come up with a caterer at the last minute?"

Jenny gave a startled laugh, but Marcy went on before she could comment.

"This is just like Candy," Marcy said darkly. "She

always hated me. She hasn't changed a bit since she was head cheerleader at high school—she can't stand not being the center of attention."

"I really doubt she planned going into labor just to inconvenience you and ruin our faculty party."

"You don't know her like I do. I wouldn't put anything past her."

Jenny didn't know her at all, she just knew Allen was a great caterer she'd already used twice since she came to Pine Gulch.

"What are we going to do?" Marcy wailed. "Oh, this is a nightmare! Between yesterday's blizzard and now Candy's selfishness, this party is going to be a total bomb."

"Calm down. We'll figure something out. I can't imagine Allen didn't have at least some of the prep work done for the party, since it's only in a few hours."

Marcy drew a breath and Jenny could picture her moving into one of the calming yoga moves from the class she took from Marjorie Dalton that she practiced in times of stress. When she spoke, some of the hysteria seemed to be gone from her voice.

"He tried to tell me everything that was ready for the party but I could hear Candy yelling at him to hurry up in the background and he was so flustered I couldn't make sense of half of it. He did tell me where the spare key is to his kitchen, though."

Jenny rose and started pacing the room, lost in administrative problem-solver mode.

"Okay. Here's what we're going to do. You've got the key and the menu we agreed on. You can run over to Allen's place right now and see if you can figure out how much prep he's finished and how much we still have left to do."

"I can do that. It's only a few blocks away. Better yet, why don't you meet me there? We could do this faster with two of us."

She turned around and saw Seth lounging against the pillows watching her with that light in his eyes again. She abruptly realized she'd left the sheets behind on the bed and was pacing the room dressed in nothing but her cell phone.

She cleared her throat, knowing she would look more foolish if she scrambled back under the blanket, as she wanted to do. Instead she reached for the closest article of clothing—his shirt—and slipped into it.

"Well, there's a bit of a hitch there. I was, um, stranded in Jackson last night by the storm."

"You're in Jackson?" All the panic—and more—returned to Marcy's voice and she spoke the last word about three octaves higher and several decibels louder than the first two. "When I called your house and your dad said to call you on your cell, he didn't say anything about you being out of town!"

"I'm out of town for now," Jenny said, hurrying to calm her. "But I'm sure the roads are clear now and I'll be heading back to Pine Gulch as soon as I can, I promise. I can be back in..."

She gave Seth a questioning look and almost dropped the phone at the expression in his eyes, something murky and unreadable that sent her stomach twirling and had her pulling his shirt more tightly around her.

Those gorgeous shoulders rippled as he shrugged and held up three fingers.

"Three hours," she told Marcy. "Though I'll do everything I can to make it in two and a half."

"That's still not enough time for us to get everything ready!"

"It will all be okay, I promise. Try to call Allen at the hospital to figure out where things stand and see if he can walk us through whatever recipes are left."

Marcy was only slightly mollified to have a plan of action. "Ten hours, Jen. That's all we've got."

"I know. We'll figure it out, I promise."

"We'd better. You know how important this is."

She thought of her faculty and how hard she had worked to earn their trust and acceptance. A good school administrator could accomplish nothing without the support of her teachers and she still had a long way to go for that. She hoped this party might melt some of their reserve.

"I know."

"I hope so. This is my one big chance with Lance and I can't afford to blow it!"

Okay, perhaps she and Marcy weren't quite on the same page here, she thought with a smile. She was desperate to build a team with her faculty while Marcy's motives had more to do with a certain physical education teacher she was interested in.

"You know how long it took me to work up the nerve to ask him to be my date tonight," Marcy went on. "I wanted so much to impress him by throwing this really terrific party and now it's all going to be ruined because of stupid Candy Grumley."

"We'll get through this, I swear. Lance won't know what hit him, okay? Just call me on my cell when you've had a chance to assess the situation in Allen's kitchen."

"I don't want to call you when you're driving, especially in these conditions. I'm sure the roads will still be slick."

She didn't want to tell Marcy not to worry about that since someone else would be at the wheel—especially when that someone was a presently naked and extremely gorgeous Seth Dalton.

She felt herself blush. "Don't worry about that. Just call me."

She wrapped up the call a few moments later and closed her phone to face Seth, who was still watching her with that lazy smile.

She wanted desperately to climb back into that bed with him but she knew it was impossible.

"I've got to get back. I'm…I'm sorry but it's an emergency."

"Sounded urgent."

"That faculty thing I was telling you about. We're having a holiday party tonight. Allen Grumley is catering it for us and his wife has apparently gone into labor three weeks later. Marcy thinks she did it on purpose."

"Candy always was a prima donna."

She picked up a pillow and smacked him with it. "Not you, too! For heaven's sake, can't a woman even go into labor without the world assigning ulterior motives?"

He laughed and fended off her attack, then grabbed her and pulled her to him.

She let out a sigh, regret a heavy ache inside her that she wouldn't share this magic with him again. "I'm sorry, but I really do have to get back to deal with the crisis."

He arched an eyebrow. "In that case, maybe we'd better save time and share the shower."

Sharing a shower turned out not to be the world's most efficient idea after all.

She hadn't really expected it to save any time, but she also hadn't been able to resist one more chance to kiss him and touch him. They made love with slow, almost unbearable tenderness, and she had to hope the shower spray hid her tears.

At last they were on their way. Seth drove his pickup through the snow with his usual competence even under the snowy conditions and she was grateful for his presence.

She spent most of the drive making lists and trying to figure out what they still needed to accomplish to pull off the party.

An hour or so from Pine Gulch, Marcy called again. "Is this an okay time for you to talk on your cell? The roads aren't too slick?" she asked.

"It's fine," Jenny assured her. "I'm not driving."

In the pause that followed, she could almost hear the wheels in Marcy's head turn as she tried to figure out who Jenny might have gone to Jackson with, but to her relief, her assistant said nothing. She was grateful, since she didn't want to have to lie.

"Okay, things aren't quite the disaster I feared," Marcy said. "The desserts and the appetizers are done and so is the salad. Allen only had about half of the au gratin potatoes ready. Knowing how fast those go around here, I was thinking of having some baked potatoes set out when they're gone."

"Great idea."

"Even I can handle baked potatoes. My mom has two ovens in her kitchen and I can set them on a timer to be finished just as the party's starting. And I can cook the ham at my place, too. He's got those all ready to go."

"Wonderful. It sounds like you've got everything under control."

"Not everything. Here's the sticky part. Remember we were offering ham and Allen's famous coq au vin? He has all the stuff for the chicken but I've got no idea how to throw it together."

Jenny's mind raced. Her skills in the kitchen were not the greatest, though she figured she could follow a recipe if they had one. Coq au vin sounded more than a little challenging. Just the name was enough to make her break out in hives. "Is there something else we could substitute?"

"Any ideas?"

She thought through her poultry repertoire, which was pretty limited to roast chicken and a moderately good recipe for grilled lemon-herb chicken breasts.

"See if you can find a recipe somewhere in Allen's kitchen. I'll be there as soon as I can. Between the two of us, we can probably figure something out. Thanks so much for everything you've done so far. It's a lot of work and I owe you big-time."

"I won't let you down, I promise."

"Just make sure you leave enough time so you can get ready and put on all your sparkly stuff for Lance."

"Are you kidding? I'm not going to all this work to impress him, just to show up in an apron and a pair of jeans!"

Jenny laughed and hung up.

"If we pull this off, it's going to be a miracle," she said after she'd folded her cell phone.

"Anything I can do?" Seth asked. "I'm not a whiz in the kitchen, but I can take orders."

The Pine Gulch gossip mill would just about start spinning off its axis if she showed up at Marcy's house with Seth Dalton in tow as a sous chef.

She mustered a smile. "I think we'll be okay. But thanks."

A muscle tightened in his jaw, but he said nothing for several more miles. Finally when they were nearing the outskirts of town—near where Cole had crashed the GTO—he spoke in a deceptively casual voice.

"Why aren't you taking a date tonight?"

The unexpected question had her pen scratching across the list she had been making.

"How do you know I'm not?"

It was a stupid thing to say, but her only excuse was that he'd flustered her. Something dark and formidable leaped into his gaze and she swallowed, struck once more by how easy it was to forget his easygoing nature covered a hard, dangerous man.

"Are you?"

"No," she admitted. "I didn't…it didn't seem appropriate."

"Why not?"

"I don't know. I guess because I'm the principal." And because the only man she wanted to take was the last one she ever could.

He was silent for another block or so, then he cast her a long look across the cab of his truck. "Even if you *had* decided to ask a date, you would never in a million years have taken me, would you?"

She did *not* want to have this conversation right now, so close to home and all the things she had to deal with there.

"Seth…" she began, but had no idea where to go after that, so her voice trailed off.

In that single word, Seth heard the hesitation in her voice and knew his suspicion was true. Despite everything, despite these last few wonderful weeks and the incredible night they had just shared, she still was ashamed to be seen with him.

Hurt and anger poured through him in equal measures and his hands tightened on the steering wheel. He wanted to lash out at her, to attack and wound until she bled as he did.

Just then the truck slid on some slush and he had to concentrate to keep control in the slick driving conditions. By the time he did, the hurt had just about overwhelmed the anger.

"I get the picture now," he said quietly. "A guy like me is fine for a little romp in the sack but when it comes to anything deeper, you're not interested."

"That is not true."

"Isn't it?"

"You know things are complicated for me right now."

"Your precious reputation. Right."

She bristled at the scorn in his voice. "I have nothing else *but* my reputation right now, as far as my faculty is concerned. It would be different if I'd been here a year or two and had some kind of track record with them—if they knew me and my capabilities. But right now I'm a wild card and my every move is endlessly dissected and analyzed in the faculty lounge."

"And of course we wouldn't want anybody to suspect you might have a pulse."

"It's more than that! I can't afford for my judgment to be questioned on anything."

"Being seen with me would certainly show lousy judgment on your part. I get it."

It was only a party. Why was he making such a big deal about it? Intellectually, he knew his reaction was out of proportion to the situation. But he couldn't seem to hold back the tide of hurt washing over him.

The whole thing had an oddly familiar feel to it. He tried to figure out why and was almost to her father's house when it hit him like a snowplow coming through the windshield.

It felt familiar because he'd been down this road before. Many times before. He had spent the first twelve years of his life trying to win the approval and acceptance of someone determined to reject him at every turn.

Hank Dalton had been a bastard who'd treated all three of his sons with varying degrees of cruelty.

He had tried—and failed—to mold Wade into a carbon copy of himself. He had disregarded all of Jake's dreams of being a doctor and completely dismissed his middle son's intellect and quest for knowledge. As for Seth, he might as well not have existed for all the notice Hank paid his sickly youngest son.

He remembered how he used to follow his father around, copying his every move—from his cocksure walk to the way he wore his hat to that hard-ass, screwyou stare his father had perfected.

All for nothing. His father hadn't noticed a damn thing except the asthma Seth had no control over.

His jaw tightened. He wasn't that weak, puny kid eager for any scrap a bastard like Hank Dalton might toss at him anymore. Long before the year he turned twelve, when Hank had died, he'd given up on his father ever seeing him as anything other than a worthless runt, always out of breath and clinging to his mother.

He'd come a long way since those days, so far he thought he had put all that behind him. So why did Jennifer Boyer's blunt rejection seem so painfully familiar?

He thought of the night they'd just shared, the heartbreaking intimacy of it and the connection he had never experienced with anyone else. He replayed again the pure, incomparable sweetness of holding her in his arms while she slept and he was astonished and terrified by the raw emotion welling up in his throat.

He swallowed it down, forcing it back by concentrating on the road.

"I see," he said when he trusted his voice again.

She sent him a searching look and he gave a casual shrug, determined not to let her see how she had eviscerated him. "No big deal. I've got plenty of things I could do tonight."

He must not have been completely successful at hiding his hurt because her eyes darkened.

"I'm sorry, Seth. But please try to see this from my perspective."

"Oh, I do," he assured her. "Nothing possibly could be worse than letting the faculty and staff at Pine Gulch Elementary see their new respectable principal hanging out with the town's biggest hellion. What a nightmare that would be for you."

"You don't need to use sarcasm."

"Yeah, I do." The tenuous rope he had on his emotions frayed abruptly. "Dammit, Jen. How can you even care what other people think, after what we've just shared?"

"What did we share? I slept with you, but that certainly doesn't make me unique among the female population of Pine Gulch."

Ah. Direct hit. He almost swayed from the force of it, but drew in a breath to steel himself against the pain. "It was more than that and you know it."

Her hands clenched in her lap and she was trembling as though she was standing out in the snow with bare feet.

"It was a mistake," she said quietly. "A lapse of judgment on my part brought on by the storm and the enforced intimacy of the situation. One that won't happen again. I can't see you anymore, Seth."

He should have expected it, but somehow he hadn't been prepared for the panic burning through him, raw and terrifying. He wanted to rage and yell and beg her not to cut him off from something that suddenly seemed as vital to him as breathing.

There was nothing he could say, though, nothing he could do to fix this and he could only be grateful they had reached her father's house.

He pulled into the driveway and sat there, his hands on the steering wheel.

"That's probably for the best," he finally said, though everything in him howled in protest at the outright lie. "I won't be your guilty secret, Jen. Some kind of stud you turn to when you're bored or lonely. I care about you. Hell, I think I might even be in love with you."

Her gaze flashed to his and he saw shock and disbelief there but he plowed forward.

"I don't know. This is all new to me." His laugh was rough and scored his throat as though he'd swallowed a dozen razor blades. "Can you believe that? The hellion of Pine Gulch has never been in love before."

He didn't give her a chance to respond. "But if that's what this is, I don't want it. At least not with you. I can't love a woman without the guts to take a chance on something that could be wonderful."

"Or miserable," she whispered.

"Or miserable," he agreed. "But we'll never know, will we? Because you've decided I'm not good enough for you."

"That is not true!"

"Isn't it?" He felt a hundred years old, suddenly. Old and tired and terribly, terribly sad.

On bones that seemed to creak and groan, he climbed out and walked around to her side of the truck, opening the door pointedly. "Goodbye, Jen. You've got a whole list of things to do before your big party so I'm sure you'll forgive me if I don't come in."

She didn't move for a long moment, the only color in her face the shiner Cherry had delivered. Finally she slid down, hesitated for just an instant—just long enough for him to pray she would fall into his arms, that she would kiss him and make all of this go away.

But she didn't. She didn't even look at him again. She just seemed to square her shoulders, then she walked away.

He waited just long enough for her to open the front door, then he climbed back into his truck and backed out of the driveway—heading toward the misery he knew was the rest of his life.

Chapter 15

It was tough to get a good drunk on at one in the afternoon. Oh, he tried, but all he had in the house was beer and he didn't feel like driving back into town for something harder.

After two Sam Adams, he decided it was pretty pathetic to sit there in his cold house with only Lucy for company, wasting perfectly good beer when he wasn't at all in the mood.

Driven by emotions he didn't know how to deal with, he finally decided to channel all this restless energy into trying to catch up on the work he'd neglected in order to take Jenny shopping. He grabbed his coat and hat, whistled for Lucy and headed out through the cold to the indoor arena.

It didn't help much, he decided an hour later atop a

big, rawboned bay mare he was training for a client. A little but not much.

His chest still ached and he couldn't quite keep the knot out of his throat, but at least he wasn't sitting around feeling sorry for himself.

He was roping one of the iron calf heads they used for training when Lucy suddenly barked a happy greeting. The loop landed yards shy of the mark as he turned quickly in the saddle to see who had come in.

The hope in his chest died a quick and painful death when he saw his oldest brother leaning against the top rail of the arena gate.

He gave a mental groan. This was just what he needed. His brother tended to see far too much and was never shy about doling out advice, wanted or not.

As tempted as he was to ignore Wade and just keep on roping, he knew he would only be delaying the inevitable. He took his time coiling the rope, then nudged the horse toward the fence.

"She's looking good," Wade said when he neared.

He dismounted. "Yeah. I imagine Jimmy Harding will be pleased with her when I'm done."

"For what he's paying you to train her, she ought to be able to stand on her back legs and salute the flag as it goes by."

He bristled. Here was the fight he was itching for. How considerate of Wade to hand deliver it. Though the fence was between them, that didn't stop him from climbing in his brother's face. "Are you implying Harding's not going to get his money's worth?"

Wade sniffed, then raised an eyebrow at the half-empty beer bottle Seth had brought along and left on the railing a few yards away. "Not at all. I just wondered if your usual training method involves working with a horse when you're half plastered."

"I had exactly two and a half beers! What are you, working for the state alcohol commission?"

"Nope. Just a concerned brother."

"Who should learn to mind his own damn business," Seth snarled, yanking the saddle off the horse.

Wade just watched him for a long moment while Seth led the horse back to her stall.

"You want to talk about it?"

"What?" He grabbed a brush and started grooming the horse.

"Whatever has your boxers in a twist."

"Nothing."

"You sure?"

"Fairly, yeah," he drawled. "Contrary to popular belief, I think I know my own mind."

"I never said you didn't. But do you know your own strength? Because if you tug that brush much harder, Jimmy Harding is going to look mighty peculiar riding his bald horse."

He froze when he realized what he was doing. He let out a breath and eased up a little then pulled off the bridle and gave the horse one last pat before he let himself out of her stall to face his brother.

"You want me to talk about what's bothering me? Sure. I'll talk about it. How's this? I've got this brother with a beautiful wife and three great kids, one more on the way. His life is frigging perfect, which makes him annoying as hell to be around, especially since he thinks he knows every damn thing in the universe."

Wade seemed in a particularly jovial mood because even that direct attack didn't seem to get his goat, to Seth's frustration. He only gave a cheerful smile that made Seth want to take out a few teeth. "If I knew everything, I wouldn't need to ask what has you drinking two and a half beers in the middle of the afternoon, would I?"

Seth released a slow breath. None of this was Wade's fault. Venting his hurt and rage at Jenny on his relatively innocent brother was unfair and slightly juvenile.

He was bigger than this. A few years ago he probably couldn't have said the same thing, but he'd come a long way in those few years, thanks in great measure to Wade's astonishing confidence in him.

If not for his brother's encouragement and support, Seth might never have found the courage to follow his dreams and build this horse arena, diverting Cold Creek resources in an effort to diversify and build up the equine operations of the ranch.

His brother had placed a great deal of faith in him the last two years. He deserved better than to be sacrificed to the sharp edge of Seth's temper.

"Don't worry about it," he managed after a minute. "I'm sure I'll be fine in a day or two."

He paused, feeling awkward as a brand-new boot. "Sorry to take my bad mood out on you."

Wade studied him and he had to wonder how much of his turmoil showed up on his features, especially at his brother's next words.

"Does your lousy mood have anything to do with the lovely new elementary school principal you took to Jackson yesterday?"

He could feel a muscle work in his jaw and he fought the urge to pound his fist into that support. With his luck, he would probably not only break his fist but send the whole barn tumbling down around his ears.

"You could say that."

"The great Seth Dalton having woman trouble? This has to be one for the record books."

"Yeah, yeah. Hilarious, isn't it?"

Something in his tone had Wade giving him an even longer look. Whatever his brother saw had him straightening. "Whoa. I was joking about the woman trouble, but this is serious, isn't it? Trouble with a capital L-O-V-E."

Seth made a scornful, snorting kind of noise that didn't convince Wade for a second.

"Carrie said this one was different," his brother said, shaking his head. "She predicted after that day we went up the mountain for Christmas trees that you were going to fall hard, but I couldn't see it. I should have listened to her. That means I owe her dinner at the Spring Creek Ranch. Man, you know how much that place costs?"

He stared at his brother, appalled. "You and your wife bet on my love life?"

Wade grinned, looking worlds different from the surly widower he'd been until Caroline Montgomery blew into their lives. "Yeah, I should know better, shouldn't I? Carrie knows a mark when she sees one. I guess that's what comes from growing up with a con artist for a father."

Quinn Montgomery, Caroline's father and their mother's second husband, had enjoyed a fairly profitable career on the grift until the law had caught up with him a few years before he'd met Marjorie.

Despite his somewhat shady past, all the Dalton sons had come to have a deep affection for the man. How could they help it when he plainly adored their mother and had given her the joyous life she'd been deprived of in her first marriage?

"So what's going on with Jennifer Boyer?" Wade asked. "I'm assuming the shopping trip to Jackson and your unexpected stay didn't go well."

The understatement of the whole damn year.

"Why should I tell you? Remind me again when we became best girlfriends, here?"

"If you can't get advice from your brother with the frigging perfect life, where else can you turn?"

He had a point. Though his brother was only six years older than he was, Wade had been more of a father figure through most of his life than Hank had ever been. The Dalton patriarch had died of a heart attack on Wade's eighteenth birthday and from then on, Wade had stepped up to show Seth by example how a decent man should live his life.

He hadn't always followed his brother's lead but he had always respected him and at least listened to his advice. It couldn't hurt, he decided.

"All right. You want to know what's wrong? I'll tell you. You'll appreciate this, I'm sure. You know how you've spent the last twenty years telling me my wild, reckless ways were going to catch up to me some day? Guess what? Big surprise, you were right."

"Yeah?"

"Did you know my reputation is somewhat tarnished in Pine Gulch?"

"Don't know if I'd say tarnished. Maybe dented a little in spots."

"Well, Jenny Boyer is looking for a saint, apparently. And too bad for me, I lost my halo sometime around my sixteenth birthday."

He waited for some wisecrack from his brother, some "I-told-you-so" kind of gloat but Wade just looked at him, and the sudden compassion in his eyes turned the lump in his throat into a damn boulder. He worked to swallow it, fighting back the horrifying emotion burning his own eyes.

"I'm sorry, man."

"Yeah. It sucks."

"She's wrong about you," Wade said after a moment, looking about as uncomfortable as Seth was with this conversation. "You might not be a saint but beneath all those dents, you're a good man."

"Uh, thanks. I think."

"You are. You're a hard worker, you're about the most honest man I know, you always dance with all the wallflowers at any party, and you're the first one I'd pick to back me up in a fight. I'm proud of you, Seth. I haven't said that nearly enough over the years, but I am."

He placed a hand on Seth's shoulder for just a moment then let it drop, to Seth's vast relief. Much more of this and he'd be bawling like a just-weaned calf.

"Come on down to the house for dinner, why don't you? Caroline's fixed a roast and some of those twice-baked potatoes you like so much. I think Nat might have even made a cake."

He mustered a smile, wondering if he'd always be the bachelor uncle his brothers would have to leave a place for at the table. "Thanks anyway, but I've got some things to do here. I'm not very good company anyway."

"You know the kitchen's always open if you change your mind."

"Right. Thanks."

Wade left and Seth leaned against the stall railing for a long time watching Jimmy Harding's mare munch her feed and wondering how long it took to heal a broken heart.

"Everything is perfect. I can't believe we pulled it off!"

Hundreds of twinkling lights reflected off the tiny sparkles of glitter in Marcy's upswept hair but they didn't hold a candle to the brilliant glow in her eyes.

From somewhere deep inside, Jenny forced a smile for her giddy assistant. "You did all the work and you deserve every bit of the credit."

"Ha. I was a wreck. You're the one who came through with the coq au vin. Everyone's been raving about it and they can't believe you fixed it all by yourself! I don't know how you did it."

Jenny had to admit, she had no idea. She had been so numb after her fight with Seth that she could barely remember anything after he dropped her off and drove away.

I care about you. Hell, I think I might even be in love with you.

As they'd been doing for hours, his words seemed to ricochet through her mind, bouncing off every available surface.

It couldn't be true. He was only saying that because he was like a thwarted child, willing to say anything to get his way.

No. That was unfair and didn't mesh at all with the man she'd come to know these last weeks. He had never lied to her and she couldn't imagine he would start with such a whopper.

Did that mean he had been sincere?

Despite the room full of people she knew she should be working hard to impress with her warmth and wit, she couldn't seem to think about anything else but those stunning words.

"Is everything okay?" Marcy asked, jerking Jenny back to their conversation.

"Sorry. Everything is great. Look what a wonderful time everyone is having and it's all because of you."

It *was* a great party, one she was sure everyone would remember for years. The food had been delicious, the company entertaining and everyone but her seemed to be in a holiday mood.

"I mean it, Marcy, you saved my bacon on this one."

Her assistant looked pleased with the compliment but she continued to look at Jenny with concern.

"Too bad you're not enjoying it," she said.

Jenny started. Was she that transparent? "Of course I am!" she lied. "Why would you say that?"

"You've only been looking at the clock every five

minutes and you haven't left the kitchen for long all night. Keep it up and your faculty is going to think you don't want to spend time with them."

"That's not it at all," she exclaimed, horrified she might have given that impression. "I just… It's been a rough day, that's all."

Marcy arched an eyebrow. "Does your rough day have anything to do with the shiner you got from one of Seth Dalton's ex-girlfriends?"

The platter of finger food she'd been replenishing at the buffet table nearly slipped out of her hands and she looked around frantically to be sure no one else overheard.

"You know?" she hissed

Marcy gave her a rueful look. "My cousin Darlene works at the Aspen during the ski season. She makes major cash in tips, let me tell you. One time Harrison Ford came in and left her fifty bucks! She said he's even better-looking in person than on-screen. Anyway, she said she saw you and Seth Dalton having dinner. She knew Seth, of course—who, by the way, she says is better-looking than even Harrison Ford. And she recognized you because she dropped her little brother off one day at school. He's in Mr. Nichols's fifth-grade class."

Marcy snagged a chicken roll from the plate and popped it into her mouth before going on. "So, Amy says you were enjoying your meal when suddenly another waitress's roommate comes over and starts making this big scene about how Seth dumped her. Amy was in the kitchen and didn't see the whole thing but she said this girl tried to slug Seth but hit you instead."

Jenny couldn't seem to breathe and knew her cheeks

must be ablaze with horrified color. "Does everyone know?"

Marcy shrugged. "I doubt it. Everyone's been asking me if I knew what happened to your eye and I just told them the same story you told, you know, about slipping on an icy step. I figure it's none of their business."

Before Jenny could thank her for that, at least, one of the third-grade teachers approached them.

Susan Smoot was a widow who had taught at the school for thirty years. Rumor had it the other woman had had her eye on the principal's office for a long time and Jenny knew she had been one of her most vocal critics when the school board opted to go outside the district to hire her.

She was a formidable enemy—though Jenny had a feeling she could be a powerful ally, as well.

"Thank you for the party, Ms. Boyer. Everything was delicious."

Though she was still rocked by Marcy's revelation, Jenny managed to put it away for now and smile. This was the warmest snippet of conversation she'd ever received from the woman and she didn't want to ruin it.

"Thank you, Susan. Please, I've been here for three months now. When do you think you might consider calling me Jennifer?"

The teacher's mouth twitched but Jenny couldn't really tell if it was a smile. "If you do this again next year, you might want to have it someplace where those of us who don't like the loud garbage that passes for music these days can find a place to hear ourselves think."

"Great idea," she said.

Susan's gaze fixed on the black eye that stood out

no matter how she tried to camouflage it with makeup. "And you know, the best thing for icy steps is to sprinkle a little kitty litter on it, Jennifer. Works better than salt and won't kill your flowerbeds in the spring."

"I'll keep that in mind. Thank you."

As soon as the other woman left, Jenny turned quickly back to Marcy and dragged her into the kitchen for a little privacy. "Who else do you think knows I was in Jackson with Seth Dalton?" she asked.

Marcy looked taken aback by the frantic note in her voice. "I don't know. Why does it matter?"

"How can you ask that? Of course it matters! Do you think Susan Smoot would find it an amusing little anecdote that I was decked by one of Seth's jealous ex-lovers? Or even that I was in Jackson having dinner with him in the first place?"

Marcy made a scornful noise. "Let me tell you about Sue Smoot. Most of the time her husband, Carl, was a fine, upstanding citizen. President of the Lions Club, first tenor in the church choir, the whole thing. But every once in a while he'd go on a holy tear and get completely loaded. Before he retired, my dad was the police chief and he used to come home with all kinds of stories about that crazy Carl Smoot. One time he took a shotgun and sprayed every single stop sign in town. Every one! Sue stuck by him through it all. I figure she can't throw any stones at you just for having dinner in Jackson with Seth Dalton on the same night some woman decides to go mental."

"I shouldn't have been there with him. It was a mistake."

"Are you kidding? Any woman who finds herself

on the receiving end of that man's undivided attention ought to get down on her knees and consider herself blessed."

She stared at her assistant. "He's a player! Everybody says so. He dates a different woman every day."

"Not true. Maybe he used to a few years ago but ever since the Cold Creek started their horse operation, he's been a different man. He still likes a good party, but he's settled down a lot now that he has some focus."

"I heard you talking to Ashley Barnes that day in the office when she was upset he didn't call her back. You told her about the Seth Dalton School of Broncbusting. You said he was a dog!"

"No, *Ashley* said he was a dog. If you remember, I said he was a good guy, just a little on the rowdy side. He is. His blood might run a bit hot, but that's not such a bad thing, if you ask me, as long as he finds the right woman to help him channel it."

"I'm not that woman!"

Marcy smiled, the sparkles in her hair reflecting the recessed lights in the kitchen. "I don't know. Darlene said he looked whipped in the restaurant before the big scene with the other girl. She said the two of you were holding hands and everything."

I care about you. Hell, I think I might even be in love with you.

She shivered but before she could say anything, Lance Tyler poked his head inside the kitchen. "Marcy, why are you hiding out in here? Are you going to make me dance with Mrs. Christopher all night?"

"Sorry. I'm coming."

She gave Jenny a quick hug and took one last parting shot. "You know," she whispered in her ear so the P.E. teacher couldn't hear, "somewhere out there is a rider who can tame even the wildest bronc. You'll never know if you don't climb on."

After she left, Jenny leaned against the counter, her mind whirling.

I can't love a woman without the guts to take a chance on something that could be wonderful.

His words echoed in her ears, louder than the music from the other room, louder than the dishwasher busily churning away beside her.

The ache in her chest seemed unbearable and she pressed a hand to it, then felt something crack away under her fingers, something hard and brittle.

She was a fool. A scared, stupid fool.

She loved him. With all her heart she loved him, and she was throwing away any chance they might have together because she was too afraid to trust him—and more afraid to trust herself and her own instincts.

She was so worried about what other people thought that she refused to pay attention to those instincts. She didn't deserve the respect she was so desperate to earn from her faculty, not if she couldn't make up her own mind about what was good and right and couldn't stand up for those decisions, even if she faced criticism for them.

Seth was a good man. A kind, decent, *wonderful* man, who had done nothing but open his life and his heart to her and her family.

Sweet assurance flowed through her and she remembered the tenderness in his eyes the night before, how safe and warm and cherished he made her feel.

She straightened from the counter. She had to find him, right this moment, to see if she had completely ruined everything or if there might be any chance they could salvage something from the wreckage she had left behind with her stupidity.

She rushed out of the kitchen and blinked, a little disoriented to find the lights and the music and the people. The party was still going strong—her party, the one she had thought so vitally important.

How could she leave in the middle of it?

No, she was going to trust her instincts on this one. She had to find Seth now, tonight, before she lost her nerve.

Marcy and Lance danced by at that moment and she stepped forward and grabbed her before she could whirl away again.

"Marcy, I have to go. I…I'm sorry. I'll explain later."

Her friend gave her a careful look, then grinned with delight. "I don't think you need to explain."

She smiled back, the first genuine one she'd felt since she walked away from Seth.

"You were right. I want my eight seconds. No. More than that. I want forever."

Chapter 16

Seth stood just inside the doorway to the Bandito, wondering what the hell he was doing there.

For some crazy reason, he thought his favorite haunt would be just the thing to lift him out of his misery. Usually he loved walking inside the honky tonk—the clink of pool cues setting shots, the music, loud and raucous, the smell of barley and hops and people having a good time. Most of all, he loved the chorus of greetings he received every time he walked in.

This had always been his place, the one spot where he wasn't just Wade and Jake Dalton's wild and reckless kid brother.

But now as he looked at the string of blinking Christmas lights strung across the mirror behind the bar, the cheap foil garlands hanging from the tables and the same faces he'd been seeing here since he was old enough to drink, all he felt was the bitter sting of his own loneliness.

This wasn't what he wanted.

What do you want? he asked himself, but he knew the answer before the question even entered his mind.

Jenny.

He wanted Jenny Boyer, in his arms, in his heart, in his life.

He pushed that dead horse off him and was just about to walk back out into the cold when a buxom blonde wearing a skimpy Mrs. Santa Claus outfit approached him.

"Hey, Seth!" Twice divorced, Dawna McHenry was ten years his senior—and she'd been hitting on him since he turned sixteen. "Haven't seen you around in a while."

"Hey Dawna. It's been a busy few weeks."

"Well, you're here now. That's the important thing. What do you say to a dance?"

One of Alan Jackson's rollicking holiday songs was playing on the jukebox, but Seth couldn't manage to summon even the tiniest spark of enthusiasm to rip up the wooden dance floor right now.

"Sweetheart, you know how much I hate to disappoint a lady. It's nothing personal, I swear, but I'm not much in the mood for dancing tonight. Can I take a rain check, though?"

"You know my umbrella's always open for you, darlin'," she purred, but her smile had slipped a little.

Maybe his own miserable mood opened his eyes a little, but for the first time he saw through her bright cheer to the emptiness beneath. She was just looking for somebody to take away the pain for a while and he was sorry it could never be him.

He wanted to make it better for her, but he didn't know how until his gaze landed on the middle-aged man sitting at the bar. Roy Gentry was another of the Bandito regulars. A shy cowboy with a small plot of land and his own herd, he never said much to anybody—and became even more tongue-tied when Dawna was near.

"You know who I bet could use a little of that cheering up you're so good at? Roy over there."

Dawna cast a look at the bar. "You think?"

"Oh, yeah," Seth answered. "I bet he gets real lonely all by himself in that big house his folks left him, especially this time of year. Why don't you go see if he wants to dance?"

Dawna looked again and he hoped this time she saw beyond Roy's shy awkwardness to the man who never had a mean word to say about anybody and who always put a little extra in the bartender's tip jar.

She gave the cowboy another considering look. "I wouldn't want anybody feelin' bad this time of year. You know, I might just do that."

She flitted away from him and headed toward the bar. Seth lingered long enough to watch her lean in and say something with one of her bright smiles. He couldn't hear over the music but he saw Roy give a quick, forceful shake of his head, then Dawna tugged him off his bar stool anyway and dragged him over to the dance floor.

He wanted to think it was divine providence—or at

least a gift from the King—but right at that moment, Elvis starting singing "Blue Christmas" on the juke box. Dawna threw her arms around the cowboy for a slow dance, and poor Roy looked like he didn't know what hit him.

If he'd had a beer right then, he would have lifted it in a salute to the man. *I'm right there with you, brother,* he thought, hoping he and Elvis might have just planted the seeds of something.

Good deed accomplished, he turned to go when he heard a woman's voice calling his name in a question.

For about half a second, he thought about pretending he didn't hear whoever she was and just continuing on his way. But she called his name again and he turned slowly with a sigh.

The ready excuse on his lips slipped away when he saw the tall brunette in slacks and a holiday sweater beaming at him.

"It is you! Hi, Seth. Remember me?"

"My word. Of course I do. Little Amy Roundy." He hugged her, stunned that this pretty, self-assured woman was the same girl he'd known since kindergarten.

"It's Amy Underwood now."

"That's right. Where is the lucky man?"

She made a face. "Pool table. I imagine my brothers are trying to hustle him out of our traveler's checks by now. They have no idea what they're up against. George plays the part of a mild-mannered, polite, slightly clumsy Brit but he'll rip them apart."

He smiled and knew he couldn't leave now, much as

he might want to. Amy had been one of his best friends in elementary school and he hadn't seen her in years.

By tacit agreement he steered them both to the only empty booth, where he took the seat across from her. "I hadn't heard you'd crossed to this side of the pond and finally come back for a visit," he said when they were seated. "How's life in the British Isles?"

"Just ducky, love." She smiled and dropped the accent. "Seriously, I love it. I miss my family and the mountains sometimes, but George and I have made a home there."

"What about kids?"

"Three girls. I've got pictures and everything."

She pulled out her cell phone, punched a few buttons, then held it out to him. He spent a minute admiring the image on the screen of three gorgeous little girls with blond curls and their mother's smile.

"What about you? Is there a Mrs. Dalton?"

He summoned a smile from somewhere deep inside. "Two of them. Both married to my brothers."

"You haven't made the big leap?"

He started to make some flippant remark but Amy's stern look caught it before it could escape. He suddenly remembered he could never hide anything from her. She and Maggie Cruz, Jake's wife, had been his best friends in grade school. They were the only kids in his class who hadn't bullied the wheezy runt he'd been.

Hank had just about popped a vein when he found out his youngest son's two best friends were girls but that had only made Seth more determined to keep them.

"No. Not yet," he managed.

Marriage. Now there was something he hadn't given much thought to. His parents' marriage had been a nightmare, enough to sour anybody on the institution. But his brothers had managed to move on and build amazingly happy lives.

For the first time, he started to wonder if he could ever do the same. He thought again of how he'd felt waking up with Jenny in his arms that morning and he suddenly wanted that every day, with a fierce and terrible ache.

Only too bad for him, the woman in question wanted nothing to do with him anymore.

He shifted his attention back to Amy, wondering what she saw in his face to put that soft, sympathetic look in her eyes.

She touched his hand. "You would make a wonderful husband, Seth."

He forced a laugh at that outright hyperbole. "Right. I'm willing to bet if you took a poll of all the women in this room, you would probably be the only one with that opinion."

She looked at him for a long moment then shook her head. "It doesn't matter what they think. If you find the right woman, her opinion is the only important one."

Didn't he just know it?

He must have made some sound because Amy sent him another sympathetic look. "Want to talk about it?"

No. He wanted to hop in the GTO and drive as far and as fast as he could to outrun this pain, this hollow fear that he would be spending the rest of his life alone.

No, he didn't want to talk about it. But something

about his old friend's compassion made him want to confide in her.

"How long do you think it will take your Brit to clean up over there at the pool table?"

Jenny drove through the streets of Pine Gulch, a strange mix of anticipation and anxiety churning through her. Would he even be willing to see her when she reached the Cold Creek after the hideous way she had treated him?

She had to try. Even if he slammed the door in her face, at least she would not have to live the rest of her life with regrets, knowing she might have touched the stars.

On the outskirts of town, she drove past the bright lights of the town's single tavern. The Bandito was doing a brisk business tonight, she thought, then took a closer look and nearly drove off the road.

She knew that red car in the parking lot. Seth's brawny GTO hulked in the corner, shiny and sleek and so distinctive she couldn't possibly mistake it for anyone else's car.

So much for sitting at home pining over her.

He was inside the tavern probably having a wonderful time while she was out here dying inside.

She pulled her SUV into an empty space in the parking lot, trying to figure out what she should do. She had two choices. She could go back to the faculty party and get on with the business of forgetting about him, as he had obviously decided to do about her.

Or she could grab hold of the rigging and climb on. She owed him an apology. By putting so much stock in gossip and rumor about him, she had treated him with terrible unfairness and she had to let him know she was sorry for it.

Even if he decided not to accept her apology, she would at least know she'd tried to offer it.

She turned off her vehicle and slid out, suddenly aware as she stepped onto packed snow of her holiday cocktail dress and high heels. She was going to look conspicuous, foolish, walking into the honky tonk like this.

People would wonder what she was doing there—and when the people in the packed tavern saw her with Seth, rumors would start flying before she would even have time to sit down.

She almost climbed back into her car, then she shook her head. No. She was strong enough to face a few rumors. She wasn't ashamed of her feelings for Seth. She loved him and she wouldn't hide it. Let the whole town see, she thought.

That defiant energy carried her to the front door of the Bandito and just inside, but there she stopped as the panic and self-doubt started to nip at her like an unruly puppy.

She scanned the crowd, already painfully aware of the stares. She didn't see him at first, then when she found him, that little yip of self-doubt turned into a pack of ravaging wolves.

He was sitting in a booth, cozying up to a brunette Jenny didn't recognize, someone tall and shapely and beautiful. Their heads were close together and the woman was laughing at something he said and Jenny felt like her heart had just been ripped out and thrown on the dance floor for everyone to stomp on.

This was stupid. Humiliating tears welled up in her eyes at her own idiocy and she wanted frantically to get out of there, but she felt frozen in place by this wild storm of emotions.

She was just trying to force herself to move when his gaze suddenly shifted from the woman beside him to the doorway where Jenny stood, exposed and heartsick.

Whatever he was saying to the other woman died as he stared at her.

Everything else in the bar—the laughter, the bright lights, the loud, pulsing music—faded away to nothing as their gazes caught and held.

Jenny couldn't breathe suddenly, stunned by the raw emotion in his eyes, pain and joy and something else she couldn't identify.

Her husband had never looked at her like that, she realized. Not once, in all their years of courtship and marriage, had he ever looked at her like she was his salvation, his entire world.

How could she turn away from this? She loved this man. She loved his strength, she loved his goodness, she loved the sweet and healing laughter he had brought into her life.

And she suddenly wanted everyone to know it.

Her pulse sounded louder than the music blaring from the jukebox as she forced herself to move forward on legs suddenly weak and jittery, until she stood at the edge of their booth.

Once she reached her destination, she didn't know where to start. She might have lost her nerve completely except that Seth hadn't looked away from her, even for a second. They stared at each other for a long moment, until the brunette actually broke the silence.

"Hi. You must be Jennifer."

That had her blinking and she managed to wrench her gaze from Seth to look at the woman, who actually seemed very nice, with warm brown eyes and an approachable smile. Too bad Jenny might just have to take a page from Cherry Mendenhall's book and deck her.

"Seth has just been telling me all about you," the woman went on.

She thought she heard Seth make a groaning kind of sound but she couldn't be sure.

"Has he?" It was all she could manage to say.

The other woman gave a smile Jenny would only have called mischievous if had come from one of her students. "Oh, yes. I'm Amy Underwood, an old friend. Sit down, won't you? Here, you can have my seat. I was just leaving to find my husband."

Husband. Right. Husband was good.

"He's sexy and British and I'm crazy about him," the strange woman added with a laugh. "Just in case you were wondering."

"Amy," Seth said in the chiding voice one reserved for old friends.

She laughed again, getting to her feet. "What did I say?" She didn't wait for an answer, just blew him a kiss. "We're in town until after the day after New Year's. Come and meet George and my girls. I want to know how the story ends."

"Yeah," he muttered. "So do I."

She walked away but Jenny remained standing by the booth, unsure where to go from here.

"What are you doing here, Jen?" he said after a long moment. A note of cool reserve had entered his voice and she winced from it even as she knew she deserved it.

"I was wondering if you would like to dance."

He gazed at her and she saw a host of emotions sift through his eyes. "Here?" he finally asked, looking around the crowded tavern.

"Here. Or at the faculty party. Or wherever you would like."

He gazed at her, stunned by her words, by the offer he knew must have cost her dearly.

Already, he was aware of the curious stares in their direction. Tongues were certainly going to wag with tales of the elementary school principal showing up at the local tavern in party clothes and a black eye and immediately sidling up to his table.

She must have known the gossip would start up before she even walked into the place, yet she had come anyway. She had faced her fears, had all but begged for the very scrutiny she claimed to be so eager to avoid.

For him.

He had never been so humbled.

Joy and sweet relief exploded in him, washing away the hurt and bitterness and angry. She was here, coming to him despite her fears and her uncertainties. He had no choice but to take the precious gift she offered and hold it close to his heart.

He reached for her hand and almost yanked her into

his arms right there in the Bandito in front of half the town but he knew that would be pushing things. Instead he uncoiled from the booth, threw some money on the table for his drink, and headed for the door, tugging her along behind him.

"Where are we going?" she asked a little breathlessly.

In answer, he pulled her out of the tavern. The cold December air blew through his jacket and he realized he hadn't given this a whole lot of thought, driven only by the need to be alone with her.

He had to kiss her in the next twenty seconds but he wasn't going to make her stand out in the cold for it, not in her skimpy cocktail dress. Thinking fast, he bundled her into the GTO, then slid into the driver's seat and started the engine.

The heater churned out blessed heat and at last he pulled her into his arms and kissed her as he'd been dreaming of doing since the moment they left the inn in Jackson.

She returned his kiss with a warmth and enthusiasm that took his breath away and they embraced there like a couple of hot-blooded high-school kids at an overlook. Much more of this, and they would be steaming up those windows, he thought.

"I've never made out in a muscle car before," she said after a long, heated moment. "It's kind of sexy."

"That's the whole idea," he managed, then lost his train of thought when she trailed kisses down his jawline to the curve of his neck, then back up.

"Can I just say, for your first time, honey, you're doing *great*," he drawled.

He felt her laughter against his skin and wanted to taste all of it. He dipped his mouth and caught hers again. Despite their playfulness, there was a poignant sweetness to her kiss, a gentle healing that seemed to wash away all the hurt of the afternoon and evening.

"I'm sorry about today," she murmured after a long moment, framing his face with her hands. "I'm so sorry I hurt you. It was never about you, Seth. It was me and my own insecurities. I was too afraid to rely on my judgment, to trust that the man I was falling in love with would be willing to catch me on the way down."

He almost couldn't speak, overwhelmed by her words. "What changed?" he finally asked, his voice hoarse.

She was quiet for several moments, the only sound the whirr of the heater and the distant bass throb from the music inside the bar. They would have to leave soon, he thought. They couldn't stay in the Bandito parking lot making out all night, but for now he didn't want to move, more content than he'd ever been in his life.

"Did I tell you about the nightmare I had after Morgan's bad asthma attack, the night my car wouldn't start and you drove us to the clinic to meet Jake?"

He shook his head, shifting so he was leaning into the corner of the seat and her cheek was resting against his chest. He held her close, his hand playing in her incredible hair. It wasn't the most comfortable position but he didn't mind as long as he could hold her.

"I dreamed I couldn't find Morgan," she went on. "She was sick and she needed me and no one would help me look for my child. It was a terrible, helpless feeling. I was just about to hit bottom when someone suddenly appeared out of nowhere and starting shoving away obstacles and pushing people back so I could reach my destination and find my child. I couldn't see his face but I knew even before he turned around who it was."

She touched his face, her eyes soft and a tender smile hovering around that lush mouth. Him? She dreamed of wild and rowdy Seth Dalton coming to her rescue like some kind of hero out of a movie?

"My subconscious has always known what I've been afraid to admit. I need you in my life. I need your strength and your kindness and your laughter."

He pressed his lips to her fingers, wondering if it was possible for a man to burst with joy.

"I love you, Seth. With everything in my heart I love you and I want everyone in the world to know. I want to run ads in the newspaper and send up hot air balloons and climb to the top of a water tower somewhere so I can graffiti it on the side."

He laughed, completely charmed by this side of her.

"Then you would get arrested for vandalism and I'd have to come pay you conjugal visits—which would be hot and all at first but would probably get old after a while. How about you just settle for whispering it in my ear for the rest of your life?"

Jenny blinked at him. The rest of her life? That certainly sounded…permanent. Was the hellion of Pine Gulch actually proposing?

"I know it's early in the game here," he went on, and she could swear there was a hint of color on his cheekbones in the dim light, "but I just want you to know where I stand. I might just have to put my foot down on this one. I love you and I want everything. The house, the dog, the kids, two cars—three if you count the GTO, which we might have to lock up for a few years until Cole learns to drive a hell of a lot better."

He smiled again and kissed her and all her worries and insecurities seemed to curl up and float away. He loved her. This strong, wonderful man loved her, quiet, boring Jennifer Boyer.

She still didn't quite understand it but she wasn't going to waste any more time doubting it, not when his eyes promised a future of laughter and warmth and joy.

"I love you, Jenny," he repeated. "I want everything."

She smiled and touched his face again, those wild and gorgeous features she loved so dearly.

"You drive a hard bargain, cowboy," she murmured. "But I'll see what I can do."

Epilogue

"Call me crazy, but aren't you supposed to be enjoying yourself?"

Seth swallowed the miserly sip of beer he'd just taken, set his tankard down and aimed a cool look at his older brothers across the table at the Bandito.

"I *am* enjoying myself," he answered Wade. "Who says I'm not enjoying myself?"

If he sounded a trace defensive, he had to hope neither Wade nor Jake noticed. To his chagrin, his brothers didn't miss much. Wade raised an eyebrow at Jake and they both snickered.

"I'd say the evidence speaks for itself," Jake answered, "considering you've been nursing that same beer all night and by my count, that's the third woman you've turned down for a dance in about ten minutes."

It was the fourth, but he wasn't about to point that out.

"I guess I just don't feel like dancing tonight," he said, wondering why the lights in the tavern seemed so harsh, the music uncomfortably loud. "Since when is that against the law?"

Jake and Wade looked at each other again, then both of them laughed.

"I wouldn't say it's against the law, exactly," Wade said with a particularly annoying smirk. "Just against the natural order of things where you're concerned. This is your last night to solidify your reputation. I can't believe you're not taking advantage of it. You're breaking all those poor girls' hearts."

Friday night at the Bandito was hopping. A live band from Sun Valley rocked the place and the battered dance floor teemed with locals and tourists looking for a good time.

Six months ago, he would have been one of them but it was amazing how a few months could change a man. It had changed this one enough that he suddenly decided he'd had enough of the stuffy tavern, especially when he knew the June night outside would be cool and sweet.

He slid out of the booth and stood up. "I appreciate the thought behind this little party but I think I'm going to head on home now. Thanks for the beer."

His brothers both stared at him like he'd stripped naked and started boot-scootin' across the tabletop.

Jake was the first one to speak. "This is your bachelor party and it's barely nine o'clock! I told Maggie not to expect me to roll in until after closing time."

He waited for some similar comment from Wade but his oldest brother was giving him a careful look. "Your feet feeling a little chill there?"

He raised an eyebrow. "Just because I don't feel much like ripping up the town doesn't mean I've got cold feet about getting married tomorrow."

He'd be lying if he didn't say the whole idea of marriage still scared the heck out of him. But he was crazy-mad for Jenny Boyer—more than he'd ever believed it was possible to love someone—and he couldn't even bear the thought of any kind of future that didn't include her.

The last five months had been as close to paradise as he'd ever imagined and he knew things would only get better.

"I don't have cold feet," he repeated.

Before he could say more, his old friend Dawna McHenry approached their table with a big smile on her face.

"Hey there, Seth!"

"Hey, Dawna." He kissed her cheek, thinking how pretty she looked in her pink flowered sundress. Since Christmas, when she'd started dating Roy Gentry, Dawna seemed different. Her hair wasn't so brassy now and she wore it in a softer style.

"Is Roy with you tonight?" he asked.

"Of course. He's over at the bar," Dawna said. Seth followed her gaze and found the quiet cowboy smiling in a bemused, besotted kind of way in their direction. He smiled back, feeling a definite kinship to the man. If Jenny were here, he'd be looking at her with that same expression in his eyes.

Dawna tucked her hand through his arm. "So tomorrow's your big day. I'd ask you to dance but I saw all those other girls who came over here walk away with big old dejected looks on their face."

"Dawna—"

She shook her head and gave his arm a squeeze. "That's all right with me. I just wanted to tell you how happy I am for you and Ms. Boyer. She's one nice lady."

"Thank you. I'll tell her you said so."

"You do that. Good luck tomorrow." She gave his arm another squeeze then kissed him again and turned back to her quiet cowboy.

"Man, I hardly recognize Dawna McHenry these days. I wonder what's gotten into her lately," Wade said.

"She's in love," Jake said. "It changes a person."

He looked at his brothers and thought how those words certainly applied to the Dalton brothers. Wade wasn't the stressed, workaholic widower he'd been before Caroline Montgomery blew into their lives. Since marrying their neighbor Magdalena Cruz, Jake had learned not to be so serious all the time, to find a little enjoyment in life besides his patients.

Seth had probably changed more than either of them. He wanted far different things out of life than he had before Jenny Boyer and her children captured his heart.

Where this would have been his idea of a good time six months ago, now he just wanted to go home and wait out the last few hours until their lives merged.

He smiled at his brothers. "Like I said, I do appreciate the effort you boys took to wrench yourself away from your women for the night but I don't think any of us are really enjoying this. I don't really need a bachelor party. Why don't we call it a night?"

He was a little annoyed to see neither brother was paying attention to him. Their gazes were both fixed on the door.

"Uh-oh," Jake said, his voice sounding oddly strangled. "Here comes trouble."

Seth turned around to see what they were both so fascinated by and just about tripped over his boots. Three women had just walked into the Bandito. Like plenty of other women in the tavern, they looked more than a little wild—heavy makeup, teased hair, tight jeans.

His heart seemed churn right out of his chest, especially when the redhead in the middle caught his gaze. She gave him a long, sultry look and sauntered over to their table, her partners in crime right behind her.

Seth suddenly discovered a pressing need to take a long sip of his neglected beer to soothe his parched throat.

"Well, aren't you three a sight?" Wade drawled and the woman on the right gave a pleased grin.

"Aren't we, though?" Caroline said, looking pleased as a little filly with a new fence post. She leaned forward a little and though Seth couldn't seem to wrench his eyes away from the little redhead who owned his heart, he thought he heard Wade swallow hard.

"We decided we were bored with our little bachelorette party, just us girls," Caroline went on. "We thought this might be the place to find us some rowdy cowboys."

"And you got all dressed up and everything," Jake murmured.

"You can blame Marjorie for that," Maggie said, sliding into the booth next to her husband. "We were just playing around with lipstick shades trying to find a good one for Jenny to wear tomorrow and Marjorie seemed to think it was a real hoot to lay it on thick and heavy. We all got a little out of control and before we knew it, here we were looking like we just stepped out of a bad country music video."

"For a pregnant woman, you're pretty hot," Jake said.

"I do what I can," Maggie purred.

Seth continued to stare at Jenny, falling in love with her all over again. It wasn't because she made one heck of a sexy party girl. It was that light in her eyes that hadn't been there five months ago, the joy and the happiness he saw in her face every time she looked at him.

"Hey, cowboy. Feel like dancing?"

The words were barely out of her mouth before he grabbed her arm and hauled her out onto the dance floor. The band obliged them by starting up a slow song—not that it mattered since he would have held her close no matter what they were playing.

He pulled her against him and suddenly he didn't mind the stuffy air or the loud music. With her here, with her soft and sweet in his arms, everything felt right again.

"Sorry we crashed your bachelor party," Jenny said into his ear, her voice pitched just loud enough to be heard over the music. "I thought we should leave you boys alone tonight but I was overruled. I hate to tell you this, but the women in your family are on the formidable side."

"Yeah, you're going to have a real tough time fitting in, aren't you?" he said drily.

She made a face. "Hey, I got all tarted up to come down here. I deserve points for that, at least."

"You can have all the points you want, sweetheart."

He leaned close and whispered in her ear, the way he knew drove her crazy. "I've got a muscle car parked out front. What do you say we drive up to the lake and make out all night?"

She gave that sexy sigh of hers and he was humbled all over again to know this smart, beautiful woman had somehow chosen him.

"That's a tempting offer, cowboy, but I'm afraid I'd better not. I'm getting married in the morning and I'm not sure I could look Father White in the eye with razor burns and love bites."

He grinned, only a little disappointed. They had the rest of their lives and he intended to fill every day of it showing her how much he loved her. "Despite appearances to the contrary right now, I guess I just might make a respectable woman out of you after all, Jenny Boyer."

"Not too respectable, I hope."

He pulled her closer. "That's a promise."

* * * * *

We hope you enjoyed reading

DALTON'S UNDOING

by *USA TODAY* bestselling author

RaeAnne Thayne

This story was originally from our
Harlequin® Special Edition series.

◆HARLEQUIN®

SPECIAL EDITION

Life, Love and Family

Harlequin Special Edition stories show that every chapter
in a relationship has its challenges and delights, and that
love can be renewed with each turn of the page.

Look for six new romances every month
from Harlequin Special Edition!

Available wherever books are sold.

On New Year's Eve, tycoon Wyatt Fortune—looking for a fresh start—crosses paths with a beautiful woman who also wants to reinvent herself....

Enjoy a sneak peek from USA TODAY *bestselling author Allison Leigh's new Harlequin® Special Edition story,* HER NEW YEAR'S FORTUNE, *the first book in* THE FORTUNES OF TEXAS: SOUTHERN INVASION, *a brand-new six book miniseries.*

Sarah-Jane could hardly think straight. Wyatt looked like he'd stepped out of the pages of some movie-star magazine. And if his stupefying good looks weren't enough, his fingers were burning a hole right through to her spine. Every inch of her was tingling. "I got my MBA from the University of Texas at Austin."

"Impressive." His hand left her back and he gestured. "I'm parked over there."

She was vaguely surprised that he didn't use the valet parking. But then again, when she thought about those well-worn boots he'd had on that morning, maybe she wasn't surprised.

Wealthy and gorgeous or not, something about Wyatt struck her as decidedly down-to-earth.

Then she reminded herself that "Savannah" would at least know how to carry on a conversation with a handsome man. "What, uh, what did you study in school?"

"Besides the girls?" He grinned crookedly. "Finance at MIT."

"Impressive," she returned.

His eyes crinkled as he opened the door for her and she sank into the passenger seat. She knew it was silly, but she was stupidly charmed by the action. Nobody had ever opened her car door for her before.

Savannah, on the other hand, probably had doors opened for her all the time.

Just be Savannah for a night, she reminded herself. One night. And then the fantasy could end. Would end.

Her hand swept over the leather seat next to her legs. She was having a hard time keeping her gaze from creeping back to him. "Nice car."

"It'll do for a rental. So tell me what an MBA is doing playing hostess at Red?"

Sarah-Jane wanted to cringe. *What a tangled web we weave…* "It's a job," she evaded. "I overheard you at Red, you know. About staying in Red Rock. I wasn't trying to eavesdrop."

"But you *are* trying to change the subject." He gave her an amused glance that she could see despite the darkness. "What'd your mama teach you about men? That they like mystery?"

Sarah-Jane didn't even want to think about her mother just then. "Do they?"

He slowed at a stoplight and looked into her eyes.

Her breath stopped in her chest all over again.

His voice seemed to drop a notch. "Let's just say I'm beginning to see the appeal."

Could Wyatt be on the verge of changing his bad-boy ways? Find out in HER NEW YEAR'S FORTUNE by Allison Leigh.

Available December 18, 2012, from Harlequin Special Edition.

SPECIAL EDITION

Life, Love and Family

Save $1.00 on the purchase of
HER NEW YEAR'S FORTUNE

by *USA TODAY* bestselling author
Allison Leigh,

available December 18, 2012,
or on any other Harlequin® Special Edition book.

Available wherever books are sold, including most bookstores,
supermarkets, drugstores and discount stores.

- ✂

Save
$1.00

on the purchase of
HER NEW YEAR'S FORTUNE by *USA TODAY*
bestselling author Allison Leigh,
available December 18, 2012,
or on any other Harlequin® Special Edition book.

Coupon valid until March 19, 2013. Redeemable at participating retail outlets
in the U.S. and Canada only. Limit one coupon per customer.

Canadian Retailers: Harlequin Enterprises Limited will pay the face value
of this coupon plus 10.25¢ if submitted by customer for this product only. Any
other use constitutes fraud. Coupon is nonassignable. Void if taxed, prohibited
or restricted by law. Consumer must pay any government taxes. Void if copied.
Nielsen Clearing House ("NCH") customers submit coupons and proof of sales to
Harlequin Enterprises Limited, P.O. Box 3000, Saint John, NB E2L 4L3, Canada.
Non-NCH retailer—for reimbursement submit coupons and proof of sales directly
to Harlequin Enterprises Limited, Retail Marketing Department, 225 Duncan Mill
Rd., Don Mills, ON M3B 3K9, Canada.

U.S. Retailers: Harlequin Enterprises
Limited will pay the face value of this coupon
plus 8¢ if submitted by customer for this
product only. Any other use constitutes fraud.
Coupon is nonassignable. Void if taxed,
prohibited or restricted by law. Consumer must
pay any government taxes. Void if copied. For
reimbursement submit coupons and proof of
sales directly to Harlequin Enterprises Limited,
P.O. Box 880478, El Paso, TX 88588-0478,
U.S.A. Cash value 1/100 cents.

® and TM are trademarks owned and used by the trademark owner and/or its licensee.
© 2012 Harlequin Enterprises Limited

NYTCOUP1212

REQUEST YOUR FREE BOOKS!

2 FREE NOVELS
FROM THE ROMANCE COLLECTION
PLUS 2 FREE GIFTS!

YES! Please send me 2 FREE novels from the Romance Collection and my 2 FREE gifts (gifts are worth about $10). After receiving them, if I don't wish to receive any more books, I can return the shipping statement marked "cancel." If I don't cancel, I will receive 4 brand-new novels every month and be billed just $5.99 per book in the U.S. or $6.49 per book in Canada. That's a saving of at least 25% off the cover price. It's quite a bargain! Shipping and handling is just 50¢ per book in the U.S. and 75¢ per book in Canada.* I understand that accepting the 2 free books and gifts places me under no obligation to buy anything. I can always return a shipment and cancel at any time. Even if I never buy another book, the two free books and gifts are mine to keep forever.

194/394 MDN FELQ

Name	(PLEASE PRINT)	
Address		Apt. #
City	State/Prov.	Zip/Postal Code

Signature (if under 18, a parent or guardian must sign)

Mail to the **Reader Service:**
IN U.S.A.: P.O. Box 1867, Buffalo, NY 14240-1867
IN CANADA: P.O. Box 609, Fort Erie, Ontario L2A 5X3

Not valid for current subscribers to the Romance Collection
or the Romance/Suspense Collection.

Want to try two free books from another line?
Call 1-800-873-8635 or visit www.ReaderService.com.

* Terms and prices subject to change without notice. Prices do not include applicable taxes. Sales tax applicable in N.Y. Canadian residents will be charged applicable taxes. Offer not valid in Quebec. This offer is limited to one order per household. All orders subject to credit approval. Credit or debit balances in a customer's account(s) may be offset by any other outstanding balance owed by or to the customer. Please allow 4 to 6 weeks for delivery. Offer available while quantities last.

Your Privacy—The Reader Service is committed to protecting your privacy. Our Privacy Policy is available online at www.ReaderService.com or upon request from the Reader Service.

We make a portion of our mailing list available to reputable third parties that offer products we believe may interest you. If you prefer that we not exchange your name with third parties, or if you wish to clarify or modify your communication preferences, please visit us at www.ReaderService.com/consumerschoice or write to us at Reader Service Preference Service, P.O. Box 9062, Buffalo, NY 14269. Include your complete name and address.

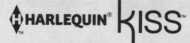

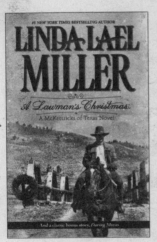